"STOP RIGHT THERE, BART KENDALL!"

Jo leveled her rifle at the man. Kendall and his men drew their horses to a halt and Kendall grinned. "Well, well. If it isn't the pretty little lady from Lawrence." He frowned. "Is it true you left there with the mountain man?" He laughed lightly. "Ol' Clint Reeves does have a way with the ladies, it seems."

"You shut your filthy mouth," Jo answered, her rifle steady. "What I do is none of your business. But what you do is *my* business when it comes to stealing my horses!"

Kendall's eyebrows shot up in surprise. "*Your* horses? Why, hell, ma'am, me and my men here found these horses running wild. Didn't we, boys?"

The men nodded in agreement, grinning.

"You've got two Appaloosa mares and one big, shaggy, red gelding in that herd that belong to me," Jo told Kendall. "I'd know them anyplace. I need those horses, Kendall, and I intend to take them."

Kendall shrugged. "I say finders, keepers. You dumb farmers ought to brand your animals. I say the horses belong to me, and I intend to sell them. And I don't think you really intend to pull that trigger, Mrs. Masters."

"Don't I?" Jo fired, sending a bullet whizzing dangerously close to Kendall's hat. "I killed a man during Quantrill's raid. Somebody told me once that after the first one, it gets easier. I think maybe they were right. . . ."

Bantam Books by F. Rosanne Bittner

Montana Woman
Embers of the Heart
In the Shadow of the Mountains
Song of the Wolf

and coming soon in paperback
THUNDER ON THE PLAINS

Montana Woman

F. Rosanne Bittner

BANTAM BOOKS
NEW YORK • TORONTO • LONDON • SYDNEY • AUCKLAND

To my father, Frank Reris.
I love you, Dad.

MONTANA WOMAN
A Bantam Fanfare Book / March 1990

FANFARE *and the portrayal of a boxed "ff" are trademarks of Bantam Books,*
a division of Bantam Doubleday Dell Publishing Group, Inc.

ISBN 0-553-28319-7

Published simultaneously in the United States and Canada

Bantam Books are published by Bantam Books, a division of Bantam Doubleday Dell
Publishing Group, Inc. Its trademark, consisting of the words "Bantam Books" and the
portrayal of a rooster, is Registered in U.S. Patent and Trademark Office and in other
countries. Marca Registrada. Bantam Books, 666 Fifth Avenue, New York, New York 10103.

PRINTED IN THE UNITED STATES OF AMERICA

OPM   10 9 8 7 6 5 4

A NOTE FROM THE AUTHOR

MONTANA WOMAN is set in Kansas and Montana in the 1860's. At the time of this story, Montana was not yet a state. It was actually a part of a vast section of land called Nebraska Territory, which stretched from present-day Montana through Wyoming, Nebraska, and part of Colorado. A few people did refer to the northern part of this territory as Montana, and to avoid confusion, I have done the same in this story.

MONTANA WOMAN is entirely fictitious, except for locations that are named, and, of course, the Civil War and the raid on Lawrence, Kansas, by William Quantrill. It might be interesting to the reader to know that there are many records of single women settling in the American West under the Homestead Act: brave, determined women who were unique for their time. Women of the West of the 1800's enjoyed much more independence than their peers in the East and the South. They were the first women to be allowed to vote, and also were among the first women to break into professions that traditionally belonged to men.

She stands in tall grasses, her skirt blowing in the relentless wind. Her face shows the loneliness she suffers; a trace of unspoken fear shows in her eyes; and she is weary from long days of hard work. Yet she perseveres. She is strong, brave, determined. And she will not give up the beautiful land she has come to call home. She is a Montana woman, and the man who wins her heart must be just as strong, just as brave, just as determined.

Chapter One

1863

Joline lifted her skirt to step over mud and horse dung as she made her way to the other side of the street. Wagons clattered past and she darted out of the way to avoid being splattered. A recent rain had done little to cool the sultry August weather, and had left the streets of Lawrence a mess.

Jo patted perspiration from her brow, the humidity making breathing difficult. She reached the boardwalk in front of STYLES'S MERCANTILE, then hesitated, staring at the sign for several long seconds and trying to decide how she should approach Howard Styles about an extension on her farm payment.

"Things have been difficult because of the war, Mr. Styles," she practiced inwardly. *"I can't get any good help. If I could just have an extension on this month's payment, I'll have more money the first of next month. A man is coming to town who might buy some of my horses."*

It all sounded perfectly logical, and Howard Styles was a fair man. And surely a man of Styles's wealth could afford to get by without her money for a couple of extra weeks. She only wished her father had not left her with these debts. Just before going off to war he had taken a loan against the farm to pay for horses and equipment, and for enough cash, he thought, to support his daughter until he returned. But he had not returned, and he never would. He had died at Shiloh, and so had Joline's husband.

Now Jo was getting desperate. She hated the thought of

selling any of the horses. She loved her animals, had
grown even more attached to them now that she was all
alone. But she told herself she also had to be practical if
she wanted to hang on to the farm. She could get by if she
sold all the horses, except Chester and Hercules, her two
draft horses. She would need them for plowing and planting.

She took a deep breath for courage and started inside,
but was easily distracted when a woman she knew from
church called out to her. Jo was almost grateful for the
excuse to put off what must be done.

"Good morning, Joline!" old Sarah Grant called out.
"How are you doing, child?"

Although Joline was twenty-two and already a widow, to
Sarah she was a "child." And the Grants always insisted on
calling her Joline instead of just Jo, the nickname she had
grown up with.

"I'm fine, Sarah," Jo answered.

Sarah approached, her aged but still-strong husband on
her arm. Jo greeted Bradley Grant, and the old man
looked at her with concern in his eyes.

"You still determined to run that farm all alone, Joline?"
he asked.

"I'm managing, Bradley."

"Well, it just don't seem right," the old man told her,
shaking his head. "A pretty little thing like you trying to
run that place alone. Your pa and your husband ought not
to have gone off to the war like that."

Jo felt the ache that was still fresh in her young heart.
Was it really two years already since her father and Greg
left the farm—and a whole year gone by since she learned
of their deaths?

"They did what they thought was right, Bradley," Jo
answered.

"And what about your sister, Joline? Why, she's been
gone at least two years now, hasn't she?"

"Three," Jo answered. "She's coming to visit in just a
few days, all the way from Columbia, Missouri."

"Oh, Joline, is that safe, with all the border raiding
that's going on?" Sarah Grant frowned. "And for her to
come to Lawrence—well, this is a town of Free Staters—
and Anna is married to a Confederate man."

Jo felt the old defenses rising, recalled the hurt that had

surrounded her sister's leaving Lawrence. "Darryl didn't join the war on the Confederate side until he was accused of being a Bushwhacker," she answered sharply. "People in this town ran Anna and Darryl right out of here, and Darryl was a good physician, Sarah. It wasn't fair the way they got treated. And it's only logical he would join the southern cause. After all, he's from Georgia." She sighed, suddenly feeling the tears wanting to come. "Yes, it's dangerous for Anna. But she's written that she's determined to come. We were always close, Sarah, and Anna left with hard feelings. We're still sisters, and we have some fences to mend."

Sarah put a hand on Jo's arm. "Of course you do. We didn't mean anything against Anna. We're just concerned for her safety is all."

"I know. Thank you for your interest, Sarah."

"Will we see you in church Sunday?"

Jo patted her hand. "I don't know. I haven't seemed to find time to come often enough myself. And if Anna is here, it might be best if she didn't come to church."

Sarah shook her head. "It's a sad thing when even the church is affected by the hatred and misunderstanding this war has created. God be with you, Joline, and with Anna, too."

"Thank you, Sarah." Jo nodded to Bradley Grant, and the old couple went on about their business, but Jo was left with the old, heavy sadness in her heart. How she hated references to "the war." A person couldn't get through the day without someone talking about it. Some called it a Civil War, but there was nothing "civil" about it. The South called it The War Between The States. No matter what it was called, it had a way of affecting everyone's lives—financially, emotionally, physically. Her father was dead because of "the war," and so was Greg.

Losing her father had been bad enough, since her mother had been dead for several years now. But losing Greg, too. . . . They had only one year together before Greg left in 1861 to fight for the Union. His death pierced her heart as though it had happened only yesterday, and she still sometimes had trouble realizing he was gone forever.

Now the shuddering dread and grief passed through her again, along with the knowledge that Greg Masters would never again hold her, make love to her. She would never again see his smile, hear his voice. That was what would make Anna's visit difficult, even though she wanted very much to see her sister again. Both of them had lost a father, and Jo had lost a husband. Yet Anna's husband was a Confederate. How strange that she and Anna shared the same grief over losing family members, yet by no fault of their own, they had ended up on opposite sides in this war. They had always been so close, until Anna married Darryl Kelley, a young doctor come to town—a man whose parents were wealthy plantation owners in Georgia. The war and the hatred that it spawned had brought the awful accusations that had made Darryl and Anna leave Lawrence three years ago.

Jo turned back to face the doors to STYLES'S MERCANTILE. It was time to do what must be done. She ignored an argument that was taking place several yards away over slavery. Such arguments seemed a daily event now in Lawrence, usually followed by fist fights. But Kansas had made its choice. It was a free state. Those who didn't like it could get out and move south.

Today Jo didn't care. She only cared that she was losing the farm her father had so dearly loved—the farm Greg had helped with and learned to love after he married Jo—the farm Jo was determined to keep alive for both men. She had discovered that in some ways she liked her new independence more than she thought she would. It was not that she would have wanted it this way, but it felt good to own something in her own name, and she liked the challenge of keeping the farm alive.

She folded her parasol and walked inside the store. "Good morning, Mrs. Masters," came a voice from behind a counter.

Jo turned her wide, dark eyes to Hank Bitters, who was Howard Styles's right-hand man. She nodded. "Good morning, Hank. Is Mr. Styles in? I need to talk to him."

Bitters glanced at a door at the back of the building. "Well, he's in, but he's got company. And I have a feeling he'll be in a right bad mood once this man leaves."

Jo frowned, discouraged. She didn't need Howard Styles to be in a bad mood. "I think I'll take my chances," she said, and headed toward the back room.

"It's up to you," Bitters called after her, studying her slender waist as she walked. Joline Masters was a pretty young woman, with long, dark hair and a nice roundness to her body that made men look twice. Bitters remembered that ever since she was a little girl, Jo had been spunky and independent compared to most other women, and he admired her efforts at hanging on to her father's farm. But he wondered if she was brave enough to handle Howard Styles today.

Jo approached Styles's office, and her courage did indeed fade when she heard the terrible shouting that was coming from inside. She recognized Styles's voice and felt a chill at his angry words.

"You never should have taken her there! This isn't the fault of the Indians! It's *your* fault! *You* killed her! You killed *both* of them!"

Jo's eyes widened with curiosity and embarrassment. She had never heard Howard Styles raise his voice before, and she suddenly felt like an intruder. She heard another voice then, low, growling, a voice that meant business.

"I ought to kill *you* for those words! If it weren't for your disapproval of our marriage, I never would have had to take Millie away from Lawrence!"

There followed a scuffling sound, then a grunt and a loud crash. Hank came running back toward the office just as the door was jerked open. A tall, broad-shouldered man in buckskins stood there, his dark, handsome face alive with hatred and anger, his dark eyes appearing watery with tears. Hank backed off as though afraid of the man, but Jo just stared. She had never seen anyone quite like him: a little wild-looking, but strikingly handsome, a powerful man whose eyes darted about like those of a cunning wolf who thought he might be trapped.

The stranger glanced at Jo for a moment, and to her surprise he looked suddenly apologetic.

"I'll see you dead, Clint Reeves!" Styles shouted from his office.

The man in buckskins glanced backward, the look of hatred returning to his eyes. "I've already died a thousand times over," he answered, his voice low and full of terrible grief. He glanced at Jo once more, then stormed out of the store.

"Mr. Styles!" Hank rushed into the office, and Jo stepped into the doorway and saw that everything on the man's desk had been knocked askew. Styles was bent over, picking up his chair, which lay flipped onto its back. When he turned, Jo noticed a red lump forming on his left cheek. The man straightened his chair and plopped into it, putting his head in his hands. To Jo's surprise, he began sobbing.

"My God, she's dead, Hank. My daughter and grandson both are dead. The damned Indians—"

"I'm so sorry, Mr. Styles."

"It's *his* fault," Styles groaned. "If Reeves hadn't taken her to Minnesota, Millie would still be alive. The bastard! Bastard! I never even got to see my grandson."

Jo turned away. This was obviously not a good time to talk to Howard Styles about her own predicament. She walked out of the store, her heart heavy at Styles's sobbing; but it was obvious he was not the only one feeling the grief. The tall man in buckskins must have been Styles's son-in-law. The grief on his own face had been evident.

"I've already died a thousand times over," the man had said.

At the sadness in his voice, Jo wanted to grieve all over again for her father and Greg. Now Millie Styles was dead. She remembered Millie, but hadn't known her well. Jo was only sixteen when rumors had buzzed around Lawrence that Howard Styles's daughter had run off with what everyone called a "mountain man." So, the man she had just seen must have been the culprit.

Clint Reeves, Styles had called him. Jo remembered people saying Styles didn't think the man was good enough for his Millie; so the two of them had run off. Jo faintly remembered that Howard Styles had conducted a special manhunt for the couple but had been unable to find them.

She picked her way back across the street and unhitched Chester. The draft horse was so big and strong, he was the only horse she needed to pull the wagon. She climbed into the wagon seat and drove to a feed store, then climbed down and tied the horse before going inside. She stopped short when she went through the door, noticing a familiar figure standing at the counter—the same broad shoulders and slightly worn buckskins.

"I just want to get as far away from things as I can," the man was telling Lou Peters, the store owner. "I just came back here to tell Millie's father about her death—and Jeff's. I thought it was only right to tell him in person."

"I'm right sorry about the loss, Clint," Lou replied. "Must have been terrible for you. I remember when you used to come in here whenever you were around Lawrence, remember how you used to talk about Millie Styles. None of us knew where you had gone, or that you'd had a son. How old was—"

"I'm sorry, Lou, but I don't want to talk about it," Reeves interrupted, picking up a sack of oats. He slapped some money on the counter.

"Sure, Clint. I didn't mean to get you upset."

"You meant well. I know that." Reeves sighed, taking his change and slipping it into a pocket sewn into the buckskin pants. "Jeff was only three," he said then. He cleared his throat, as though the words had stuck there. "I'm heading east to see a few old friends I haven't seen in a while. Then I'll be back through Lawrence before I head for Montana. I'll be needing more supplies then."

"I'll be here."

Reeves turned, and again his eyes fell on Joline Masters. He looked surprised, and a sudden half-grin passed over his lips. Jo reddened, wondering if he thought she was following him. She wanted to explain it was simple coincidence that their paths had again crossed, but an explanation was unwarranted and would only make her look ridiculous. He walked past her, nodding slightly before walking out. Jo approached the counter, where Lou Peters was still staring at the door.

"That's a sad situation," he muttered.

Jo could not ignore her curiosity. "Was that the man who ran off with Millie Styles six years ago?" she asked. "I saw him leaving Mr. Styles's store, and I heard some terrible words exchanged."

Lou nodded. "I expect they were terrible all right— Clint comin' here to tell Styles his daughter and grandson were killed by Indians. But I know it was a terrible loss for Clint, too. I feel sorry for him." The man squinted at her over his wire spectacles. "You remember when all that happened, Joline?"

"Just bits and pieces."

Lou removed the glasses and leaned on the counter. He was a man who loved a good story and enjoyed showing others how much he knew. "That there Clint Reeves, he used to come in here a lot when he came through Lawrence. He's originally from St. Louis, but the way I heard it, he ran away from home when he was only fourteen or fifteen years old. Joined up with a wagon train headed west and ended up staying out there for better than ten years. Worked as a scout for wagon trains and some for the army at that time—knows the west like the back of his hand. Then one time when he was in Lawrence he met Millie, and that girl fell head over heels in love with that big, handsome mountain man."

The man straightened and took a deep breath. "Well, I don't have to tell you what Howard Styles thought of that. You know the man yourself. Only the best for his wife and young ones. There was no way he was going to let Millie marry what he considered a wild, unsettled man like Clint Reeves. So the two of them ran off."

Jo didn't usually pay attention to Lou Peters's rattling. He was a man who talked a mile a minute, barely letting another get a word in, and usually he talked about nothing important. But the incident at Styles's supply store made Jo want to listen.

"It was the talk of the town," the man went on, his eyes lighting up with the pleasure of boasting that he personally knew the man who was the center of his story. "I'm surprised Clint came back here at all; but then that's like him—a man who's not afraid of anything or anyone. Too bad Styles didn't just let them marry and settle here. The way Clint tells it, he turned into a settling man after all, had a nice little spread up in Minnesota. But then the Sioux took to raiding last year—you remember the headlines, don't you? Most of the white settlers in Minnesota got the heck out of there. But I guess Clint didn't leave fast enough. I have a feeling what hurt the most was losing his boy. That goes hard on a man."

"Yes, I'm sure it does," Jo answered. She actually felt a lump in her throat at the story. She didn't know Clint Reeves at all, yet she found herself wishing she could somehow comfort him. After all, she knew the grief of losing a spouse.

"I need a couple sacks of oats, Lou," she said then. "I used up my own supply already and my oats and rye aren't quite ready to harvest. Besides that, I don't think I'm going to have a very good crop. I only hope I can find some help when it comes time to harvest."

Lou put his glasses back on. "I don't know how you keep that place going all by yourself, Joline. You ought to sell it and move closer into town. You could get work easy here. That farm is too much for a woman alone."

Jo bristled, her defensive pride surfacing at the term "woman alone." She had come to hate it, tired of being treated as though she were a child needing guidance. She forced herself not to show her anger, aware that Lou was simply expressing his kind concern.

"I did as much on that farm as Father and Greg when we all worked it together," she answered. "And now that they're dead, I just don't have the heart to sell it—not yet. But things aren't going well financially. It isn't because I can't do the work. It's all the outside problems—the war, lack of help, hardly any rain this summer."

"Well, I'm right sorry to hear that, Joline." The man walked around the counter and heaved two sacks of oats over his shoulders. "I'll just bill you for this. You can pay me later," he told her. "Open the door and I'll put these in the wagon for you."

"Thank you, Lou." Jo opened the door and followed the man out. Peters plunked the oats into her wagon and gave her a grin. "Have a good day now. I hope things improve for you, Joline. Say, what ever happened to your sister Anna? She still married to that southern rebel?"

"He's not a rebel, Lou. He's a doctor. He can't help it if he's from the south."

"Well, he's down there doctorin' those Confederate soldiers, isn't he?"

"Yes. But he's just a physician. He's from Georgia, Lou. You can hardly blame him for doctoring other men from his own territory."

"Well, seems to me like after losing both your pa and your husband to those gray-coats at Shiloh, you wouldn't have much use for him *or* Anna."

Jo stiffened. "Anna is my sister, Lou. We were always close. No matter what is happening in this war, she is still my sister. In fact, she's coming to visit me."

The man's eyebrows shot up in surprise. "That so? That husband of hers still alive?"

"Yes, as far as I know. And to Anna he is just a man, Lou—the man that she loves. This war has torn apart too many families. It almost tore ours apart. Now there is no family left—just Anna and me. I hope to patch things up while she's here. She's all I have left."

"Well, I can understand that. But she'd be best to lay low while she's here and don't go toutin' about how her husband is from Georgia and his folks own a big plantation and slaves and all. You know how things are in Lawrence right now. People are a might touchy."

"Yes. I know." Jo knew there was no sense in pursuing the subject with the man. Lou Peters loved gossip, loved to know every detail of people's lives. She vowed she would give him no details about Anna's visit. It was too personal—too special. She was so lonely now, and the thought of her sister coming was welcome indeed, no matter what had driven her away.

She unhitched Chester and headed for her farm east of town. Her emotions ran wild, with thoughts of the terrible story about Clint Reeves, thoughts of her own losses, and the joy of knowing Anna was coming. She whipped Chester into a faster gait, little noticing that a tall man in buckskins was standing on the boardwalk watching her pass, curious about the slim, pretty young woman he had run into twice in one day.

"Who's that woman driving the wagon?" he asked a man standing beside him.

The man looked up, grinned and shook his head. "That there is Joline Masters. She runs her pa's farm east of town all alone. Lost both her pa and her husband at Shiloh."

Clint Reeves stared after her. Between Indians and the Civil War, he wondered sometimes if there would ever again be peace and happiness for people like Joline Masters—or for himself. He turned and walked back into a nearby tavern. Whiskey seemed to be the only thing that eased his haunting memories and helped him sleep. For

Clint Reeves, at least until he could get over this terrible grief, peace and happiness came in a bottle.

Jo patted the sides of her dark hair, which was swept up into curls on top of her head and decorated with a small blue silk hat that matched her blue dress. She didn't often wear the dress. It was her best one, saved for special occasions and church; but since she learned of her father's and Greg's deaths, she hadn't gone to church as often as before, nor had she attended many social events. And running a farm alone left little time for such things.

She wondered now if she had overdressed for her sister's arrival. The ruffled crinoline skirt of the dress seemed to make too much of a rustling noise as she nervously paced the boardwalk in front of the stage station. She wasn't sure why she had felt compelled to look her best, except that Anna would surely look beautiful herself. Anna was just one year younger, and she was the fair one, with blond hair and blue eyes. Since marrying into wealth, she would surely wear the best in clothes.

Still, Anna's letters had suggested things were not going so well with Darryl gone. She had written of how she and Darryl would one day visit the beautiful plantation where Darryl's parents lived, as soon as the war was over. Then Darryl would return to a private practice, and they would surely lead an elegant life. But now that Darryl was off to war, Anna had been living with the wife of one of Darryl's friends from Georgia. The friend owned a restaurant in Columbia, Missouri, and when he, too, left to fight for the Confederates, Anna and the man's wife, Fran Rogers, ran the restaurant, and it was not easy work. But Anna was always hinting at how wonderful things would be once the war was over.

Jo hoped Anna was right, that everything could be the way it used to be, when the war ended. But she had her doubts. She wanted to be happy for her sister, but she could not help some of the bitterness that continued to plague her. How could Anna have married a man whose parents owned slaves—a Confederate—the very kind of men who had killed their own father, and Greg? Still, it would be good to see Anna again, and it pained Jo's heart

to remember how close they had been when growing up
on the farm, only to be torn apart by this ugly war.

The coach approached then, and Jo's heart pounded
harder. Everything else aside, she was lonely. Seeing
Anna would be welcome, and she was relieved to see the
coach had arrived safely. Raiding along the Kansas/Missouri
border between Jayhawkers—men who were against
slavery—and Bushwhackers—men who supported the
South—had been intense since before the war, making life
dangerous for settlers and travelers alike. Most of the
Jayhawkers had joined the Union once the war started,
and the Bushwhackers now were Confederates. But many
did not join the two armies, remaining behind to continue
their raiding. To Jo and a lot of others, the raiders were no
more than outlaws now, using the war and its cause as an
excuse to murder and steal.

The coach drew up in front of the platform. Hot weather
had quickly dried out the ground that had been soaked by
all the rain several days before, and dust rolled in a great
cloud past Jo, making her cough and turn away.

When the dust cleared, a pretty and familiar face peered
out from a window in the side of the coach. Jo waved,
telling herself she must put aside her sorrow over Greg,
the vision of Confederates shooting him down at Shiloh.
Horses whinnied and snorted as the driver climbed down
from the coach and opened the door. Anna was the first
passenger to exit. She approached Jo slowly, their eyes
holding. Three years had gone by since they had seen
each other; and their last words had been cruel and hurting.

"Hello, Jo." Anna spoke first.

The stage driver unloaded two brocade bags and set
them beside Anna. Jo noticed she had dressed simply,
wearing a soft green day dress, its full skirt decorated
with embroidered roses in a row down the front in darker
green.

Jo walked closer. "Hello, Anna." She saw tears in Anna's
eyes.

"I'm so sorry about Pa, and Greg," Anna said anxiously.
"Darryl couldn't have . . . he's just a doctor, Jo. He doesn't
fight with guns. All he does is help the wounded ones . . .
even Union—"

"You don't have to explain, Anna. It's just good to see

you." Jo reached out for her, and in the next moment they embraced. For several minutes they were unaware of the activity around them, or the stares. They were Joline and Annabelle Barker, daughters of Tom Barker, sisters. Both wept. Both hated the war and what it had done to them.

"Oh, Jo, I'm so sorry for the things that were said when Darryl and I left Lawrence," Anna sobbed, pulling away slightly. She took a handkerchief from her handbag, and Jo did the same.

"I'm sorry, too, Anna," she answered. "And I'm so glad you came. I've been so lonely."

Anna blew her nose and wiped at her eyes. "Jo, you should come to Columbia and stay with me, or at least move into Lawrence. With all the raiding, it's dangerous for you to be out there all alone. Why do you insist on trying to keep that old farm alive? It's too much for you."

"I'll manage," Jo answered, wiping at her own eyes. "Pa and Greg loved it. That's why I stay, Anna. And I like running the farm—I really do."

"But they wouldn't have expected you to handle it all alone."

"Things will get better when the war is over."

"If it ever *gets* over. Sometimes I wonder, Jo, if this country will ever be one again, be at peace again. It's all so horrible. Darryl writes me letters, and he says unless you're out there in the battlefield, you can't imagine what it's like—all the pain and suffering and death." Anna decided she would not burden her sister with the fact that she had not heard from her husband in over a year now.

Jo turned away and picked up her sister's bags.

"*At least your husband is alive to write you those letters,*" Jo thought. She reminded herself again to let go of the bitter feelings. She wanted to enjoy this visit. "Let's go to the house," she said aloud. She walked to the wagon and Anna followed. Jo threw the bags into the back of the wagon and climbed into the seat, and Anna climbed up the other side, looking too pretty and fragile to ride in the old farm wagon.

"I remember Pa taking us to town in this wagon," she said, brushing away more tears. "Oh, Jo, if only we at least had a grave to visit."

"I know. That's the worst part," Jo answered sadly. "At

least we can go and visit Mother's grave later." She sighed deeply. "I guess that's another reason I stay on, Anna. I can visit Mother's grave, and being on the farm makes me feel closer to Pa . . . and Greg. Greg loved working with Pa." She picked up the reins and kicked off the brake.

"Jo, you can't keep living in the past, you know. As long as you stay on that farm, you'll be waiting for Pa or Greg to come walking through the door, and that will never happen. You're only twenty-two. You have to think about your future, think about marrying again some day."

Jo shook her head. "I don't want to marry again. I never want to care like that again and then lose the man I love. It hurts too much, Anna."

Jo turned Chester and headed for the farm, forcing back the hurt, forcing herself not to blame Anna. This was her sister, the little girl with whom she had grown up, the only family she had left. And God only knew when she would see Anna again after this visit.

"How was your trip, Anna? No problems with raiders?"

"None. I was a little bit afraid, though."

A few people stared at Anna, and she moved her hand to grasp Jo's arm. "Maybe I shouldn't have come at all."

"Of course you should have. I'm so glad you're here, Anna." Jo turned to meet her sister's eyes and saw tears there. "I really am."

Anna smiled sadly. "Everything is different, isn't it?"

Jo held the reins in one hand and put the other hand over Anna's. "Only the things that don't matter. We're still sisters. Let's go home and just be that—sisters—like it used to be. Things will get back to normal once the war is over."

Anna swallowed and sniffed. "I hope so, Jo. I hope so." *If only I would hear from Darryl.*

Chapter Two

"Everything looks the same," Anna commented as she sipped tea and gazed around the big, airy kitchen.

Jo had changed into a plainer dress and prepared a pie for that night's dessert. She put the finishing touches to the pie and then opened the oven door of her wood cookstove.

"In appearance everything *is* the same," she answered. She set the pie inside the oven. "But nothing is really the same at all," she finished. She turned to face her sister. "Pa isn't barging in here with an armload of wood. I'm not making supper for two men anymore." She walked to the cupboard to get herself a cup. "And I sleep alone." She sighed, swallowing back an aching lump in her throat. "Sometimes I think, if only Greg and I had had more time together—just a little more time. I only had him one year, Anna."

"I know." Anna blinked back tears. "I had hardly more than that with Darryl. He left for the war not long after Pa and Greg did. I haven't seen him since. For all I know—" She sniffed and drank some more tea, finally deciding to admit her own worry. "I haven't had a letter for quite a while. And the last one . . . I don't know. It just didn't sound like Darryl. I know he's awfully worried about what might happen to his parents and their plantation. He says the South can't win this war. The North has all the factories and all the money."

She looked at her sister with tear-filled eyes. "Jo, I just know that if it weren't for this awful war, Pa and Greg and

Darryl could have been great friends. I just know it. And Darryl is a good doctor, Jo. It isn't right the way the people in this town ostracized him."

Jo stirred her tea. "That's just the way things are right now, Anna. People who ought to love each other are fighting. When the ones closest to you are being hurt, you strike out."

Suddenly Clint Reeves came to mind again, and to Jo's surprise the thought of him made her heart tighten and her blood rush. She realized that if not for the diversion of Anna's visit, she would have been unable to stop thinking about the tall man in buckskins. Even with the visit, she had thought about him during the night almost as much as she had thought about seeing Anna again.

"Do you remember Millie Styles—when she ran off with what people called a mountain man?" she asked aloud.

Anna frowned. "I remember a little bit about it."

Jo set down her spoon. "The man came back to Lawrence yesterday. I went to see Mr. Styles about—" She hesitated. She didn't want Anna to know her financial predicament. Anna would want to lend her money, and Jo wanted no handouts. "About some things I needed for the farm," she finished. "And I heard this terrible shouting in his office. Mr. Styles was accusing this man of killing his daughter and grandson."

Anna's eyes widened. "What happened to them?"

Jo was quiet for a moment, realizing the event had actually helped her feel better about her own losses. "Well, it seems Millie Styles went to Minnesota with this man and they married and had a son. Last year, when the Sioux raided, Millie and the boy were killed. Her husband came back here to tell Mr. Styles, and Mr. Styles said it was all his fault for taking them up there."

"The poor man! What a terrible thing to say to him!"

"I know. He walked out of Mr. Styles's office and looked right at me. And I never saw such sorrow in a man's eyes." Jo spoke the last words softly, with great pity. She stared at a salt shaker for several long seconds, and Anna watched her carefully, frowning.

"Joline Masters, I swear this husband of Millie's got to you somehow. Do I see something special in your eyes?"

Jo looked at her and blinked, realizing she had momentarily been lost in thought—thoughts of Clint Reeves. She
reddened slightly and rose from the table, carrying her
cup to the sink. "No. It was just such a sad thing to see,
and I felt bad witnessing it. I felt so sorry for Mr. Reeves."

"Reeves? That's his name?"

"Clint Reeves. I saw him again in the feed store,
and the man who runs the store told me about him. He
roamed the west for over ten years—led wagon trains,
scouted for the army, things like that." She turned and
faced Anna. "The most pitiful part was that he waited all
these months to tell Mr. Styles about Millie and the boy.
The man at the feed store said it was because after it
happened, Clint Reeves went off alone. He figures Mr.
Reeves must have been just about out of his mind for a
while." She shrugged then. "Of course I have to feel sorry
for Mr. Styles, too. What terrible news. But he should
want to be close to the man who loved his daughter. That's
what I mean about lashing out at people when we lose a
loved one."

Their eyes held. "I don't want that kind of hatred between us, Jo," Anna said. "I want us to be close, the way
we used to be."

"I want it that way, too, Anna." Jo smiled. "Come
upstairs and see your room. It's just the way it used to be.
I wish you could stay forever."

Anna blinked back tears. "Sometimes I wish it, too. But
we aren't little girls anymore. So much has changed.
Even so, I'd stay, Jo, and help you here. But Darryl could
come back any time, and I have to be there for him."

Jo nodded sadly. "Of course you do. And I hope he
comes back safely, Anna. I mean that. I know how it feels
to lose the man you love and I wouldn't wish that on
anyone else, certainly not my sister."

Anna pushed a strand of blond hair behind her ear. "I
know you mean that. It isn't just to wait for Darryl that I
have to go back. I'm needed at the restaurant. I hate
leaving Fran alone with all that work. She's like you—
determined to keep that place going for her husband while
he's gone. He worked so hard to build up his business."
She sighed deeply. "I feel almost guilty knowing my own

husband is still alive, while your Greg is dead. It seems like lately everywhere I turn, someone loses a loved one."

"Anna, that's the fault of the war, not you or Darryl. And don't forget you've lost your own father."

Anna came over to her. "You don't know what it means to me to see love in your eyes and not hatred, Jo."

They embraced, and Jo kept an arm around Anna's waist and led her up the creaking wooden stairs of the old Barker farmhouse. The smell of fresh-baked pie filled the house with its aroma, reminding them of days when they were small and their mother let them help her bake. For a little while they must try to forget about "the war" and all their losses. Both realized how precious time was now, how tentative life could be. And both needed to stop and remember better days, happier times.

"Let's try not to talk about the war for the next few days," Jo told her sister as they approached the landing. "Let's go visit Mother's grave tomorrow, and then we'll just talk about the old days, when we were little and didn't know anything about war and death."

"Yes. I'd like that," Anna answered softly.

Anna's intended three-day stay turned into nearly two weeks. When it came time to leave, they shared a new closeness that both knew neither time nor circumstance could destroy. Reluctantly, Jo loaded her sister's belongings into her wagon, the bags stuffed fuller than when Anna arrived. Jo had given her some old toys from their childhood—mementos that had been left behind when Anna departed so quickly two years earlier. And Jo had crocheted several doilies and knitted a sweater for Anna as gifts.

Jo pulled the wagon to a stop near the pick-up station for the stagecoach. "Whoa, Chester," she called out to the horse.

Anna grinned, remembering how Jo always insisted on naming all the animals on the farm, even the hogs and chickens. But there were no more hogs and chickens, only a few horses, and Anna was concerned. She turned to Jo before her sister could climb down from the wagon.

"Are you sure you won't let me give you a little money?" Anna asked. "Darryl left me some."

"I wouldn't think of it," Jo interrupted. "For one thing, with a war going on and all, a person can be wealthy one day and destitute the next. You might need that money yourself, Anna."

"Are you sure? Don't let pride get in the way, Jo. I know you."

"I'm sure." She met her sister's gaze. "Right now we're each on our own, Anna. The word is survival. We're grown women now, and in these days of turmoil we have to think of self-preservation. I've got the farm. Even if it fails, I have things I can sell, and I can always get work in town. You keep whatever money you have and use it wisely."

Their eyes held, both of them realizing it could be years before they saw each other again. They hugged, both of them quietly crying.

"I guess we can't put this off any longer," Anna sniffed. "It looks like the coach is about to leave."

"I suppose." Jo pulled away, wiped her eyes, and climbed down from the wagon to tie the horse. Her legs felt like lead as she walked with Anna toward the waiting coach. Two other passengers were already inside.

Two little girls ran past Jo and Anna, giggling and holding hands. Memories of summer days on the farm, of climbing trees and playing with dolls, became painfully vivid for both sisters.

"Be sure to let me know when Darryl gets back and if he's all right," Jo said. "I hope you at least get a letter soon."

"I'll let you know. And you write me if you need anything, Jo. Anything at all. You can always come and live with me, you know. I still wish you'd get rid of the farm."

Jo hugged her again. "I told you not to worry about me." She kissed Anna's cheek. "I love you, Anna."

"I love you, too. God be with you, Jo."

The driver picked up Anna's bags. "Time to be going, ma'am."

Anna reluctantly pulled away. "Good-bye, Jo." She squeezed Jo's hands.

Jo thought of asking the driver to wait a little longer. But she realized the pain of parting would not be made any easier by adding a few minutes. "Bye, Anna."

Jo's stomach ached and her chest felt tight. She remembered another sad parting, remembered again that awful day when Greg and her father left. Why was life so full of good-byes? Jo held Anna's hand until she was inside the coach and the door had to be closed.

"I'm so glad you came, Anna," Jo told her through the window.

"I'm glad, too. Everything will be different when the war is over, Jo, won't it?"

"I hope so."

The driver whipped the horses into motion and the coach lurched forward. Tears were running down Anna's face. "Bye, Jo!" She waved from the window.

Jo waved back. "Bye, Anna," she repeated. She felt a sudden wave of dread, her whole body shuddering from a fear she couldn't even name. She walked back toward her wagon, her heart heavy, thinking how much more lonely the house was going to seem now with Anna gone.

She untied Chester and climbed into the wagon, picking up the reins. She was too engrossed in her own sorrow to notice at first that a man in a long black coat had been watching. Suddenly he grasped Chester's harness, hanging on and barking at the horse to stay put.

Jo kept hold of the reins and frowned at the man, recognizing Bart Kendall, who was known to everyone in town as a Jayhawker. Kendall was not trusted, and it was suspected by many that he participated in raids against Union sympathizers, stealing horses from his own neighbors. But no one could prove it. Kendall had come to Lawrence four years earlier as a drifter, his background unknown, and had earned the nickname "Black Coat" for the coat he always seemed to wear, no matter what the temperature.

Jo didn't know Kendall well, but she knew who he was and considered him a worthless drifter. "Let go of my horse!" she ordered.

Kendall just grinned; his teeth were brown from chewing too much tobacco. "Mornin', Mrs. Masters." He turned to glance at the coach that had just left town with Anna on it. "Have a nice visit with your sister?"

Jo pushed off the brake. "That's none of your business. And I said to let go of my horse."

Kendall kept hold of the harness and pushed back his hat. "Folks might consider your sister's visit a little strange, after her being gone so long, what with her husband being a Confederate and all. The two of you wouldn't be some kind of spies now, would you? She come here for information to take back to Bushwhackers?"

Jo's eyes widened with indignation. "That remark doesn't even deserve an answer!" She jerked on the reins, forcing Chester to back up. The horse was so big that Kendall could do little to stop the animal then. Chester whinnied and shook his head in a sudden jerk, banging it into Kendall's head and knocking the man down. A few people who had stopped to watch laughed at the accident. "Serves you right, Kendall," one of them shouted.

Jo turned Chester to leave, and Kendall leaped to his feet, grabbing the side of her wagon. "Spy!" he shouted to her. "I say you're a spy, and so is your sister!"

Jo was in such a hurry that she didn't notice another wagon coming. Someone grabbed at Chester just in time to keep the animal from running right into the side of the oncoming wagon. The horse whinnied and reared, but the man who had stopped him was big and knew how to handle horses. In her anger and near tears, it took Jo a moment to realize that the man who had grabbed the horse was Clint Reeves.

"Whoa, there!" Reeves ordered Chester. "Settle down, boy." He stayed with the horse until the other wagon passed, then patted its neck, talking soothingly to the animal. He turned to Jo. "You all right?"

Jo reddened at her own quickening heart when she met his eyes. Here he was again, appearing in her life at an unexpected moment. "Yes, thank you."

"You're all spies!" Kendall began shouting. "Bushwhackers!"

"Why don't you shut up, Kendall," someone from the street shouted back. "Mrs. Masters already lost a husband at Shiloh, and he fought for the Union."

"And her sister is married to a *Confederate*. What was she doing here?"

By then Clint Reeves had walked around to the side of the wagon where Bart Kendall was ranting and raving.

"She only came for a visit." Jo spoke up defensively. "She's my *sister*."

Kendall raised a fist. "Tell that to loyal Jayhawkers!" he yelled.

Clint grabbed the man's upraised arm. "Why don't you do like the man said and shut your mouth?" he warned. "Unless you'd like me to shut it for you."

Kendall spit tobacco on Reeves's shirt. "Who are you to tell me to shut up? I know who you are, mister. And you as much as murdered Millie Styles—taking her away from Lawrence like you did. You got no right being in this town, Reeves."

In an instant Clint Reeves's big fist landed in the man's face. Kendall went flying, landing on his back in a watering trough with a resounding splash. The small crowd that had gathered laughed, and a few men helped pull the sputtering Kendall out of the trough. They gave him a shove away from Jo's wagon.

"Go have a drink, Kendall," someone chided. "That's the only thing you're good for."

Kendall stumbled away, carrying on about getting his coat wet. People dispersed, and Clint turned to look up at a shaken Jo.

"You didn't have to do that," she told him. "I'm sorry."

Clint picked up a little sand from the street and rubbed it over the spot where Kendall had spit on his buckskins. "I'm afraid the punch was for me, not for you," he answered. "I didn't care for that last remark."

Again Jo felt pity for him, and an odd attachment she couldn't quite explain. She put out her hand. "I'm Joline Masters."

He brushed his hand off and reached up, shaking her hand. "Clint Reeves."

"I know. I asked that day at the feed store."

He grinned, a handsome, unnerving smile that made Jo feel warm all over. "Well, I already knew your name, too." His smile faded. "Sorry about that day at Styles's store. I didn't know you were out there." He held her hand a moment longer than necessary before letting go. He glanced up the street to see Kendall disappear into a tavern. "Men like that—" He turned back to meet her eyes. "I think they just use this war as an excuse to make trouble."

"I agree. He calls himself a Free Stater and a Jayhawker, but as far as I'm concerned, he's nothing but a drifter and an outlaw. Not many people around here like Bart Kendall, as you could see."

Clint grinned again. "Well, I hope he doesn't give you any more trouble. If he does, I won't be around to help out. I'll be heading for Montana pretty quick."

Jo kept the reins pulled tight to keep Chester still. "Montana? That's so far away—cold, wild country, I've always been told. Why Montana?"

Clint shrugged. "The farther from here the better. I've got no interest in this unnecessary war. I've had my fill of death and fighting. At any rate, they've found gold up in Montana—and since there are so few soldiers left out there to protect white settlers and miners, good scouts are needed. That's one of my few talents. It's either stay busy or go crazy, so I guess I'll go up there and see if they need me."

Jo smiled gently. "Well, I wish you luck, Mr. Reeves. And thank you for intervening, although you really didn't have to. If Kendall had kept it up, I would have used my whip on him."

Clint laughed. "I don't doubt you would have found a way to take care of him. I hear you're a pretty self-sufficient woman. I admire your determination, Mrs. Masters."

"Thank you. And good luck in Montana, Mr. Reeves."

Their gazes held for a moment, each tempted to say something more. "Good luck to you, Mrs. Masters."

Clint backed away, giving Jo a nod as she whipped Chester into motion and drove off. Jo secretly chided herself when she realized she actually wished Clint Reeves wasn't leaving at all. She didn't look back to see that he was still watching her.

The next two days only grew hotter and soggier with humidity. With Anna gone, the hours seemed even lonelier for Jo. Now that she had had a taste of having someone around to visit with, the old farmhouse felt too big and empty again.

She busied herself with chores from sunup to sundown, going beyond what she really needed to do. She wanted to keep moving, to shut out the loneliness, and to keep her

mind off the recurring vision of Clint Reeves. He was
probably gone by now—gone to that remote territory called
Montana.

The past night had been especially hot and muggy. She
had awakened before sunup to a pleasantly cooler breeze,
and decided to bake bread. Baking had always been an
outlet for Jo. She found a special joy in kneading the soft
bread dough, or in forming cookies and decorating cakes.
The smell of something baking gave her a warm, loved
feeling. There had been a time when she dreamed of
baking for her own children, the way her mother used to
bake for her. But those dreams were gone, just as Greg
was gone.

She bathed and dressed before going to the kitchen,
where she prepared a large bowl of dough from memory.
She no longer needed to follow a recipe. She set the bowl
on a small table by a window on the east side of the house.
The morning sun would warm the dough and help it rise
faster. She covered it and went out onto the front porch to
sit down in a rocker.

The sun was just beginning to peek over the wide, flat
horizon. She put her head back and dozed off for a moment, the restless night finally catching up with her and
bringing on a much-needed sleep. She suddenly jerked
awake, unsure at first how long she had slept. She felt
alarmed but couldn't understand why she should feel such
a pressing, urgent sensation. She remembered that just
before falling asleep she had realized she still had to talk to
Mr. Styles. She was already late with her payment, and
that depressed her. She thought at first that was what had
made her awaken so suddenly, but quickly she realized it
was something more.

On the far horizon she noticed riders approaching. She
sat up straighter and saw they were riding hard. It was
difficult to tell how many there were, but she guessed
there were close to two hundred men heading toward
Lawrence, maybe more.

Jo slowly rose and watched for a few more seconds,
feeling a distinct sense of danger. Her heart began pounding faster as she reminded herself the country was at war.
What other reason could there be for men riding fast
toward Lawrence than something to do with that war?

Lawrence had been raided before. It could happen again, and she was a woman alone. She couldn't take the chance that the men approaching were friends and not the enemy. They would come past her place before they reached Lawrence.

Now she could actually catch the thundering sound of the horses, hear the clanking of sabers. She felt perspiration breaking out all over her body. She ducked into the house and bolted the door. She grabbed her Henry repeating rifle and a box of ammunition, then ran to a window to watch. As the riders came closer she realized there were far too many of them for her to consider fighting. To fire at them would only set them all against her, and instinct told her what they would do to her before they killed her.

She hurried to the back door and went out. She ran through soft grass to the fruit cellar under the stone foundation of the house. Lifting one of the heavy, flat doors, she quickly climbed below, closing the door after her.

In the darkness below, Jo felt her way to an old pickle barrel Howard Styles had let her have. She removed the wooden lid and set her rifle inside the barrel, then raised her skirt and managed to climb over the edge of the barrel. Her skirt caught on a nail and she hastily yanked at it, ripping her dress. She reached out and with great effort picked up the heavy lid to the barrel, then ducked inside and lowered the lid over the top.

In moments the ground literally shook with the pounding of horses' hooves. She could hear men shouting and yipping like Indians, then the sound of shots being fired, glass breaking.

"We'll check the place out," someone yelled. "The rest of you head on into town!"

There was more shouting, voices of men obviously out for blood. Jo's throat was so tight she thought she might choke, and she struggled against tears of terror. But the terror turned to anger when she heard pounding footsteps right above her, heavy boots worn by men bent on destruction. They were in the kitchen, she could tell. She could hear crashing and scraping sounds. Dishes were being broken, the precious dishes that had belonged to her mother.

She could hear gruff voices and muffled laughter. Her chest ached with agony as she pictured the men destroying everything she had of any value. She wondered what the others who had gone on to Lawrence were doing. She could dimly hear a lot of shooting in the distance, but she didn't dare leave her hiding place now.

Jo's bent legs ached, and she felt nauseous at the lingering stench of pickle juice inside the barrel. Breathing was becoming more and more difficult. She felt around the sides of the barrel, discovering the thin crack that had made the barrel useless to Mr. Styles. She pushed her nose against the crack, and inhaled fresh air as best she could while she prayed she would not be found. She forced herself to remain calm, but as the destruction above her and the men's shouts grew louder, terror again overcame anger.

After several more minutes Jo realized everything was quiet. She waited, praying the men had all left. But then she heard the familiar squeak of the cellar door being opened. She cringed, clinging to her rifle, ready to shoot whoever found her first.

"Where are you, woman?" a gruff voice shouted. "We know you're around here someplace. Ain't nobody but a woman would have fresh bread dough sittin' out to rise. Come on out, now. All we want is for you to bake that bread for us."

There came several snickers.

"We won't hurt you none," came another voice.

"Let's torch the place and get going!" came a voice from outside. "If there was a woman here she must have run off. Quantrill said to hit every place fast and get out. He'll be waiting for us."

"Yeah, come on, Dooley. There's plenty more women in town," came a voice closer to the barrel.

"The woman's got to be down here!" an angry voice answered. "I don't like bein' out-did by a Yankee woman."

"The hell with it, Dooley! I'm leavin'. And you better find her quick, 'cause I'm settin' the torch to this place on my way out."

"Go on then!"

Jo heard heavy steps scrape against the old wooden stairs as someone left. She waited then, her heart pounding so hard she was sure that if anyone was out there they would hear it. She heard and felt horses riding away. Again everything was silent, until she heard a shuffling sound. Someone had stayed behind in the cellar! Was it the one called Dooley? She clung tightly to her rifle, barely breathing for fear of being detected.

"Damned Yankee bitch!" the man cursed. She heard fruit jars being smashed. As far as she could determine, only the one man had stayed behind. He kept rattling off profanities as he smashed everything he came across in the dark cellar, and Jo wrapped a finger around the trigger of her rifle.

Suddenly she gasped when something slammed into the barrel, startling her. She heard laughter then.

"Okay, lady, the game is over. I heard that pretty little whimper. I know you're in there. Come on out now. I won't hurt you."

He banged on the barrel again with something heavy, and Jo cringed in terror. "Come on, woman. All I'm gonna do is make you feel good—get me some satisfaction and be on my way. It won't be so bad. You might even like it. Come on now. Your house is on fire. You don't want to stay in here and burn to death, do you?"

Jo could hear the snapping noises, the devastating sound of flames licking at the old farmhouse that she loved so much. Her anger knew no bounds. She understood without looking that the other men had destroyed her precious crops and had probably stolen some or all of her stock. She would be ruined. There would be no hope now of keeping the farm.

The stench inside the barrel was suffocating, but Jo was determined not to come out, fire or no fire. Let her attacker come to her. Let him take off the lid and look inside the barrel! She prayed that he would.

"This is your last chance, woman," the man said then. Jo guessed he had been drinking, and she hoped she was right. That would make his reactions slower. "Come on out willingly now, or I'll have to hurt you if you make me drag you out of there."

Jo looked up at the lid, keeping her eyes adjusted to the darkness. The man banged on the barrel again, and Jo prayed for the courage to do what she must do if the man

opened the lid. It seemed she had been in the barrel for
hours, but it had only been twenty minutes.

There was another moment of silence, except for the
crackling fire. Jo sensed the man was very close. Suddenly
the lid to the pickle barrel was flipped off and a man's face
slowly peered over the edge.

Jo fired. At the same moment she heard the shot go off,
blood and tissue sprayed over her face. She screamed as
the man's head bounced up and back. She heard the thud
of his body falling and she kept screaming at the feel of
pieces of his skin and spatters of his blood on her face and
in her hair.

She rose up, shaking her head, hitting wildly at bits of
flesh on her face and neck. After several seconds she
reminded herself she had to stay calm, had to think fast
now, had to bear the horror of what had just happened
and keep her head about her. She clung to the rifle,
allowing her eyes to adjust until she could see a middle-
aged man lying sprawled on the cellar floor. Sunlight came
through the half of the cellar door that remained open,
and Jo could see that most of the man's face was missing.

She just stared for a moment, hardly able to believe she
had killed a man. She slowly climbed out of the barrel,
again shaking her hair and brushing frantically at the front
of her dress. She moved cautiously around the body and
broken fruit jars. She heard the sound of things falling
above and looked up to see an orange glow through the
floor cracks. In moments the floor would catch fire and
collapse. She had to get out of the cellar, and she prayed
all the other men had left.

Jo lifted her dress and climbed the short ladder to the
sunlight above, cautiously sticking her head out to see if
anyone was around. One saddled horse stood in the distance, nibbling at some grass. She quickly climbed out of
the cellar and ran to the nearby woods, jumping down into
a hole she had dug for garbage. She stood on top of old
potato peelings, ignoring the bugs and flies, hardly aware
of them when she saw her precious farmhouse almost
completely engulfed in flames already.

"Pa," she whimpered. Tears stung her eyes as the roof
caved in, right over the room Anna had so recently used.
Everything that represented happy memories was crum-

bling before her eyes. She could see from where she stood that part of her corn field had been trampled, and the rest of it had been set to flames. Horses had trampled through her garden, and she had no doubt the raiders had also ridden through her fields of oats and rye. She saw none of her cattle and only a couple of horses.

She felt suddenly numb, as all her possessions and means of living disintegrated before her eyes. One wall of the house fell in, and soon the rest of the walls followed. She knew that in moments the floor would give way onto the man in the cellar. She was glad.

"Let him burn in hell," she muttered. It was then she noticed smoke rising from some of the buildings in Lawrence. Minutes later it thickened and spread, and flames licked at most of the buildings she was able to see from the half-mile distance to town.

"My God, they're burning down Lawrence!" she groaned. She leaned against the sandy wall of the garbage pit and wept.

Chapter Three

For hours Jo waited in the garbage pit, watching the change in the shadows of the trees that told her at least six hours had passed since she heard the last gunshot from town. Her nostrils stung with the smell of charred wood. She had remained turned away from the sight of the burned farmhouse. At times smoke from the still-burning buildings in Lawrence had darkened the sunlight.

Everything was eerily silent now, and Jo finally gathered the courage to climb out of the pit. She stumbled toward the debris of what was once her home, shivering at the realization that a man lay in the cellar, dead by her own hands, his body probably burned beyond recognition.

Through vision blurred by tears she could see there was nothing left to salvage. She had lost everything. She felt strangely numb, void of all feeling for the moment. Her mind scrambled to think what she should do now. She didn't even have her clothes. All she had was what little savings she had in the bank, and she prayed that had not been stolen by Quantrill's men.

William Quantrill. Everyone in Kansas knew the name. He had once actually lived in Lawrence and had been a Jayhawker, but one the people of Lawrence didn't trust. Like Bart Kendall, it had been suspected Quantrill stole horses from his own neighbors. When he was finally caught he became a man wanted by his own former friends. Quantrill had turned traitor and joined the Missouri Bush-

whackers, forming his own gang, each man armed with up
to five revolvers, plus rifles and sabers.

Quantrill and his followers had become the terror of the
border, but a year ago he and his men had left to join
Confederate soldiers. Everyone along the border, includ-
ing Jo, thought with relief that they were finally rid of
William Quantrill. They had learned the hard way that
Quantrill was back.

Jo shuddered at the thought. She had seen Quantrill
once, back in 1859. She had never forgotten his face. He
was not a big man. In fact he had a pale, sickly look about
him. It was his eyes that she remembered best, blue,
intense, a cold glare to them that she knew now revealed
the killer that was inside.

Jo walked around the burned house, desperately hoping
to see at least one item she could recover. She knew she
would not forget this day for the rest of her life. The war
had come right to her doorstep. There was apparently no
escaping it. It had once seemed remote and unreal, a
terrible distant battle that had stolen away her father and
Greg. Now she had been a part of it. She had even killed a
man.

She choked in a sob, then bent over and vomited,
realizing that the blood and dried particles that were stuck
to her dress and face and clotted in her hair belonged to
the rebel lying in her cellar. She could smell the remnants
of garbage on her shoes and the hem of her dress, mixed
with the stink of pickle juice.

For several minutes she wept and was sick. Then anger
reclaimed her. Quantrill and his men had no right to do
what they had done! How dare they attack innocent people who were not involved in any battle! To wear a uni-
form and carry a gun into actual combat was one thing.
But this was an act of pure, vicious vengeance against
peaceful, unsuspecting people, some of them people
Quantrill had known. She had no doubt many had died,
and she was relieved Anna had gone back to Columbia.

Her mind whirled with what she should do next. She
would wire Anna and make sure she had got home all
right. She would have to tell her sister what had happened. It would break Anna's heart.

She straightened, wiping angrily at her tears and hold-

ing her chin high. She told herself she must not let men
like Quantrill defeat her. And she would not go running to
Anna for help. Anna had enough problems of her own.

She breathed deeply, telling herself she had to be calm,
that there had to be a solution to her problem. She would
lose the farm, but if she sold the land she would have a
little money left over after paying off Howard Styles. And
maybe once she got cleaned up, she could ask some men
to help her find whatever might be left of her scattered
horses. But she didn't doubt most had been stolen by the
outlaws, never to be seen again. Those she could find
would have to be sold now. Somehow she would have to
start over.

She struggled not to break down all over again at the
realization that everything her father and Greg had worked
for was gone—everything she had fought to hang on to.
The house. All the things that had belonged to her parents. Thank God she had given a few things to Anna. Even
the outbuildings were burned. Her whole farm had been
leveled, and she could see that half of Lawrence lay in
smoking ruins.

She needed help but had no idea where to turn. There
was nothing to do but go to Lawrence and see what was
left. She picked up her rifle and walked toward town, her
legs feeling like rubber. The half-mile seemed like ten
miles, and along the way she saw dead bodies scattered
here and there. As she came closer to town the scene was
even worse. Men were running about trying to save the
few buildings that were still burning. Children and women
walked around crying, and dead and wounded bodies lay
everywhere she looked.

In spite of her disheveled and bloody appearance, few
people noticed Jo. There was so much destruction and
havoc, one more straggling woman simply fit into the
scene. Jo stepped over dead horses and dogs, as well as
bodies. Her heart went out to a little boy who stood near
an overturned wagon. He was spinning a free wheel, a
vacant stare on his face. A man's body lay under the
wagon, and Jo knew he was dead without going to look.
She wondered if the man was the boy's father. She had
started to ask when a woman came running toward them,
crying "Johnny!" The woman stopped short, stared at the

man under the wagon, then screamed and knelt beside him. The little boy turned to look at her. "Mama," he said quietly, squatting at her side.

Jo walked on, noticing that miraculously STYLES'S MER-CANTILE remained intact, as did a few saloons, a boarding house, a bank, and a hotel. Jo closed her eyes and thanked God that the bank was the one where she kept her money.

There was little else left. Lou Peters's feed store was in ashes. Jo spotted Peters sitting nearby, his head in his hands. She wanted to go to him, but her own devastation left her unprepared to help anyone else. She looked up the street, trying to decide what to do, where to go. She had never felt so lost and confused, not even when she had heard her father and Greg were dead. At least then she still had the farm, still had a home.

Suddenly she felt a hand on her shoulder. Jo whirled, lifting her rifle, and a man in buckskins stepped back, putting his hands out defensively. "Don't shoot, Mrs. Masters. I only want to help."

Jo looked into the handsome face of Clint Reeves. She noticed it was stained with soot, and the left sleeve of his jacket was torn and bloodstained. His dark eyes moved over her and Jo felt suddenly embarrassed, realizing what a smelly mess she had to be. Genuine concern came into Reeves's eyes.

"Are you all right, ma'am? Are you hurt?"

Jo blinked, trying to think straight. "No . . . I . . . they burned my house, my outbuildings . . . ruined my crops."

He lowered his arms, stepping closer. "What about you? Did they attack you?"

She shook her head, tears coming to her eyes then. "I killed one of them." She looked down at her rifle. "With this." She looked up at him. "I hid . . . in a pickle barrel. He found me. I . . . shot him. His blood . . . skin . . ." She reached up with a shaking hand to feel her face again and shuddered with horror. "I've never . . . killed a man before."

In the next moment Clint Reeves was taking the rifle from her hand. "The hotel where I was staying wasn't burned. You can use my room to clean up," he told her.

"A couple of stores are still in good shape. I'll go find you some clothes. Come with me."

She followed him blindly, hardly aware of what was happening. He took her into a hotel and up to his room. People were so lost in their own tragedies, no one paid any attention to the fact that Joline Masters was going up to the room of the "mountain man."

Once in the room, Clint made her sit in a chair while he filled a wash basin with water. He knelt in front of her then. "Can you wash by yourself? I'll leave you alone, but only if you'll be all right. There's a shirt hanging over the chair that you can put on until I get back with some clothes. You can climb right in that bed there and get some rest. Don't try to think about what you should do just yet. You need to rest."

Jo stared at him, confused, surprised, and touched. She glanced at the ripped shirt again. "You're hurt."

"I'm all right. I think I wounded a couple of the raiders. If they hadn't taken the town so early in the morning with such surprise, there wouldn't have been this much destruction." He frowned. "You telling the truth? They didn't . . . abuse you?"

She knew what he meant by the remark and she reddened. "No. I hid . . . in the pickle barrel. They all left . . . all except the one who found me. He's lying in the cellar . . . probably burned up by now."

He sighed deeply, and Jo could sense his anger. "Bastards!" he muttered. He rose. "Can you clean up on your own? There are towels and wash rags over on the stand."

Jo nodded. "I'm all right."

He touched her shoulder. "I'll leave your rifle right here against the wall if it will make you feel better. I'll be back in a little while. Bolt the door. I have a key."

Jo said nothing as he left. She rose then, going to a mirror and gasping at the sight she saw there. "Dear God!" she groaned. She was covered with bloodstains and bits of flesh. She let out a deep sob and began ripping off her clothes as fast as she could, wanting desperately now to get out of them. She shoved them into a corner and ran to the wash basin, dipping her hands into it and washing her face and arms vigorously, rinsing her hair as best she could.

She scrubbed like a madwoman, then suddenly stopped, holding a towel in front of her, realizing she was standing stark naked in the room of a man she hardly knew! She hurried to take the shirt from the chair and pulled it on, thinking that Clint Reeves could come back any moment. The sleeves were much too long, the shoulder seams hanging below her shoulders. The bottom of the shirt came nearly to her knees.

She wondered just what Clint Reeves's intentions were; whether she should be here at all. But she had no place else to turn. She felt suddenly weak and spent. She didn't want to think about what had just happened, about the fact that she had nothing left, that she had killed a man, that she was in a stranger's room. All she wanted was to sleep—blessed sleep. If she slept, she wouldn't have to think about all the heartache, all the terrifying realities.

She walked to where her rifle sat and picked it up, then went over to the bed, which was unmade and a rumpled mess. She straightened it a little, then lay down on top of all the blankets except the bedspread. She pulled that over herself and rested her head on a pillow, positioning the rifle right beside her so it would be ready to use.

She closed her eyes, and in moments the exhaustion of the day took over. She fell into a welcome sleep, totally unaware when Clint Reeves returned. He unlocked the door and came inside to find her lying in a deep sleep, the rifle beside her. Clint grinned at the sight, his heart going out to her. He studied the pretty face, the thick, dark hair, and deep urges stirred inside him at the sight of one bare leg that was revealed where the bedspread had fallen away.

He chided himself for letting his eyes linger on the slender thigh. She had been through hell, and he had no right taking advantage of the fact that she didn't know he was there. He laid a package of new clothes on the chair, then walked over and picked up her old ones, curling his nose at the smell of pickles and garbage. He carried them out, locking the door behind him. He took the clothes out back and threw them into a trash can. He looked up at the window of his room. His original plans had been to leave Lawrence this very day, but Quantrill's raid had foiled his plans. Now something else had interfered with those plans—a pretty little woman named Jo Masters.

Jo could hear the thundering horses, see the crackling fire, feel its heat. She tried to run, but her legs would not move. It was as though each leg had a heavy weight tied to it. Suddenly she was in a dark place. An ugly face leered at her and she tried to scream. She fired a gun, and blood poured over her. Again she struggled to scream, until a groan coming from her own throat awakened her and she sat bolt upright, drenched in sweat. She stared around a strange room, trying then to gather her thoughts.

She looked down to see her rifle lying beside her. She ran a hand through her hair, trying to remember the sequence of events since the raid, wishing it had all just been a tragic nightmare like the dream she had just had. But the reality of it set in all over again, just like the waves of grief that consumed her whenever she remembered Greg was dead. The farm and all her assets were gone.

She saw now that it was dark outside. Someone had left a lantern dimly lit on a dressing table. She struggled with her memories of the past terrible day. This morning seemed like many days ago. She vaguely remembered wandering into town; someone had found her, brought her up to this room. She blinked and moved to the edge of the bed. Clint Reeves! It had been Clint Reeves. She looked down at herself to see she was wearing the stranger's shirt, and for a moment she panicked at the thought that Reeves might have done this—might have seen her naked. But then she remembered ripping off her clothes. She glanced at the corner where she had thrown them. They were gone.

She slowly rose then, noticing the package on the chair beside the bed. She thought she remembered Clint Reeves saying something about bringing her some new clothes. She tore open the brown paper to find a soft blue dress inside, as well as bloomers and a slip, some stockings and a support undergarment. She reddened, wondering how he had guessed her size.

She carefully laid out the clothes on the bed, and a brush and a tiny bottle of perfume fell from the folds of the dress. She stooped to pick them up, smiling at how thought-

ful Clint Reeves was, wondering why he had bothered.
She went to the mirror to look at herself again and realized
she still hadn't gotten all the stains off her face. She
noticed that someone had emptied the wash bowl, and she
filled it with fresh water from the pitcher and washed
again, wishing she had some cream to put on her face. She
dressed in the new clothes, then lightly touched the perfume to her throat and wrists. It felt good to smell decent
again. She walked back to the mirror and had begun
brushing out her long, dark hair when someone knocked
at the door. She heard a key in the lock, and she rushed to
pick up her rifle from the bed.

"You awake yet, Mrs. Masters?" a male voice asked. He
opened the door just a crack. "It's me—Clint Reeves."

Jo kept hold of the rifle. "Come in."

Reeves entered, and she slowly lowered the rifle. "I had
to be sure," she told him.

He nodded. He was still covered with soot and blood.
His eyes moved over her appreciatively. "You look much
better than when I found you a few hours ago. I've been
back a couple of times—lit the lantern for you."

"Thank you. I . . . I don't know why you bothered."
She looked down at the dress, touching it. "I'll pay you
back. I—still have some money in the bank."

"Don't worry about it." He closed the door, and his
huge frame seemed to fill the room. "I'll be taking my
things to a little room in the attic. I was going to leave
Lawrence tomorrow, but I think I'll wait a few days. There
are more people who need help. I told the clerk downstairs this would be your room now. You'll need a place to
stay until you decide what you're going to do."

Jo frowned. "Oh, but this is your room! I can't take it
from you. I can't even afford it now."

"Quit worrying about what you can afford. I'll see the
clerk gets something. For now he's not charging. There
are too many people who need a roof over their heads.
People are camped out all over the floor in the lobby."

"But . . . it just doesn't seem right. I can camp out like
the rest of them—or go back to the farm and find some
shelter—"

"I said not to worry about it. After something like this a
woman alone is in more danger than in peacetime. You're

a lot safer up here than staying at that burned-out farm or sleeping with a bunch of homeless people. Sometimes people get strange ideas when they're destitute. There's going to be looting. Right now people aren't thinking too clearly."

Jo folded her arms. "I . . . don't know what to say. I'm so grateful for the clothes, Mr. Reeves—"

"Clint. Call me Clint."

She felt her cheeks reddening against her will, his virile good looks stirring her with unexpected desires. She turned to face him. "Then please call me Jo." She smiled nervously. "How on earth did you know what size clothes to get?"

His smile faded, and the strange sadness she had seen in his eyes that day in Howard Styles's office returned. "My wife . . . was built about like you."

Their eyes held. "I'm sorry about your loss, Mr.— I mean, Clint. Believe me, I know how you must feel. I lost both my father and my husband at Shiloh."

He quickly turned away. "I'll get my things together."

"Please—let me bandage that arm," she told him, realizing the last thing he wanted was to talk about the deaths of his wife and son.

"It's all scabbed over by now. Not much can be done about it. I caught it on a damned nail when I whirled to shoot at one of Quantrill's men." He opened a dresser drawer and threw a couple of shirts onto the bed. "I'll never understand how men can do something like this to peaceful, innocent people. He ought to be hanged by his—" He walked over and picked up a saddlebag from where it lay in a corner of the room. "I'd like to get my hands on Quantrill."

"So would a lot of others." She put a hand to her stomach at the memory of shooting one of his men. "I suppose I should tell the sheriff about the man in my cellar."

"I already did. The body will be taken care of."

Jo sighed. "Thank you. But I don't know why you're doing all of this for me. It really isn't necessary. You hardly know me."

"*You look so much like my Millie,*" he wanted to tell her. "You needed help so I helped you. A man doesn't need a reason. I'll come get you in the morning and take you over to the bank and we'll try to scramble up a breakfast. If we can't find a place to cook us one, we'll make a fire and cook our own. How about now? You hungry?"

His dark eyes met hers, and again she felt strangely drawn to him. "No. I've just got one big knot in my stomach."

He finished packing his saddlebag. "Well, the clerk downstairs is keeping coffee on the cookstove in back for anybody who wants any. You might want to go down there and get a cup."

She nodded. "Yes. I think I'll do that."

"Got any idea what you'll do tomorrow? What you'll do about the farm?"

Tears began to form in her eyes. "No." She walked over to the window, looking out to see an orange glow from the embers of buildings still smouldering. "I still owe money on the farm. My father had borrowed money from Howard Styles to build a barn and pay off some other debts. He gave Mr. Styles the deed against the loan. It wasn't paid off yet, and now the barn is gone. Everything is gone. I guess I'll have to sell the farm to pay off Mr. Styles."

She stopped short then, realizing whom she was talking about. She turned to see the hatred in Clint Reeves's eyes. "Too bad it's Styles you owe money to," he told her. "Somebody else might give you some time to get back on your feet. Styles won't. He's not a man to give anybody a chance to prove him or herself."

She sighed deeply. "I'm sorry. I shouldn't have mentioned his name."

He shrugged. "Your business with Styles doesn't have anything to do with my feelings about the man."

Jo wanted to ask more, wanted to hear the whole story from Reeves. But she knew better than to ask. "I'll go see him tomorrow and get it over with. I noticed his store didn't burn. I take it the man is all right."

A steely glint came into Reeves's dark eyes. "Men like Styles always make out. You just make sure you get everything that's coming to you."

"What about you? I thought you were leaving for Montana."

He smiled sadly. "I was supposed to leave this morning. Quantrill put a stop to my plans. I'll leave in a couple of days."

She put a hand to the high collar of her dress. "I can't thank you enough, Clint. I don't feel right about you giving me this room. Why don't you let me take the attic room? It must be terribly hot up there."

"I'll get by. I don't use a room much anyway. Like to be out in the open most of the time." He ran a hand through his hair, looking suddenly self-conscious. "I'll be cleaner when I come get you in the morning. The only bathhouse left in town is over at Sadie Clements's place. I reckon I can talk Sadie into letting me in there yet tonight."

Jo reddened again, feeling an unexpected surge of jealousy, an emotion entirely uncalled-for. Sadie Clements's bathhouse was not the most reputable establishment in town. There were women there who took money to give men baths, and Jo had heard they often did more than that. Reeves grinned slightly at her suddenly pink cheeks.

"I'm sorry. I forgot who I was talking to. At any rate, I'll look a little more presentable tomorrow."

"It doesn't matter. Thank you again, Clint. You didn't have to do any of this."

"Well, that's when something is the most enjoyable—when you don't have to do it." He gave her a warm smile. "I guess you didn't realize how late it is. Must be past midnight. You might as well get undressed again and get some more sleep. I'll leave the shirt you were wearing." He handed out a key. "Keep the door locked."

She walked up and took the key from him, feeling a pleasant warmth move through her when their fingers touched. Their eyes met.

"I'm sorry about your losing everything," he told her. "But I'm glad you're all right. And I'm sorry about your husband and all. We'll talk more tomorrow. If there's anything more I can do to help before I leave, let me know. I'll come by in the morning."

She folded the key into her palm. "Thank you." *"I wish you wouldn't go away,"* she felt like saying. What a foolish thought, and an even more foolish remark that would be! "Good night, Clint."

He slung the saddlebags over his shoulder. "The rest of

my things are already upstairs. Good night, Jo. Will you be all right?"

She nodded. "I think so. I'll probably have bad dreams for a while, but I'll survive."

He opened the door a crack. "You're a strong woman. Any man can see that. I admire your courage. And don't you feel bad about killing that sonuvabitch back at the farm. He deserved to die. You did what you had to do. Anybody feels bad when they kill someone—man or woman. It's natural. But you had no choice. You remember that. When a man has no choice—" He stopped short, the terrible hurt coming back into his eyes. He just nodded to her then and quickly left.

Jo quietly locked the door and went to the window, feeling as though she had stepped into another world. All that was familiar to her was gone, and now there was a new person in her life, a man who was a stranger, yet with whom she felt so comfortable and protected. After several minutes she spotted him, his big frame unmistakable in the light of lanterns that hung outside along the street. He crossed the street and moved into the shadows, most likely heading for Sadie's place. The ridiculous jealousy pinched at Jo's heart again and she turned away from the window, angrily removing her clothes again, disgusted with herself for having such silly feelings.

She pulled on the big shirt, wrapping it around herself and lying down on the bed again. But now she wasn't tired anymore. There were far too many things to think about.

Chapter Four

"If you need the money quickly, Joline, I can give you three hundred dollars right now and sell the farm later after things settle some," Howard Styles told Jo. "The way things are right now, nothing is going to sell for a while. You've lost everything. You can't wait that long for money you need just to have a place to live and clothes on your back."

Jo studied the man's pudgy, well-fed body, his thinning hair, and the look of arrogance in his cool gray eyes. Clint was right. She could expect little in the way of help from Howard Styles. "The farm is worth much more than that, Mr. Styles, even after you take what my father owed you. It's good, rich land."

The man sighed and leaned back in his leather chair. The shiny leather squeaked as he shifted, almost as though to announce it was a fine, expensive piece of furniture. "I'm aware of that," the man answered. "But for the moment I would be literally handing you three hundred for nothing. This is wartime, Joline, and Lawrence is a dangerous area to live right now, let alone the fact that a lot of other people are broke. It could take months to sell your place, considering all the buildings are gone and half of Lawrence is destroyed. If you want to wait that long, it's fine with me. But in the meantime you'll still owe monthly payments. How will you manage to meet them?"

Jo suppressed her anger, which was so intense she felt like crying. "Three hundred won't go very far, Mr. Styles."

"Haven't you heard of the Homestead Act? You could resettle on government land. Three hundred dollars would buy you two hundred and forty acres. Or you could buy a fine little house and have money left over."

"It might buy land or a house, but there is still the matter of equipment, livestock, seed, food for animals, clothes, furniture—"

Styles shook his head. "Joline, I can't go any higher. This is money right out of my pocket. I have no idea when or if I'll recover it. I'm sorry as hell about the raid, and as angry as everybody else in town. But I've taken losses, too. Several of the businesses that burned down were backed with my money or belonged to me. I stand to lose a great deal of money. I can't turn around and deal out charity to everyone who is hurting from this. You aren't alone. Even I am taking severe losses."

Jo stiffened, rising from her chair. She studied his fine silk suit and the leather chair. "Yes, I can see how destitute you are."

Styles frowned, rising himself. "I wouldn't be so flippant, Joline. I'm doing you a great favor." The man opened a drawer at the left side of his desk and pulled out a stack of money. Jo watched his well-manicured hands as he counted out the three hundred dollars, and she realized he must not have done anything to help others the night before. He was too clean. Clint had scrubbed and scrubbed, but the creases and knuckles of his hands and face still showed soot stains. "There you are," Styles said, handing her the money.

Jo just stared at him, furious at her helpless position. She grabbed the money then. "I want something in writing that I don't owe you anything," she told the man.

He shook his head, sitting back down and taking out a piece of paper. "If it will make you feel better. The deed is already in my name, so I wouldn't have given you any trouble over it."

"Nevertheless, I want it in writing."

Styles wrote out the note and signed it. "There." He handed it up to Jo and she grabbed it, almost tearing the paper as she took it from his hand. She read it quickly and folded it, shoving it and the money into her handbag.

"You're so generous," she muttered with almost a sneer.

"When you think about it, you'll realize I *am* being generous," he answered. "And I'll tell you one more thing, Joline. I saw you out the window, walking toward my place with Clint Reeves beside you. After seeing that, you're lucky you even got the three hundred. Reeves is a no-good drifter, little lady. I would advise you to stay away from him."

"I'll choose my own friends, thank you. And the way I hear it, what happened was more your fault, Mr. Styles, for not allowing your daughter to stay right here in Lawrence."

Jo whirled and walked out before the man could answer. She wanted to feel sorry for the remark, but she didn't. She marched through the store, determined not to buy any of her supplies from Howard Styles. She realized she would have to spend her money very carefully, and she wasn't even sure yet just what she would do. Clint had walked with her to the farm after breakfast that morning, and there was virtually nothing of value left except a buckboard wagon.

To Jo's joy she found two of her horses, a roan mare she called Red Lady and a buckskin gelding named Sundance. Finding the horses had helped lift her spirits at least a little. She had left the animals to graze in an outer fenced pasture where the grass had not been burned off. Now Jo had to decide whether to sell or keep them.

She walked outside Styles's store and up to Clint, who stood leaning against a support post. A hearse passed them, pulled by four horses, and several people walked behind it, weeping. Four wagons piled high with furniture and belongings passed going in the opposite direction— west—people disgusted with the war and bickering, eager to get out of Lawrence and start anew someplace farther west, where civilization, or what there was of it, cared little about slavery or states' rights or any other issue.

"It's so sad," Jo told Clint, who watched the passing funeral procession quietly.

Clint nodded. "The gravediggers will be busy the next few days." He looked down at her. "How did it go?"

She looked away angrily. "He gave me three hundred dollars."

Clint let out a long, angry sigh. "Cheating bastard!"

"I didn't have much choice. He said it could take months to sell the farm, and he's right. I can't wait that long. In a sense he's doing me a favor. Now it's his mess to clean up, not mine. At any rate, I could have waited, but then there would be the monthly payments, and until I'm back on my feet, where would I get the money?" She looked up at him. "I have another two hundred and fifty in the bank. I can get a few clothes, maybe find a place to stay, find a job."

"Where? Half of Lawrence is gone. There's no place to work."

She sighed. "I'll think of something. I've got along on my own for months now. If worse comes to worse, I can go to my sister in Columbia, but the strain would be hard, considering Confederates did this, and her husband is a Confederate. But Anna is a good woman. It's just that I hate to go crawling to anyone for help."

"It isn't crawling, Jo; it's a matter of survival."

"Well, I'll just have to find a way to survive without going to my sister. Right now I'm just going to buy a few clothes." She studied his dark eyes. Today, cleaned up and looking more his normal self, she was struck again by his rugged good looks, and by the gentle concern behind the brawny man. She realized she liked the way his hair hung past his collar, longer than most men wore their hair. She liked his smile, the warmth in his dark eyes. Her feelings for him, so sudden and too soon, frightened her; and she saw she had let herself get too close to him.

On their walk that morning she had spilled out everything about Greg, and the situation with Anna and her husband. She had talked too much about herself to this near stranger. He, in turn, had said little. She still really knew next to nothing about him except what Lou Peters had told her.

When they had reached the farm that morning, Jo had crumbled at the sight. Clint Reeves had touched her shoulders, helped her to her feet. She had felt a strange comfort and strength at his touch, and it surprised and confused her. The last thing she wanted was to care again, about anyone. It hurt too much to lose loved ones, and she had lost all she could bear to lose.

"What do you know about the Homestead Act?" she asked him now.

He folded his arms and leaned against the post. "Well, I think a person can claim something like 160 acres for around $1.25 an acre. But I think he can get it free if he agrees to live on it and develop it over a certain length of time. The government came up with the idea to get people to settle in new territory, open it up, improve it." He frowned. "You thinking of resettling under the Act?"

"I don't know yet. It will take some thinking." She watched another funeral procession move past them. "Well, I guess this is where we part," she said, looking back up at Clint. "There is really nothing more you can do for me, and you have your own business to tend to. Thank you again, Clint."

Their eyes held, and he put out his hand. Jo reddened as she put out her own and he wrapped a big, strong hand around her small one. "It's been a real pleasure knowing you, Jo Masters. You're one fine woman, brave and strong. I wish you a lot of luck."

She smiled lightly. "I wish you the same," she answered. "And happiness."

His own smile seemed forced then. "Luck and happiness don't seem to be much on my side most of the time. Maybe I'll find both in Montana."

"Maybe you will. Thank you again for the room—and for breakfast and for walking with me to the farm."

"My pleasure. I'm going to gather up some supplies of my own. There won't be much to pick from now, but I suppose I can find enough to get by till I hit the next fort."

She nodded. "Take care of yourself. It's been very nice meeting you. I'll never forget how you helped me yesterday."

He smiled for her. He was not about to tell her that he could not forget the sight of her slender, bare leg; or that he wished he could see more of her. Joline Masters was a special woman, one to be regarded highly. He knew that if he got any closer to her, it could be dangerous for him. He might start to have feelings for a woman once more, the kind that meant commitment, caring. He never wanted to feel that deeply about a woman again. He decided it was a good thing he was leaving Lawrence in the morning. He would have gone today, but he couldn't resist a few more hours around Jo Masters, nor could he bring himself to leave her before he was sure she would be all right.

"A lot of people needed help yesterday," he told her. "I just did my share." He squeezed her hand and let go.

"God bless you, Clint."

He nodded. "You, too." He tipped his hat and turned, walking toward the livery. Jo watched him: his lean hips, his rambling gait, the dancing fringes of his buckskin shirt. Suddenly her eyes misted and she turned away, heading for the telegraph office. She would have to send Anna a telegram to let her know she was all right. She wouldn't tell her sister the worst. She would break that to her later, after she had got herself settled somewhere. Anna had enough to worry about right now.

Jo lay awake through the long, restless night. She considered her options, which seemed to be few. Her life had been turned upside down, and suddenly there was nothing left for her in Lawrence. What was left of her family and memories lay in ashes, and until rebuilding took place, there was little opportunity to find any kind of job.

She thought about Anna. She could go to Columbia, but somehow that seemed like giving up. And if Darryl came home, she would be in the way. Besides that, Columbia was even closer to the war, and all Jo wanted now was to get as far away from the war as she could get. Quantrill's raid had only brought all of the ugliness to her doorstep. She wished there were someplace where she could go to get away from all of it—where she could start her life over and learn to live not only with the reality of Greg's death, but live in peace.

She had wired Anna and was relieved to know her sister too was all right. She could tell by Anna's reply that she was terribly concerned, and Jo knew she would have to write immediately and explain the whole event. Jo was determined to convince Anna she was just fine, even if she wasn't.

Jo breathed deeply, thinking again about Clint Reeves. She envied men like Clint—men who could go wherever they wanted, who knew the wild land to the west. She longed to simply go away from Lawrence, from the ugly sight of the farm she had tried so hard to hang on to, from

all the bad memories. She wondered what it was really
like farther west, if there really were mountains as magnificent as Clint had described to her that morning.

A man like Clint knew that land, the canyons, the
deserts, the plains. A man like Clint could survive anywhere. He had talked of snow on top of mountains even in
summer, of huge pine trees, and clear mountain streams.
Soon he would go into that land of mystery and beauty,
and suddenly Jo longed to do the same; to see someplace
new and different, to experience dangers and new adventures that would help her forget the agony of the past two
years.

Her thoughts were interrupted then by loud voices in
the street. Fights were a common event, but this time she
recognized Howard Styles's voice again, shouting obscenities.

"What are you still doing in Lawrence, Reeves?" the
man yelled. Several men's voices growled their agreement. A crowd had apparently gathered, and Jo knew
immediately there had been a confrontation between Clint
and his father-in-law. She rose and went to the window,
looking down into the street below. Several men were
facing off, one group behind Howard Styles, another behind Clint.

"Leave Clint alone," one man shouted. "It ain't his fault
what happened. The poor man lost a wife and son."

"My daughter and grandchild!" Styles shouted in return. "That sonuvabitch dragged my daughter off to uncivilized territory where he knew she would die! A man
doesn't do that to a woman he loves!"

Styles was apparently very drunk, and Clint, too, appeared to have been drinking. The men must have run
into each other in a saloon, and the confrontation had
moved into the street.

On Styles's last words Clint dived into the man, knocking him to the ground. He quickly jerked him up and gave
him one hard punch, knocking him down again.

"I could kill you, Styles!" he growled. "And by God if it
weren't for the law in this town and my respect for Millie's
memory, I *would* kill you!"

Styles got to his knees, spitting blood. "Get him, men!"
he sputtered. Clint stood his ground, glowering at a few
men who stepped over Styles threateningly.

"Cowards!" one of Clint's friends shouted. "It's easy to take on a man like Clint when you're all bunched together like wolves. Ain't a man among you who'd take him on man to man."

"Makes no difference when the man's a traitor!" someone shouted. Jo looked in the direction of the voice to see Bart Kendall in his ever-present black coat. "Reeves comes to town—makes friends with a woman who's got a Confederate sister—and then we get raided. What's all that add up to?"

"Nothing!" a man behind Clint answered. "Clint Reeves is a good man. Nobody helped out around here more than he did after the raid!"

"I don't know about you being a traitor, Reeves," Styles growled. "I only know that because of you my daughter is dead!"

One of Styles's friends landed into Clint then, and the fight was on. Clint held his own against three of Styles's men, while the rest of the crowd joined in the fight on both sides, some not even knowing who or why they were fighting. Tensions were high, and the crowd simply needed to let loose.

Jo watched with pity for poor Clint, but also with awe for how he handled himself. He had fended off several men before there came a gunshot. The local sheriff stepped into the melee, shooting twice more to get the men to settle down. "What's going on here?" he shouted.

Styles brushed off his silk suit, which was covered with dirt. He shook more dirt from his hair. Jo was surprised he had allowed himself to get into a brawl, but his hatred for Clint was obvious. He spit out more blood.

"I want this man out of Lawrence!" Styles growled at the sheriff.

"Now, Howard, if he hasn't done anything wrong—"

"I want him out of Lawrence!" Styles shouted louder.

"You just calm down, Howard," the sheriff told him.

"He doesn't have to worry about me leaving," Clint spit out, wiping at blood near his eye. "I'm leaving in the morning."

Styles stepped closer. "Make it bright and early. I have influence in this town, Reeves, and your hide isn't worth much right now. I could easily get you hanged as a spy!"

Clint's eyes glittered with hatred. "You know something, Styles? Millie was never happier than when she got away from *you*," he hissed. "She might have died young, but she died happy. She wouldn't have had it any other way!"

Styles grabbed at him again but Clint stepped back and the man stumbled.

"Come on now, Howard, you'd better get yourself home," the sheriff told the man, taking his arm. "The rest of you men get back about your business. We have enough problems in Lawrence without you wasting your energies in a street fight."

Clint staggered into the hotel. Jo moved away from the window and pulled on a robe. She hurried to the door and opened it as Clint walked by.

"Clint?"

He stopped and looked at her, the terrible sorrow in his eyes again. He just turned away and went up the narrow stairway at the end of the hall that led to his tiny room. Jo slipped into the hall and followed, tapping on his door.

"Go away."

Jo opened the door. "Clint, let me wash your wounds."

"The hell with it. I'm getting the hell out of here come sunrise."

She boldly moved inside and closed the door. "To Montana?"

He looked up at her. "Eventually. It's a long way. I expect I'll have to hold up somewhere and go the rest of the way next spring."

She moved closer, clasping her hands nervously. "Take me with you, Clint."

He looked at her in surprise. He thought how tiny she was, how much she reminded him of Millie. He liked brave women. And he already liked this one too much for his own good. It didn't pay to care about someone.

"Are you crazy? You don't know me *that* well. And you aren't at all prepared."

"How long does it take to buy a few supplies? I have a wagon back at the farm—and the two horses. I've worked a farm for years. I can drive horses and fix wagon wheels, and I can cook anywhere under any circumstances. I'm strong and I'm healthy, and I want to get out of Lawrence,

Clint. I want to go someplace brand new, where I can start all over and forget the ugliness of the past two years. Please, Clint. I can take care of myself. I'm not asking you to be a babysitter—just a guide. I'll gather my own wood and—"

He waved her off. "The Indians out there are still wild. And the white men are almost as dangerous. It's no place for a woman."

"You took your wife there."

The look he gave her made her regret the remark. He rose, turning to put his hands against the wall. He hung his head as he spoke. "Not that far west. It wasn't as wild and uncivilized where Millie and I settled. Things just got out of hand with the Sioux, that's all." He turned and faced her. "You don't realize what you're up against when it comes to Indians."

"I don't care. You should understand better than anyone how I'm feeling, Clint. I don't have anything left to live for." Her eyes teared. "Don't you see? I *want* the excitement, the challenge. If I die, I die. What difference does it make? At least I'll have done something I've never done before, and I'll be so busy just surviving, there won't be time to sit around feeling sorry for myself, mourning my father and my husband and all that I've lost. I *want* to go, Clint. I could claim some land there under the Homestead Act, for free. I've already had a taste of being on my own, of owning land. I like it, Clint. I like the independence. If I claim some land for free, that would leave me money for supplies to help get me started."

"At what?"

"I don't even know yet. Ranching, maybe. All I know is I've been thinking about it, and I'm going whether you take me or not. I just thought—I'd rather go with someone I know."

"You've known me all of three days."

"That's long enough for me."

Their eyes held and he shook his head. "You're really serious!"

"Yes, I am."

He studied her dark eyes, the way her hair shone in the soft light of the lantern. The last thing he wanted was to have to be with her day in and day out, for months. But he

hated the idea more of leaving her behind. She was determined to go west, and he didn't want her traveling with
strangers.

He looked away. "I don't know. I just don't know." He
wiped at the blood on his face and walked to a tiny round
window, wiping dust from it. But he still couldn't see well
outside. He turned to face Jo again, his eyes surveying
her. "You don't know what you're asking. And I don't like
the responsibility."

"You wouldn't be responsible for anything but showing
me the way. Anything that happens to me will be my own
fault, not yours." She stepped closer. "Please, Clint. I've
lain awake half the night trying to decide what to do. The
more I thought about you going to Montana, the more I
envied you. I want to get out of Lawrence, Clint. I *need* to
get out. I have nothing left here, and I won't go to my
sister. I don't want to get any closer to this war, Clint. I
just want to get out."

He studied her dark eyes, eyes he could not refuse. He
sighed deeply, taking on the look of a man defeated. "All
right. Be ready before sunup. We'll go get your wagon and
horses first. I'm not too popular around here right now so
we won't bother to stop in town to stock up on supplies.
We'll head directly west and stock up at Fort Riley."

He took a cigar from a bedstand and lit it, pacing for a
moment. Jo waited, seeing he was lost in thought. "The
quickest way to Montana is to head north on the Missouri
by steamboat, but it's expensive, and in these times not
very dependable," he said almost absently. "Besides, that
would leave us in the heart of Sioux country, which is
much too dangerous right now."

He walked to a small mirror on the wall and touched a
bruise on his cheek, wincing. Jo noticed his knuckles
looked bloody and swollen. He turned away and puffed
the cigar a moment longer. "It's also too dangerous to go
north on the Bozeman Trail from Fort Laramie. Red Cloud
is working hard at closing up that route. We'll head west,
then north a little to the old Oregon Trail out to Fort
Laramie, then stay on the Oregon to Fort Bridger."

Jo's heart pounded with excitement at the thought of
the journey. Even Clint sounded more excited as he spoke.

"We'll probably have to hold up there for the winter. Then we'll head north into Montana following the Rockies."

He turned to face her again. "You'd just better be damned sure this is what you want. I'll not be responsible for another woman dying out there."

"It's my decision. I told you, whatever happens is on my shoulders, not yours."

His eyes moved over her again, as though sizing her up. "Yeah, well that's easy to say. But a man still feels responsible." He ran a hand through his hair. "You'd better get some sleep. Tomorrow is going to be a long day. We'll cover a lot of miles."

Jo smiled. "Thank you. Somehow I'll see you get paid."

He shook his head. "I don't want any pay."

"It's only right. I'll see you in the morning then. Please don't change your mind and leave without me."

He wondered if he had just made the most foolish decision of his life. "I'm a man who keeps his word."

Their eyes held a moment longer and she opened the door. "Good night then."

"Good night."

She smiled at him and left, heading for her room, wanting to run and jump. Her heart felt lighter than it had in months. She was going to Montana!

Chapter Five

Jo stuffed her few belongings into a potato sack she had gleaned from the hotel kitchen. It was all she had in the way of luggage. She wore a simple white blouse and brown cotton skirt, and leather work boots on her feet. She was glad now that she had taken her money out of the bank the day before, for fear that with Lawrence so devastated, robbers and pillagers might ride through the town and try to steal what was left.

It sickened her that she was able to stuff all that she owned into one potato sack, and she wanted to cry. But she refused. She told herself she had to face the fact that nothing could be done about any of it now, and crying would not bring back her belongings or the people she had lost. It was time to move forward.

She only hoped she would find the strength to get through this first day; she couldn't have slept more than two hours. After leaving Clint, she had spent over an hour writing a letter to Anna, trying to explain why she was making this journey, telling her she would let her know where she finally settled. After that she had tried to sleep, but the excitement over what she was about to do had kept sleep from her doorstep until the wee hours of the morning, just before she had to be up to join Clint.

It pained her heart to think of the possibility of never seeing Anna again, yet she was suddenly never more sure of anything than that it was right to leave Lawrence. The loss of the farm seemed like a sign that her life had to change. After all, she had already lost all her loved ones. There was nothing left to hold her here.

The only drawback was her attraction to Clint Reeves. She told herself to be careful, for if she was going to start a new life, it had to be her own. She had suffered too much hurt and was not going to let herself care again as much as she had cared for Greg. She reasoned that her attraction was simply due to loneliness, and she had to ignore it. She could never love another man the way she had loved Greg. And the thought of surviving on her own held the lure of an exciting challenge, which made her eager to prove not just to others, but to herself, that she could do this.

There came a light tap on her door, and she felt a wave of relief. Clint had kept his word to take her with him. She opened the door, and again she felt a deep stir at the way his dark eyes moved over her. He stood there in buckskins, loaded saddlebags slung over his shoulder, a rifle in one hand. "Most of my things are at the livery," he told her. "You ready?"

"I said I would be. I just have to drop off a letter downstairs to be sent to my sister."

He nodded. "Let's go then."

She followed him down the stairs and paid a clerk to see that her letter got to Anna. She hurried out behind Clint then, walking fast to keep up with his long stride. He was quiet, and she could feel the anger that still boiled in his soul. It was obvious he still had not got over the incident of the night before, nor did he want to talk about it. She said nothing as he saddled his horse at the livery and loaded on his supplies, but she could tell he was in some pain. The bruises on his face were more evident, and she could see he had trouble using his sore hands.

"I usually take a second horse for a packhorse," he told her. "But the one I had recently went lame, and I had to shoot it. I figured I could put some of my stuff in your wagon, if it's all right with you."

She held up her potato sack. "I think I can find room."

He finally grinned a little. "We'll pick up more things at Fort Riley. We can get there in a couple of days." He mounted the horse. "Climb up behind me. We'll go get your wagon and horses. I hope the wagon is in good shape."

"It is. I greased the axles only a few days ago."

He grinned a little at the remark, trying to picture her doing what was traditionally a man's work. He reached down and grasped her arm, moving his foot out of the stirrup so she could put hers into it. She grasped his upper arm and pulled herself up, settling into the saddle behind him. He struggled to ignore the feel of her legs straddled behind his own, and Jo in turn leaned back slightly, afraid to let herself lean against him, afraid of how good it would feel to rest against someone strong again.

Clint bid farewell to the livery owner, Marcus White, who nodded to him, then gave Jo a look of disdain. The "mountain man" was riding off with another woman from Lawrence. Jo realized what White must be thinking, but she didn't care. As far as she was concerned, she would never see the man again. Clint turned his big gelding, a fine, sturdy Appaloosa, and rode out.

Jo's heart pounded with apprehension and excitement. She was really riding out of Lawrence! In minutes they reached the farm. The sun was still nothing more than an orange glow in the east, and the burned house and outbuildings were ugly, dark shadows against the sunrise. Jo could still smell the stench of charred embers. She forced herself not to think about it, not to let herself get nostalgic over the fact that she might never set foot on this piece of land again.

As Clint rounded up the horses, Jo thanked God that the last time she used the wagon she had thrown the harness onto the seat rather than hanging it in the barn where it belonged. Otherwise there would be no way to hitch the horses. Her heart lightened even more when Clint returned with four horses rather than two.

"These two belong to you?" he asked her. "I found them grazing near the other two outside the fence."

Jo hurried over to the horses, hugging a roan mare around the neck. "Yes! These are my draft horses, Chester and Hercules! Oh, thank God! Now I have a little more property to bargain with."

"We'll use the draft horses then to pull the wagon. We'll tie Red Lady and Sundance to the back of the wagon to make sure they don't stray. Help me harness these two."

Jo urged the two broad-chested horses into place. Both sturdy animals were gray-and-black geldings. Chester nodded his head and whinnied, and Jo smiled. "I think they're as anxious to get going as we are," she told Clint. "The one with the black tail is Chester. The gray-tailed one is Hercules."

Clint grinned and shook his head at the names.

"Does your horse have a name?" she asked him as she lifted one of the heavy leather harnesses.

Clint took the harness from her. "I don't believe in naming horses. Just makes you get too attached. You never know when you'll have to sell them. Once you name them, they're like part of the family. Now go tie the mare and the buckskin to the back of the wagon."

"Oh, I think every animal should have a name."

"Well, ole Chester and Hercules here, or else those two back there, are going to have to be traded at Fort Riley for a couple of oxen. Horses don't have the stamina for pulling weight over mountains. On our way, you'll have to be thinking about which ones you want to trade."

Jo lost her smile. She couldn't imagine selling any of them, they had been so faithful during her long months alone on the farm. But she didn't want to start their trip being a baby about anything. If Clint said she had to have oxen, then she had to have oxen.

"We'll find a wheelwright at the fort to make you some iron supports to go over the top of the wagon, then put canvas over that so you'll have something like a covered wagon," Clint was saying then. "There will be times when you'll be glad to have that canvas, especially if we get caught in a storm."

Jo nodded, tying the two extra horses. "Whatever you say."

"Take that extra gear from my horse and throw it into the back of the wagon, will you?" Jo obeyed the direction, her heart still hurting at the thought of selling any of her horses. Clint finished harnessing them and Jo climbed up into the wagon seat. He handed her the reins. "I'm sorry about the horses," he told her then. "That's just the way it is. You've got to have oxen. They have a lot more

endurance. I know the draft horses seem big and strong
enough, but few horses are up to the long haul—the daily
struggle it takes to pull a wagon. You've got to remember
that from here westward you're basically going uphill all
the way. When you see the Rockies, you'll understand
even better why we need oxen. There's less oxygen, and
there are climbs that will make your heart stop. It's no job
for horses."

Jo nodded. "I understand."

Clint climbed onto his own mount. "Let's get going."

He rode out, and Jo whipped the horses into motion.
She wondered if Clint would get tired of having to slow
down because of the wagon. Alone on a horse he might
even be able to make it all the way to Montana before
winter set in, but not with a wagon trailing behind. She
felt a little guilty for asking to go along, but her mind was
made up now. No matter how inconvenient it was for
Clint Reeves, she was going with him to Montana.

The sun rose higher, casting a red-gold glow on a line of
trees to the west. She tried to imagine what the Rocky
Mountains might look like. She had never seen mountains
before. She yawned and stretched, urging the horses to go
a little faster, and already feeling the ache of not getting
enough sleep the night before. She kept her eyes focused
west, refusing to look back at the burned-out farm and
familiar places she might never see again.

"Good-bye, Anna," she whispered, biting back tears.
Her throat ached, and she wanted to scream at Clint to ask
him to wait just a little longer. But what was the sense in
putting it off? And what was there to look back upon? It
was all gone. She wanted a new life, and it lay ahead of
her, far away in the west.

A rest stop for "lunch" did not come until three o'clock
in the afternoon. Clint seemed relentless in wanting to
cover as many miles as possible that first day. Jo fought an
urge to complain, sure he was only testing her, trying to
make her change her mind in time to turn back for
Lawrence.

But the more Clint pushed, and the more tired she got,
the more determined Jo was to keep going without saying
a word about rest. She would show Clint Reeves she

could be just as strong and stubborn as he. Her hands were already getting callused, and she decided she would buy gloves at the fort.

Earlier in the day she had held the reins between her knees while she tied on her slat bonnet against the hot prairie sun, deciding not to ask Clint to stop for such a "womanly" need. She was overjoyed that she had left the bonnet lying under the wagon seat so that it survived the fire, for there had been no time to buy a new one; she was sure her brains would be thoroughly cooked by now if she had not been able to put it on.

Her shoulders screamed with pain from driving the wagon all day, and all afternoon she fought against the desire to fall asleep right on the wagon seat. She was so tired that after several hours the wagon's jolting and bouncing were not enough to keep her awake, and the constant, rhythmic creak of the wagon wheels began to lull her.

All day Clint had ridden ahead of her, watching the horizon, keeping an eye out for snakes. Finally he rode back to the draft horses, grabbing hold of one harness and helping Jo halt the animals. He pointed to a stand of trees on the Missouri River. "Head over there and we'll eat something and rest a couple of hours," he told her.

The words were like music to Jo's ears. She drove the wagon to a stand of trees and climbed down, every bone and muscle stiff and sore. "I'll gather some wood," she told Clint, feeling like a walking dead person as she headed into the trees. She found a spot where the sun shone through the leaves onto soft, green grass. A fallen branch of cottonwood lay nearby, so brittle it could be broken into pieces.

Jo sat down on the grass, intending to sit there just a moment to gather her strength. She reached over and pulled the branch toward her, wincing as the blisters on her fingers touched the wood. A gentle breeze cooled her hot face, and she removed her bonnet, enjoying the shade. She lay back to rest for a moment, but almost instantly her eyes closed and she drifted off to sleep.

When she awoke, Jo realized someone had covered her and had put a blanket under her head. It was dark, and somewhere not far away an owl hooted. She sat up, pulling the blanket closer, gathering her thoughts. Was she alone? In a panic she called out Clint's name, and moments later she heard someone walking through the nearby brush.

"It's all right. It's me—Clint," came a voice.

"Oh, Clint, what happened? Where are we?"

"We're still where we stopped this afternoon."

"What! You mean—I *slept* all this time?"

"You needed the rest. I decided another day wouldn't cost us that much."

"Oh, no! Oh, I'm so sorry! I just—last night I didn't sleep at all. It won't happen again, Clint." She was glad it was too dark for him to see her red face. She felt devastated. She had tried so hard to prove she could keep up with him. How could she have let this happen?

"Don't worry about it. This is your first day."

"But I've had days when I worked from sunup to sundown on the farm—and worked hard."

"I said don't worry about it. It's just one of those things." She felt him helping her up. "Come on over to the campfire. There's some food and coffee left."

"Oh, this is terrible! You had to tend the horses and gather the wood and fix the food. I should have helped with all that."

He grinned at her concern. "You can do all that tomorrow. Right now just eat and get some more sleep. You'll feel a lot better tomorrow. And I want you to wear a pair of my gloves. They'll be big on you, but your hands will be so raw you won't be able to drive at all if you go gloveless again tomorrow. I noticed how blistered they were when I covered you up."

"I have some cream I can put on them." She stopped and looked up at him. "Oh, Clint, I really am sorry."

He studied her in the moonlight, a sudden, terrible desire to kiss her sweeping through him. It angered him. He quickly walked ahead of her. "Don't worry about it. It happens. It's only your first day," he said brusquely.

She quickly followed him to the campfire, sure he was angry over her falling asleep, for he was suddenly cool and distant again. He handed her a tin plate and cup and pointed to the coffee pot and a pan that sat over the fire.

"There are some beans in the pan and some biscuits in the leather bag next to it. I picked the biscuits up yesterday in Lawrence, so we'll have to eat them up first before they get stale." He moved to his bedroll and settled down with his head against his saddle. "You can stretch out wherever you want when you're through. You might want to sleep in the back of the wagon."

She choked down a piece of biscuit. "Shouldn't one of us keep watch or something?"

"The animals are hobbled. As far as intruders, we're not likely to be bothered by anybody way out here. At any rate, my ears hear everything, asleep or awake."

She took comfort in his abilities on the trail. But she felt angry and depressed that she had upset him by falling asleep. She quickly scooped up the beans and finished a biscuit, then washed the food down with strong coffee. She wanted to tell him she had to go relieve herself, but his eyes were closed, and she didn't want to bother him again. She fished around in his gear for some paper, then walked off into the shadows, hoping he wouldn't come looking for her while she was in a compromising position. When she finished she moved to the wagon and climbed up into the bed she had made and lay down.

The night was filled with strange sounds, but Jo felt safe and protected. She told herself she had to get used to this loneliness, to night sounds under the stars. After all, Clint Reeves would not always be at her side to protect her. She chided herself for falling asleep earlier in the day, and she made a personal vow never to let such a thing happen again.

They rolled into Fort Riley the third day after leaving Lawrence. Its limestone buildings were a welcome sight, especially the supply house. There were many things Jo needed, most of all a pair of gloves that fit her, if she could find any. She hoped to find a supply of women's necessities. Although this was an army fort, travelers often stopped here for supplies, or so Clint had told her. She noticed several emigrant wagons camped outside the fort, including, she guessed, other people who had decided to leave Lawrence.

As they approached the wagons, Jo noticed a few familiar faces, people she had seen around Lawrence but didn't know very well. She nodded to them, and she felt their stares. She was a woman traveling alone with the "mountain man" who had stolen away Howard Styles's daughter, and she could just imagine what those who knew her were thinking. She drove straight ahead, following Clint into the fort and to one of the several stables, where he spoke to a civilian he apparently knew, explaining the work he wanted done to Jo's wagon. They unhitched the draft horses and packed their gear onto them, leading all the horses back outside the fort.

"Let's hope it doesn't rain the next couple of nights," Clint said. "We'll still be sleeping under the stars."

"Joline!"

Jo turned to see Sarah Grant approaching her.

"Sarah!" Jo hurried up to the woman and they embraced. "What are you doing here, Sarah?"

The woman's eyes teared instantly. "We're heading west, child. Our daughter, Bess, and her husband have come along. You know Bess and Johnny Hills, don't you—and my grandsons, Lonnie and Joey?"

"I remember them from church."

The older woman wiped at her tears. "We lost most everything in the raid, Joline. Johnny always did talk about going to Oregon, so we decided this was as good a time as any. All our crops were ruined by the raiders, but at least our home didn't burn all the way down. We managed to save a few things but we're getting out of Lawrence. We've had our fill of living in constant fear."

"Oh, I know what you mean, Sarah. I'm leaving, too. I'm headed for Montana."

"Montana! Oh, child, such wild country!" Sarah glanced at Clint, then turned questioning eyes to Jo. "Why Montana?"

"I'm not even sure, Sarah. I just want the challenge, I guess, and there is land there that can be claimed under the Homestead Act. Mr. Reeves knows how to get there. I've hired him as my guide."

Sarah grasped her hand. "Such a brave girl you've always been—and so independent." She sighed deeply. "Men here at the fort tell us we can't possibly get all the way to Oregon this year, but at least we'll have a head start. Bess and Johnny are using the covered wagon behind our farm wagon over there." The woman pointed to two wagons nearby. A younger man and woman sat near it, and two young boys were playing tag. "Lucky for us we kept the covered wagon we used to come to Kansas from Illinois," Sarah added. "And between what we saved and what we were able to purchase here, we should be well set for our journey. How much did you lose in the raid, child?"

"Everything, Sarah, except what little money I had in the bank and a few horses, and my wagon, of course. Mr. Styles bought the farm from me, and I've decided to get as far away from the war as I can get. With my husband Greg dead, I want to start over someplace new." She turned to Clint. "Forgive me for not introducing you. Clint, this is Sarah Grant. She and her husband attended the same church as Greg and I. Sarah, this is Clint Reeves."

The woman squinted from the sun shining behind Clint. She put out her hand. "Hello, Mr. Reeves. I've heard about you."

Clint shook her hand gently. "Nothing good, I expect. But I'm not as bad as people say."

"Clint is a good man, Sarah," Jo told the woman. "He helped me a great deal right after the raid. And he's made a living at scouting, knows the west well. I decided I couldn't be in better hands."

"Oh, how fortunate for you." The woman put on a smile for Clint. "I'm afraid we'll be hunting our own way out west."

"Well, good luck to you," Clint told her. He looked at Jo, appearing suddenly anxious to get away. "I'll go tend to the horses and make camp, Jo." He turned and walked away, leaving Jo with Mrs. Grant.

"You're so lucky to have a good guide, Joline," the older woman told her. "Do you think it's safe, though, traveling alone with a man you hardly know?"

"I know him well enough, Sarah," Jo answered defensively. "He's the only person who helped me after the raid. He even gave up his room at the hotel for me—bought me some clothes. He was so kind. He helped a lot of people that first night, and he got hurt fighting Quantrill's men. I trust him."

"Oh, well, if you're sure." The woman glanced at Clint again, watching his long stride. "It's . . . just the two of you then?"

Jo bristled. "Yes. It's just a business arrangement, Sarah."

"Oh, I understand! I wasn't asking because of that. I was just wondering . . . won't you have to follow the Oregon Trail most of the way? My husband showed me a map he has of the west. To go to Montana you would have to go quite far west before you head north."

"What are you saying, Sarah?"

"Well, I . . ." The woman's eyes watered. "Joline, none of us in our little group truly knows the way, or the land out there, what dangers we'll face. And we certainly don't know much about Indians. Mr. Reeves looks like such an experienced man. Anyone who has ever heard of him knows he traveled that land for years. And it seems such a coincidence, a godsend, you might say, that he shows up here where we're camped, all of us wishing someone would come along who could guide us on our journey."

Jo frowned. "You mean . . . you want Clint Reeves to guide you?"

The woman's eyes grew pleading. "Do you think he would? We could pay him."

Jo looked in Clint's direction. She had already burdened him enough asking to go with him. The man was a loner. "I don't know, Sarah. I had to beg him to take *me* along. I'm not sure he'd like the idea of taking on more people. Besides, he's not going to Oregon."

"Well, he'll be going *most* of the way. Will you at least ask him for us?"

Jo knew what Clint would think of such an idea, but she didn't have the heart to say no to Mrs. Grant. Fear of the journey ahead was evident in the old woman's eyes, and she and her family had lost so much. Jo knew the feeling of desperate homelessness. "I'll ask him," she answered.

"Oh, thank you. It will be best for you, too, Joline, to have some woman company."

Jo realized it would be much safer emotionally if she could talk Clint into guiding all of them. After all, if she continued for weeks traveling alone with him, her feelings might get dangerously out of control. She could not allow herself to care too deeply for Clint Reeves. And Mrs. Grant was right. How did she know how Clint himself would behave after weeks alone with a woman. He might get ideas. She had noticed how he looked at her some-

mes, had caught a look of admiration that bordered on
esire in his dark eyes more than once. He was a lonely
.an, she reasoned. He had not yet recovered from the
.ss of his wife.

She headed toward a grassy spot under a sprawling
.ttonwood tree, where Clint was unloading the horses. Jo
.rew a deep breath for courage and approached him,
.raying he wouldn't be so angry that he would leave all of
.em behind, including herself.

"Clint?"

He turned, then set down a saddle. "What is it?"

"Mrs. Grant . . . the old woman you met a moment
.o."

Clint glanced in the woman's direction, noticing she was
.atching. "Seems a bit nosey to me."

Jo swallowed. "It isn't that at all. She only stopped us
.ecause . . . Clint, they've lost so much—all these people—
.ke me."

He straightened and met her eyes. "And?"

She folded her arms. "And they're going into a land
.hey don't know anything about. They aren't even sure
.hich way to go. I mean, I suppose by now the Oregon
.rail is pretty easy to follow, but—"

"It is," he answered, turning to take the blanket off his
.orse.

"Clint, they need a guide. They're willing to pay."

He kept his back to her, slowly lowering the blanket
.nd sighing deeply. "Jo, all I want is to get to Montana. I
.asn't even crazy about taking *you* along. But I agreed
.ecause—" He hesitated. Because she looked like Millie?
.Ie thought how ridiculous that remark would sound. Be-
.ides, she might get romantic ideas, and that was the last
.hing he wanted. "Because I knew you could pull your
.wn weight. Some of those others don't have what it
.akes."

"Clint, there are old people, and little children along. I
.eel sorry for them. And isn't there some kind of safety in
.umbers?"

"Only if they know how to use a rifle and how to stay
.alm and obey orders."

"I think they're all capable of those things."

He sighed deeply, turning to face her. "It's been a long

time since I headed up any wagon train, Jo. And it isn
just the Grants and their family. There are other wagor
here. They'll all want in on this. I'm really not in the moo
for having a lot of people around."

"Will you . . . at least think about it? We have to sta
until the wagon is ready anyway. Maybe you could at leas
talk to them—explain some of the things they shoul
watch out for. You could do that much, couldn't you?"

He studied the pretty face, the full lips. How was h
going to control his feelings after spending weeks alon
with this woman? He glanced at the others camped nearby
saw the look of hope on Sarah Grant's face. The last thin
he wanted was to have a bunch of greenhorns along. But
it meant being able to keep his distance from Jo Masters
maybe it would be worth it. He wondered how he man
aged to get himself into this mess. He wished now he ha
got out of Lawrence before the raid. Then he never woul
have had occasion to help Jo Masters.

"I'll think about it," he told her aloud. He turned bac
to unloading his gear, cursing his weakness for big brow
eyes and a pretty smile.

Chapter Six

Jo shivered and held her blanket around her as she built a fire. The eastern sky was a red glow from the impending sunrise. Since they weren't going anywhere this morning, she knew she was up earlier than necessary, but an aching back from lying on the hard ground had made it impossible to continue sleeping. She wished more than anything that she could take a hot bath; but it was obvious that bathing and other luxuries would be rare for the next several months, and she told herself she had better get used to this life for a while, backaches and all.

She got the fire going and ground some coffee beans with a hand grinder Clint had purchased at the fort. Her own grinder had been lost in the fire. She carefully poured some ground coffee into a small cloth bag, making sure not to spill any of the precious grounds. She still couldn't get over the fact that coffee beans could be purchased already roasted. All one had to do was grind them before making the coffee. It was a wonderful time-saver. She put the cloth bag into a pot of water and set it over the fire.

She opened a tin can of bacon grease and spooned some into a heavy black fry-pan, then began slicing some potatoes into it, happy to have the new utensils and a better supply of food. She knew there were many more things she needed to purchase before leaving the fort, but she realized she would have to be very careful how she spent what little money she had. It would have seemed like a lot of money if she wasn't forced to replace virtually everything a person needed to live decently.

The coffee pot began to steam, and the potatoes were frying. Jo glanced at Clint, who seemed to be still sleeping soundly. He had said next to nothing to her the night before, after agreeing to lead the others west. He had seemed restless and troubled, and Jo wished she knew a little more about his past. She was sure something very important was being left out in the story about his wife's and son's deaths, and she wondered why, if they were killed by raiding Indians, Clint hadn't also been killed. Surely he would have fought to the death for his family. Perhaps he wasn't around when it happened. But she was afraid to ask for details.

She noticed that old Mrs. Grant was already up, building her own fire. The woman looked in Jo's direction and nodded, and Jo gave her a wave. Clint stirred then and sat up. He glanced at the fire and the frying potatoes.

"Good morning," Jo said.

"Morning." He pulled on his boots and walked off for several minutes, returning to retrieve a brush from his saddlebag and run it through his thick hair. "Not light enough to shave yet," he muttered.

"I know," Jo answered. "I haven't even combed my hair."

"I might be able to talk one of the officers into letting you use the bathhouse if you'd like," he told her. "It will be a couple of weeks before we hit another town. If we were going straight west we'd run into a few more towns. But we've got to head north from here to catch the old trail."

Jo thought how odd it was that they were discussing personal things like bathing and shaving, as though they were husband and wife, or sister and brother. She had constantly to remind herself she had known Clint Reeves only six days.

"I'd love a bath," she told him. "Thank you for thinking of it."

He rubbed at his eyes. "You'd better make up your mind about those horses," he told her. "There's a trader here who'll bargain with you on some oxen. You've either got to buy them or trade a couple of your horses for them, like I told you."

Jo stirred the potatoes, glancing over at her four tethered horses. She had wrestled with indecision all night over whether to spend some of her precious savings, or get rid of the draft horses. If she settled in Montana, she would need the draft horses again if she wanted to break ground for planting. Still, she had to get to Montana first, and if Clint said oxen were needed for the journey, then she had no choice but to buy some.

"What about the other travelers?" she asked then. "I see six wagons and only four oxen. Most of them are apparently using horses."

Clint sat down near the fire. "That's their problem. They'll figure it out soon enough. When they do, they'll find the oxen they need. The trail to Oregon has been pretty well used now for twenty years. There are other forts and a few towns along the way where they can get hold of oxen."

"Are you saying now you won't guide them?"

"All they have to do is follow the ruts."

"Clint, it isn't just a matter of following ruts. I already know that and we've only been traveling three days. And the more people, the more there are to help out if something goes wrong. And there are Indians to be considered. The newspaper in Lawrence was full of stories about the Sioux raiding gold camps in the north."

He frowned, anger in his dark eyes. "This is a fine time for you to bring that up. I know all too well about raiding Sioux, remember?" His eyes flashed at her. "Don't you realize where you want to go is right in the thick of the problem? I never should have agreed to take you, let alone consider leading a whole train. You've got no business up there, Joline. If I agree to lead these people, it will only be if you agree to stay with them once we hit Fort Bridger, and go on to Oregon with them. There is an Indian danger most of the way, but not as dangerous as farther north."

"But I don't *want* to go to Oregon. I want to go to Montana."

"Why? There is nothing there but wild Indians and wild animals and wild miners. It's no place for a woman!"

She almost winced at the remark, realizing how quickly his mood could change when Indians were mentioned. She faced him squarely, her own anger showing then. "Well *this* woman knows hard work; and *this* woman handled Quantrill's raid and lost everything, and she isn't beaten yet! *This* woman knows how to shoot straight, and she has nothing left but to start all over."

"Then why not start in Oregon?"

"Because Oregon is already heavily settled. I don't *want* that! I want the *challenge*, Clint. It will help me forget the pain of the past. Surely you understand that better than most!"

He leaned closer, his eyes almost menacing. "Oh, yes, I understand, all right! And I understand a lot better than you what Indians can do to white women! I don't want that responsibility again, Joline. You don't know what you're asking of me!"

"It *isn't* your responsibility. Why do you keep bringing that up? Your job is simply to show me the way. The rest is up to me."

He told himself she was right. Why did he care what happened to her? He straightened. "Fine. If you want to commit suicide, it's your privilege."

"I'll be just fine. And you already promised you would take me. I thought you said you were a man of your word."

He rolled his eyes and turned away. "Make up your mind about the horses," he grumbled.

"What about the others? Can I tell them you'll guide them?"

He sighed deeply, as though beaten. He turned and faced her then. "You know, a few days ago I was alone and perfectly content. I intended to get to Montana before winter set in. Now I'm guiding a whole wagon train of greenhorns west. Just how did I get into all of this?"

Jo felt like crying as she stirred the potatoes. "I'm not sure how I got into it myself. Life takes some strange turns sometimes."

"Yeah, I guess it does. You make up your mind about those horses and we'll go see the trader about the oxen." He looked past her at Mrs. Grant, who was hesitantly approaching them. Clint frowned with irritation as she stood staring at them both. Jo turned with his gaze and rose to greet the old woman. "Good morning, Sarah."

"Morning. I . . . I was just wondering. I told my husband last night about Mr. Reeves, and he is in full agreement, if Mr. Reeves will guide us. I couldn't help hearing you argue, and I'm sorry if we caused problems. Have you . . . decided?" The woman looked at Clint. "We collected some money. It isn't much."

Clint looked from Sarah Grant to Jo, his jaw flexing with repressed agitation. His eyes moved back to Mrs. Grant. "I'll guide you," he told her. "And you can keep your money. I was going that way anyway. You'll need to buy supplies, all the nonperishable things you can pack. And tell the others they'll need to buy some oxen somewhere along the way—trade your horses for them—or you can use mules. Horses don't have the stamina for pulling heavy loads over mountains. And if anybody with you is sickly or any women are carrying, they go back to Lawrence. We'll have enough problems without starting out with them. We'll leave as soon as Jo's wagon gets outfitted with some canvas, either tomorrow or the day after. And if I'm going to be your guide, I expect everyone to listen to what I tell them and do as I say."

The woman smiled. "Thank you so much, Mr. Reeves. I'll go tell the others."

Sarah left, and Clint looked at Jo. "Well, this turned into quite a parade, didn't it? All I can say is, if anybody has problems and lags behind, they can just wait for the next wagon train that comes along because I'm not waiting. Is that clear?"

"Does that include me?"

"It most certainly does." He turned and walked toward his horse.

"Where are you going?" Jo asked him.

"I don't know. Just riding. I like to be by myself in the early morning. I reckon it will be quite a while before I get *that* pleasure again!" He slipped a bridle on the horse and moved with ease onto its bare back, riding off without another word.

Jo watched after him. She felt guilty for putting this burden on him, but she also felt sorry for the travelers at the fort. And she realized Clint Reeves was a deeply troubled man. She wondered herself what she had gotten into. Maybe he was right about Oregon; but his remark about a woman not being able to make it in Montana only angered her and made her even more determined.

She stirred the potatoes again, wondering if he would come back to eat them.

It was two hours before Clint returned. He found the coals of the fire still glowing, and some potatoes left in the fry-pan. He poured himself some coffee and winced at how strong it was, then looked around, wondering where Jo had gone. It was then he saw the two oxen, ambling from the far side of the fort, where the corrals and the horse trader were located. At first it looked as though the animals were wandering on their own, but then he heard a woman's voice shouting "Git! Git up there!"

Clint grinned, losing his anger at the sight of Joline hanging onto a rope that was tied to the oxen. She was literally being pulled along behind them, struggling to stay in control of the animals as she used a staff she held in her other hand to poke at them and keep them moving. He hurried over to help her but she angrily refused. The other travelers stared at her tiny frame as she poked and shouted at the big, lumbering animals until they were far enough out into the grazing field near her campsite to be fettered.

"Let me hold one while you fetter the other," Clint told her then, taking the ropes from her hand. "You'll get stepped on."

She grudgingly let him help. "I can tell you right now I don't like oxen at all," she grumbled. "They're ugly and stubborn, and the man I traded with says I'll have to walk with them most of the way. I can't drive them like a team of horses. You never told me that, Clint Reeves."

He laughed lightly. "There is probably someone along with the others who can drive them for you. And I guarantee you'll like them well enough before this trip is over. You trade the draft horses for them? I don't see them around."

"Yes," she said sadly, already missing Chester and Hercules.

"Well, when you get to Montana, these oxen will do you

as much or more good as those horses if you want to break ground. They're damned strong animals."

"Well, I want to learn to drive them myself."

"That's fine, but you'll want to let someone relieve you once in a while, or you'll walk all the way to Montana."

"Others have probably done it."

"They have." He helped fetter the other oxen, giving it a slap on the rump. "You did pretty well. They look healthy."

"They're only four and six years old, so the trader told me." She backed away and studied the huge but gentle beasts. "They're freshly shod, too." She looked at Clint, glad to see he was apparently in a better mood again. "Did I really make a good deal? I had to give the man fifty dollars as well as the harness to the horses so I could get a yoke for the oxen. You'll have to help me carry it. They *must* be strong to walk all day with that heavy piece of wood on their backs."

Clint walked back to the campfire. "I'll help just as soon as I eat these potatoes," he told her. "By the way, do you always make your coffee so strong?"

"Keeps a man, or woman, alert, my father always said. Greg liked it strong, too." The words came out so naturally, and it irritated her that the thought of her dead husband could come to her in such unexpected moments, piercing her again with the pain of his loss. Clint took a fork from his gear and knelt down to stab at some of the potatoes.

"What was he like?" he asked.

Jo swallowed, her throat suddenly aching. "He wasn't a tall man, but he was stocky, very strong, a hard worker, but a gentle man, too. He and my father worked the farm together." She sat down across from him, pouring herself some coffee. "I met Greg in 1859, when he came to Kansas from Illinois. He was twenty-five, I was eighteen. We married a year later, and we had just one year together before he and my father went off to fight for the Union. Several months later they were both killed." She swallowed some coffee. "That was a year ago," she said thoughtfully. "It's hard to believe it's been over two years since I said good-bye to Greg. For a long time I kept expecting to see him show up at my doorstep, hoping it was all a mistake." She looked at Clint. "It's hard to have someone you love die so far away, where you can't be with them, hold them in their last minutes of life, comfort them. I have no idea how much he suffered, if he called for me." Tears came into her eyes.

Clint stared at the glowing embers of the fire. "You should be glad it happened that way. To be right there . . . to witness it—" He suddenly threw his fork into the pan and slugged down the rest of his coffee. "Let's go talk to the others and find out who we'll be traveling with."

She watched him, wanting to ask him to tell her more. So close. He had come so close to explaining what had happened. So, he had been right there, had watched his wife and son die. How did he escape alive? It was obvious he had told her all he intended to. He was already walking toward the Grant wagons, and Jo followed.

Sarah quickly gathered her own family, sending one of her grandsons to tell anyone who wanted to travel with Clint Reeves to come together. Men and women left breakfast fires to gather near the Grant wagons, and Jo could see the fear and sorrow in the eyes of the women. They had lost homes, just as she had. Some had probably lost loved ones in the raid. Their lives had been suddenly and dramatically changed. Suddenly "home" no longer existed.

"I'm Clint Reeves," Clint spoke up, wondering if he had lost his mind agreeing to do this. "I've traveled all over the west and I know the Oregon Trail well. I've promised Mrs. Grant that any of you who wants to travel with me as a guide is welcome. But I don't want any sick or injured people along, or any woman who's carrying. Are most of your wagons in good shape?"

A man nodded. "Most of us were farmers." He spoke up. "Had to keep our wagons in good condition. I'm Donald Sievers and this is my wife, Martha, and my daughter, Rose. Rose is fourteen."

Jo studied the dark, stocky man and his wife and daughter, both plain and shy. She had seen all these people at one time or another in Lawrence, but the Grants and their daughter, Bess Hills, were the only ones she knew reasonably well.

"I'm Bennett Kiehl." Another man spoke up. He was a short, skinny man with a balding head. "I'm a farmer, too.

This here is my son Bobbie. He's seventeen. If anybody needs a hand driving their wagon, Bobbie can help."

Clint glanced at Jo. "Mrs. Masters might need some help," he answered, looking back at Kiehl. "Does Bobbie know how to drive oxen?"

"Yes, sir."

Jo wondered how Bobbie could be so tall. He towered over his father. She also wondered how someone so bony could be strong enough to handle oxen.

"You got a wife?" Clint asked the man.

"She's been dead six years now."

Clint nodded. "Sorry." His eyes moved to a man standing alone. He looked as though he were in his late thirties. "And you?" Clint asked.

"I'm Bill Starke—bootmaker." A look of terrible loneliness shone in the man's eyes. "My wife was killed by Quantrill's men. She was only eighteen."

Jo's heart tightened. She remembered seeing Betsy Starke in town only three weeks earlier. The young woman had not been married long, and she was shopping for more things to put a woman's touch to her house. Starke had been a bachelor for many years, and she remembered Betsy Starke mentioning how badly his home needed decorating.

Clint and Bill Starke just looked at each other for a moment, sharing the pain. "Apparently just about everyone here has lost loved ones," Clint said aloud. "I guess that's one thing we all share in common."

Starke frowned. "You're the one who was married to Millie Styles, aren't you?"

The others watched curiously.

"I am. Millie and our son were killed by the Sioux up in Minnesota last year."

Starke nodded. "I was real sorry to hear about that," he answered. "And you're right. Most all of us have known that kind of loss. We know Mrs. Masters there lost her husband and father in the war."

Clint quickly moved his eyes to another couple, wanting to drop the subject of death. "We're Bess and Johnnie Hills," the pretty blond woman told him. "I'm Sarah and Bradley Grant's daughter. You've already met my mother." She put her arm through that of an older man. "This is my father. And the man standing with the boys there is my husband. The youngest boy is Joey. He's eight. Lonnie is ten. We all know Joline pretty good."

Clint moved his eyes over all of them, counting. If he included the last couple, who as yet had not introduced themselves, there were five women, six men, three young boys, and one young girl. There would be seven wagons along, none of them too heavily loaded, as most of these people had been burned out before leaving Lawrence and didn't have much in the way of personal possessions. He studied the last couple, a strong-looking and very stern woman with jet-black hair pulled into a tight bun at the back of her head, her big bosom corseted up so stiffly that Clint wondered how she could walk.

"I am Marie Boone," the woman told him; her thin lips remained in a hard line, with no hint of a smile. "This is my husband, Sidney." She nodded in the direction of a short, skinny man who appeared shy and mousy. Joline wondered who was the stronger, Sidney or Marie. She suppressed a smile. "We owned a men's clothing store in Lawrence—got burned out," Marie said matter-of-factly. "Managed to save a few things. I've got lots of material along. I intend to make clothes and get started over again in Oregon."

The woman spoke as though it were all up to her and her husband had no say in the decision.

"Makes no difference to me what any of you intends to do when you get to Oregon," Clint told them. "My job is just to get you to Fort Bridger. That's the farthest I can take you, since I'm heading into Montana after that. You can probably find a guide to take you the rest of the way from Fort Bridger; but you'll have to wait out the winter there. You'll never get over the mountains in time. I want all of you to stock up on supplies as best you can, and like I said, you need oxen. If there aren't enough here, we'll hit more forts and towns along the way where you can trade. Anybody lags behind, they can wait up for another wagon train. I fell into this job and I don't feel I have to wait on anybody."

"What's in Montana?" Starke asked.

"Gold," Clint answered. "I don't intend to dig for it myself. Just intend to guide men up into the mountains, find odd jobs. It's pretty country and a place where a man can be alone if he wants. I've got no real purpose for going there. I just want to get away from civilization."

"What about Indians?" Marie Boone asked, her face still stern. "If you lost your wife and son to them, do you know how to handle them?"

Jo cringed at the words.

"Marie!" the woman's husband spoke up, embarrassed.

"It's a necessary question," the woman spouted.

Clint glared at her, easily understanding why the couple was childless. He wondered what ever possessed Sidney Boone to marry such a black crow. If she were a man, he would be sorely tempted to land a fist in her face, and he didn't doubt she could probably take it like a man.

"I've dealt with Indians for years," he told her, the anger evident in his voice. "I've traded with them, lived among them, called some friend. I've also done battle with them. If we are attacked, my orders are to be followed exactly. Is that understood?" His eyes scanned the group and they all nodded. He looked back at Mrs. Boone. "The situation involving my wife was different. A lot of people died in those raids last year—people caught alone and unsuspecting."

"And how is it you lived?" the woman asked.

Jo's eyes widened with anger and surprise. Clint stepped closer to the woman, towering over her. The look of arrogance left the woman's dark eyes, replaced by fright. "I have my scars," Clint growled. "And I don't owe you any explanations. If there is something about me you don't like, lady, you can stay behind and wait for another wagon train to come along!"

The woman sniffed and held her chin defiantly. "I just want to be sure we're relying on the right man," she told him. "I am sorry if I offended you."

Clint fought an urge to put his hands around her thick neck. He turned, his eyes meeting Jo's. "We'll have another meeting later," he told her. He walked off, heading toward the fort, and Jo marched up to Marie Boone.

"You're a very rude woman, Mrs. Boone," she told her flatly. "Mr. Reeves is doing us a favor. He didn't even take the money Sarah Grant offered him."

The woman looked her over. "I apologized." She folded

her arms. "We all know about the mountain man, Mrs. Masters. His past is very fuzzy. If I were you, I would be careful being alone with a near stranger."

"Well you're *not* me, so you don't have to worry about it."

"Mr. Reeves's background, or the people Joline chooses for friends, is not our business," Sarah Grant told Mrs. Boone, stepping up beside Jo. "We have a good guide now, and that is all that matters."

Marie Boone held her chin haughtily and marched back to her wagon. Her husband looked at everyone apologetically and turned to follow his wife. Jo turned to Sarah. "Thank you," she told the old woman.

Sarah put a hand on her arm. "We're just glad to get a little more organized. And this will be better for you, too, Joline. A woman should have other women to talk to on such a long journey."

Jo smiled. "Please call me Jo."

Sarah patted her arm. "I'll try to remember."

Jo started to return to her own camp, then she spotted them—three men headed into the fort, one wearing the black coat that unmistakably belonged to Bart Kendall. She frowned with irritation that the man would show up here, of all places. Kendall and the men with him were leading several horses ahead of them, and Jo recognized three of her own horses among them, two Appaloosa mares and a shaggy red gelding.

"He stole them!" she muttered. Sarah Grant turned in the direction of Jo's stare and recognized Bart Kendall. Most everyone in Lawrence knew the man.

"Stole what, dear?" she asked, turning back to Jo.

"My horses!" Jo hurried off to get her rifle, and Sarah called to her husband.

"You'd better go find that Reeves fellow," she told him. "I think there is going to be trouble."

Bradley Grant hurried inside the fort, and Johnny Hills walked up to his mother-in-law to ask what was wrong.

"Jo says that Kendall and those men have some of her horses."

Johnny watched as Kendall and the men herded the animals into an empty fort corral, whistling and shouting until all fifteen horses were inside.

"By God, I think I see a couple of my *own* horses!" he exclaimed. "That thieving scum went around and rounded up horses after the raid, I'll bet. He probably figures on selling them here—make a profit off what belongs to *us!*"

A soldier closed the gate to the corral, and Kendall and the two men with him headed toward the command post to talk to whoever was in charge about selling the horses to the army.

All three men were met by a small young woman holding a Henry repeating rifle; Johnny Hills and others were gathered around her.

"Stop right there, Bart Kendall!" Jo ordered, leveling her rifle at the man.

Kendall and his men drew their horses to a halt, and Kendall grinned. "Well, well," he said, tipping his hat. "If it isn't the pretty little lady from Lawrence—the one with the Confederate sister." He frowned. "Is it true you left Lawrence with the mountain man?" He laughed lightly. "Ole Clint Reeves does have a way with the ladies, it seems."

"You shut your filthy mouth!" Jo answered, her rifle steady. "What I do is none of your business. But what you do is *my* business when it comes to stealing my horses!"

Kendall's eyebrows shot up in surprise. "*Your* horses? Why, hell, ma'am, me and my men here found these horses running wild." He turned to the other two men. "Didn't we, boys?"

Both men nodded in agreement, grinning.

"You went out and stole horses that were scattered after Quantrill's raid!" Johnny Hills spoke up then, fists clenched.

"You've got two Appaloosa mares and one big, shaggy, red gelding in that herd that belong to me," Jo told Kendall. "I'd know them anyplace. One Appaloosa has a black patch over its eye, and the other has a white star on its forehead. And there's no mistaking the shaggy red one. There isn't another horse around here like him. I need those horses, Kendall, and I intend to take them."

"Mine, too," Hills added. "You've got three of them."

"And two more are mine," Donald Sievers spoke up then. He was headed in their direction from the corral, where he had taken a look at the fresh stock. Sievers's wife and daughter scurried behind the man, looking frightened.

Kendall shrugged. "I say finders, keepers. You dumb farmers ought to brand your animals."

"We don't need to," Jo answered. "We know which horses are ours. And if somebody else's stray onto our property, we take them back. That's the way it is. People of honor on such small farms don't need to brand their animals."

"That's too bad," Kendall said, shaking his head. "I guess it's your loss then. Without proof they belong to you, you've got no more right to them than anybody else."

"You know our papers got burned up in the raid," Jo said, her voice steady and her anger intense. "You're just a lazy, worthless human being who gets along by sucking the blood of others. But you'll make no profit on what belongs to me or any of these other people!"

Kendall snickered. "Well, I say the horses belong to me, and I intend to sell them to the fort commander. And I don't think you really intend to pull that trigger, Mrs. Masters."

"Don't I?" Jo fired, startling everyone and sending a bullet whizzing dangerously close to Kendall's hat. All three men struggled for a moment with whinnying, rearing horses.

"I killed a man during Quantrill's raid, Kendall," Jo warned. "Somebody told me once that after the first one, it gets easier. I think maybe they were right. I've lost everything, and all I have left for financial survival is those horses! I'll kill to get them if I have to!"

Kendall steadied his horse, his face red with rage. "Why, you little bitch!" he snarled. "I ought to—"

"Ought to what, Kendall?" Clint approached the scene, heading out of the fort with Bradley Grant hurrying behind him. Clint carried his own rifle. He leveled it at Bart Kendall. "You a woman-killer on top of all your other fine qualities?"

Kendall swung his horse around. "You stay out of this Reeves! This isn't your business!"

"I'm guiding these people west. That *makes* it my business. Now get down off that horse and we'll let the commanding officer here at the fort decide what to do. But it's pretty obvious these horses are *all* stolen. You've never worked a day in your life, and you don't own more than the clothes on your back and *maybe* the horse you're sitting on. Anybody from Lawrence knows the kind of lowlife you are."

"Lowlife?" Kendall dismounted and stepped closer to Clint. "You want to talk about lowlife, I'm looking at one! Any man who would take a nice lady like Millie Styles off to the wilds to be raped and murdered by Indians—"

The man didn't get a chance to finish. Clint swung his rifle, in a split second landing its butt end across the side of Kendall's face. Jo winced at the cracking sound, and others gasped as Kendall went down hard, out cold. Clint held his rifle on the other two men and ordered them to dismount and leave their rifles on their horses. The men obeyed, one of them going to examine Kendall while the commanding officer at the fort approached the scene.

"Clint!" the man called out.

The two men shook hands, and Jo was relieved to see Clint apparently knew the commanding officer.

"Hello, Lieutenant," Clint answered. "I came to see you last night when we first arrived, but you weren't around."

"I got back late last night from patrol. When we heard about the raid on Lawrence, we rode out to see if we could maybe round up Quantrill and some of his men. But they're probably well into southern territory by now." The man frowned as he looked at the bleeding, groaning Kendall, then scanned the crowd. "Clint, I'd ask where in hell you've been the last few years, but it looks like there is something more important here to discuss first," the officer said. "I'm Lieutenant Mark Cleaver." He spoke up louder to the others.

Kendall began coming around, moaning louder and managing to get to his knees while the settlers explained the situation to Cleaver. Cleaver ordered one of his soldiers to keep an eye on Kendall and his men while the settlers went to the corral to point out the horses that belonged to them. Two belonged to Donald Sievers, and three to Johnny Hills, as well as the three Jo had recognized as hers. The officer told the settlers to take what was theirs and ordered one of his men to wire Lawrence.

"Have the newspaper in Lawrence run an ad," he told the man. "Tell the people there that horses suspected to be strays belonging to settlers who were burned out in the raid are here at the fort to be examined and/or claimed."

"Yes, sir," the soldier answered, hurrying away.

Cleaver turned to Clint. "I can't see buying any of these animals. From the story your people have told me, I doubt any of the horses belong to Mr. Kendall. And I know you're an honest man, Clint. These people just want what's theirs. I don't intend to buy stolen stock."

Clint nodded. "Thanks, Lieutenant."

Cleaver glanced at Jo and the rifle in her hand. "And who is this? My man came running to say a woman was facing off some horse traders."

Jo reddened slightly, lowering her rifle and putting out her hand. "I'm Joline Masters. I just wanted what belonged to me, Lieutenant."

"Obviously," the man answered, shaking her hand. He turned to the others. "Go ahead and take what's yours, folks. Just be sure to leave something in writing for me, showing which horses you took and signing your names."

"Thank you, Lieutenant," Johnny Hills answered. He and several others headed for the corral, and Cleaver turned to Clint.

"So, what are you doing around here, Clint? The last I heard, you had married and gone off to Minnesota."

Clint sobered. "Millie and our son were killed," he answered. "Sioux."

The lieutenant frowned. "I'm damned sorry to hear that, Clint. Hell, there's more talk around here about the Indians than there is about the war. You'll have to be mighty careful taking these people west. Stay away from the far north. Red Cloud has some of those mining areas pretty well bottled up. There is even talk of vacating the forts up around the Bozeman Trail in Montana."

Clint looked at Jo with an "I told you so" look in his eyes. She sighed and looked away.

"I'll remember that," Clint told the soldier.

Kendall was helped to his feet by his friends, and Cleaver ordered all three men to be taken to the guardhouse.

"You can't do that!" one of the others growled. "Those horses weren't branded! We had a right to round them up! You can't say we stole them!"

"And you didn't try very hard to find out who the

owners were either, did you?" Cleaver answered. "You had to know most of them were just scattered from the raid. And I don't intend for any of you to make trouble for the rest of these people here. As soon as they're well on their way, you'll be released. But you're damned lucky you aren't arrested and hanged for horse-stealing."

Kendall glared at Clint. The side of his face was already swollen and turning purple, and he was obviously in a lot of pain. "I'll get you for this," the man hissed. He spoke through one side of his mouth, unable to open his jaw all the way. He moved his eyes to Jo. "You, too, little lady!"

Jo gripped her rifle tighter, and Clint stepped closer to Kendall. "You ever give Joline Masters trouble again, and it will be more than your jaw that will be hurting, Kendall! In fact, you might not be feeling any pain at all, if you get my meaning!"

Kendall just glared at Clint, then winced with pain as a soldier grabbed his arm and herded the man away, two other soldiers pushing Kendall's two friends along behind him.

Lieutenant Cleaver turned to Jo. "Ma'am, with you around to stand up for them, I think these travelers will be just fine." He looked up at Clint. "Come on over to my office for a drink when you get the time, Clint."

"I'll do that."

"You think maybe you'd like to do some army scouting again?"

"If I do it won't be for a while. I've got these people to take care of for now."

"Well, they're in good hands." The lieutenant nodded to Jo again and walked off.

Clint turned to Joline. "That was quite a display of courage, and probably a little foolish," he told her.

She held up her chin. "They were my horses. At least now I don't feel so bad about trading Chester and Hercules for the oxen." She sighed. "But thank you for stepping in. I'm not positive I really could have shot him if I had to."

He smiled softly. "Well *I'm* not positive you *wouldn't* have shot him. And I didn't want you to have to." His smile faded. "You had another nightmare last night. You didn't wake up, but I knew what was on your mind. You might be able to set the raid aside in your thoughts by keeping busy, Jo, but you aren't over it. I remember the shape you were in when I found you."

She shrugged, hating any signs of weakness. "I'm all right." She turned. "Let's go get my horses."

She felt a strong hand on her shoulder. "Jo, I want you to think again about Montana. You heard what Cleaver said."

The strength in his hand, the memory of the way he had knocked Kendall flat just moments before, made her long for his full supportive strength; to be held close to him and told everything would be all right. But it had also felt good to stand up to Kendall herself, to feel more independence than she had ever known before. She looked into Clint Reeves's handsome face, forcing herself to ignore the broad shoulders, the virile qualities about him that made her want to be a woman again in the fullest sense.

"I heard. But I'm not going to change my mind." She ignored the little voice that told her the only reason she wanted to go to Montana was because that was where Clint Reeves was going.

Clint watched the way her dark hair blew gently in the morning breeze as she walked away from him. There was a strength about her that made him want her more than he had wanted any woman since Millie. In many ways Joline Masters was much stronger than Millie. Millie had followed him to Minnesota just to be with him. She had depended on him, leaned on him. But Jo was going for herself, not for a man. Millie would never have held a rifle on a man, or gone into the wilds alone.

He slung his rifle over his shoulder and followed her to the corral.

Chapter Seven

They headed directly north, ferrying across the Kansas River and aiming for Alcove Springs, where more of the travelers hoped to find oxen or mules. Bennett Kiehl and his son were the only ones who already had oxen when they arrived at the fort. Since seventeen-year-old Bobbie knew how to drive a team, he drove Jo's oxen for her, but Jo walked with him, watching how he used the whip, paying attention to his "gee's" and "haw's" and "whoa's" and "git-up's," watching how the oxen responded. After two days she took short turns guiding the animals herself, and as soon as she realized what grand and patient beasts of burden they were, she began to feel an attachment to them, naming them Brute and Goliath.

Sidney and Marie Boone, and the bootmaker, Bill Starke, procured oxen at the fort. With the three extra horses retrieved from Bart Kendall's stolen herd, the Hills family and the Grants managed to continuously rotate their horses so as not to tire any of them unnecessarily before oxen or mules could be purchased at Alcove Springs. Extra horses were tied to the backs of wagons.

At times Jo wanted to laugh at the strange mixture of people she and Clint had picked up on their journey. She thought of Clint as a kind of Moses, leading them into the western desert; but she knew better than to voice her fantasy. It would only make him angry. So far Mrs. Boone had grumbled nearly every step of the way; Martha Sievers and her daughter stayed inside their wagon most of the time, as though hiding; and Bess and Johnny Hills and Sarah and Bradley Grant were cooperative, but they all seemed to talk more than necessary. Both their wagons had cages full of chickens tied onto their sides, and between the constant squawking of the chickens, and the chattering among family members, they were a noisy but friendly bunch. Bill Starke kept to himself and hardly talked at all. Bennett Kiehl and his son seemed very close but were also both very quiet.

Because it was late August, the ground was dry and made traveling easier on the animals. But that meant they were getting a very late start. Every day, every hour, was important. With precious savings, most were able to stock up on the necessities of flour, coffee, bacon, beans, sugar, and the like at Fort Riley. Some had saved more belongings than others from Quantrill's raid, making their little group a grand mixture of those who "had" and those who "had not." Those who "had" willingly shared some of their belongings with those who could not afford to stock up on every necessity. But Marie Boone refused to share anything with anyone, saying a person had to look out for herself, never knowing what dangers lay ahead.

Jo tried not to dwell on her contempt for Marie Boone. She tried to concentrate only on good thoughts, for enough problems lay ahead for all of them. At least she had canvas over her wagon. The wheelwright had fashioned iron bars into half circles and bolted them to the sides of her wagon, and he had charged her far less than his work was worth, at Clint Reeves's request. It seemed that Clint knew a lot of these men, and everyone he knew liked him.

Jo was still full of a thousand questions about Clint, but for now the days were too full of work and travel to ask questions. By midday the heat was unbearable, and there was no relief to be found in the shade of the canvas wagon, for it was even hotter inside. Jo's feet were blistered but she refused to acknowledge the pain, nor did she complain about the heat. Every discomfort was like a godsend, something to help keep her mind off the raid and her personal loss and heartache.

As they walked, everyone gathered pieces of dead wood whenever they neared a stand of trees so that they would have plenty for a night fire. Whenever buffalo chips could be found, Clint ordered that they also be gathered.

"They make hotter coals and create less smoke," he told the travelers. "You won't find many this far east, but farther on there will be more."

"I'll not pick up the manure of those shaggy beasts," Marie Boone announced.

"Then don't plan on warming your feet at someone else's fire," Clint told her. "You're the one who said it's everyone for himself, Mrs. Boone. Take your own advice. And with your attitude, I wouldn't expect much help from anyone else."

The woman grudgingly picked up a few chips that day, and the memory of it made Jo smile.

On the fourth day they reached Alcove Springs, where Clint told them they would be following the Independence-St. Joe Road north to the Oregon Trail. They made camp outside the small settlement, and that night Clint and Jo were both invited to share supper and campfire with the Grants.

Clint had kept to himself once they left Fort Riley, and it was the first time even Jo had a chance to sit down and visit with him. He sat near her, and the ease with which Jo thought she had managed to stop thinking about him turned again to a burden.

He had bathed first in the Big Blue River, and he had shaved. Jo caught the faint scent of leather and sage, and she noticed his strong hands as he took a plate of food from Sarah Grant. She realized with a sudden pain that she actually missed being alone with him, missed the gentle attention he had given only to her those first couple of days after the raid. She half regretted talking him into guiding the others, yet she realized that her intentions had been realized: it had helped put a stop to the dangerous closeness that was developing between them. She had wanted it that way, and she had a feeling Clint wanted it that way, too. She wondered if that was the reason he had finally agreed to the job. Clint told stories of earlier days, how much harder it was for the first wagon trains. He made them all feel a little better that their only problem so far was the heat.

"That doesn't mean you won't face dangers and starvation yourselves," Clint warned. "A lot depends on how much game we find, the weather, the mood of the Indians. Any of you who want to go back can still do it. It will be easy to find the way."

"Not us." Old Bradley Grant spoke up. "I might be old, but I'm strong. Been workin' hard all my life. My daughter wants to go to Oregon, and my wife and our daughter have never been separated. I don't aim to be separated from the grandkids, neither."

Clint finished chewing a piece of rabbit. "You're a lucky man, Mr. Grant, to have such a nice family."

"Well, you got a lot of years to have one of your own, you know. Life has to go on, Mr. Reeves. A man has to look ahead. You'll marry again."

"Pa, maybe he doesn't want to talk about it," Bess Hills interrupted.

Jo glanced at Clint, who threw aside a rabbit bone. A skinny stray dog that had begun following the wagon train picked it up and ran off. Clint guzzled down some coffee and rose.

"Thanks for the meal, Mrs. Grant," he said. "I'll try to find some game once we're on the trail again. You should be able to find a few more supplies here at Alcove Springs. We'll head out again day after tomorrow." He walked off and Bess looked at her father.

"See, Pa? You got him upset."

"Don't worry about it, Bradley," Jo told him. "He isn't angry. It's just hard for him."

The old man nodded, looking apologetic. "He's not an easy man to get to know."

"No, he isn't. But the lieutenant back at Fort Riley said he's the best man for this job, and that's what really counts. I don't know him well myself, but I think he's an honest man. And the incident over the horses shows he'll stick up for us."

Jo finished her meal, enjoying the chance to visit with Bess and Sarah, but unable to get Clint off her mind. Darkness fell, and she limped back to her wagon, allowing the darkness to hide her pain. She climbed wearily into the wagon and lit a lamp, sitting down in the bed of the wagon and unlacing her boots. Suddenly Clint loomed into the light, standing at the back of the wagon.

"Blisters?"

Jo reddened. "A few."

"I saw you limping."

She smiled wearily. "You weren't supposed to."

He laughed then. "You wouldn't have had to limp for me to know it. It always happens. Get your boots off. I have a liniment that will help."

He disappeared. She wanted to object, yet she couldn't resist the pleasant feeling of having him all to herself for just a few moments. He returned carrying a brown bottle.

"Lie back and stretch out your feet," he told her. "I'll rub this on for you. It will be a lot more relaxing to let someone else do it."

She blushed again, feeling a sudden flutter of desire. "I don't think it would look right."

"The hell with that. Lie back."

She wanted to argue, but her feet ached so badly that the thought of getting relief overwhelmed all other emotions. She lay back, and Clint lowered the wagon gate, sitting on it and putting one of her feet over his legs. In the next moment strong hands began massaging her feet with the cool liniment. She sighed with the glorious comfort, but fought the sensual urges his touch aroused. He was so strong and rugged, yet could be so gentle. He rubbed his thumb on the inside of her arch and over the balls of her feet. He gently squeezed her toes and massaged her ankles.

"Don't get all stiff and angry now, but it will help to rub the calves of your legs, too," he told her.

"How can I object?" she told him. "I admit it. Everything hurts. If it will help, go ahead."

He pushed her bloomers up to her knees, and fire ripped through her as the cool liniment and the strong hands brought new life to the muscles in her calves. He brought the other foot over his lap and massaged it. His own desires brought an ache to his insides much worse than being in the saddle all day. Her feet were pretty and slender, her legs slim and soft. He had not forgotten the bare leg he had seen that first night when she slept in his hotel room. He wondered how any man could forget something like that, and he could not help thinking now how easy it would be to move his hands farther up her legs.

He had a terrible urge to try it, to climb farther into the wagon and lie on top of her, to taste her lips and move his hands under her slender hips. She had been on his mind almost constantly, and he had fought the feelings. He felt it was much too soon to love again, and he was so lonely he couldn't even be sure his feelings were real. Besides that, he knew Joline Masters well enough by now to realize that if he did try to kiss her, she would probably raise a commotion that would arouse the entire camp.

He splashed more liniment on his hands and rubbed her feet again. "I used to do this for my wife," he told her.

Crickets sang loudly, and Jo thought he looked even more handsome in the soft lantern light. She smiled, glad for his sudden attempt at talking about his wife. "You made her walk to Minnesota?" she teased.

He grinned. "No. But she worked hard helping get our farm started. And she was the type anyway who liked to have her feet rubbed."

He squeezed her feet gently, and Jo felt a sudden wave of jealousy at the thought of Clint Reeves lying with another woman, loving her, touching her, desiring her, creating a child with her. There was a time when she had planned a big family of her own. She and Greg were going to have a lot of children. Life was going to be so good. She was so glad to be moving farther and farther from the war.

"You seem like a loner," she told him then. "You must have loved Millie very much to decide to settle."

He nodded, looking at her feet, afraid to look into her pretty, dark eyes. "Who knows what compels a man to settle? I never thought it would happen to me, but it did. I ran away from home at fifteen. My parents were both dead by then and I was raised by an aunt who didn't care much about having me around, so I left. I always had a wandering bug, never finished school. I traveled all over the west for years. Then I met Millie." He shrugged. "I guess I thought it was time to have some kind of purpose in life. Now here I am wandering with no purpose again. Life sure can hand a man some strange turns."

"A woman, too." She wanted to ask about the Indian attack, but she knew better. It seemed the minute anyone mentioned Millie's death, he immediately left, refusing to talk. She decided he would tell her some day on his own, when the time was right.

He finally met her eyes. "Yeah. A woman, too."

"Fate has a way of messing up the best-laid plans."

He watched her for a moment, every nerve end alive, his mouth tingling with a desire to kiss her. "Sure does."

She sat up, and he quickly turned to hang his legs over the back of the wagon, putting a cork back in the neck of the liniment bottle.

"Thank you, Clint," she told him. "If you need anything— some clothes washed or mended, whatever, please tell me. Let me do something for you. You've done so much for me, and you didn't have to do any of it."

He jumped down from the wagon gate and closed it, then leaned on it, looking into the wagon. "When we leave, you ride in the wagon for a couple of days until your feet are healed. That's an order, not a request."

"Yes, sir."

"You could ride one of your own horses, you know."

"I will at times. But for such a long journey I think they're better off not being ridden. That will make it easier on them. I need healthy horses when I get there."

"True. But you don't weigh much." He moved away from the wagon gate. "And don't forget you have time to change your mind about Montana."

She smiled in amusement at his continued effort to make her go to Oregon. She wondered if he was really concerned about her safety, or if he was simply afraid to have her near him. Her feelings vacillated between desire, with thoughts of a more serious relationship with him, and a determination to absolutely forbid herself to care. Too much had happened to her too quickly for her to trust her feelings. "I'll remember that," she told him.

He walked off into the darkness. Jo turned and took out a quill pen and a piece of paper. She laid the paper over a book on a crate and set the lantern closer, then began the letter.

"Dear Anna,

"I have already sent you a letter explaining that I am going to Montana. I hope you weren't too upset by my decision, but the farther I go, the more sure I

am I've made the right decision. I found three more
of my horses. The ironic part is that some men stole
them and tried to sell them at the very fort where
we were camped. My guide taught their leader a
good lesson with the butt of his rifle, and now I have
my horses, which will help a lot. Mr. Reeves and I
came across several more people headed west, and
they are now traveling with us, so we are not alone
and you shouldn't worry.

"Anna, I told you in my first letter that Clint
Reeves was the man who would take me to Montana. We had talked about him when you visited. I
have to tell you about my feelings for Mr. Reeves,
which are terribly confused. He is not the kind of
man a woman easily ignores . . . ."

It was not long before Jo realized that the worst part of
the journey was not the weather or the danger or the
walking. It was the monotony. Every day it was the same
routine: wake up at daybreak, yoke the oxen, try to get a
fire going and eat sparingly so as to ration supplies, pack
everything back where it belonged, wash clothing and
dishes in streams whenever possible, make camp again at
sunset. While on the move, there was a constant search
for fuel.

The only respite from the monotony was the skinny
stray dog that continued to follow them. It was a male, a
medium-size, black-and-white, flop-eared mixed breed that
apparently had no special home, and it seemed to have
adopted Jo, since it was she the dog followed beside most
of the time. Jo warned herself not to get attached to it; the
dog could disappear just as quickly as it had appeared. But
it had a sad look about its big, brown, hopeful eyes, and
she found herself throwing him bones and occasionally
dropping a crust of bread, unable to ignore her love of
animals.

Her feet healed, and Jo could not think about the night
Clint had rubbed them without wondering how gentle he
must be making love. As soon as the thought entered her
head, she chastised herself, deciding that she had been
without a man for so long that her feelings and needs were
running away with her. She reminded herself there was no

room in her life now for such things. She had a whole new life to build, and she was more and more determined to prove to herself she could do this alone.

Clint had told them they would be taking a new road called the Overland Trail, which ran just south of the Oregon Trail between Nebraska Territory and Utah. Parts of it even dipped into eastern Colorado Territory. Because it was south of the Oregon Trail, it was safer from Indians; and there were a few settlements along the way. Clint had heard about the trail from someone at Alcove Springs. He warned everyone that it didn't veer much south until they reached eastern Colorado, so the threat of Indians would still be a problem while moving through Nebraska Territory.

They stayed to the north of the Little Blue River, but followed it closely so that they were able to water the stock and bathe and wash clothes often, a luxury Clint warned they would not always have, and one that helped relieve the awful heat. But other than the high temperature, the weather remained their friend, allowing them to keep the pace Clint said was required if they were to arrive at Fort Bridger before winter.

They were only two days from Fort Kearny in Nebraska Territory when the weather took a sudden turn. Dark clouds rolled toward them from the west, appearing many miles away at first but approaching much faster than expected. A cold wind moved just ahead of the clouds, the temperature dropping close to thirty degrees in minutes. Suddenly Clint was riding hard from his position far ahead, headed for the wagons.

"Get out of the wagons!" he was yelling. "Get out and lie flat!" He reached Jo's wagon. She and Bobbie Kiehl stood watching him in confusion. "Get down in the ditch over there!" Clint ordered. "This could turn into a tornado!"

Jo's heart tightened. She was not afraid for her life, but if a tornado destroyed her wagon and newly gained belongings, she would be truly destitute. And how would she be able to go on to Montana? She ran for the ditch, noticing Marie Boone fly past her at a pace she never thought the hefty woman capable of running. She looked back to see her oxen bow down their heads against a cold sheet of rain mixed with hail that burst from the black clouds, and she felt sorry for the poor animals and for her

horses. It was then she noticed that Clint was still on
his own horse, riding to the wagons that had extra horses
tied to the back and quickly cutting the ropes so the animals
would be free should a wagon be carried away by the
storm.

"Clint, get over here!" she screamed, but her words
were lost on the wind. She lost sight of him in the heavy
rain, and in that one quick moment she remembered the
ugly pain of losing a loved one. She ducked down as the
rain and hail pelted her back; and in that moment of
realizing Clint Reeves was just as vulnerable to death as
any other man, she knew why she had not allowed her
feelings to run away with her better sense.

The wind roared, and water gathered in the ditch where
Jo knelt, forming a stream that ran in a muddy mess over
her knees. She felt something poke at her and heard a
whining in her ear; she turned her face to see the stray
dog nudging her. Jo grasped him around the middle and
pulled him under her arm to protect him. Just then she
heard a groaning sound and something flew past her. In
the next moment someone was kneeling beside her, throwing a blanket over her. "Keep your head down," she heard
Clint's voice say. He was under the blanket with her, his
face close to hers. "It will be over soon," he told her, the
words close to her ear.

Then there came a louder roar, unlike anything she had
ever heard. Having grown up in Kansas she knew about
tornadoes, had heard of their destructive powers. But she
had been lucky enough not to have witnessed one first-
hand. Clint's arms were around her then, and she cowered
against him while the wind and rain raged. Minutes later
the wind calmed as quickly as it had risen, and the air
temperature rose again, though it remained cooler than
before the storm.

Joline raised her head and looked into Clint's face for a
moment. She saw by his eyes that he was thinking the
same thing she was. How easy it would be to care, and
how wrong; how quickly loved ones could be lost. For a
brief moment she had enjoyed the comfort of his strong
arms, but the storm was over now. Still, there was a storm
in her heart that might not end so quickly.

"Bradley! Where's my Bradley!"

When they heard Sarah Grant's moaning words, Clint quickly threw back the blanket and left Jo, walking toward the old woman in his soggy buckskins. Jo rose, her hair and dress drenched. She set down the dog and watched Sarah climb out of the ditch, looking dazed, while her daughter kept hold of the woman and her son-in-law began running around searching for Bradley Grant.

"He never made it to the ditch," Johnny Hills was yelling to Clint. "Somehow in the rain we got separated."

Everybody searched. Jo noticed most of the horses were gone, but miraculously there was no damage to the wagons except that canvas had curled back on a few. Some pots and pans and other items that had been tied to the sides of wagons lay scattered; and chicken feathers coated the ground under the bird cages, but the chickens appeared to be all right.

"Pa!" she heard Bess Hills cry out. She turned to see the girl running toward a body lying some distance away. Martha Sievers helped Sarah Grant walk toward the body. Jo stood frozen, the pain of death revisiting her with a sudden wave of sickening reality. She watched old Sarah Grant crumble next to the body, and she knew Bradley Grant must be dead.

A cool breeze blew Jo's dark hair back from her face as she stood over Bradley Grant's grave while Donald Sievers read from the Bible. Johnny Hills had thought his father-in-law was right behind him in the storm when he let go of the old man's elbow to scoop his son Joey into his arms. Bess had her mother and Lonnie to watch after. They were all in the ditch and the tornado was nearing before they realized Bess's father was not with them.

Whether the man had fallen and couldn't get up, or a flying object had knocked him down, no one would ever know. He was found with a gaping gash on the back of his head, and it had killed him. Sarah Grant would travel with her daughter now, since there was no one to drive the Grant wagon. As much as the Hills wagon could carry was added from the Grants' load. The rest was distributed to the other settlers, and each man or woman paid Sarah Grant for what he or she received. Wood was torn from the Grant wagon to fashion a coffin for Bradley, to keep wild animals from digging up his grave and getting to the body. Johnny Hills made a cross out of wood and carved his father-in-law's name into it.

Jo wondered how long it would take the elements to wear away the name and cause the cross to fall and be lost to the earth, leaving an unmarked grave no one would ever know had existed. Her throat ached so badly that the pain hurt her ears. She wondered if she was getting sick from the wet and cold of the storm, or if the ache was simply from sorrow. She had not known Bradley Grant very well or been close to him. She simply felt sorry for poor Sarah Grant, forced to leave behind the grave of a man she had lived with for thirty-five years. She wondered which was worse: having a man for just a short time, like Greg; or being with him most of a lifetime before losing him.

The men lowered the coffin into a deep hole they had dug. Jo wished that she knew where Greg was buried. Perhaps she wouldn't have had such a lost, floating feeling when she found out about his death, if she had only been able to visit his grave. It was like unfinished business, and it made her feel almost guilty, even though there was nothing she could do about it.

She watched Clint, noticing the strained look on his face as he helped lower the coffin. She knew the burial brought the same bad memories for him as it did for her. Sarah Grant stood weeping bitterly, her daughter's arms around her. Jo wished she knew how to comfort the woman, but she still felt the pain of her own husband's death. Maybe it would help the old woman to tell her she understood the loss. But did she truly? She had never had the chance to have children with Greg, to grow old with him.

All too soon it was time to be on their way. They would take a rest stop at Fort Kearny. The men had rounded up the scattered horses and had mended the canvas. Jo had bought two quilts and a few tools from the items Sarah Grant no longer needed; and since her own wagon was still not full, she had offered to store some of Mrs. Grant's things so the Hills wagon would not be overloaded. Mrs. Boone, of course, needed none of the "used" items belonging to Mrs. Grant, and Jo noticed the woman's eyes held the same stern look as always. She wondered if Mrs.

Boone had any sympathy for poor old Sarah, or if she was simply upset that the tornado and the burial had hampered the journey.

Sarah sat quietly weeping in her daughter's wagon as they got underway again. Just as she had refused to look back at her old farm, Jo refused now to look back at the desolate grave. Poor Sarah would never see it again. In spite of the cool breeze, Jo felt hot. She asked Bobbie to stop the wagon for a moment and she dipped a cloth into a barrel of water. She held the cloth to her face while Bobbie got the oxen moving again. Jo put the cloth to her forehead and held it there as she walked. Her throat ached more and more, until by the time they made camp for the night, she could hardly get air past her throat to her lungs. But she didn't want to complain. She managed to make a fire. She had promised Bobbie she would make him fresh biscuits. The young man was quiet and helpful, and he had walked the entire trip so far, driving her oxen for her.

Jo got out some flour, then leaned against the wagon, feeling suddenly very tired. Before she could start mixing the biscuits, Clint came riding back to her wagon. He dismounted and walked up to her with a concerned look on his face.

"Bobbie tells me you look sick."

"I'm all right," she answered, quickly straightening.

Clint grasped her arms. "No you aren't. Your face is as flushed as if you had a sunburn." He put a big hand to her face. "My God, Jo, you're burning up! Does anything hurt?"

She was too tired and hot and aching to fight it. "My throat. It's . . . hard to swallow."

In the next moment she was lifted in his arms and he was putting her in the back of the wagon. "Don't you move," he ordered. "I'll get Martha Sievers and her daughter to help you undress."

"I'll be all right," she argued.

"Not if you don't stop pushing yourself," he answered. "This is probably from getting so wet. I'm surprised others haven't gotten sick."

"I'm . . . sorry, Clint," Jo said weakly.

He leaned closer, placing his hands to either side of her face. "Don't be sorry. Just do what I tell you, all right?"

Her eyes watered. "I'm . . . scared. My throat—"

"Don't talk. And don't panic. Try to relax. We'll find something to make your throat feel better. You'll be all right, Jo." He leaned down and kissed her forehead, and Jo felt better at his concern.

Clint climbed out of the wagon, his heart tight with worry. He suddenly realized how devastated he would be if anything happened to Joline Masters, and he was angry with himself for allowing himself to care so much. It was stupid and wrong, and he intended to fight his feelings every mile of the journey. But it didn't help to see Jo suffering. He hoped it wasn't cholera or measles or some other disease that could wipe out the whole train. Still, if Jo died, what difference would it make if the others were lost too? He was making this journey for her and no one else. He knew how badly Jo wanted to get to Montana, and now, seeing her so sick, he wanted more than ever for her to finish the journey.

He hurried to get Martha Sievers.

Chapter Eight

Jo lay struggling against the terror of not being able to breathe. Sarah Grant insisted on taking over her care; she wanted something to do to help her get over her own grief. In her sickness, Jo imagined that Sarah was the mother she had lost so many years ago. She realized how much she missed having a mother, and in her weakened condition she found herself crying often, wishing she could go back to the days when she and Anna were little, and their mother was still with them; the days when they played on the old farm and never considered that life could be anything but carefree and happy. What a hard lesson they had both learned.

For the first time she wondered if she had made the wrong decision leaving Lawrence, but she told herself it was only because she was sick. Clint came inside the wagon whenever they made a stop, and each time she begged him to promise he would write Anna if she died, to let her know when and where it had happened. She had heard so many stories about people dying on the way west, she was afraid she would be another statistic.

"Put a stone . . . marker . . . on my grave," she told Clint the second night of her illness. "Don't let it . . . be lost forever. I want Anna . . . to be able to find it . . . if she wants to."

"Don't talk foolish," Clint told her. "There won't be any grave."

He listened to her labored breathing, then put a hand to

her face. It felt hotter than ever. "My God," he muttered. Jo began tossing and moaning, muttering senseless words. Clint looked at Sarah. "I think she's going into a convulsion. We've got to get her cooled down or the fever could affect her brain. I've seen this kind of thing before."

He gently maneuvered Jo to the back of the wagon and lifted her down. "Get a blanket and come with me," he told Sarah. The woman obeyed, grabbing a blanket and climbing out of the wagon.

"What are you doing?" she asked.

"I'm taking her to the river. Have your daughter put on some sassafras tea, will you? And have some more liniment ready."

Sarah hurried to tell her daughter to make the tea, then followed Clint to the river.

Clint had already carried Jo down to the riverbank and behind some brush. She groaned as he pulled her cotton nightgown over her head, and she began to shake. "No. Don't," she muttered.

"I've got to get rid of this fever, Jo," Clint told her. "But I don't want you in wet clothes afterward."

Jo was naked under the gown, and for a brief moment Clint let his eyes drink in the sight of her small but nicely rounded body, the firm, full breasts and the flat belly. He knew he would not soon forget what he saw, but his concern for her health was too great to look on her with normal manly appreciation.

She thrashed at him and struggled to get away as he picked her up again and carried her to the water. "It's all right, Jo," he told her. "I'm trying to help you." He dipped her into the water and held her there against her groaning and her effort to get away. As soon as the cool water touched her, her eyes widened in shock, and she wiggled to get free. But his strong hands held her down.

In her delirium, Jo thought someone was attacking her. She sensed she was naked. Was she going to be raped? She pushed at someone but was much too weak to get free, and suddenly the cool water felt good. The terrible heat of her fever seemed to subside, and for some reason she could think more clearly. She lay still, letting the water flow through her hair and cool her head. Only her

face was out of the water. Someone supported her head.
She opened her eyes to see Clint bending over her.

"I had to get the fever down, Jo," he told her. "This was
the best way I could think of."

Her breathing quickened and she felt humiliated. "Don't
look at me!" she squeaked.

He sighed, leaning closer. "The only thing that matters
to me right now is that you live. You want to get to
Montana, don't you?"

Her whole body jerked in a sob, and she nodded her
head.

"And you'll get there, if you do what I tell you. Now I'm
going to hold you here for a few more minutes and then
wrap you in a blanket and take you back. Mrs. Grant is
here with me."

Jo looked around, and Sarah smiled at her. But Jo could
see the distant sadness in her eyes. "I'm sorry . . . to be
such a burden, Sarah."

"I don't mind, Jo, dear. Right now I need someone to
care for. And you'll be all right. Bess is making some tea
and we'll put more linament on you when we get you
back."

"We're going to get you through this, Jo," Clint added.
"You want to be well when we get to Plum Creek Station.
Why, they might even have a dance there."

She watched his eyes. They did not stray to observe her
nakedness. He kept them on her face. "Do you . . . dance?"
she asked him.

He grinned. "Depends who you ask. I don't think most
would call it dancing."

"Will you dance . . . with me?"

Their eyes held. He was absolutely miserable over the
feelings he was developing for her. What a fool he was.
"Sure I will, if your toes are strong enough to take it."

She actually managed a smile. For the first time in the
past forty-eight hours she began to think she might live.

"I think you've been through the worst, Jo," he told
her. "If we can break this fever, you'll be all right."

Her eyes teared. "When I . . . feel like this . . . I can't
help . . . wondering . . . how much Greg . . . suffered
before . . . he died."

"Don't think about sad things, Jo. Think about Mon-

tana. Think about life. You've even helped Mrs. Grant.
Looking after you is helping her forget her own sorrows.
She's a woman who needs to be doing for others." He
dipped one hand into the water and trickled some over
her face. After several minutes he noticed a more natural
color return to her skin, the scarlet look receding. "We
just have to hope that once I take you out of the river the
fever won't come back," he told her.

"If my throat . . . would just stop aching . . ."

"If you'll rest like I tell you, it will get better. Nobody
else has got sick, so I don't think you have any dangerous,
contagious disease."

"I . . . swear, Clint. I . . . almost never . . . get sick. I
swear. It won't happen . . . again."

"It's just one of those things. I've had my share of being
laid up too. When you live under the stars most of your
life you run into poison water, your food rots, you get wet
in weather that won't let you dry out, your feet get cold as
blocks of ice, and a cut can turn into a life-threatening
infection. The list is a lot longer, but those are just some of
the things that get a man down, let alone eating the wrong
berries."

"The . . . wrong berries?"

He dipped a little more water over her forehead. "The
kind that make it almost impossible to keep your pants on,
if you know what I mean."

She thought for a moment as he lifted her out of the
water. She smiled then in spite of the pain in her throat,
understanding his quip about the berries.

Sarah wrapped the blanket around her as Clint set her on
her feet for a moment. Jo felt weak and dizzy, but more awake
than when he had brought her to the river.

"Use the blanket to dry yourself and we'll put your
gown back on," Clint told her. "Bess should have that tea
ready about now."

He helped rub her down, and the feel of his strong
hands over the blanket reminded her of the way it felt
when he had rubbed her feet with liniment. Clint Reeves
was as much man as any woman would want, sure, experienced, strong. She was still too sick to care very much that
he had seen her naked. She only knew she was grateful for
his quick action, and for his concern. She tried to ignore

the little voice that told her she might be falling in love. For one thing, to love another man somehow seemed traitorous to Greg's memory; and to love a man like Clint Reeves meant running the risk of losing him to an early death.

He picked up her gown and handed it to Sarah. "Help her get this on, will you?"

Sarah took the gown, and Clint turned around while the woman helped Jo put it on. Every move was agony, and she soon felt dizzy again. "Clint," she muttered. He turned and quickly lifted her again, carrying her back to her wagon.

Mrs. Boone watched from her own campfire, mumbling to her husband about the indecent way Joline Masters conducted herself around Clint Reeves. "Letting that man take her to the river!" she sputtered. "Has she no shame? He probably stripped her stark naked, and *she* probably didn't even mind!"

"She's sick near to death," her husband answered, irritated at his wife's eternal pettiness. "If he thinks dunking her in the river will help get rid of that fever, then it's got to be done."

"It will probably kill her off for sure."

"We'll see."

Clint lifted Jo into the wagon, and she managed to pull the covers over herself. Clint waited at the wagon gate while Sarah brought the hot sassafras tea, then helped her climb up inside. Jo sat up to drink the tea, letting the hot liquid soothe her sore throat.

"You look much better, dear," Sarah told her. She put a wrinkled hand to Jo's cheek. "The fever is gone."

"For now," Clint answered for Jo. "If it comes back I'll have to cool her down all over again. We'll be at Plum Creek in another four or five days. If she isn't better by then, maybe there will be a doctor around. Thanks for your help, Mrs. Grant. I'd better see how everyone else is doing."

He walked off, eager to get away so he wouldn't have to look at Jo Masters anymore this evening. He had seen all he needed to see to haunt him for the rest of the journey, and he realized it was more important than ever to keep their relationship strictly business. He would have gladly let someone else put her in the river, but no woman would have been strong enough to carry her or hold her down in her delirium; and he knew that if it had to be a man, she wouldn't have wanted it to be any of the others.

"Damned fever," he muttered, refusing to look back at her.

By the time they reached Plum Creek, Jo's sore throat was gone, but she remained weak. She insisted on dressing with Sarah's help and getting out of the wagon, wanting to see what there was outside the monotonous wagon. Jo climbed down and saw several log buildings and a few soldiers milling about. Most of the others in her group were heading for one building in particular.

"Where is everyone going?" Jo asked Sarah.

"Mr. Reeves tells us this place is famous for their buffalo steaks," Sarah answered. "They're going to have some. Are you hungry?"

"A little."

Jo noticed Clint in the distance, talking to some soldiers. So, he knew about the buffalo steaks here. It seemed he knew everything about this land. She reddened at the thought that he had seen her naked and wondered just how much he saw or remembered. It was strange to think about; in some ways they had been so intimate, and yet they hardly knew each other at all.

The stray dog trotted up to Jo and she smiled, kneeling down to pet it. "You still around?"

"That dog stayed right by your wagon the whole time you were sick," Sarah told her.

"Well, I guess I have a permanent friend, don't I?" Jo patted the dog's head and stood up to walk with Sarah to the little log restaurant. Everyone inside greeted her warmly when she entered, all but Mrs. Boone. They congratulated her for being up and around, and Bill Starke gave her his chair. A skinny, bearded man who looked like he needed a bath took their orders. Jo wondered what kind of a cook he could be, but when he began bringing out the steaks, the room was full of exclamations of pleasure.

Jo cut a piece and tasted her first buffalo meat. She was surprised at its succulent flavor and tenderness, and she wondered how it had been prepared. Soon there came a round of boiled potatoes and carrots, as well as biscuits, and everyone ate heartily, after having rationed food for weeks. There was apple pie for dessert, which quickly disappeared. The bearded man, who simply called himself "Cook," told them he was "fairly decent" at playing the fiddle, and that he'd gladly play for them later on.

"Maybe we'll get us a little dance goin'," he told them.

Everyone applauded the suggestion, and there was more camaraderie among the little group than there had been on the entire trip. Clint came inside as they all sat back rubbing their full stomachs, and Jo felt her cheeks go hot when he came over to ask how she was feeling.

"Pretty good," she replied, averting her eyes. She cursed her sickness for leaving her weak in his eyes, and for letting Clint Reeves see her naked. In a sense it gave him an upper hand, had made her dependent on him for that moment. It was the last thing she wanted, and she vowed never to be in such a position again. "I'm sorry about the whole thing. I won't be any more bother to you. After all, I'm the one who got you into all of this."

Clint sensed her embarrassment, and a keen sense of sympathy mixed with desire made him want to hold her. He wanted to ease her embarrassment but didn't quite know how.

"Nobody can help getting sick, Jo."

He touched her shoulder before leaving her to go to the front of the room. Jo knew he was just trying to make her feel better, but the touch only made her angry and frustrated, for it again made her feel dependent on him.

"Mr. Reeves only wants you to be well, dear," Sarah told her, patting her hand. "I must tell you, I really think the man is quite infatuated with you. You shouldn't discourage such a fine man."

The remark only made Jo more frustrated. "I hired him as a guide and that's all there is to it," Jo answered, turning to face the front of the room. She saw Clint put one foot up on a chair and lean on his knee, his dark eyes moving over the little group of travelers.

"We need to talk," he announced, raising his voice. Everyone stopped talking and turned their attention to Clint.

"We're going to wait here a couple of days for a train of

freight wagons headed this way," Clint told them. "I've been talking to the soldiers outside, and they say that until we head a little farther south at Julesburg, we'll be in danger of Indian attack. There are too few of us, and not enough with experience at Indian fighting, to travel safely. We need more wagons and more guns."

His eyes moved to Jo. "If any of you wants to turn back right now, I would suggest you do so. Sometimes you can deal with the Indians, trade with them, whatever. But I can tell you better than most what they're like when they aren't in the mood for trading or making any other kind of deals. Right now they've been enjoying the upper hand." His eyes scanned the rest of them. "We might get lucky and not have any trouble at all. Then again, it might be a battle all the way across Nebraska Territory."

"If we wait for the freighters, we'll be pretty safe, won't we?" Donald Sievers asked.

"Safer than we are now. But the freight wagons are also a prime target. They'll be carrying two things Indians love—tobacco and whiskey. And we have something with us that they would also like to get their hands on—something they can use for bartering with white men for guns and supplies." His eyes moved to Jo again. "Women and children. Some captives don't get terribly mistreated." His eyes took on the agonizing sorrow again. "Some do," he finished. He headed for the door then. "All of you talk about it. You have a couple of days to make up your minds."

Clint walked out and everyone looked at each other, their gaiety of the moment before dampened by the news.

"I think the man is exaggerating," Marie Boone said haughtily. "Of course, his own wife and child were killed by Indians, but we don't know all the details. After all, the man lived. Doesn't anyone here wonder why? He could have traded his wife and child to save his own life. How do we know he wouldn't do the same using one of us?"

Jo's fury knew no bounds. She rose, her anger making her forget her weak condition. "How dare you talk like that about Mr. Reeves!" she cried. "Anyone can tell what a terrible loss it was for him just by the look on his face when his wife and son are mentioned. And anyone can tell he's a capable man, an honest man. He isn't the type who would do less than fight to the death for his family!"

"And you only see him through romantic eyes," the woman answered.

Jo's eyes widened with indignation. "And you're a gossiping old bat who wouldn't know the *meaning* of romantic! Nor would you know anything about love and sacrifice and family!" she blurted out.

Mrs. Boone's lips pressed into a tight line, her eyes sparkling with anger and her cheeks crimson. A few others snickered, agreeing with Jo.

"I've lost a father and a husband, Mrs. Boone," Jo said boldly. "And Sarah here lost her husband only a few days ago. Mr. Kiehl has lost a wife, and Mr. Starke lost his wife in Quantrill's raid. And everyone here lost nearly everything they owned to that raid! What have *you* ever suffered, Mrs. Boone! You saved most of your belongings. Who are you to sit there and judge others, especially a man like Clint Reeves, whom you know nothing about? And you have no business insinuating there is something between me and Mr. Reeves. He is simply a good man, a man who helped me after that horrible raid. And I might add he helped a lot of others that day, and he suffered a wound himself. I heard he was going to Montana, and I just wanted to get out of Lawrence, so I begged him to take me with him. There was nothing *romantic* involved! How *dare* you sit there on your pompous . . . pompous back end and judge others!"

Marie Boone rose and looked around the room, breathing deeply for self-control. "Perhaps Mrs. Masters is right." She spoke up. "Perhaps I have no business judging her or Mr. Reeves. But the fact remains we are headed into Indian country, being led by a man whose wife and child died in an Indian raid while he survived. I feel we have a right to know just how that happened. Would any of you want to be used as a ransom, to be handed over to savages to save the lives of others? How do we know Clint Reeves wouldn't do such a thing?"

The room was quiet, until Cook stepped forward. "You folks is talkin' about somethin' you don't know nothin' about. That there Clint Reeves is the best man you could have for a guide. The little woman there who stood up for

him is right. He's a good man. And anybody who says he
might have traded his wife and son for his life ought to be
handed over to the Indians themselves."

The old man's eyes bore into Marie Boone's. "Woman,
you don't know the half of what you're talkin' about. I've
knowed Clint Reeves a long time. When he come through
here on his way back to Lawrence, he done told me about
what happened. When it's one man against forty, what's a
man to do but fight to the death? That's what he done—at
least that's what the Indians who wounded him thought
when they *left* him for dead. I reckon he ain't let any of
you see him with his shirt off. If he did, you'd get sick at
seein' the scar across his shoulder and chest. Ain't many
men who would have lived through the wound he suffered
that day."

Cook stepped closer to Mrs. Boone. "Your Mr. Reeves
will fight to the death, even for a stuck-up old biddy like
you, ma'am. He fought for his wife and kid till he was so
bad wounded he couldn't do nothin' but watch them bein'
carried off. *That's* how he lived and they died."

The man looked around the room then. "Any other
questions?"

The room was so quiet Jo was sure a person could have
heard a feather move. Her heart swelled with sympathy
for Clint, and gratitude to Cook.

"Now I suggest to all of you that you don't say nothin' to
Clint about what I just told you," Cook warned. "He don't
like to talk about it, and he'd be upset if he knew. He ain't
a man to be talkin' about his personal business." The man
turned to the rest of them. "Now, you folks have a hard
trip ahead of you. I think you should forget about the
Indians and what I just told you and enjoy yourselves
tonight. Get rid of any hard feelin's. There ain't room for
them on a trip like this. You've got to stay together.
Tonight there will be fiddle music, a little whiskey, and
some punch for the ladies. We got supplies here, so stock
up and do a little celebratin' tonight."

The old man went back into his kitchen and everyone
stood around with either guilty looks, or condemning stares
at Marie Boone. Mrs. Boone walked out of the room in a
huff. Jo felt tears stinging her eyes at the thought of what
had happened to Clint and his family. No wonder he had

told her she was better off not seeing her husband suffer. Had his family been killed before his eyes?

The room felt suddenly stuffy. Jo walked outside and saw Clint talking to some soldiers and studying a new rifle. He raised it, getting a feel for its weight. He sighted it, then handed it back to a soldier. Jo realized he was preparing for possible Indian trouble, and she understood more than ever how difficult that would be for him.

Cook whined out a slow tune on his fiddle, and a thousand stars hung in the night sky. Jo watched Bess and Johnny Hills dance, and Martha and Donald Sievers. Bobbie's father, the widower Bennett Kiehl, politely asked Jo to dance, and she obliged.

"Glad to see you're feeling better, Mrs. Masters," the man told her.

"Thank you. But don't you think we could all start calling each other by our first names? You can call me Jo."

The man smiled. "Then call me Ben." They turned to the music, and Ben looked out into the darkness. "You going ahead with the trip?"

"I certainly am."

The man frowned. "Still determined to go to Montana? Oregon is more settled, you know."

"I know. But I don't want that. I have this . . . I don't know . . . a kind of need to prove I can fend for myself in the wilderness. I've had so many people tell me it's no place for a woman that I've decided to prove them wrong."

Ben laughed lightly. "Well, I have a feeling you just might do that. I like the way you stood up to Marie Boone earlier."

Jo blushed. "When I get angry I tend to blurt out the first thing that comes to mind without thinking." She noticed Clint then, standing outside the circle of people and wagons, watching quietly. The dance ended, and Jo made a point to approach Clint. "Aren't you going to join us?"

He looked at her strangely. "You and Bennett Kiehl make a fine-looking couple." How he wished she would fall in love with some man and give him an excuse to stop thinking about her.

"Bennett Kiehl?" She smiled. "We had one dance. And

he's much too old for me." She folded her arms. "I believe you promised me a dance, Mr. Reeves."

His dark eyes traveled over her, and an unexpected desire rushed through her at the memory of when he had made that promise. How much did he see? How much did he remember?

"I guess I did, didn't I?" he answered. "It's your risk. You've already had sore feet from so much walking. You sure you want me to make them worse?"

Cook whined out another tune, and the music drifted across the prairie. Clint put a hand to Jo's waist and led her into the firelight. Their eyes held as he turned with her. His step was easy to follow.

"You dance just fine," she told him.

He wished he could grab her close, but he warned himself to beware of his feelings. He had to remember Millie—how she died. "You're just good at following," he replied.

Jo caught the smell of whiskey. "You've been drinking," she said quietly.

"Same as a lot of the others. A man needs a little whiskey once in a while."

"I suppose—as long as he isn't using it to soothe hidden wounds." She watched the defenses rise in his dark eyes.

"Every man has a reason for drinking. For some it's a nagging wife. For some it's a way to feel better about himself. For others it's just a bad habit. And for a few, it does just what you said it does—soothes inner wounds."

"Well, I know yours isn't the first reason. My guess is it's the last."

He whirled her around, and she felt a sudden power in his hand at her back, as though he either wanted to grab her close or angrily shove her aside. His face took on a harder look.

"Clint, sometimes it helps to share the pain. You can't hold everything in forever, and you can't run forever."

"And you aren't running? How many women choose to go to a place like Montana?"

She smiled. "I suppose you're right in a sense. But I'm out to start a whole new life—to forget the past and get on with life. I don't think you're ready to do that. You're a man who's just wandering with no thought for the future, no real purpose."

The dance ended, and he stood there staring at her. "You're right, Mrs. Masters," he answered, a cold ring to his voice. "I had a purpose in life once. I had a future, in the form of a little boy. That was all taken from me, and I'm not about to let myself be fooled into thinking I can ever have that again."

He turned and walked off into the darkness. Jo followed, calling out his name, but there was no reply. There was only the sound of a horseman riding off.

Chapter Nine

The freight wagons lumbered into Plum Creek Station, and the sight of the six wagons and the eight men with them was a welcome relief to Jo and the others, who were more than apprehensive about the rest of the trip. But now they wondered if their own leader would show up in time to leave in the morning. Clint had not been seen since the night of the dance.

"My guess is he's on a drinking binge," Marie Boone told the others at a meeting the evening before they were to depart. "Before the dance I saw him off sitting alone with a bottle of whiskey."

Jo wondered if what she had said had angered him so much he didn't intend ever to come back. She didn't doubt that Marie could be right, but she was not about to tell the others. Clint Reeves had been drinking that night, and he had obviously been wrestling with ugly memories. He was a troubled man, and Jo didn't know how to help him without getting too involved emotionally.

"A man has a right to whiskey," Bill Starke put in. "Especially a man who has been through what Reeves has. I understand that better than most of you. But he'll show up. He gave us his word, and I believe his word is good."

"So do I," Jo put in. "He'll be here."

She looked at Sarah. "You should stay with your own family tonight, Sarah. I appreciate all your help, but I think I'm well enough to handle things. Your grandchildren must miss your company after losing your grandfather."

Sarah smiled sadly. "Yes, I suppose you're right. Thank you for your thoughtfulness, Jo. And be sure to come get me if you need anything at all, child."

"I will, Sarah." The two women hugged. "Thank you for all your help, Sarah," Jo said.

"Oh, I don't mind. It was good for me, anyway. You just take good care of that nice Mr. Reeves. He's a man who needs looking after, even though he doesn't admit it."

Jo frowned, pulling back. "Sarah, it isn't my place to take care of him. He's just our guide."

Sarah smiled slyly. "So you say, child. So you say." She gave Jo a wink and walked off; Jo just grinned and shook her head. She walked back to her wagon and stirred her campfire, pouring herself some coffee. She wished she were more tired. Tomorrow would be a long day, and she needed her rest. But she was too nervous about what might lie ahead to sleep. She was glad she at least felt much better physically. She would need her strength.

She set down her coffee and walked to her wagon, taking out her Henry repeater and bringing it back to the fire to check the gun and make sure it was loaded.

"Getting ready to shoot at Indians?"

Jo looked up to see Clint standing across from her.

"You're awfully good at sneaking up on people."

"Have to be out here. Indians are even better at it. Remember that."

Jo set her gun aside. "Want some coffee?"

He rubbed at his eyes. "I think I'd better drink the whole pot. They say coffee helps rid a man's system of whiskey."

She poured some of the brew into a tin cup. "Then you *did* go on a drinking binge. Some people have been wondering if you'd show up in time."

He took the cup and shrugged. "I heard. I was standing in the shadows." He drank some of the coffee. "Like Bill Starke said, every man has a right, long as he isn't hurting anyone. Don't worry. When we're on the trail and there's danger, I'll be sober and ready."

"Was it something I said the other night, when we danced?"

He sipped more of the coffee. "Just a combination of things. I don't want to talk about it."

Jo sighed. "All right. But I just want to say one thing. You have to face your tragedies and learn to live with them, Clint. You can't drown them forever in a whiskey bottle. It will never work. Every time you sober up, there they are again, staring you in the face. You just have to go on."

He guzzled down the rest of the coffee and met her gaze, and in the firelight Jo was sure she detected tears in his eyes. "There are some things a man just can't forget, Jo—ever," he answered. "You don't know all of it. In your wildest imagination, you couldn't know." He closed his eyes. "Leave it be, will you? Just leave it be."

She felt a lump rising in her throat at what he must have seen and suffered. "All right. I just want you to know I care. A lot of us care. Don't pay any attention to that battle-ax, Mrs. Boone."

He grinned a little, quickly wiping his eyes and clearing his throat. "I've been around that kind before, a heart as cold as a block of ice. Howard Styles is like that. It's a miracle Millie was as loving and—" He stopped talking and handed out the cup. "Give me a little more," he said.

Jo filled the cup again and he stared at the coffee a moment. "How do you do it?" he asked. He drank some of the coffee and met her eyes again. "You lost your pa, your husband. I never had much in the way of family, but I have a feeling you were real close to your father, wanting to keep his farm going and all. I admire your courage, Jo. To lose your husband, watch your farm burn down and all. You're a strong woman."

Jo looked at the fire. "I don't know if it's strength or plain-out stubbornness. Pa was a stubborn, ornery man when he wanted to be—always said his piece. I tend to take after him. My sister Anna, she's different. Pa always said she was more like our mother, more gentle and soft—she even has our mother's blond hair and blue eyes." She sighed, blinking back tears. "I'll miss Anna. I pray her husband comes back from the war alive, and a whole man." She met his eyes again. "Did you get involved in the war at all?"

He shook his head. "Like I told you back in Lawrence,

I've got no use for it. Sometimes I wonder if they even know what they're fighting about. It's mostly politics, you know. They like you to think it's over slavery, but it's a lot more than that. I've had my share of fighting just being out here fighting Indians and outlaws. At any rate, I was busy homesteading when the war broke out. That was part of the problem in getting protection from the Indians. Most of the soldiers went back east and left us on our own."

"Was that the first time you ever tried settling?" Jo spoke cautiously, never sure when something she said might send him running again.

He drank a little more coffee. "Yeah. I figured it was time. I'd been wandering the mountains for years. I'm not a man who easily gives up his freedom, but when you find the right woman—" He stared at the flames of the campfire for several silent seconds, then looked at Jo. *"A woman like you,"* he wanted to say. "At any rate, she's gone now, and so is my boy. So, it's back to the only life I was probably meant to lead anyway." He rose. "You'd better get some rest. We can't waste any time once we get started again." He finished the second cup of coffee. "You feeling all right now?"

"Yes. Still a little weak but that's all."

His eyes flickered over her. "Good. Thanks for the coffee."

"You're welcome."

He handed back the cup and their fingers touched. Jo sensed a thousand things being left unsaid. And she knew it was partly her fault. She was just as afraid of saying them as he was, and neither of them was about to speak first.

"Good night, Clint." *"I wish you would lay with me and hold me,"* she was thinking.

"I want to come to your bed tonight, Joline Masters," he thought. "Good night," he answered.

He quickly left, and Jo felt a painful ache deep inside, the kind of ache she once felt for Greg. She turned and climbed into her wagon, lying back into the new feather mattress she had purchased at the Plum Creek supply store. Tears welled in her eyes. This trip was turning into something more than she had wanted. She told herself to concentrate on Montana and nothing else. She pulled the blankets over herself and curled into the mattress, more keenly aware than she had been in months of how much she missed having a man hold her in the night.

They left in the morning, after deciding that the two groups of wagons would take turns being at the head of the train. No one wanted to be at the end of the train day after day, eating the dust of the others. Every other day the freight wagons would lead. Their leader, Dusty Hagan, didn't seem to mind taking on the extra travelers, as long as none of them held up the freight delivery.

"I've got a load to get to Fort Bridger, and I aim to get there before too much snow flies," he told Clint.

"We have the same intentions. And you can't argue there's more safety in numbers. You'll be helping us, and we'll be helping you. Besides, your men won't mind some woman-cooked meals, will they?"

Hagan laughed and shook hands with Clint. "Mister, I've never met you, but I've heard about you. I've made this trip many a time myself. Between the two of us, we'll get there all right."

Jo was relieved there was no animosity between the two men and no hard feelings on the part of the freighters over having the settlers tag along. She rode in the back of her wagon that first day, wanting to be sure she had no relapse. On the second day she walked, and her heart felt lighter at having the extra men along. Clint was usually nowhere in sight, riding far ahead of the train, keeping an eye open for mud, Indians, game, anything that might mean danger or might be needed by the travelers.

For several days the trip was actually enjoyable. The weather remained cool and clear, and for the moment they had plenty of meat. There was no trouble from Indians, and two of the men among the freighters played banjo and fiddle. Every night there was music, singing, and dancing. Because she was single and traveling alone, Jo was the most popular woman with the freighters, who admired her beauty and her courage. Every night she danced nearly every dance, aware that Clint was watching from the shadows and ready to pounce on any man who treated her with disrespect. But she received a great deal of respect from all of them. They passed through Willow Bend, a stage station and supply stop. There had been so much Indian trouble that the stagecoach had not been that far west all summer. Game had been scarce, and they were unable to purchase any meat; nor had Clint and the other men found any game to shoot. Clint warned that belts would have to be tightened, and meals would have to consist of biscuits and beans for a while. There were supplies in the freight wagons, but those were meant for Fort Bridger and had to be preserved unless they became desperate. Besides that, most of those supplies were in the form of material, pots and pans and such, with only two wagons carrying staples like flour and sugar.

Many of the travel stations at which they stopped had originally been built for the Pony Express, which was no longer in operation, since telegraph lines stretched all the way to Denver in Colorado Territory. At Midway Station Jo found a man who was carrying mail back east. She quickly finished a letter to Anna, telling her about her adventures thus far, about the tornado, her sickness, and what she had learned about Clint Reeves. She gave the letter to the carrier, paying him an outrageous price of seventy-five cents. But she had no choice, and she wanted desperately for Anna to get the letter and know she was still all right.

They ate well at Midway. It was here the Platte River parted into North and South Platte. The wagon train remained south of the South Platte and continued on to Gilman's Station, where cedar trees provided shade, and a dozen log buildings housed soldiers. Gilman's had turned into a military post, both to protect the area against Indians, and to keep an eye on possible attempts by the Confederates to gain territory in the west. Rumors quickly buzzed about the Confederates trying to get their hands on gold out of Denver, badly needed for buying weapons and supplies.

It was at Gilman's that Jo saw her first wild Indians. She had seen a few Indians around Lawrence, Christianized ones who dressed like white men and had farms. But there

weren't many. Most of the settled Indians were in Indian
Territory south of Kansas. Now, just beyond Gilman's settlement there was a circle of tipis, smoking campfires, and
half-naked Indian men sitting around the fires, a few of
them drinking whiskey.

Clint and Dusty Hagan both rode out to the Indians. Jo
walked on with the wagon, then helped Bobbie unhitch
the oxen and fetter them in a spot where they could graze.
She gathered clothes and bedding that needed washing
and carried them in a crate to the river, along with
some lye soap. Other women were already gathering to
scrub their own family's clothes. Bobbie brought the
wash for himself and his father, setting the clothes down
beside Jo.

"You sure you want to do this, Mrs. Masters?" he asked.

"Of course. It's the least I can do for having you drive
the oxen for me. But as soon as I'm stronger, I'll have to
try it myself, Bobbie. Once I leave Fort Bridger and head
north I'll be on my own."

The boy shook his head. "You ought to go on to Oregon,
ma'am."

"No, thank you. It's Montana for me." She looked past
him then at Clint, who was walking with four Indian
braves and Dusty Hagan. She wondered how Clint could
face any Indian without wanting to kill him. They walked
to the top of a hill, and one of the braves pointed, moving
his arm then to span the landscape.

"Indians," Bobbie muttered. "You reckon Mr. Reeves
knows how to talk to them?"

"I suppose he does. He told me he lived with Indians
for a while, years ago."

"That's strange, ain't it? I mean, he can talk to them,
maybe had some for friends, but it was Indians killed his
wife and kid."

"Well, Bobbie, I suppose there's good and bad in Indians, just like white men. Some you can trust and some you
can't."

They watched as Clint handed something to one of the
braves. From where she stood the Indians seemed a grand
specimen of man, hard-muscled, with long, shining black
hair, sometimes wound with beautiful beads. Two of them

wore fancy beaded shirts and leggings. The other two were nearly naked, wearing no shirts, their leggings slung low across their bellies and open at the sides, revealing bare hips. They seemed to be having a good time with Clint, bantering good-naturedly, although Jo could not understand what they were saying. They all walked toward the tipis and disappeared.

Jo saw no sign of Clint until later that evening, when he joined their circle around one central campfire. Their little group had begun gathering every night for music, a habit that kept their spirits up and brought them all closer together. Clint and Dusty both joined them, and the four braves and one woman were with them. Everyone stared at the Indians as they stood behind Clint and Dusty, who sat down. The woman wedged herself between the white men, taking both their arms. She was not beautiful, nor ugly. Jo guessed her to be perhaps twenty, and she looked longingly at Clint, then lay her head on his shoulder.

Jo felt an instant jealousy so powerful it surprised her. She immediately looked away, afraid Clint would see the look in her eyes. An Indian woman! He had probably had lots of Indian women, considering how he used to live. But how could he touch one now, after his wife? Still, white men had killed her own father and husband. That didn't mean she could never love another white man.

"These braves behind me are Southern Cheyenne," Clint told the others. "They tell us their northern brothers and the Sioux are roaming everywhere, causing a lot of trouble. These Southern Cheyenne are peaceful."

The woman said something, petting his arm, and he pushed her hand away. "This is Prairie Flower, an Arapaho woman. She, uh, likes white men, so you women had better keep an eye on your husbands."

Some of the men chuckled, but Marie Boone sniffed and rose, walking off to her wagon. The Indian woman pointed at her and said something in her own tongue. Clint nodded in agreement and the woman giggled.

"It's important to get along with any Indians we meet from here on, if that's possible," Clint told the rest of them. "If Indians at the various rest stops want to trade with you, trade with them. Don't insult them in any way."

He looked at Sidney Boone. "That goes for your wife, Boone. Can you make her understand that?"

"I can try."

"Do it. These Indians are peaceful, but they're all like old dynamite right now. Anything could set them off. No one knows what started the slaughters that took place up in Minnesota. It might have been something as slight as a white man spitting on an Indian. These are hard times for them. If you can put yourself in their place for a moment, you'll understand. They're starving. Most of the buffalo are gone, and the buffalo are their lifeblood. They depend almost completely on the animal. On top of that, whites are settling in places where the Indians used to roam freely. One treaty after another has been broken. They can't trust white men, and they're afraid for their women and children. Most of them are being put on reservations and forced to live a life completely foreign to them. They're dying, by the hundreds—from white man's diseases, hunger, too much whiskey, broken hearts. We'll have enough trouble ahead of us without one of you starting something unnecessarily."

"How can you sympathize with them after what they did to your wife and kid?" Johnny Hills asked him.

"Same as I can call another white man friend even if some of them hurt me or my own. I can't hate all Indians for what some did, and I can even understand why they did it. I know how they think. I brought these five braves over so you'd get used to being around Indians because you're going to be around them from here on, all the way to Oregon. It's Indians who will help you across rivers farther north: Shoshone, Chinook, Nez Percé, Cayuse, Yakima. Whatever they ask, you pay. At certain places it will be the Mormons who will help you, but most of the time it will be Indians. Some might seem offensive to you, but they know what they're doing and they'll get you across the rivers and show you the right way to go. Just remember that most of the way you'll still be in *their* country, not yours."

Jo studied their faces, proud, rather haughty. One of them said something to Clint in their strange, grunting language. Clint answered in the Indian tongue and motioned toward the Indian woman. The Indian man barked something at her and she immediately got up and left, pouting.

"This is Red Wolf," Clint told the others. "Any of you men willing to play a game of hands with him? I warn you, he's good."

"What's a game of hands?" Johnny Hills asked.

"He puts a bead under a walnut shell. He shuffles the shell with several others and you try to guess under which shell the bead is hidden."

"Oh, that sounds easy," Johnny answered. "I'll play."

Everyone gathered around as Dusty went to one of his wagons and got out a board. He brought it to the circle of travelers and laid it on the ground near the fire. Red Wolf sat down cross-legged in front of the board and laid out his shells and the bead, showing everyone where the bead was. He began quickly shuffling the shells, then pointed to Johnny, who scratched his head and studied the shells. Jo moved in closer to watch. Johnny pointed to the fourth shell and Red Wolf raised it. There was no bead under it.

Red Wolf grinned broadly and slapped Clint on the arm. Both men laughed, and the rest of the men from the wagon train began betting on the game. Before long Red Wolf had collected a kettle, some tobacco, a few coins, and Bennett Kiehl's shirt.

The gambling went on until they heard a scream for help coming from Marie Boone's wagon. Everyone ran toward it, where they found Mrs. Boone and the Indian woman wrestling on the ground. Mrs. Boone's hair was tumbled from its usual tidy bun and was full of dirt and grass. She kept grabbing for something in the other woman's hand, while the Indian woman kept her fist closed tightly, soundly socking Mrs. Boone across the side of the head.

The Indian men held back; a couple of them grinned but Red Wolf and the other brave remained sober. Clint and Dusty stepped into the melee, each man grabbing one of the women. Clint held on to the struggling Prairie Flower, while Dusty kept a tight grip on Mrs. Boone.

"What the hell is going on here?" Clint shouted at Mrs. Boone.

"That heathen woman stole my brooch!" Mrs. Boone shouted. "You make her give it back!"

Clint said something to Prairie Flower, who quieted and looked up at him. She held out the pin and spoke to him in her tongue.

"She says she saw it lying on a barrel and she just picked it up to look at it. Indian women like pretty things," Clint told Mrs. Boone.

"They're all thieves! She was going to steal it! If I hadn't come along she would have run off with it!"

"You don't know that for certain!"

"You're just sticking up for her because you have an eye for her!" Mrs. Boone shouted back. "You're as wild and heathen as they are! I'm beginning to wonder about that story about your wife and child, Mr. Clint Reeves! You seem to be able to become Indian yourself whenever it's convenient!"

Jo shivered at the look that came into Clint's eyes. He grunted an order to Prairie Flower, then pushed her aside. The Indian woman still clutched the brooch. Clint stepped closer to Mrs. Boone, towering over her.

"What story are you talking about, woman?" he growled.

Sidney Boone was so shaken by the incident, and so frightened by the look in Clint's eyes, that he didn't try to stand up for his wife. But Marie Boone faced Clint squarely. "The story Cook told us—about the Indians leaving you for dead and that's why you couldn't help your wife and son."

"I don't owe you any explanations, woman!" Clint snarled at her. "But if you're going to put doubts in the heads of these others, then I'll show you the proof!" He unbuckled an ammunition belt he wore slung over his shoulder and dropped it to the ground. Reaching down and grasping the bottom of his buckskin shirt, he pulled it up over his head. The light of the fire near Mrs. Boone's wagon revealed a magnificent build, muscular shoulders and back. But a deep, ugly scar seared across his chest, from his left shoulder, down across his nipple nearly to his belly.

People gasped and Jo looked away for a moment. Mrs. Boone stared aghast at the remnants of a terrible wound.

"Are you satisfied now?" Clint seethed. "Does this look like a wound that might have rendered a man helpless?"

The air hung silent.

"Red Wolf and the others call him Man Who Looked At Death," Dusty told them, his voice sounding strangely out of place.

"This scar was made by a hatchet, Mrs. Boone," Clint told the woman, "wielded by a warring Sioux brave who was out for blood! I won't even begin to try to explain to you about Indians—about the good and bad side of them— not much different from a lot of white men! I do know one thing: you get them riled, and it takes them a long time to cool down. So I suggest you put on a smile and tell Prairie Flower that she can have the pin as a gift."

Mrs. Boone sucked in her breath and hesitated.

"Do it!" Clint shouted the words. "Or by God I'll strip you naked right here in front of everyone and offer every bit of your clothing to her as well as the pin!"

Jo's mouth fell open. If not for the gravity of the situation, she would have laughed; and she would dearly have loved to see Clint act on his threat. Mrs. Boone deserved it. The woman stared wide-eyed at Clint.

"You wouldn't dare!"

Clint grinned an almost evil grin. "Wouldn't I? You said yourself I could be as wild and heathen as the Indians. Don't tempt me, Mrs. Boone. I'm not going to make enemies here! These Indians have plenty of friends a few miles from this station."

Marie Boone breathed deeply and looked at Prairie Flower. She forced a smile and told her she could have the pin as a gift. Clint interpreted, and Prairie Flower looked from him to Mrs. Boone, her dark eyes on fire with anger from the insult of being called a thief. Finally she nodded, clutching the pin and running off toward the little tipi village in the distance.

"Now I suggest, Mr. Boone, that if you have some tobacco, and some other trinket, or maybe some pretty cloth, you offer it to Red Wolf here. Prairie Flower belongs to him."

Jo frowned. How could a man "own" a woman, then offer her to another man? Clint pulled his shirt back on while Sidney Boone scrambled to find more gifts for Red Wolf and Prairie Flower. Then he strapped his gunbelt over his shoulder again, talking the whole time to Red Wolf and trying to explain the misunderstanding. Sidney Boone brought the Indian a plug of tobacco, some bright pink material, and a woman's belt with a silver buckle. Mrs. Boone climbed into her wagon and said nothing, while her husband asked Clint to apologize for his wife's behavior. When Red Wolf finally seemed satisfied, he walked off with the other three braves. Clint turned to Mr. Boone.

"If we run across Indians out on the trail, you keep that woman out of sight, understand? I don't care if you have to tie and gag her. You're responsible for your wife, Mr. Boone, and if she makes trouble, it's the two of you who will pay, not the whole wagon train."

"Yes, sir. I'll keep her away."

Bennett Kiehl stepped forward, looking embarrassed. "Clint, none of us . . . I hope you realize none of us doubted you for a minute. You didn't have to show us the scar. We know it's a private matter to you. I'm damned sorry that woman forced your hand."

Clint bent over and picked up his leather hat, which had got knocked from his head while he held on to Prairie Flower. "Don't worry about it. Now you all know and that's the end of it. While we're on this journey we have to try to get along with those Indians we run into or we'll never make it. That's just the way it is, and that's why I'm being friendly with this bunch. All of you just be sure to do what Dusty and I tell you."

Kiehl nodded and everyone went their own way, some still seemed stunned by the sight of Clint's scar. Moments later only Jo was left standing near him. He saw the deep sympathy in her dark eyes and he scowled.

"Don't say it," he grumbled.

She quickly put on a smile, but she wanted to cry. "Oh, I . . . I just wanted to ask you . . . would you really have stripped Mrs. Boone right in front of everyone?"

"You *bet* I would."

Jo couldn't help a laugh. "Oh, I wish she had dared you."

She saw a smile begin to show at the corner of his mouth. "I kind of wish she had myself."

He grinned and Jo laughed harder, reaching out and hugging him as naturally as if it were something she always did. Clint chuckled and put an arm around her shoulders. She looked up at him, and suddenly they both sobered. For a moment she thought he might lean down and kiss her, but instead he stiffened and moved back.

"You'd better get some sleep," he told her. "We move out in the morning. I'm going to Red Wolf's camp to make sure no feathers were left ruffled."

He quickly left, and Jo wrestled with painful emotions— desire mixed with jealousy. Would he sleep with Prairie Flower tonight just to keep her happy? It was none of her business whom he slept with, and she shouldn't feel this awful love and sympathy over the terrible scar. She realized it was a good thing he had not tried to kiss her, or she might have melted and let her emotions run away with her.

Her heart and mind were filled with confusion over whether she merely felt sorry for him, or felt genuine love. The second choice frightened her. She headed for her wagon, climbed inside, and dropped the canvas flap that closed her in. She didn't want to see Clint return— didn't want to know how long he spent at the Indian village. She heard a soft whining then and pulled the flap aside to look down at the stray dog.

"Where have you been?" she asked. "I haven't seen you for a couple of days."

The dog wagged his tail and Jo reached into a wooden bin inside the wagon and took out a biscuit. When she dropped it on the ground the dog immediately devoured it. He looked up at her gratefully and Jo smiled.

"You know, you're the best kind of friend to have," Jo told him. "You don't expect much and you're uncomplicated. All you need is some food and a little attention. And you're dependable. You don't run away every time I look cross-eyed at you. That's more than I can say for some people I know."

She glanced in the direction of the Indian camp, then jerked the canvas shut, disgusted with her feelings. She removed her shoes and dress, and lay down into the feather mattress, closing her eyes. But all she could see was the scar—the ugly scar. What had Clint witnessed? What had he suffered? There still was something unfinished about his story.

Jo curled into her blankets, and in the distance she heard a strange call. It was hard to tell if it was a coyote, or perhaps a wolf . . . or maybe it was an Indian. She tried to imagine what it must be like to be alone, surrounded by painted, screaming Indians, knowing they intended to kill all your loved ones—to feel the horrible crunch of an Indian hatchet, to see your loved ones dragged off right before your eyes, and not be able to help them.

Her eyes filled with tears. "Oh, Clint," she whispered.

Chapter Ten

The wagon train limped into Cottonwood Springs, with the Kiehl wagon rattling on broken springs, and one freight wagon propped up with boards shimmied across the right rear axle at an angle, dragging like an Indian travois. The boards replaced a broken wheel, which would have to be fixed at Cottonwood Springs.

Everyone gratefully filled their barrels with the plentiful supply of fresh water from a well at the way station. There was a large corral, where the animals could be turned loose, a log stockade surrounding the station, and three log cabins inside, as well as a telegraph office. Jo saw no Indians camped nearby, but there were several unsavory-looking white men.

Clint approached her as she carried two buckets of water back to her wagon. He took the buckets from her.

"You shouldn't be exerting yourself so much yet," he told her.

"I'm fine now. I can carry my own water."

"Well, I'm carrying these two. You can get the next load." He set the buckets down near her wagon. "Besides, I want to talk to you," he added. "You've probably already noticed some of the men hanging around here. This place is known to be used by outlaws at times, including Bart Kendall's gang. Stay close to your wagon or you might find something missing. And tell the others not to be too careless."

"I will." She looked up at him. "Do you think that Bart Kendall will try to follow us?"

His eyes darted around the station with hawklike awareness. "Wouldn't surprise me. He's not going to forgive either one of us for a time, that's sure. I wonder if his jaw is working right yet."

Jo smiled at the memory of Clint whacking the man flat with his rifle. "I hope it's so injured that he couldn't eat and he died of hunger."

"Joline! Such talk from such a tiny, gentle woman."

"I'm not gentle when it comes to men like that. He's no better than the man who tried to attack me in the cellar the day of the raid. I shot him, and I'll shoot Bart Kendall if I have to."

He frowned and shook his head. "Remind me never to get you riled against me."

She laughed lightly. "You've been too good to me. How long will we be here?"

He pushed back his hat. "A couple of days. You might as well wait and finish filling the barrels just before we leave so the water is good and fresh. Your oxen holding up all right?"

"Brute and Goliath are fine and healthy, as far as I can tell."

He grinned and shook his head. "Why do you insist on naming everything?"

She shrugged. "Everything deserves a name. It's a matter of respect. They're living beings, with their own spirits."

He leaned against her wagon wheel, grinning. "You'd get along great with Indians. That's the way they look at things. To them everything has a spirit, even the earth, the trees, the sun. They have a very beautiful, poetic attitude toward life. Everything on this earth and in the sky is a gift from the Great Spirit, put here to give man life."

She folded her arms and frowned, trying to ignore his disturbing masculinity. He wore a sleeveless vest that covered his scar, but revealed powerful arms, the skin sun-darkened. "It's interesting that you can talk about them that way," she said, "that you understand them, in spite of what happened to you."

"I never said I hated Indians, Jo. There are some I

greatly admire, and some I'd just as soon kill as look at. But even the friendly ones, once they've been pushed over the edge, can be more vicious than your wildest imagination. When they reach that point, I'd sink a blade or a bullet into them as easy as they'd do to me. It's when some damned fool does something stupid and starts a war that you don't dare trust them, even the ones you called friend."

"Were some of those in Minnesota ones you once called friend?"

The pain returned to his eyes, and he turned and took the lid off her water barrel. He picked up one of the buckets and poured it into the barrel. "A couple of them were. But one of them—his family had been murdered. One thing led to another; someone convinced him I was some kind of traitor, that I had something to do with his family being killed. So he decided to pay back the crime. He was called Two Moons."

Jo shivered. "An eye for an eye," she said quietly, her heart aching for him.

"A wife and son for a wife and son is more like it." He set down the bucket and picked up the other. "I wish our conversations wouldn't always lead to what happened in Minnesota."

"You have to get it out, Clint. You have to talk about it. You should have explained more to Millie's father."

She saw the anger then in his eyes as he set down the second bucket. "He didn't deserve an explanation. And you don't know it all, Jo. You still don't know it all."

She watched him sadly. "What don't I know? I want to help, Clint. I want to understand."

He picked up the buckets and handed them to her. "It's your turn. Remember what I said about watching your wagon. Tell the others."

He left, and she realized she had chased him away again. She chastised herself for always asking about Minnesota, and she promised she would not let the subject come into their conversation again.

The screeching of crickets filled the night air, which hung hot and muggy. In the distance Jo could hear men laughing, gambling and drinking into the night. She had

seen some of the men who hung around the fort playing
cards earlier in the day. They sat around a large, square
piece of wood set on top of a barrel. Barrels also served as
chairs. Clint played cards with them, but Jo suspected it
was only to keep an eye on them.

She wondered if he was still with them. Most of the
men from the wagon train were asleep, weary from the
long day's journey and from working to prop up the broken freight wagon. As Clint had ordered, Jo had stayed
near the wagon, and so had most of the others. There had
been no problems, but Jo still shivered at the way one
man looked at her as he rode past with several others.

She threw off her covers and unbuttoned the top buttons of her nightgown, wishing she could just lie naked,
because of the heat. But in these parts a person never
knew when he or she might have to jump out of a wagon
in the middle of the night, and a woman couldn't be
caught unprepared.

She thought she heard footsteps outside her wagon, but
more laughter from the distance shrouded any nearby
sound. Jo frowned, sitting up and listening carefully. There
had been several nights when she had caught Sarah Grant
walking outside; the old woman had trouble sleeping because of her grief over her dead husband. Many times Jo
had climbed out of her wagon and talked quietly with the
woman, feeling sorry for her.

"Sarah? That you?" she asked softly. She moved to the
back of the wagon and leaned out.

In the next instant a hand came over her mouth in a
powerful grip. Strong fingers squeezed her jaw, holding
her whole face with one big hand while a big, dark figure
quickly climbed into the wagon. Jo flailed at him, but his
arm was so long she couldn't reach his face. Her heart
pounded wildly as she began kicking at him; at the same
time she tried to grasp for her rifle.

Now she could smell whiskey and sweat. The powerful
figure pushed her down into her feather mattress, still
holding her face painfully with one hand while he ripped
at her nightgown. Gathering a handful of the material, he
released his hold on her face just long enough to shove the
material into her mouth, before she could let out a scream.

His body was so heavy against her that Jo couldn't

budge. It was impossible to reach for her rifle. She screamed through her nose, but the sound was not nearly loud enough to alert anyone. She was choking on the material in her mouth, and she was sure she was going to vomit and probably choke to death. With her free hands she scratched at the man's eyes, until a hard fist landed against the side of her face.

Everything whirled then, the light of a bright moon coming through the canvas, the dark shadow of the man hovering over her. She tried to push at him as she felt him raise up her nightgown and grasp at her bloomers, but nothing seemed to work right.

"Now you just stay real still, you pretty little thing," came a voice. Jo tried to scream again through her nose, and she could taste blood in her mouth and throat. He jerked her arms behind her back and held them with one hand, while he tore at her bloomers and pushed a hard knee between her legs, forcing them apart. Jo attempted to scream again as she arched upward, struggling violently to get her hands free.

"In just a second now you're gonna be glad I'm here, little woman," the man was saying. She felt a fumbling between her legs, but suddenly his weight was gone. She heard a grunt and watched through blurred vision as her attacker rose up and was tossed out of the wagon by an unseen figure. She heard punches and grunts, then voices as others apparently gathered outside.

Jo sat up, yanking the material out of her mouth and coughing. She quickly pulled up her bloomers and pushed down the skirt of her gown, grasping at what was left of the bodice to cover herself as she crawled to the back of the wagon.

Men had gathered around and a few of them held up lanterns. They had been roused by the vicious fight that was now taking place between Clint Reeves and one of the men Jo had seen earlier in the day, the one who gave her the chilling look. Clint was landing severe blows to the man's midsection and face, but Clint himself was bleeding profusely from the mouth.

Jo watched wide-eyed as her attacker finally went down and didn't get up. Clint, filthy and panting, bent over, grasping his ribs and wiping at the blood on his mouth.

Suddenly the other man went for his gun. Before Jo could manage to find her voice through the phlegm in her throat, Sidney Boone yelled, "Mr. Reeves, look out!"

People screamed as the gun went off, catching Clint's shoulder. He whirled, and in a split second came back around. A knife landed in the other man's chest, pulled and thrown so quickly that no one even saw the movement. Jo's attacker, still on the ground when he fired the gun, just stared at Clint for a moment, then looked down at the knife in his chest before his eyes rolled back and he fell dead.

The crowd stared in shock. Clint grasped his wounded shoulder. "Get him out of here!" he growled. "He attacked Jo Masters."

Several pairs of eyes turned to look at Jo while Clint staggered up to her attacker and yanked his knife out of the dead man's chest. He wiped it off on the man's coat and turned to cast a dark look at others from the fort who had gathered around. He waved the knife. "Any of you want to avenge this sonuvabitch's death? I'm ready!"

A couple of men who had apparently been friends of the man walked up to the body, carefully avoiding Clint. "We'll bury him," one of them told Clint.

Clint eyed the rest of them. "Any of the rest of you tries to rob or bring personal harm to anyone on this train, he'll answer to me! Is that understood?"

The men backed off, and Sarah came rushing up to Jo. "Oh, Joline, are you all right?"

The left side of her face ached fiercely, and Jo could tell it was swelling without even touching it. "I think so," she told Sarah. She looked at Clint. "Clint, come inside and let me and Sarah have a look at that wound."

He shoved his knife into a sheath worn around his calf and stumbled to the wagon. Sidney Boone walked up and asked if he could help. Clint looked at the man with a frown. "You probably saved my life when you yelled out."

"Well, I . . . I hope I did. Maybe it will make up for the problems my wife has caused." The man put out his hand and Clint shook it, leaving dirt and blood on Boone's hand. "That was quite a fight, Mr. Reeves. I guess we don't have to worry about your skills in that area."

Clint just stared at him in surprise for a moment before

climbing into Jo's wagon while Sarah lit a lantern. "I'm a mess," Clint told Jo. "I'll get everything dirty."

"It doesn't matter, as long as you're all right." Jo reached for an old shirt to cover herself and let go of her gown long enough to put it on. Clint caught sight of the white fullness of one breast almost fully exposed from the torn gown. He also noticed ugly red scratches on the white skin. Jo quickly pulled on the shirt and buttoned it, and then she felt a big but gentle hand touching the side of her face.

"Bastard!" he muttered. "I was playing cards and all of a sudden I noticed he was gone. He'd been asking about you earlier in the day and I told him your affairs were none of his business. I had a feeling this was where he'd gone." He touched her hair. "I'm sorry, Jo."

"Sorry! You got him away from me."

"I should have been watching closer. He didn't . . . he didn't . . . get to you, did he?"

She dropped her eyes. "No." She wondered how one man's touch could be so repulsive, and a moment later another man's touch could be so soothing. "It's you who's hurt worse," she said then. "Take off that vest."

He looked at his shoulder. "I don't need to. Besides, it's just a graze. Most of it is exposed. Just pour some whiskey on it and wrap it. I need to rinse the blood out of my mouth though."

Jo looked at Sarah, who knew where things were in the wagon after caring for Jo when she was sick. The woman already had out a bottle of whiskey, which Jo kept for medicinal purposes, and some clean gauze. "I want to take care of it, Sarah. I can do it. I'll be all right."

"You sure, child?"

"Yes. You get some rest."

Sarah patted her shoulder. "You do the same. Thank God for Mr. Reeves here."

Jo met his eyes. "Yes."

Sarah got out of the wagon by climbing over the front seat, since she couldn't move past Jo and Clint in the cramped quarters. Jo doused a cloth with some whiskey and held it against the ugly gash across the top of Clint's shoulder. He winced with pain, then took the whiskey bottle from her.

"Hold on," he told her. He tipped the whiskey bottle to his mouth and rinsed, moving to the back of the wagon and spitting out the whiskey. He rinsed once more, then drank some of the whiskey. "Damn," he sighed as he settled back into the wagon. "When I knew he was in this wagon . . ." He handed the bottle back to her. "Someone should be tending to you, not me."

"I'll be all right. But you're bleeding." She pushed his vest away and dabbed at the wound again, realizing he didn't want to remove the vest because he was self-conscious about his scar. She pressed the cloth tightly against the wound.

"I don't know what I would have done if he had killed you," she told him, her eyes misting. "It would have been all my fault. All I've done is make trouble for you ever since we left Lawrence. I'm sorry, Clint. All I wanted was to get to Montana."

"And you'll get there. You can't help any of the things that happened."

She thought about the foul breath of her attacker, the rough whiskers and the hard punch. She shivered at the memory of how close he had come to raping her, and she couldn't stop the sudden sob that welled up from her soul.

In the next moment she felt an arm come around her and she was quietly crying against his chest. Clint closed his eyes, the agony of being so close to her more painful than the wound to his shoulder. He could smell the clean scent of her hair, and fury surged through him again at the thought of another man touching her. He didn't want any other man to lay hands on her, yet he was desperately afraid to let his feelings go, to put his own hands on her the way he would like.

"I couldn't . . . get to my rifle," she sobbed. "It happened . . . so quick."

"It's over now."

She curled up against the ugliness of it, amazed that another man could be so comforting. He ran a hand over her shoulders.

"My first duty is to you. You're the one who asked me to bring you out here. These others come second. From now on I'll keep a better eye on you. But this should show you the dangers there are out here, Jo."

She straightened, wiping at her eyes. "It won't happen again. I did a foolish thing. I thought it was Sarah, and I stuck my head out without even thinking. From now on I sleep with my rifle right beside me, and I ask questions first and have my gun ready when I hear noises in the night."

He leaned closer. "Why? Why are you doing this? Are you trying to prove something to someone?"

His face was so close that every nerve end, every desire came alive in her. She moved away from him, angry for again showing weakness. "Just to myself, I guess. I felt I would go crazy if I stayed in Lawrence and tried to start all over again. A woman can wander, looking for her purpose in life, just the same as a man. All I ever knew was the farm and Lawrence. I had a taste of love and marriage, and it ended almost before it had a chance to begin. I loved Greg and then he was gone, and everything I thought I wanted in life was destroyed with him. It all just got turned upside down, and I feel so . . . so lost."

Their eyes held. "I know the feeling," he told her.

She sat rigid as he leaned closer, and then his lips were suddenly lightly touching her own. He parted her lips, his tongue sliding along their outer edges as he grasped her hair with one hand and held it tightly. He left her mouth and kissed her bruised cheek. "We're two of a kind, Jo," he said softly. "We both know what we want but we're both afraid of having it again, losing it again." He kissed her gently once more, then drew back. He let out a strange sigh, as though disgusted with himself. "My God, what am I doing? I'm sorry. I had no right."

Before Jo could say a word he quickly climbed out of the wagon. "I'll have Sarah wrap my arm," he told her before quickly disappearing.

Jo touched her lips with the back of her hand, and her eyes burned with tears. What a beautiful kiss it had been. He had suddenly interrupted all her plans, destroyed her design for being strong and independent, for never loving a man again. She ached to feel his arm around her, but she knew the meaning of his remark. He wanted her, but he would never allow himself to go that far. He had risked his life for her, but he would not let himself love her.

*   *   *

Clint kept his distance during the rest of their stay at Cottonwood Springs, and Jo knew he was embarrassed and angry with himself for kissing her. She wished she could forget that kiss, wished she could understand the man who had kissed her. She wanted to tell him it was all right, yet it wasn't all right at all. He had completely disrupted her original plans, totally destroyed her vow not to care.

After two days the train got underway again. As Jo walked beside her wagon on the third day past Cottonwood Springs, Clint rode up beside her. He kept his eyes forward, refusing, perhaps afraid, to look at her.

"I want to apologize about the other night. You were so close and you were hurt and upset. I just . . . I guess I wanted to tell you everything was all right—that I wouldn't let anybody hurt you again. Besides that, I haven't . . . it's been a long time. I kind of lost control."

Jo tried to ignore the passion his presence stirred in her soul. "No apology is necessary," she told him. "Circumstances make people do strange things sometimes. We just have to remember while we're out here that . . . that conditions sometimes make it difficult to think straight." *"I wanted you to kiss me,"* she wished he had the courage to say. *"I think I could love you, Clint Reeves. But I'm so scared to love again. And so are you. But we could try—together."*

"I think of you as a good friend, Jo. I think you understand me better than most. I guess . . . it just feels good to know somebody understands. When it happens to be a woman . . . out here emotions can run a little wild. I had no right, and I blame myself for it. I don't want it to come between us."

She looked up at him, but he still looked forward avoiding her eyes. "It won't. The fact is, I guess I needed a strong arm around me just then, even a kiss. There's nothing wrong with friends kissing, I suppose. I deeply appreciate your concern—your risking your life for me."

"I couldn't bear the thought of another man touching you," he wanted to tell her. He still felt a deep anger seeing the bruise on the side of her face. "I said I'd get you safely to Montana, and I meant it. What happens after that is up to you."

She looked up at him again, wondering if he really meant it. "Yes. I'm on my own. That was the agreement." Her anger began to rise then. Oh, he was trying so hard to act as though he didn't care. If he wanted it to be that way, she could be just as good at pretending as he. "I never asked for any more than that. Your life will finally be your own again. But I hope you'll come and see me once in a while, out of friendship."

He finally looked down at her. A smile moved across the corner of his mouth, and she could remember the taste of his finely etched lips. "I'd be glad to call on you once in a while, Mrs. Masters," he answered, his voice very formal. "It will be very interesting to see how you do up there in the wilds alone." He smiled more then and rode off, and she wished she could hit him.

Again he was gone more than he was present. As long as they were on the trail, he knew she was in no danger from outsiders, and his job was to hunt and scout ahead for trouble. Again water and food ran low, and people pulled in their belt buckles. They found more water at Fort McPherson, and farther on at Morrow's Ranch they stocked up on food supplies: sardines, tomatoes, peaches, with the men getting a new supply of whiskey and bitters. From the talk of old-timers like Dusty Hagan, Jo realized she was lucky she was making this journey in the 1860's rather than the 1840's, when there were hardly any harbors like forts and ranches along the way. At Morrow's Ranch she met Jack Morrow, another man Clint knew well, and who had an Indian wife.

Nearby several Sioux Indians were camped. Marie Boone stayed in or near her wagon, keeping well away from the Indians; but while they camped there, Clint spent most of his time with the Indians, determined to stay on their good side. Jo and Bess and Sarah mended quilts and washed clothes, along with the shy Martha Sievers and her daughter. Marie Boone kept to herself, and Jo wondered if the woman was still suffering embarrassment over the incident with Prairie Flower back at Gilman's Station. She figured it served the woman right to be embarrassed still, and she wondered how anyone could live so selfishly and without friends.

They headed out again, still experiencing no real Indian

trouble as they passed through the Sand Hill Stage Station and the Old California Crossing, where there was another trading post but few supplies. The well there was nearly dry, and they could fill their barrels only halfway. It was several days out of Old California Crossing when their first Indian problem arose. Clint came riding back to the train at full gallop, telling everyone to form a circle and stay inside it.

"There's a tribe of Sioux up ahead. They have women and children along, so they aren't looking for trouble, but we can't be sure. Everybody do as I say. Dusty, come with me."

The two men rode out again, and Jo watched anxiously. The dog that had followed her wagon through most of the trip sprang after Clint and Dusty.

"Come back, boy," Jo called out to it, suddenly wondering why she had never named the poor thing. The dog stopped and watched the horizon, as did everyone else as soon as the wagons were positioned. It was not long before the horizon was lined with what looked like several hundred Sioux. Jo felt her heart sink, and she reached for her Henry to make sure it was loaded.

Chapter Eleven

Everyone stared, rifles ready, as the huge tribe of Sioux approached; young warriors rode in the lead, older men rode behind them, while most of the women walked. They led horses burdened down with supplies and pulling travois loaded with tepee hides, more supplies, and children. Other children walked, and many women carried cradleboards on their backs. Some travois were pulled by dogs.

Jo felt some relief that there were women and children along. As Clint had told them, this was obviously not a war party. But there were enough of them that everyone realized caution was the word. The warriors in front had proud, daring looks on their faces, obviously realizing they had the upper hand as they pranced their painted ponies around the wagons, as though sizing up what they would take from the small group of frightened travelers.

Marie Boone stuck her head out of her wagon and gasped. "Oh, my God!"

Jo hurried over to the woman's wagon, rifle in hand. "Don't you dare come out of that wagon, Mrs. Boone."

The woman scowled. "Who are you to give me orders?"

"It doesn't matter. I mean it. If you come out of there I'll sock you."

The woman's eyebrows arched in surprise and indignation. "Well! Such impudence from someone young enough to be my daughter."

Jo met the woman's eyes boldly. "I mean it! We could

all die from one wrong word or gesture! Now get inside
and don't even let them see you!"

The woman sniffed and ducked inside her wagon. Jo
moved back to her own wagon, staying behind it and
watching Clint. She realized that being surrounded by so
many Indians had to be a terrible strain on him. He was
talking in sign language to one of the old chiefs, or at least
that was what Jo imagined the old man to be. Dusty sat
beside Clint on his own horse. Sometimes he would do
the talking. The old man seemed to be demanding something, and Clint and Dusty were trying to reason with
him. Jo prayed it was not women captives he demanded.

While they talked, the younger warriors kept circling
the wagons. One stopped at Jo's wagon, eyeing her closely.
She didn't feel he was looking at her hungrily, the way the
vagrant white men had back at Cottonwood Springs. It
was more a look of curiosity, as though trying to figure out
these white women, what was different about them, perhaps wondering why they dressed so differently from Indian women. The stray, unnamed dog was sitting beside
Jo. It stood up and barked at the Indian. He scowled at
the dog and rode to the back of Jo's wagon, starting to
untie the two Appalaoosas, Patch and Star.

Jo's heart pounded. She needed those horses badly. She
set her rifle aside, afraid to point it at the young man for
fear of instant retaliation by his friends. "No!" she shouted.
"They're mine! Take something else."

She tried to grab the ropes out of his hands, but he
placed a moccasined foot against her chest and shoved, not
viciously, but just enough to warn her to stay away. The
move caused her to slip backward and land on her rump.
By then some of the young man's friends had gathered
around and were all grinning at the sight, as though it
were an amusing joke on the white woman.

Clint heard the commotion and left Dusty to dicker with
the old Indian. The chief was demanding supplies before
he would let the wagon train pass.

Clint rode into the dangerous confrontation between Jo
and the young warrior. Jo was scowling as she got to her
feet and dusted off her skirt, which had become ragged at
the bottom from walking so many weeks and miles through
grass, rocks, and brush. Her eyes were gleaming with

tears, but Clint could see she was struggling to remain calm.

"Clint, he's taking my horses! Tell him he can't!"

Clint sighed and looked at the young warrior, saying something to him in a combination of sign language and the Sioux tongue. The young man looked from Clint back to Jo, frowning in curiosity again. He said something to Clint then, and Clint looked at Jo. "He wants to know if the dog belongs to you."

Jo looked down at the poor, faithful animal that had followed her halfway across the country. She suddenly loved it and wished she had named it. "I . . . no. It doesn't really belong to anyone."

"I told him you're a woman traveling alone, without a man. I told him it isn't honorable to steal horses from a lone woman. He respects you now as a woman of great property. There is nothing more valuable to an Indian than good horses. He'll give them back, but if the dog doesn't belong to you, he wants it."

Jo frowned. "Whatever for?"

Clint removed his hat and ran a hand through his hair. "Probably to eat it. It's fairly young, and you and the others have fattened it up."

Jo eyes widened and filled with more tears. "*Eat* it! Oh, Clint, I can't hand over a poor animal to be eaten! Dogs are for pets, not eating!"

"Not to the Indian. They're for pulling travois, and some are for eating. It's their way, Jo. No different from our killing a deer or some other animal for food. This is no time to get sentimental over a stray dog that doesn't even belong to you. We're in a tight situation here."

The Indian grunted something and rode closer to Jo, handing her the ropes to her horses. She pressed her lips together to keep from crying as she took the horses and led them back to her wagon. The dog followed her, wagging its tail and looking up at her trustingly. More tears came, so that she could not keep them from spilling down her cheeks. She bent over and picked up the dog, giving it a hug. It licked at her tears. She petted it gently and looked at Clint.

"I can't do it," she told him. "Tell him he can take one of the horses instead. I won't give him the dog."

"Jo, it's just a dog."

"No it isn't! He loves me and trusts me! I won't let him be killed and carved up for someone's dinner!"

Clint suppressed an urge to laugh. He looked at the Indian and tried to explain. It was obvious the Indian was amazed at Jo's decision. He stared at Jo and the dog for a moment, then moved his eyes to Clint. He said something more in his own tongue, then turned and rode off with the others. Clint grinned and looked down at Jo. "This is your lucky day, Jo Masters."

She held the dog close to her breast, quickly wiping at her tears. "Why didn't he take the dog?"

"He said you and the dog are apparently one in spirit. He said it's obvious the Great Spirit means for the dog to remain with you. And he said you are an unusual white woman. Others would have handed over the dog gladly."

She smiled through tears. "You mean he's not going to take it?"

He shifted in his saddle. "Nope. And you might as well name that mutt. I think you're stuck with him."

"Oh, thank goodness!" Jo hugged the dog close and kept hold of him, walking back to her wagon. She looked back at Clint. "I'm sorry about the horses. I mean, I probably shouldn't have tried to stop him. It could have made trouble."

"They admire bravery. You did all right." He grinned and rode back toward Dusty. More Indian braves circled the wagons while Clint and Dusty talked to the old leader. One young man took a wash tub, another grabbed a hatchet. Two young men began banging on the chicken cage attached to Bess and Johnny's wagon, laughing at the way the chickens clucked and squawked and fluttered about inside the cage whenever they hit it. Bess stayed hidden inside the wagon, and Johnny eyed the men carefully but made no move. Everyone seemed to understand they didn't dare strike out at the volatile warriors.

Clint rode back to the circle of wagons, ordering everyone to hand over whatever they could spare in the way of food without being left destitute. "They especially like sugar and honey and tobacco," he told them.

"Damn thieves," Bill Starke muttered.

"Stay calm," Clint told them. "This was their land first.

Remember that. We've taken just about as much from them as one man can take from another. You can't blame them for demanding something back when they have the upper hand, and they *do* have the upper hand. Remember that."

"We need this stuff," Donald Sievers complained. "I thought you were an Indian fighter."

"When it's necessary, Sievers. If they attack us, we'll *have* to fight them. But there are times when common sense is all we can use. We have to watch out there. We'd end up with our wagons burned, every man dead, and every woman either dead or wishing she was. If we can get through this by doling out a few supplies, then we're damn lucky. Now quit complaining and hurry it up. The sooner we put some miles between us and them, the better."

"What's to keep them from following us and begging for more—or sneaking up on us in the night and stealing our stock?" Bennett Kiehl asked.

"Not a damn thing. We just have to hope they won't do either one. I know the old man there and I think he respects me enough that this will be the end of it. From some of the things that have been happening to other travelers, I'd say we're doing damn good getting out of here with our scalps."

Everyone began setting food and blankets outside the circle of wagons. Some of the Indian women approached cautiously then, picking up the articles and loading them onto travois. Jo noticed a strange sadness in the eyes of some of them, and she realized there was not a fat man or woman among them. Some looked much too thin. Were they starving? She saw with sudden clarity the situation of the Indians. As more and more whites settled this land, where would the Indians go? Their whole way of life would have to change. And indeed, they must think of this as their land. Why shouldn't they? She and the others were intruders, yet they all thought they had a right to settle wherever they chose. She didn't feel guilty, for she knew that if it weren't she, there were a hundred others ready to leave eastern lands and take her place. It was going to happen, whether the Indians liked it or not. But

it had to be a sad and frightening realization for the
Indians.

A few of the Indian women looked at Jo curiously.
When one turned, Jo called out for her to wait. The
woman knew by Jo's gesture what she meant, and she
stopped for a moment while Jo peered into a cradleboard on
the woman's back to admire an infant peering out at her
with wide, brown eyes.

"Your baby is very beautiful," she told the woman,
smiling at her and hoping she understood. She held up
her hand, signaling her to wait a moment longer. She
climbed into her wagon then and dug out some ribbons
she had brought along. She wouldn't have much use for
ribbons and pretty attire in Montana. She climbed back
out and handed the ribbons to the young woman, whose
eyes lit up with joy. She spoke something in her own
tongue which Jo reasoned was gratitude, and reached behind her neck to untie a necklace made of quills, beads,
and bone, held together with a strip of rawhide. She
handed the necklace to Jo, who stared at it in surprise.

"For me?" She pointed to herself and the Indian woman
nodded.

Jo took the necklace, sensing it was an honor. The
Indian woman nodded again and left, clinging to the ribbons.

It seemed hours, although it was only perhaps thirty
minutes, before the Indians finally seemed satisfied and
began moving past the wagon train. Everyone waited nervously while the huge tribe moved around them; the only
sound was the plodding of their horses and the scraping
sound of the travois poles. Jo wondered if they always
traveled so quietly, and she realized they probably had to,
so they wouldn't be seen or heard by soldiers.

Everyone breathed a sigh of relief when the Indians
moved on, but there was a lot of muttering about "thieving savages" as the group prepared to get moving again.
Clint rode up to Jo, his own relief obvious. "What did the
Indian woman give you?"

"A necklace." Jo took it from her skirt pocket and held it
up.

Clint nodded. "Could come in handy sometime. If you're
ever threatened by other Sioux, show them the necklace. I

don't know if it would help or not, but it can't hurt. You
did real good today, Mrs. Masters."

"I'm just glad there wasn't any trouble over the horses.
I reacted too quickly. I need them more than any of my
other supplies."

"Well, it worked out. You never can be sure how an
Indian will react to something like that. God must be
keeping a good eye on you."

He rode off, whistling at oxen and mules, helping men
get their animals moving again. Jo hurried up to her
wagon before it got underway and slipped the necklace
into a pocket in the side of the canvas. She checked to be
sure the horses were properly tied to the back of the
wagon, then bent down to pick up the stray dog.

"You just missed being some warrior's supper, boy," she
told the animal. She hugged it close, glad the animal had
been spared, but more glad that Clint had survived. "That
Indian said we share the same spirit, boy, so that's what
I'm naming you—Spirit." She set the dog down and hurried up to walk next to Bobbie. Spirit barked and ran up
beside her, his tail wagging and his head held proudly, as
though he knew he now belonged to someone.

The wagon train broke south along the newer Overland
Trail, moving on to Julesburg, a town that had sprung up
when gold was discovered five years earlier in a place now
called Denver, Colorado Territory. Julesburg was a supply
stop for prospectors, and a welcome sight to the weary
travelers. The town was a stage stop, and it also had a
telegraph office, a supply store, a blacksmith shop, ware-
houses and stables, and more saloons than it seemed could
be filled. Clint advised the travelers to camp outside of
town and the women to stay in groups.

There was more mending to be done to the wagons, and
Bill Starke had to purchase more oxen. One of his had
died two days from Julesburg, dropping in its tracks for no
reason the men could figure out. They were relieved that
so far none of the other animals seemed sick. But one of
the oxen pulling a freight wagon stepped in a hole and
broke its leg and had to be shot. Both animals were left
along the trail, and Jo thought it sad that they had to lie
there to be eaten by buzzards and wolves.

All along the trail they continued to pass the carcasses and skeletons of other animals who had not lasted. They also saw the remnants of graves of people who had gone before them, graves which might never be visited again by friends and relatives who managed to get to their destination. They would lie forgotten, eventually disappearing from the elements. The thought made Jo's heart heavy, and she prayed her own grave would not be among them.

She wrote another letter to Anna, letting her know she was still all right, and telling her about the incident with the Indians. She didn't tell her about the attack at Cottonwood Springs. It would only worry Anna, and Jo had decided she would never be caught off guard like that again.

She also decided not to tell Anna about the kiss, the beautiful kiss Clint Reeves had given her and which she could not forget. That kiss had haunted her deep in the night, and she wondered how much it haunted Clint. Was it really just a sudden emotional reaction, a meaningless gesture? That was a lie. The kiss had lingered too long for that explanation. It was not something quickly stolen, a peck on a sudden whim. It had been much more than that, but Clint Reeves didn't want to admit it; and she didn't want anything to do with a man who was so far from ready to love again. She told herself it was best forgotten, if that was possible. After all, that was the way Clint wanted it.

Men began gathering animals together to have new shoes put on those that needed them. The blacksmith would be a busy man for the next couple of days, and Jo supposed he was also a rich man. He surely got all the business he wanted by the time people got this far along on their journeys west. She untied her own horses, deciding to take just one of the Appaloosas and Shag, the big, shaggy gelding she had got back from Bart Kendall. She would have the blacksmith look at those two first, then she would bring the rest. She had checked their hooves herself, and the two horses she led toward the blacksmith's were in the worst shape.

Johnny Hills walked with her, leading two of his oxen, and Bennett Kiehl and Donald Sievers followed. Kiehl hurried up beside Jo, striking up a casual conversation. Jo knew that the widower, whose son had been driving Jo's oxen, was interested in her, and she wished she could feel something for the man. But he was at least forty, if not older; and although he was a handsome and strong man for his age, she had no special feelings for him, not like she had once felt for Greg, and not like—

Her chest tightened at the realization that as she talked to him she was comparing him to Clint. What a stupid thing to do, as though there was room for a Clint Reeves in her life. She would have enough problems without taking on a man as troubled as Clint. She didn't really want any man at all, for it would only mess up her plans for Montana. Bennett Kiehl struck her as the kind of man who felt a woman's place was behind her man, obedient and passive. She was not ready to be either, and no man was going to stop her from going to Montana.

She realized it would be easier to forget about Clint's kiss if he were more like Bennett Kiehl. But he had a freer spirit, and she knew deep inside that he admired her own spirit, her courage and determination. He wouldn't expect a woman to be passive and meek. If she were ready for a man, she would want him to be a man like Clint.

She turned to Kiehl and smiled, talking about silly things as she led her horses up to the blacksmith.

"I think these two are the worst," she told the blacksmith. "My name is Jo Masters, and—" She halted when a man stepped out of the blacksmith's shed and stared at her. Her heart nearly stopped beating when she saw the yellowed teeth and the black coat.

"Well, well, lookie here!" Bart Kendall sneered, stepping closer. He eyed the horses, then moved his gaze back to Jo. "If it ain't the little slip of a woman who stole my horses from me."

"You're the horse thief, Bart Kendall, and you should have been hanged. What are you doing in Julesburg?"

He shrugged. "Man's got a right to go where he pleases. And he can travel pretty fast when he's not bogged down with a bunch of greenhorn settlers and heavy freight wagons. Why, I thought you folks would never get here."

Jo frowned. "What do you care if we got here or not?"

"Oh, I don't." His steely blue eyes raked over her as though she were naked. "I just waited out of curiosity, hopin' maybe the Indians would give you a bad time of it, maybe carry you off and do with you what ought to be done with you."

"You watch your mouth, Kendall," Ben Kiehl spoke up. "Mrs. Masters is a lady. And she's right. You should have been hanged back there at Fort Riley. Now get out of here. We've got things to talk over with the blacksmith here."

Kendall removed his hat and bowed. "Be my guest." He stepped closer to Kiehl. "But don't ever try to order me around again, farmer, else I'll look you up when you least suspect it and shove your teeth right down your throat."

The two men glared at each other, while Jo waited with a pounding heart, terrified that Kiehl would get hurt on her account. Kendall suddenly grinned, looking down at Jo. "That mountain man you took up with around?"

Her face grew red with fury. "I haven't 'taken up' with any man. And if you're referring to Clint Reeves, you'd be wiser to stay away from him. Or have you forgotten what happened the last time the two of you met?"

She noticed his face looked slightly crooked, and he put a hand self-consciously to his jaw. His eyes turned to a frightening glare. "I ain't forgot, missy. Why do you think I'm keeping track of him? Next time it's *my* turn."

"Clint Reeves is twice the man you'll ever be," Jo answered boldly. She shoved past him and handed the ropes of her horses to the blacksmith. "This is Shag and Patch. I'll bring two more tomorrow. Is that all right?"

"I'll try to get to them. I've got my work cut out, ma'am, but I've hired a man to help. He's inside right now working on some oxen."

Jo could hear the heavy blows of the blacksmith's hammer. "Thank you. I'll pay you when the work is done."

She waited for Ben and Johnny to talk to the smithy about their own animals, all the while feeling Bart Kendall's eyes on her. She refused to look at him. When Ben and Johnny were ready, the three of them walked back together to the wagons. Bart Kendall just stood and watched them.

"Nice to see you again, Mrs. Masters," he called out, sending shivers up Jo's spine. "Maybe we'll meet again—in Montana."

The words both frightened and infuriated her. How dare he spoil her plans and dreams by threatening to give her problems in Montana! She wouldn't let him do it. If she ever saw him anywhere near her property, she would shoot him on sight. After all, there was no law in a place like Montana. No one would care if she shot a man like Bart Kendall. He deserved to be hanged anyway. She told herself she could shoot him if she had to. After all, she had shot the man called Dooley, hadn't she? She had protected herself that day, and she could do it again. A woman had to be hard in this land. There was no room for weakness or softheartedness. And Bart Kendall would be just another challenge.

"Don't let that man bother you, Mrs. Masters," Ben was telling her. "We'll keep an eye out."

"It's all right. I chose to make this trip and I can take care of myself." Kiehl tipped his hat to her as he went on to his own wagon, thinking what a fine wife she would make if she weren't so stubborn and independent. His romantic thoughts about Joline Masters were fast fading. She was more woman than he cared to fuss with.

Jo made a fire and dug through her meager supplies to scrape up some supper. She realized she would have to buy more supplies here at Julesburg, and she worried she was spending her money too fast. She put on some coffee and beans, then got her rifle and sat down on a log to watch the food cook. She set the rifle beside her, her lingering anger at Bart Kendall making her want to cry. Suddenly the hardships of the journey seemed to catch up with her, and she felt agonizingly weary. She wished she could just walk up and shoot Kendall. It had been exciting and refreshing to reach Julesburg; now it was all spoiled. She put her chin in her hands, pressing her lips together to keep the tears from coming.

A moment later she saw familiar leather boots and deer-skin leggings step up to the fire. As usual she had not even heard him approach. Clint knelt by the fire and reached for the coffee pot.

"It's not ready yet," she said quietly.

He looked at her and frowned. "You look like a little kid who just got her candy stolen away. Something wrong?"

She sighed, worried not just for herself, but for Clint. "I saw Bart Kendall," she told him.

Instantly anger and concern crossed his face. "Kendall is here in Julesburg?"

She nodded. "He said he waited purposely to see if we'd all show up. You be careful, Clint. He's looking for you."

He turned and poked at the fire. "That doesn't concern me in the least. I've handled many a man like Bart Kendall." He looked back at her. "The bigger concern is you. Did he say something? Do something?"

She shrugged. "He just accused me of stealing those horses. I'm afraid I said a few things I shouldn't have. Mr. Kiehl and Johnny were with me. We were at the smithy's. It's all right. I wasn't in any real danger."

Clint looked around, then back at Jo. "What did he say, Jo? You haven't told me all of it."

She stared at the fire, swallowing, determined to look brave and uncaring. "He said he'd see me again—in Montana."

"He did, did he?" He rose. "Well, I guess I'll have to change his mind about that."

"Clint, leave it alone. It's not your concern. I made this choice. I'll take care of myself."

"Don't be a fool. It's one thing to start out on your own up there with the normal dangers. Why bring trouble with you when we can avoid it? I'll make sure Mr. Bart Kendall thinks twice about giving you any trouble in Montana."

He started past her and she grabbed his wrist, looking up at him. "Clint, please don't. It makes me feel guilty and weak."

He looked down at her, gently pulling away from her grip. "Then think of it as something I'm doing for myself, which I am. You said he was looking for me. Fine. He'll find me sooner than he thinks."

He walked off, and Jo stayed by the fire. She didn't want to watch.

Everything remained quiet into the evening. No one came running to tell about a fight. Jo ate lightly and cleaned her wagon, shaking out bedding and sorting the clothes she would take to the river to wash with Bess and

Sarah in the morning. She forced herself to keep busy, wondering if Clint was dead or alive, how he could have taken care of Bart Kendall without anyone mentioning a fight.

Night fell, and she could hear the laughter of both men and women coming from town, accompanied by piano music. The wagon camp was quiet; everyone sat around their own little campfires, and several of the freighters had gone to town to gamble, since it would not be necessary to rise early. Jo walked over to visit with Bess and Sarah, and she listened while Bess read a story to Lonnie and Joey. Both boys fell asleep before she finished, and Jo walked back to her wagon. She sat down by the fire, keeping her rifle beside her.

"Still awake?"

She turned to see Clint standing behind her. "Where have you been! What happened?"

He pulled a thin cigar from his vest pocket and put it in his mouth, walking up to the campfire and leaning forward to light it. His arms seemed to shine by the light of the fire, their muscles glowing. He puffed the cigar for a moment and sat down on a log across from her. "Had a little talk with our friend Kendall."

"A little talk?"

He puffed the cigar again. "That's what I call it. Mr. Kendall might have a different name for it."

Her eyes widened. "You didn't . . . kill him?"

He grinned a little. "He might *wish* he were dead, but he isn't. I simply made a point to inform him what would happen to him if he ever bothered you again—ever. So you be sure to let me know if you ever run into that man again."

"What did you do to him?"

"You don't need to know. But I don't think he'll bother you anymore."

"Where did you have this . . . little talk?"

"Outside of town. I advised Mr. Kendall to keep riding, once he feels better."

She looked him over, seeing no bruises. "But . . . you don't look like you've been in a fight or anything."

"Let's just say it was a little one-sided."

"But how? I don't understand."

"Quit trying to. Remember how quiet I can be?" He puffed the cigar and rose. "I know you want to take care of things yourself, Jo, but some things are men's business and that's all there is to it."

She put her head in her hands. "You shouldn't have had to do anything. You're just a guide, not a bodyguard. I feel like a fool. I hate not being able to handle things myself."

He stepped closer. "Jo, *nobody* can handle *everything* by him or herself. That's why all of you people are traveling together. That's why I lost my family, because I couldn't handle all those Indians alone. Things like that happen, that's all. You've done damn good, better than I thought you would. I never knew a woman to try what you're doing. You're going to make it to Montana, and you'll do all right."

Her heart felt suddenly lighter at the remark. He had faith in her. He didn't look down on her as frail and helpless. He respected her determination. She looked up at him gratefully. "Thank you. I needed to hear that."

He grinned. "I've thought it all along. I just didn't say it because I didn't want you to get too cock sure of yourself and get careless."

She smiled a little. "Thank you—for whatever you did with Kendall."

"Anything for you, Mrs. Masters." He tipped his hat and disappeared into the night.

Jo stared at the fire a while longer, feeling reassured by his remarks. But the thought of finally arriving in Montana and settling there alone—saying good-bye to Clint Reeves—left a heavy feeling in her heart. This had all turned into something much more challenging than just survival.

Chapter Twelve

At Fremont's Orchard the wagon train left the South Platte for the first time since their journey began. They headed north, out of Colorado Territory and to Big Laramie, Rock Creek, Elk Mountain, and Fort Halleck.

Before they reached Julesburg, the country had begun to change; the flat land was lined on the northern edge by magnificent hills that Jo was sure were the beginning of the Rocky Mountains. She had no idea what to expect when she finally saw mountains, and she was disappointed when the land was again flattened around Julesburg. But as they headed north into what some called Wyoming, the land again began to change. It turned to great, swelling hills that made hard work for the oxen as well as the humans who walked, and from the crest of one of those hills Jo caught her first sight of real mountains, which at first she thought were dark, low-hanging clouds. The hills over which they traveled grew more difficult, becoming the foothills of grander mountains to the west; and by the time they reached Fort Halleck, they were in the midst of the mountains.

Jo felt surrounded by God himself. Her heart took joy and hope in the land to which she had come, for dangerous as it might be, it was magnificent. She felt as excited as a little girl when Clint told her and the others that these mountains were not nearly as high as those over which they would travel farther west, nor as beautiful as the Tetons of northwest Wyoming, which Jo would pass on

her way north to Montana. And his description of the
Bighorns, the mountains in which Jo planned to settle in
Montana, filled her with eager anticipation.

But she would not reach those mountains until the
spring. It was nearly the end of October now, and the
more mountainous the land became, the colder it got. At
night, water in the barrels would freeze over, and Jo
began to wish she had brought more blankets. Still, it felt
good to be cold instead of sweltering in the heat of the
prairie. And the change in scenery gave Jo new vitality.
The mountains here had a velvety look to them, with
colors of green and purple blanketing the land. The cottonwood trees that lined Cottonwood Creek near Fort
Halleck were bathed in splendid gold, although some of
them were nearly bare. In the morning there was frost on
the ground, and the day they left Fort Halleck they had
snow.

Clint warned that it was possible they could be socked
with a blizzard before they reached Fort Bridger. From
here on the weather would be unpredictable because of
the mountains. Also, drinking water had to be rationed.
Once they crossed the North Platte River, which dipped
directly south out of central Wyoming and would cross
their path, they would see little water until reaching the
Green River near Fort Bridger.

Every day the wind blew, endlessly battering at their
faces. Clint warned Jo to get used to the wind, telling here
there were few days in the foothills east of the Rockies that
were still, no matter what the season, especially in Wyoming. But in spite of the wind, and a drop in temperature
that brought inclement weather, Jo was grateful she had
got this far, and that all her animals were still healthy.
Spirit followed the wagon faithfully day after day, and at
night he slept curled up against Brutus. It was an amusing
sight, and everyone was surprised that the big ox didn't
mind the intrusion of the small dog.

The bitter wind did little to spoil the magnificent scenery. Jo was becoming more sure again that she had done
the right thing. Frequently she spotted elk and antelope
grazing in distant grassy valleys, and Clint and the men
who hunted with him managed to keep the travelers in a
supply of meat.

At night the air was filled with frightening sounds, the howling of wolves, the hooting of owls, the yips of coyotes, and occasionally the chilling, threatening growl of a mountain lion, which always made the animals stomp and scuffle their feet and brought snorts from the oxen and whinnies from the horses. Mixed with the haunting, howling wind, the sounds of the night robbed the nervous travelers of sleep, but Clint reassured everyone that as long as they kept fires lit and the animals close, they were in no danger.

Jo told herself she had to get used to the sounds, and sometimes Clint would sit with her after dark and tell her what each sound was so that she wouldn't be afraid of them. When she heard a sound almost like a woman screaming, he told her it was only the call of the elk.

"At certain times of the year up in the Bighorns, you can hear the clashing of the Bighorn sheep—the males— fighting for leadership of a herd of females. It's unlike anything you've heard yet—those big horns knocking together over and over, echoing through the mountains. I don't know why, but it always makes me feel kind of small and insignificant. The forces of nature are much more powerful in this land than man will ever be. It's beautiful country. I've never been able to stay away from it for very long."

They were camped on the east side of the North Platte, where the river dipped directly south. Tomorrow they would cross the river.

"What if nothing had happened to your family?" Jo asked. "Would you have brought them out here?"

He watched the flickering flames of fire, and in the distance a wolf howled its mournful wail, answered moments later by a friend, or a mate.

"Probably. Millie was a little afraid to come this far west. As it turned out, we'd have been better off to head west in the first place."

She wondered if a man like Clint could really settle in any one place for good, and she told herself she was being wise to keep her feelings in check.

"Have you ever come across a bear in all your adventures out here?" she asked.

He grinned. "More than once. I'll give you some advice about bears. If you're headed uphill, you can probably outrun a bear. They get winded real easy. If you're headed downhill, you're better off to lie down and play dead. The bear might paw you around and sniff at you, but they would rather eat fish and berries than human flesh. A bear attacks out of fear or in protection of its young. They aren't man-eaters, but they can kill you with one sweep of a paw. If you approach a lake to fish and a bear is there, just leave. It's his territory. As far as mountain lions, they'll almost never attack unless they're trapped. They're more afraid of you than you are of them. But they can play havoc with your animals. If you see one approach your house, don't be too afraid. They're just like smaller cats—curious. One that comes near is probably just nosing around, seeing if there's anything around to play with."

She sewed a patch on one of her skirts by the light of the fire. "Will you take me hunting one day? I'm going to have to do my own hunting after I get to Montana."

"You ever hunted before?"

"I never had to. But my father hunted a lot. I used to watch him prepare to go out, helped skin rabbits and squirrels. I even helped carve up a deer once. And I've listened to plenty of stories about how he got this rabbit or that deer. I also know enough to stay downwind from the animal I'm after. I'm not completely unfamiliar with hunting. I've just never gone out and done it."

"Not many women have." He rose, pulling up the collar of his wolfskin jacket. "All right. When we get to Fort Bridger, I'll take you hunting. And when we get there I want you to get yourself a pair of Indian-made winter moccasins. They're usually made from the shaggy mane of the buffalo, turned inside out so the hair is against your feet. They're about the warmest footwear you can have out here in the winters. Your feet will freeze if you go tromping around the snow in those hard boots."

"Will there be Indians at Fort Bridger?"

"You can bet on it—mostly Crow, probably some Shoshone, Blackfoot. They're all pretty peaceful now. It's the Sioux and Northern Cheyenne that are making most of the trouble. We've been real lucky only running into that one band of Sioux so far."

"How long will we have to wait there, before we can go on to Montana?"

"Depends on the winter we have." He looked up and

sniffed at the air, like an animal completely aware of its surrounding elements. "Something tells me this will be a hard winter. The animals I've noticed have shaggier winter coats than I've seen in a long time. And a lot of elk have already come down out of the mountains. Seeing so many this far east in the lowlands is a sign of a hard winter." He gazed at a long, dark line of mountains in the distant west. "Nothing survives up in those mountains in the dead of winter," he said quietly, lost in his own thoughts. "Nothing. Even the trees won't grow after you get so high. When you see the big mountains, you'll see the tree line—then just bald rocks and snow above that."

A wolf howled again in the distant hills. "You love it, don't you?"

"Yeah, I guess I do."

It struck her how much he must have loved Millie Styles to have given up this wild life and land he loved just to marry her. He could surely never love another woman that way. The closer she got to her own destination and her own dream, the easier it was to tell herself she could and should forget any special feelings she might have for this man. He belonged free and alone now, and she had her own destiny to fulfill.

They crossed the river two days later. Normally it was shallow this time of year, but it had swelled from a heavy rain that poured for twenty-four hours the day they originally planned to cross. They had remained camped on the east side for two days, until Clint said they could wait no longer. Everyone shivered in their cold, damp wagons, as the rain finally turned to a thick snow, forming a miserable slush. By the time they crossed the cold river waters, and traveled the rest of that third day, everyone was cold and wet. Some of the wagons, including Jo's, had also got wet inside. They all built a big central fire and hung blankets and clothes around it, trying to dry things out. Jo was glad that she had placed most of her clothing high in the wagon, hanging some from the canvas top, so that her most important articles stayed dry.

The third day brought sun but little warmth, and they began to wonder why they had complained about the prairie heat. The deep slush left by the wet snowstorm

made travel difficult. The animals slipped and slid, wagons
became mired in slop, and those who walked might as well
have been walking through water. Jo temporarily gave up
her vow not to tire her horses by riding them. She didn't
want to put any extra weight on the wagon by riding
inside, since the oxen had their job cut out for them; so
she rode Patch most of the day, bareback since she still
had no saddle. She rode the animal tied to the back of the
wagon, because without a proper bridle and saddle he was
harder to control. She had no desire to be thrown onto the
sloppy ground.

The journey became more difficult than anything they
had yet endured. They were moving through this part of
the country much later than travelers with heavy wagons
normally passed through the high, cold, rocky land. Most
travelers who were headed for Oregon were just about
there by now, having passed through the Rockies in August or September.

By the fifth day the ground was drier again. The nights
were still freezing cold, but during midday it was warm
enough to take off jackets. Jo walked again, enjoying the
warm sun on her shoulders, drinking in the rock-studded
plateaus in the distance, velvety hills that looked like a
patchwork quilt. They were between two mountain ranges
now, moving through what Clint called the Great Divide
Basin. To the west, higher, rockier, snow-covered mountains rose in majestic glory. Jo was more glad than ever
that she had come. She told herself that even if she died
here, at least she had seen a part of the land thousands of
others back east would never know. She wished Anna
could see it, too, and wondered if she would ever see her
sister again. Maybe she could convince Anna to come west
once Darryl came home—if he came home.

Most of the leaves were gone from the hardwood trees,
but the surrounding hills and mountains remained green
with pine trees. The wagon train seemed to be heading
ever downward now, the mountains around them growing
higher, casting their shadow over the travelers early in the
day because the sun was quickly lost behind them. By
mid-November they finally arrived at Fort Bridger.

In spite of weariness, frozen feet, bones aching from the
cold, there was a celebration the first night of their arrival.

At last they had reached the place where they would rest
for a good three months. And they had got here without
Indian trouble. The freighters pulled their wagons up to a
log building that served as a warehouse. This was their
final destination. They would unload and head back east in
two days, hoping to stay ahead of the winter weather that
was sure to blast down soon. They intended to get back to
Fort Laramie by heading directly east along the Sweetwater
River and the North Platte, taking a shorter route to the
post where they knew they could hole up for the winter,
and have a head start on getting back to St. Louis the next
spring.

But for now it was time to celebrate. The freighters
hauled out banjo and fiddle. Men at the fort shared an elk
they had been roasting; people dropped their chores and
set aside any bad memories of the past, and they danced.

Fort Bridger was a very large post, comprised of several
log buildings as well as stone, which served as soldiers'
barracks, officers' quarters, a hospital, post office, stage
station, trading post, a Wells Fargo station, a public eating establishment, stables, and corrals. At the time Jo and
her fellow travelers arrived, most of the soldiers were
gone due to the war back east. A few remained, but the
highest-ranking officer was only a sergeant. A group of
volunteer mountain men were stationed there in case of
Indian trouble, and Clint seemed to know nearly every
one of them.

The travelers celebrated well into the night, and in spite
of her aching feet, Jo danced with nearly every mountain
man there, sensing only respect from them. They seemed
to have an understanding that Joline Masters was special
because Clint Reeves had told them she was. She wanted
to avoid being thought of as Clint's woman, but for now
she realized it didn't hurt for them to know she held a
special position in his eyes.

But throughout the celebrating Clint never asked her to
dance. He stood aside, drinking with a few old friends.
Later in the night he was nowhere to be seen, nor did Jo
see him for the next three weeks. She began to wonder
again if he had deserted her, leaving her to find a new
guide at Fort Bridger and forcing her finally to forget
about Clint Reeves. If he indeed had decided to go his

own way, she knew she would have to go on to Oregon in the spring. There would be no one to take her to Montana.

The freighters had left, and it was a sad parting, for the little band of settlers had grown attached to them, especially Dusty Hagan. It was Dusty who reassured Jo that Clint would be back. "Men like that, they get times when they have to go off alone," he told her, patting her hand. "I wish you lots of luck up in Montana, Mrs. Masters. It's a brave woman you are. Ain't a man among us wouldn't be proud to call you his, but we can all see you're a woman who can handle herself right fine alone. Maybe we'll meet again some day."

Jo watched their departure with tears. A snowstorm settled in, and the settlers were afforded the luxury of living in the vacated soldiers' barracks, a welcome relief from sleeping in wagons or on the ground. Inside they kept a fire going in wood stoves. The women took turns cooking, and they lived a communal life. Jo sometimes longed for quiet solitude, but she told herself to enjoy these friendships while she could; for come spring, she would have more solitude than she could ever wish for, and she didn't doubt she would long for company again. Even Marie Boone seemed friendlier lately.

Whenever Jo truly needed to be alone, and when the weather would allow, she would dress warmly, donning a pair of Indian moccasins she had bought at the fort as Clint had told her to do, and she would get her animals from the stables and walk them, taking a different horse each time. Indians camped and lounged about the fort, but she quickly grew accustomed to their presence. She even made friends with one old Indian woman who was always making things for the "Lone White Woman," as she called Jo. The old woman was called simply that—Old Woman—and she was forever making Jo necklaces and belts and more moccasins. Jo tried to explain that she didn't need to give her gifts all the time, but the woman seemed to enjoy it.

Whenever Jo walked her horses, the grizzly, often foul-smelling mountain men warned her not to stray too far. There was a time when men like those who hung around Fort Bridger would have frightened her. But in spite of their unwashed and unshaven condition, she had learned to trust them. She was learning a valuable lesson about men, which she knew would help once she settled in Montana. They couldn't be judged by their appearance. She learned to read their eyes, learned to sense respect or disrespect in each man.

These mountain men seemed to admire her courage, rather than look down on her independence. Back east more-settled men, and women, had names for women who chose to remain single and lead an independent life. Out here things were different. A person, man or woman, could do as he or she pleased; and women were so rare that men seemed to put them on a pedestal, holding them almost in a reverent position. But Jo was not foolish enough to think that all men in this wild land would think that way, and she never ventured out without her rifle. She had learned a hard lesson at Cottonwood Springs.

Christmas passed, and they all celebrated by cutting a pine tree and setting it up inside the barracks, decorating it with popcorn and candles and homemade decorations. Jo struggled against sadness, remembering Christmases back in Lawrence when she was a little girl, opening gifts with Anna while her mother and father both watched. And she remembered her first Christmas with Greg. Now all of them were gone. She had hoped at least to see Clint, and she had knitted him a scarf; but he was still gone. She wondered if celebrating Christmas was too painful for him. Surely he had memories of Christmases with his wife and son.

She wrote Anna another letter, sending her one of the Indian belts Old Woman had made, telling her it was her Christmas present. She prayed Anna was all right, and hoped perhaps Darryl had come home by now.

The days passed rather drearily, every day the same, since they were snowed in and the fort would be their only life for two or three more months. The women sewed and visited and cooked. The men chopped wood, smoked, played cards, and ate. Near the end of January, on an unusually mild day, Jo took Shag for a walk, leading the horse to a favorite perch she had found, a stack of flat rocks where the snow always seemed to blow free, leaving them bare. She tied Shag to a small tree and climbed up on the rocks, from where she could look down on the fort. She looked around at the magnificent mountains that surrounded her, and she felt like another person, far removed from the Joline Masters who had left Lawrence, Kansas, only six months earlier. It seemed everything had changed for her ever since she killed the man called Dooley and lost everything that was a part of her old world.

Then she saw a lone rider approaching, leading a pack horse. He was coming from the north, headed for the fort, and even from a distance she knew who it was. She hated herself for being so glad to see him. At the same time she was angry with him for just leaving without saying a word. Yet she knew he had every right, and she was determined to show him it didn't bother her at all. She climbed down from the rocks, untied Shag, and headed back to the fort, arriving at almost the same time as Clint. She walked in his direction, and intercepted him before he reached the fort.

He stopped, watching her eyes as she approached. It was obvious he had chosen to drop out of civilization completely for a while. He had grown a full beard.

"I thought maybe you had decided to just leave me here," Jo told him.

His eyes moved over her. "I thought about it."

"Where did you go?"

He looked at the surrounding mountains. "Out there. I'd had my fill of people and problems for a while. I wanted to be alone—to think."

She looked back at the pack horse. Two deer were tied across its back. "Looks like you brought a little food."

He nodded. *"I missed you, Jo,"* he thought. *"God, you look good."*

"I was so scared you wouldn't come back and I'd never see you again," Jo wanted to tell him.

"Yeah, a little. And I didn't forget my promise. You feel like going hunting in a couple of days?"

Her eyes lit up at the thought of getting away from the monotony of the long winter days spent inside the barracks listening to the constant jabber of the women and smelling the smoke from the men's pipes and cigars. She smiled. "I could go right now."

He grinned and scratched at his beard. "Well, I have to get rid of this thing and find the bathhouse first. The way

I smell right now, the animals would scent me ten miles off."

She wondered how much he still suffered on the inside. Had he been thinking about Millie and his son again? Or had he been thinking about Joline Masters, wondering what he should do about his feelings for her? They walked back to the fort together, and she said nothing more about his absence. She knew that wandering off to be alone was as natural for a man like Clint as breathing. And, after all, he was just her guide. What he did while she wintered at the fort was his business. She was just glad he was back, and she looked forward with excitement to her first hunting adventure.

It came into her sight as silently as the softly falling snow. Jo had been sitting so long she had almost fallen asleep. When she blinked open her eyes, she could hardly believe what she saw. It was a huge buck elk, its antlers looking as big as a tree.

She wasn't sure how close Clint was, but she couldn't call out to him now. This was her chance. They had been hunting for two days and had seen only a few rabbits. She liked this life, loved the adventure of being in the wild, sleeping under mounds of blankets topped with snow. She could understand how a man could want always to live like this, but a part of her knew she could never do this forever. The woman in her still longed for a home of her own, a hearth, a cookstove. She would have those things; she was determined. And it wouldn't be long. Next spring. Next spring they would head for Montana and she would have her own place. And in order to survive, she had to have food and know how to get it for herself.

She slowly and quietly perched her rifle on a fallen branch, resting its barrel and bracing the butt end against her shoulder. She lined up the elk in her sights, aiming for the spot just behind the shoulder where Clint had told her to aim if she had the chance. She said a little prayer, hating to kill the beautiful animal, but wanting more to prove she could do it, especially to Clint.

Her heart pounded so wildly she was sure the animal would hear it and bound away. But it just stood there, nibbling at the bark of a tree. She squeezed the trigger.

The gun jolted her in the shoulder, and for one brief moment she remembered the day she had killed Dooley. She could remember the pieces of flesh spraying her in the face. She shuddered and realized then that the animal had staggered. It ran a short distance, then fell.

"Jo? You all right?" Clint's voice came from somewhere behind her.

"Come quick! I got an elk! I got an elk!" She ran toward the animal, hardly able to believe she had got it with one shot. Clint was soon on her heels, and they reached it together.

"Well, I'll be damned."

"Pure luck, Clint. I was almost asleep! I opened my eyes, and there he was, like God put him there for me." She walked up to the animal, bending down to gently stroke its neck. "Isn't he beautiful? I feel kind of bad, Clint."

"Most people who respect animals feel bad killing them, but it's a necessity. Just do like the Indians do and thank its spirit for offering the animal to you. By God, you did good, Jo. Now it's time to find out if you're strong enough to gut it out."

She looked up at him, wincing. "Gut it out?"

He grinned. "If you're going to kill your own game, you've got to be able to clean it. You said you helped cut up a deer once."

She looked down and petted it again. "I did. But it was already gutted."

"Well, then, you've got that part to learn yet. It's got to be done right away so nothing spoils." He pulled out his knife, the same knife he had used to kill the man who had attacked her back at Cottonwood Springs. "Here you go."

She took the knife from him and stood up, looking the animal over. "I don't know where to start."

"Well, it's easiest to tie the front and back legs apart a little so they don't get in the way." He proceeded to spread-eagle the animal, leaving it slightly on its side so it would be easier to scoop out the entrails. He pulled up the front and back leg on the top side of the animal and tied them to tree branches to keep them up out of the way, then took the knife from Jo and positioned it just under the animal's chest, between its ribs. "Cut a straight line down to its rear. See if you're strong enough. We'll save the head when we cut it up later, and have it stuffed. You'll want to keep it—mount it over your fireplace when you get a place built."

The words were music to her ears. He said it as though he had no doubts she would have her own house. She knelt beside the animal and closed her eyes, saying a short, silent prayer, thanking its spirit as the Indians did. It made her feel a little better. She took the knife again from Clint and put it where he told her, pushing hard and telling herself not to feel sorry for the animal. It was already dead.

It took all her strength, but she slowly managed to bring the knife all the way down the animal's middle, something she guessed Clint would have done with one swift thrust. In spite of the cold, she was sweating from nervousness and excitement, and she removed her bearskin coat, which she had traded dishes for at the fort. The coat was more vital to staying alive than dishes. She saved just enough utensils to get by on for the time being.

She tossed the coat aside and took a deep breath, reaching into the animal and cutting and pulling at the guts. She felt a strange kinship with the elk, with its warm blood on her hands, and she was suddenly more sure than ever that she was going to survive in this land.

Clint watched with amusement and admiration. He had spent the last several weeks when he had gone off alone arguing with himself about Joline Masters, about daring to love a woman again; and he had decided he never wanted that kind of hurt again. As long as he didn't commit himself; as long as he didn't tell her aloud that he loved her; as long as he didn't touch her, make love to her, he could stand it if something happened to her. He would be losing a good friend, but he wouldn't be losing the woman he loved, his wife, maybe the mother of his child. He was convinced he was never meant for such things. That was why God had taken Millie and Jeff from him, and there would never be another Mrs. Reeves.

Besides, he wanted her to succeed now as much as she wanted it. He didn't want to spoil her determined dream to prove a woman alone could survive in this land. He intended to sit back and watch. He cared about her enough to want to give her the freedom to experience the wonders of this land, learn to love it as much as he did. The problem was, he was secretly falling in love with Joline Masters, and when she did things like this, the more she proved she could handle herself alone, the more he loved her. He never thought he could treasure the friendship of a woman on the same level as friendships with men. But Jo was different from anyone he had ever known, even Millie.

She looked at him then, her big brown eyes full of excitement and questions. "Am I doing it right?" she asked.

He studied her a moment, wondering if she had any idea how hard it was for him not to crawl under her blankets in the night and feel her lovely, warm body pressing against his own. He had stayed away for weeks to get over her, and it hadn't worked. He told himself to think of Millie—only Millie—and the agony of losing her.

He took the knife from her. "Not bad. I'll give you a couple of pointers."

Jo watched carefully, wanting to jump up and down with joy. She had killed an elk! Wait until everyone back at the fort saw it! She was going to be able to take care of herself, she was sure. How she wished Anna could see this. She could hardly wait to head for Montana now. She *would* have that house, and that fireplace—and she would mount the elk's head over it—her first hunter's kill.

Chapter Thirteen

"Dear Anna, We are leaving Fort Bridger today," Jo wrote. "Spring has finally arrived, and spring in the mountains is the most splendid sight I have ever beheld. Wildflowers are blooming in magnificent colors, many rising right out of lingering snow. It is possible we will be hit with another snowstorm, but Clint says that is just a chance we will have to take.

"I am so happy and excited, but my heart is also heavy over having to leave the people with whom I have traveled and lived for so many months. I will even miss Marie Boone, the woman who has been so rude to everyone. I helped nurse her through pneumonia this past winter, and since then she has been kinder, although I know she still thinks I am a woman of questionable character because of that hunting trip I took with Clint. I'm not sure what the others thought, but I don't care. I got that elk, and its head and antlers are in my wagon, headed for my new home in Montana."

Jo looked over at the barracks where everyone else still slept. She had slept in her wagon, since it was all packed and Clint wanted to leave at the crack of dawn. Jo sat on a barrel, writing on her lap, her fingers stiff from the cold air. Her eyes misted at the thought of the meal she had shared with the other settlers the night before, and the little party they had thrown for her. Sarah had baked her a cake, and had given her some doilies she had crocheted for

Jo's "new home." The old woman had cried and hugged her, and Jo had wept as though she were leaving her own mother.

She began writing again, telling Anna about the party and the gifts: a set of dishes from Marie Boone; two jars of canned peaches from Martha Sievers, carried all the way from Lawrence; a crocheted afghan from Bess Hills; and a beaded parfleche from Old Woman, who came to the little party but sat shyly in a corner away from the others.

"Bennett Kiehl gave me an ax," she continued, "a fine tool in good condition. He said I might need it if mine broke or got dull chopping wood. He told me to be sure to get in plenty of wood before next winter, and I could see he was sure I would never survive. But I will do fine. Clint believes I will, too. I think Mr. Kiehl had ideas of courting me, as he is a widower. He was always asking me to change my mind and go on to Oregon. He is a good man, but not a man I would want to marry, as he would always be telling me how to behave.

"I have told you my feelings for Clint Reeves, but he is a troubled man and a loner at times, and not a man I should allow myself to love. All I want to think about now is getting settled in Montana, and I hope some day you'll be able to come out and visit me. Clint says he thinks that some day there will be railroads coming all the way out west. It's hard to believe, but if it happens, we can take a train and visit each other.

"I must go now. We'll be leaving any time. I hope you can read this all right, as I am writing by the dim light of a lantern, and my fingers are very stiff from the cold. I love you and miss you, Anna. May God be with you. I'll write again when I am settled and let you know where I am. Love, Jo."

She folded the letter and put it in an envelope, then doused her campfire. She had already eaten a light breakfast, which she shared with Clint. She walked through a cold mist to the little post office and handed the letter to Buck Webster, a long-haired, bearded old mountain man

Jo had come to know well. Buck promised to send the letter east with the first freight wagons that came through from Salt Lake City. When Jo returned to her wagon, Clint was there saddling Sundance, Jo's buckskin-colored gelding.

"What are you doing?" she asked.

"You're riding. There are about eight men going with us, seven of the mountain men who intend to check out the prospect of gold up there, and Bill Starke." He tightened the cinch under Sundance's belly. "Starke decided with all those gold miners up there around Virginia City, he can probably make a tidy profit with his bootmaking. He's a man alone now, so it doesn't make much difference to him whether he goes north or west."

"Clint, where did you get that saddle? I can't afford it."

He checked it over, running a finger between the cinch and the horse's belly to make sure it was tight enough but not too tight. "It's a gift from me. Everybody else gave you something. This was the best thing I could think of."

Her heart went out to him, and she felt guilty over all the attention. "Clint, just agreeing to take me is enough. You've done so much for me already."

"Just accept it and don't argue about it. It's still too cold for you to walk, and you don't need to be driving the oxen every damned day. The men will all take turns driving them for you, and you can take your own turn. That way nobody gets overtired. Today you ride." He turned and faced her, putting his hand on the horse's rump. "There you go. Want a hand up?"

Her eyes filled again. "I don't know what to say. Everyone has been so good to me."

"They all want you to make it. And so do I."

She studied the handsome face, wishing circumstances were different and there was not so much loss and heartache in both their pasts. If this were another time, another place, if they had met under some other circumstances, maybe they could love each other. Maybe they could even have been husband and wife.

"Thank you," she said softly. She turned and put her foot in the stirrup, pulling herself up and straddling the horse. Her skirt caught, exposing part of her leg as she settled in, and she quickly pulled it around so that her legs were covered, but not before Clint caught sight of the slender calf. It brought back memories of the day at the river—her flat belly and full breasts—the slender legs—the beautiful body he longed to possess. He turned away, refusing to meet her eyes.

"The others are coming," he told her. "I'll get my horse. A man called Hugh Reed will guide your oxen today."

She watched him walk to a hitching post and get his horse. His pack-horse was already tied to a loop on the gear of his riding horse. The others joined him then, and Hugh Reed rode up to Jo's wagon, dismounted, and tied his horse to the back.

"Are you sure you want to do this, Hugh?" Jo asked the man.

"No problem, ma'am. We'll all take turns." The man took a whip from its perch at the side of Jo's wagon and flicked it at the oxen, which were already hitched and ready to go. He gave out a whistle and a "git-up," and Brute and Goliath were again at the task of pulling the wagon. They had got a long winter break and were strong and rested.

A few other men rode past Jo, tipping their hats or nodding to her with "mornin' ma'am" and "good day for headin' for Montana, ain't it?"

Jo knew she couldn't be in better hands. All these men were experienced Indian fighters and hunters, men who knew this land like the backs of their hands. Besides Hugh Reed, there was Moose Barkley, Larry Black, Ben Willis, Randy McGreggory, Jon DuPre—whom everyone called Frenchy—and Harold "Happy" Strickland. Jo decided it would be difficult to describe each man separately, except that Larry Black and Randy McGreggory were younger than the others, perhaps Clint's age, around thirty, or younger. The others were at least in their forties, and Jo guessed Moose Barkley and Happy Stickland were in their fifties. But they were strong, hardy men, toughened by a life under the open sky. The lot of them were clad in buckskins and fur or floppy leather hats, and an assortment of fur jackets; and every man sported a beard and an array of weapons.

Jo guessed that if not for her presence, Clint himself would be as unshaven and unwashed as the rest of them.

But this morning he was clean-shaven, and the buckskins he wore looked new. She wondered if he had got them recently from some of the Indians in the area. When she stood close to him before mounting her horse she had caught his clean, manly scent, the natural smell of man and leather that stirred her emotions with irritating persistence.

Jo and Clint joined Moose and Ben behind the others, and Bill Starke brought up the rear, walking beside the oxen that pulled his wagon.

Jo glanced back at the barracks where everyone she had called friend for months still slept. They would wait for the first wagon train headed for Oregon that came through Fort Bridger. A swift stab of sorrow swept through her at the thought that she would never see any of them again. She would especially miss Sarah; and she hated leaving Old Woman. Bess had become like a sister to her, and even the shy Martha Sievers had opened up and had become a good friend. Jo's eyes watered, and she turned away again, facing forward, remembering the awful day she quit Lawrence and had to leave the farm behind. "Life is full of good-byes, Jo," Clint told her.

She glanced at him, realizing that some day she would also be saying good-bye to Clint Reeves. "It is, isn't it?"

Their eyes held for a moment. "Come on," he told her. "Ride a little way ahead with me and I'll show you the kind of things I look for when I'm scouting for a wagon train. I'll teach you what things to be aware of when you're alone— trail signs to read, how to tell if there are Indians ahead."

He prodded his horse and rode out ahead of the others. Jo followed. It felt good to be riding a horse again. Sundance dashed out into a field of snow mixed with wildflowers. The sun was casting a red glow above the mountains to the east, although its ball of flame had not yet risen above them. But already Jo could see it was going to be a beautiful day. She hardened her heart against the sad good-byes and refused to look back again, just as she had forced herself not to look back at the old farm. She was headed for Montana now.

They moved through spectacular country, keeping to the foothills of the Rockies and heading toward the Tetons.

Jo took her turn at hunting and at driving her own oxen, a sight that brought chuckles from the men when she tried shouting at the animals with authority. She looked small and helpless next to the big oxen, but she soon proved she was capable as she walked beside them snapping the whip and shouting "gee's" and "haw's."

Flowers bloomed everywhere, and the newborn leaves of the aspen trees began to open in bright green splendor. But the nights were still bitterly cold, and Jo slept near the fire with mounds of blankets and a bearskin given to her by Moose Barkley piled on top of her, even covering her head. There was not a man among the party who would not relish crawling under those blankets with the spunky woman from Kansas, but it was only a pleasant thought, not something they had the courage to act on, for they didn't doubt Jo Masters would soon make them wish they hadn't tried.

After their first two weeks of travel they were hit with a spring snowstorm that forced them to take shelter in a cave in the wall of a deep canyon through which they had been traveling. For three days the wind blew with the fury found only in the mountains, screeching and howling through the canyon so that Jo felt as though she had left the earth and was on some foreign, desolate planet. When she went outside to take care of personal matters, it seemed the wind would blow her clear back to Kansas; and each time, she prayed she wouldn't be buried in snow before she finished and was able to get back to the warm cave.

"This ain't easy, travelin' with a pretty thing like that, Clint," Ben Willis spoke up once when Jo went outside.

"How do you think it's been for me? I've been around her for nine months, all the way from Kansas."

The men all chuckled. "You got an itch for her, don't you, Clint?" The question came from Hugh Reed.

Clint glanced at Bill Starke, who had been with the original wagon train. He looked back at the fire then, holding a stick over it with a piece of deer meat on the end. "What man wouldn't? But I'm not about to get involved again, not after what happened in Minnesota. Besides, she's an independent woman, and she's got plans of her own."

"I never knowed a woman like her," Larry Black spoke

up then. "Heck, she's not a whole lot younger than me. You think she'd take a shine to me?"

Clint forced back a sudden jealousy at the remark. "She's not looking for a man. All of you remember that. She lost her husband to the war, and she's lost a lot of other things. She wants to be left alone, so save your needs for the whores at Virginia City. Besides, you're not a settling man, Larry. She's not the kind you jump in bed with and then go off and forget. She'd never—"

Jo came inside then and the conversation ended. Every man eyed her strangely, and Jo reddened, quickly sensing they had been talking about her. She had never been afraid of any of them; still, there were moments like this one when she felt awkward, as though she were suddenly on display, naked before their eyes.

Clint grinned, handing her the meat. "Have some supper," he told her. He turned to the others. "The rest of you had better eat, too. Get out a deck of cards or something and quit gawking at Mrs. Masters. She's one of us, remember? She can ride and hunt and gut a deer as good as any of you."

They all looked away, suddenly embarrassed, some nervously coughed and cleared their throats. Frenchy snickered and took out a deck of cards. Jo looked at Clint gratefully and took the meat from him, sitting down to eat.

After two more days they ventured out into sunshine and plodded through deep snow, trying to avoid streams swollen from the spring melt. They decided to keep to lower ground, even though it was more slushy, since sticking too close to the mountains meant danger from snowslides. At times, though, they had no choice but to move back up into the mountains. Jo made riding easier by cutting one of her skirts up the middle and sewing each half together to create skirtlike pants. Now she could mount a horse without worrying about showing something that should not be seen, and she decided that when she got to Virginia City she was going to buy herself some men's pants, much more practical wear for this country. She had long since quit caring about being beautiful and dressing like a "proper lady."

She wondered sometimes if the occasion would ever

again arise when she would want to put her hair up in a fancy do and wear a frilly dress. Such things seemed so unimportant now. She was having much more fun acting like a man than she had ever had acting like a woman. But deep inside she knew there was one womanly instinct she had managed to bury that would probably some day have to be unearthed. She seldom thought about it, except when Clint Reeves stood close to her or for some reason happened to touch her. Only then did painful needs come alive to remind her she was most definitely still female, and that Clint Reeves was as devastatingly male as the species could be. She was grateful so many men were along and that they watched her so closely. It gave little opportunity for her to find herself alone with Clint, making it easier to be casual with him and stick to her personal promise not to get involved.

It took three weeks to reach the Tetons, and Jo could not stop staring at them. Once Clint even had to take hold of her horse's bridle and lead it, while Jo drank in the beauty of the spectacular, snow-covered peaks that seemed to change constantly with the sun. The ragged mountains were filled with gorges and ridges and valleys within the mountains that seemed to hang in the sky. Sometimes they were purplish blue and hazy. Then they looked smooth and shiny gray; again suddenly sharply defined and rosy, mountains within mountains.

They headed through Jackson Hole, a broad valley filled with meadows and marshes, cottonwood, aspen, and pine, lakes and streams. The Snake River tumbled through the valley, and Clint warned that outlaws were known to lurk in the area. But that afternoon it was not outlaws who came to give them trouble. They heard the yipping and shouting first, then saw them riding down on them fast—a band of painted warriors headed toward them from the opposite hill.

"Sioux!" Moose shouted.

Jo did not doubt the old man was right. After all his years in this land he could tell from a mile off what kind of Indians were coming.

"Head for that rocky hill up ahead!" Clint shouted. "Leave the wagons!" He turned to Jo. "Stay close to me!"

Hugh Reed ran to the back of Jo's wagon and untied his

horse, climbing up and riding back to Bill Starke. He gave
the man a hand, hoisting him onto the horse behind him
and riding off to join the others, the Indians close on their
heels.

Jo pulled out her rifle and rode like the wind, glad she
was on Sundance, her fastest horse. Mud and snow flew
from under the horses' hooves as they headed for the
shelter of a hill littered with boulders. They had barely
reached it when Jo felt herself being torn from her horse,
Clint Reeves's strong arm around her as he dismounted
before either horse came to a halt. He carried her in one
arm at a run up the hill and plunked her behind a large
boulder. Jo cocked her rifle while the other men took
positions. She saw Bill Starke fall from Hugh's horse, an
arrow in his back.

"Oh, my God!" she whimpered.

Hugh frantically gathered as many of the horses as he
could, quickly leading them behind more rocks and tying
them, while the Indians drew up their horses near the
wagons, riding around them and inspecting what was inside.

"Maybe they'll just take some loot and leave us alone,"
Happy said quietly to Clint.

"Don't we wish," Clint answered. "Whatever happens,
they don't get the woman. Understood?"

"Ain't a man here would let that happen," Ben Willis
answered.

Jo reddened, feeling like some kind of terrible burden
to them all. She glanced at Clint, and his face was hard-
set, his eyes full of fury as he positioned his rifle on a rock
and gripped it, ready to shoot. And she knew what must
be going through his mind.

"They're lookin' for blood, Clint," Randy shouted. "I
can see it in their eyes."

"I know the look," Clint mumbled. "Everybody hold
steady and let them get closer," he said louder. "Save your
ammunition. If we don't chase them off they could keep us
pinned down here quite a while."

Jo watched with a sinking heart as her wagon was ransacked. She could only pray they wouldn't burn it. The
Indians piled their loot together, circling the wagons once
more and then heading toward the rocks, hooting and
yipping, their faces painted in wild, frightening stripes and

colors, hatchets and rifles ready. Jo took aim herself, but waited until the others started firing before she squeezed the trigger and felt the jolt of the shot.

To her amazement, the Indian she was shooting at fell from his horse. She was so surprised and momentarily stunned that she had shot another man that it took her a moment to cock the rifle and fire again. This time she missed. She guessed there were at least thirty Indians, but every man with her was a good shot, and seven or eight of the Indians were already down. Jo tried not to think about poor Bill Starke, lying nearby with an arrow in his back. He had come all this way unscathed, and now he was dead. He should have gone to Oregon, and now she was beginning to wonder if she should have, too.

The warriors regrouped and came at them again. Moose Barkley cried out when an arrow landed in his upper shoulder. He gritted his teeth and yanked it out and continued firing, blood pouring from the wound. But there was no time for Jo to ponder how a man his age could still be so rugged and hardy. She fired again, her heart falling when she hit an Indian pony instead of its rider. And she realized she felt worse about killing the horse than she would have if she'd killed the warrior.

The horse reared and fell, pinning the warrior beneath it. The man made no movement. She stopped to reload, while Clint, keeping a steady aim, killed two more warriors. He handed her his rifle then pulled out a pistol.

"Reload for me, will you?"

She quickly obeyed without question, grabbing bullets from the gunbelt he wore over his shoulder. She was almost finished when suddenly a warrior's horse leaped right over the rock behind which she and Clint had taken cover. Jo was too frightened even to scream as the Indian leaped off his horse as it passed over and landed on top of Clint, knocking him backward. Jo saw Clint's pistol fly out of his hand. She scrambled to pick it up, having to decide in a split second whether to try to help Clint or turn and keep firing. She decided she had no choice but to keep firing.

She turned. "Look out, Jo!" Hugh Reed shouted. Jo heard the roar of Hugh's big gun, and a warrior poised on the rock behind Jo stood still for a moment, a bloody hole

in his side. He fell forward then, and Jo had to jump out of
the way to keep him from falling right on top of her. She
glanced back at Clint to see he had wielded the hatchet
away from his attacker. He brought it down into the
Indian's skull.

Jo grimaced and turned away, scrambling back to the
rock and picking up her rifle to take aim at another Indian.
He fell from his horse but got up again, his arm bleeding,
then got back onto his horse and retreated. Clint was
suddenly beside her again. He said nothing as he finished
loading his rifle, his hands covered with blood from the
Indian he had killed. He raised his rifle to take aim, and Jo
noticed a deep gash that went all the way through the
sleeve of his fur jacket. It was blood-soaked.

"Clint, your arm!"

"Don't worry about it! Just keep shooting!"

She quickly obeyed, but the Indians were circling the
wagons farther off again. They picked up the items they
had taken, and Jo watched with sickening agony as they
untied her Appaloosas, Patch and Star, as well as her
shaggy red gelding. They rode off with the horses.

"Yahoo!" Larry shouted. "We showed them, didn't we,
Moose? We must have got half of them!"

Clint watched the warriors ride off. He seemed to wither,
leaning against the rock and putting his head down.

"You think they'll be back, Moose?" Larry was asking
his friend.

"I don't think so. For one thing, they got the supplies
they wanted and they got three fine horses. They think
they've given us a good lesson. And they know we're
a damn good bunch of Indian fighters, ain't that right,
Clint?"

Clint threw his head back, breathing deeply.

"Clint, let me take care of your arm," Jo told him.

He looked at her strangely, the terrible sorrow in his
eyes again. He shoved his pistol in its holster and threw
down his rifle, walking off.

"Clint?"

"Leave him be, missy," Frenchy told her. "Just leave
him be. We will go to the wagons and see if there is
something left you can use to help Moose, *oui*? He has got
that arrow wound in his shoulder."

Jo watched after Clint. His pack horse came trotting up to him, and Clint took a parfleche from the animal and walked to a distant hill, disappearing into a cluster of pines. Hugh checked Bill Starke.

"Starke's dead," he told the others. "Let's get him buried."

Some of the others helped carry the body as they all returned to the looted wagons. Jo saw that most of her food was gone, and some of her clothes and kitchen utensils. But the saddest loss was her horses.

Happy patted her shoulder. "Don't you worry, ma'am. It's times like these you've got to be glad for the good— they didn't burn the wagons, we only lost one man, and they didn't get their hands on you. We're also damned lucky they didn't steal every single animal."

"I needed those horses bad, Happy," she said.

"I know that. But look here. We've still got Starke's wagon, and lots of things left in it. And I'll just bet that man would have wanted you to have it. That gives you extra oxen, an extra wagon, and extra supplies. He's got tools in there, too. What you can't use, you can sell at Virginia City and use the money to buy you more horses or more supplies, whatever you need. You'll be all right."

Jo looked toward the hill where Clint had disappeared. "Will Clint be all right?"

Happy shook his head. "Well, now, there's one troubled man. That there wound he suffered, and what must have happened to his woman and kid—leaves a bad scar on a man's heart. He's never told anybody the last of it—if he found his woman—how he found her—what the Indians did to her and the boy. I expect it ain't somethin' a man can bring himself to talk about. Just leave him be. He'll rejoin us in a bit. You tend to Moose's wound."

"But Clint's hurt, too."

"He can take care of himself. We all can. But long as you're here, I expect Moose would feel a whole lot better havin' a pretty woman fix him up."

Jo smiled sadly, turning to search through the mess in her wagon to find some whiskey and gauze. She had a bottle of whiskey hidden deep in a trunk that the Indians didn't find. She got it out, looking around the ransacked wagon and wondering how she would ever get it back in shape. She climbed out and tended to Moose while the other men dug a grave for Bill Starke. They buried the man, holding a little ceremony, and still Clint had not returned. The little party of travelers herded wagons and animals to higher ground where there were more rocks and trees for shelter, then made camp for the night.

Jo spent the next two hours rearranging her wagon, making a list of items taken. There was some food left in Starke's wagon, for which she was grateful. But she wanted to weep over the loss of Patch and Star and Shag. It wasn't the value loss that upset her so much as the loss of three horses she personally treasured and felt attached to.

Darkness fell, and Spirit suddenly bounded into the light of the campfire. Jo realized the dog had been no-where in sight during the Indian attack. She picked it up and hugged it.

"Where have you been, boy?"

"Smart dog." Frenchy spoke up. "Indians come . . . he goes."

They all laughed, and Jo set Spirit down and walked into the nearby woods to relieve herself. She hunted in the darkness for an extra-brushy area, aided by the bright moon. She headed up a hill, and then she saw him standing there, a tall, broad-shouldered figure.

"Clint?"

He was just a shadow as she approached him, but she knew who it was.

"Are you all right, Clint?"

He suddenly grabbed her arms and pulled her close. Her mouth was quickly covered by a warm kiss, as strong arms came around her.

Chapter Fourteen

Jo's body ached with torn desires, as old needs surged deep inside, making her return the kiss with all the fervor it was given. All the while her mind told her it was foolish and wrong. Clint groaned, moving his tongue over her mouth and bending her back, forcing her to the ground.

In that first moment of passion Jo had ignored the whiskey on his breath. Suddenly he had her on the ground, pressing on top of her. She felt the urgent hardness against her groin, and his kiss became so intense it hurt her lips. She struggled to let common sense rule, realizing she wanted him more than she had known until this moment, but that this was not the way. He was drunk, and he was thinking of someone else. She managed to turn her face sideways, pushing at him.

"Clint, don't. This isn't right."

"Why not?" he almost growled. "I want you and you want me. It would be a lie to deny it." He kissed and licked at her neck and throat, making resistance painful, but this was not the Clint Reeves she knew or wanted. He was not being gentle as his hands began groping at her breasts. She didn't want to embarrass him in front of the other men by screaming and making a scene. She grabbed his hand and pushed at him again.

"Stop it, Clint!" she whispered.

He began kissing her again. He was a man far too powerful for her to halt by simple pushing, but one she knew would never violently force her, even if he was drunk. She only had to make him know she didn't want him this way. His lips began moving down her throat, and she reared back with her fist and punched him as hard as she could on the ear. He grunted and cursed, moving off her slightly. Jo quickly rolled out from under him and stood up.

"I'm sorry," she said quietly. "But you're drunk, Clint. It isn't even me you want. You can't deny you're thinking of someone else."

He held a hand to his ear. "Damn!" He slowly got to his feet, shaking his head and rubbing at his ear again. He stepped closer, towering over her in the moonlight. "Why in hell do you think you're always right!"

She felt a sudden stab of confusion and regret. He really *had* wanted her, Joline Masters, not a memory. Should she have let him have his way? Would it have somehow comforted the agony that plagued his soul? She told herself that no matter how terribly he suffered, she was not going to sacrifice her pride and dignity just to soothe him. He had cruelly awakened painful needs in her now, and she hadn't wanted to care or to feel those needs again. "My God, what's wrong with you?" she groaned. "Why do you go off drinking like that?" Her eyes stung with tears. "Was it the Indian raid? Clint, we're all right."

He grabbed her arms in a firm grip. "Yes, *this* time! *This* time! Why couldn't they have ridden off *then*—back in Minnesota? Why did they have to take Jeff and Millie while I lay there helpless!"

"Clint, it's over. You've got to stop reliving it, stop drinking to make it go away. The whiskey won't help. It will only destroy you!"

His grip grew tighter. "You don't know," he groaned. "You don't know."

"*What* don't I know? You were hurt bad, Clint. You tried to save them but you couldn't. It's happened to others. At least they're dead, Clint. The Indians killed them and they won't suffer anymore."

He shook his head. "No." The word came out in a strange, gutteral sob. "*I* . . . killed them," he choked out. "*I* put them . . . out of their misery."

Jo's eyes widened with horror. She put her hands against his chest. "Dear God," she whispered. "Clint, I'm sorry."

Suddenly Hugh Reed called out. "You all right up there, Jo? I hear voices."

Jo could hear the man heading up her way. "It's all right, Hugh," she answered quickly. "It's just Clint."

"Clint? Well, by golly, tell that man to get down to camp so we can head out in the morning."

The man headed back down and Jo looked up at Clint. "How, Clint? What really happened? You've got to talk about it or it will destroy you."

He let go of her arms. "It already has." He walked off again and she called after him, but he disappeared into the darkness.

Jo sat down on a log, glad to be surrounded by the dark. Somewhere a wolf wailed, and it reminded her of how Clint Reeves must feel inside, crying out. The night sounds didn't frighten her anymore. She didn't care at the moment about the night and its dangers. She only cared about the horror Clint Reeves lived with—and about the agonizing passions he had stirred in her with the probing kiss; how it felt to feel her breasts pressed tight against his broad chest, and the needs he had aroused in her when his hands had touched her.

She knew without experiencing it the ecstasy Clint Reeves could show a woman once he was inside of her. She knew it must be sinful to think about those needs again, but it had been close to three years since Greg was killed, and she had not so much as held hands with another man since. Now here was a man who was the epitome of maleness, but too troubled for her to allow him into her already complicated life. If he weren't so unpredictable—if it weren't for the whiskey, and the bad memories that made him keep turning to drink. . . .

No. She couldn't let herself care for him, and she couldn't let her baser needs dictate her acts. Clint Reeves was the worst kind of man a woman could love—a wanderer, moody, troubled, and in love with a memory. And she still had plans of her own.

She touched her mouth, her breast. She wondered if he would remember touching her there. The painful reality was that she had wanted him to touch her, and for a brief moment she had even considered letting him do more. She wondered if loneliness and old desires would turn her into a wanton woman, and she reminded herself never to let go of her basic morals and self-esteem for a brief moment of passion. It had to be more than that. And she knew deep inside it *could* be more than that, if only Clint Reeves were not such a complicated, unpredictable man; if only she could be sure his own feelings were real.

She returned to the brushy area and took care of her personal business, then walked back to her wagon in a daze.

"Where's Clint?" Hugh asked.

Jo touched her hair, reddening slightly. Did they suspect? "He was on his way down here to talk to you," she lied. "But when he saw me he just told me to tell you he'd be here in the morning. You know how he can be. He just turned and disappeared again."

Hugh eyed her closely and nodded. "We'll be heading out come mornin', ma'am, Clint or no Clint. He'll catch up."

Jo turned away. Hugh noticed a few leaves caught in the back of her hair, but he said nothing.

They finished with breakfast and all the men thanked Jo for the fine coffee and biscuits.

"Those are the last biscuits you'll have for a while," Jo answered. "The Indians took most of the flour. I'll have to conserve what's left until we reach someplace where we can get more."

"That'll be a couple weeks yet," Randy answered. He looked around. "I wonder if Clint's gonna make it like he said."

"Don't worry about Reeves," Moose told him. "He'll be along."

Jo refused to look at any of them at the mention of Clint's name. She quickly cleaned up camp, hoping she could make it through the day without falling from her horse—she was so tired from a nearly sleepless night, thanks to Clint. She saddled Red Lady, her heart still heavy over losing her Appaloosas and Shag. But at least she still had Red Lady and Sundance.

They headed out, Larry leading her oxen this time, and Frenchy leading the oxen that pulled Bill Starke's wagon. Jo's heart was heavy over the thought of leaving yet another grave behind, and she wondered about the other travelers left at Fort Bridger. She realized it wasn't wise to get too close to anyone in this land. One never knew when death or some other circumstance would separate people forever. She made up her mind once and for all that this was how it had to be with Clint. In his case it was even more hopeless. If death or the elements or some other circumstance didn't separate them, Clint's own problems would.

Hugh rode back beside her then, moving his horse close to hers. "You sure Clint said he'd be here this mornin', ma'am?"

Jo met his eyes, and she saw the discerning look there. "No. I just . . . didn't want to have to explain anything in front of the others, Hugh. He was drunk and troubled. I tried to talk to him, but he just wandered off again."

"Well, then, I won't worry about him. He'll show up when he wants. If he really said he'd be here, he would have. He's a man of his word, and I'd be worried and tempted to go lookin' for him if you were tellin' the truth." He looked her over. "Did he get rough with you or somethin'?"

Jo thought about the kiss, the feel of his powerful frame on top of her. "No," she answered. "He was just . . . feeling pretty bad. He acted like he wanted to talk . . . but then he just walked off again."

Hugh noticed a red mark at the corner of her mouth that had not been there the day before. "Well, whiskey can do things to a man, you know. And most times he's sorry the next day, especially a man like Clint. But he'd never . . . I mean, even full of whiskey, he'd never really hurt a nice lady like you."

"I know that, Hugh." She looked at him then. "Don't say anything to him when he comes back." She blushed, putting her fingers to the red mark. "What do the others think?"

"Oh, nobody has said anything. We're the kind that figures a man's business—or a woman's—is their own. And they know you're a lady, ma'am; and they know what a man can be like when he's hurtin' inside and full of whiskey. Pay no mind to any of it. But I'll tell you, ma'am, I could tell right off when your wagon train first arrived at

Fort Bridger that ole Clint had some real strong feelin's for you. But he don't want to ever feel like that again. That's why he went away for so long at first. And I reckon that's why he's stayin' away again. Besides that, he's got some heavy regrets today, if that mark on your mouth means what I think it does. Just try not to blame him too heavy."

Jo put her hand to the mark again. "I don't, Hugh." She swallowed back a sudden urge to cry. "How far are we from Montana?"

"Oh, we'll be there in just four or five more days, if we keep makin' good time and them Indians don't come back for us."

Jo kept her eyes to the northern horizon. She hoped Clint would come back before they reached Montana Territory. It didn't seem right, coming all this way with him, to finally reach Montana without him.

Another freak snowstorm slowed their journey by two extra days. They camped in a wide valley surrounded by magnificent mountains and tall pines; and everywhere they looked there were bubbling hot springs and simmering mud holes. Clint had still not rejoined them.

"This place is called Yellowstone. It's a favorite spot to the Indians," Ben Willis told Jo. "So we'll have to keep an eye out. There're some places where there's warm mineral water that's great for bathin'. We'll find a spot and you can have yourself a genuine hot bath."

"In the middle of this snow?"

"Once you get in the hot water, it won't matter. Wouldn't you like a real bath?"

Jo looked around at the others traveling behind her. "With all these men around?"

Ben laughed. "We'd leave you be. It wouldn't be easy for any of us, mind you, but every woman likes a nice hot bath. You've been livin' like a man too long, ma'am. Fact is, if you'd put on a pretty dress afterward, ole Hugh there, he plays a decent fiddle. We'll find ourselves some kind of shelter and hunt some fresh meat and have us a good meal and some music tonight. Maybe you could honor each of us with a dance."

Jo smiled and shook her head. "If that's what you want.
You've all done so much for me."

They rode for two more hours, through land that seemed
to Jo unearthly in its strange, almost menacing nature.
They had to be careful where they rode, so as to avoid
suddenly stepping into hot, bubbling mud; and often the
stinging smell of sulfur made Jo curl her nose.

They finally made camp near a small pond from which
steam rose. The men quickly made a screen of blankets at
the edge of the pond, using posts fashioned out of slender
branches cut from trees. They cut slits into the tops of the
branches where they slipped the edges of the blankets to
hold them. Eventually they had a wide enough screen
behind which Jo could undress and bathe without being
seen. Jo could only pray no one would come riding in from
the other side of the pond. But the water looked too
inviting for her to let that prospect stop her.

Behind the blanket screen and several yards away the
men made camp. Happy Strickland was already off hunting. Jo breathed deeply for courage and hoped she was
right in trusting the men behind her not to come running
the instant she was naked. She undressed and quickly
stepped into the pond and walked out until only her head
showed.

The warm water was gloriously refreshing. It soothed
her aching shoulders and legs, and as she washed she
began to feel not just more human but more feminine
again. She dunked her head into the water and washed
her hair. She wished she could stay in the water for hours,
but after she had sat in it a while longer after washing, she
came out and dried off behind the blankets, already thinking about how she would write Anna and tell her about
this unusual experience.

She pulled on her undergarments in the chilly air, gazing out at the magnificent view that surrounded the valley—
deep green pines set against black and gray granite. They
had passed thundering waterfalls, the white, foamy water
crashing over rocks worn smooth from the constant flow of
water. They had passed rock formations that rose like
organ pipes into the sky, and hills with boulders hanging
precariously over their path. Coming into this valley they
had followed narrow roads, mere pathways, around the

edges of mountains, so high that Jo had felt nauseous looking down. The paths wound around the sides of the mountains like snakes, and Jo pitied the men who led the oxen at such precarious heights.

It was in the mountains that they had experienced the worst of the snow. Now those same mountains surrounded them, but they were safely in the valley, and in some spots where the ground was eternally warm, there was no snow at all. But the air was still cold.

Jo finished dressing and brushed her hair, then used a mirror to arrange it. She was surprised to see how much thinner her face was, and she realized the dress she had put on felt big on her. She had lost weight on the hard journey. She tied the cloth belt of the dress tighter, then picked up her things and returned to camp, wearing a soft green dress that was far from fancy but was at least more feminine than the brown pants-skirt she had been wearing for weeks.

The men had two rabbits roasting over a fire, and they all looked up at her. She wore the bearskin coat over the pretty dress, but the men could see the bottom of it and knew she had put on something special. Her face was scrubbed to a lovely pink-white complexion, her hair pulled up at the sides and pinned with barrettes. She wore a tiny bit of soft rouge, and to the mountain men, she was the most beautiful woman they had ever set eyes on. Her natural beauty far outshone the painted whores that were most common in those parts.

"Ma'am, you're the prettiest woman ever came to this part of the country," Larry told her, his dark eyes looking her up and down.

Larry was younger than the others, and Jo knew he had an eye for her, but she had no interest, and he seemed to respect that.

"Thank you, Larry," she answered, blushing. She turned to the rest of them. "Why don't all of you go ahead and bathe, if you want. I'll watch the rabbits."

They all sat there for a moment.

"You *are* going to take baths, too, aren't you?"

Moose cleared his throat and looked at the others. "Well, uh, sure!" He gave the others a warning look. "Come on, boys. The lady says we ought to bathe, and I reckon we all smell worse than a bear comin' out of hibernation. Let's all take that bath we've been wantin'."

They all jumped up in pretended eagerness, but a few grumbled under their breath as they took blankets or towels from their gear and headed for the pond. Jo grinned at their attempt to convince her they were anxious to bathe and soon she could hear curses and shouting as their bodies hit warm water for the first time in God only knew how long. Jo turned the rabbits, breathing in the delicious smell as drops of fat hissed against the hot coals of the fire.

At that moment she heard a horse whinny, and she turned to see a man approaching on horseback. It was Clint, and behind him he led the horses the Indians had stolen from her.

"Patch! Star!" Jo rose from the fire and ran to the horses, hugging each around the neck. Patch had a sun and a hand painted on his rump, and Star's tail was braided, with beads wound into it. "Oh, look at them! They look wonderful!" Jo exclaimed. She turned to Shag, giving him a hug also. She looked up at Clint then, tears in her eyes. "Clint, how did you do it?"

He turned his back to her, dismounting. "I can be just as sneaky as the Indians, remember? I found their camp and waited till night. Then I moved in and got back what didn't belong to them." He tied his horse and turned to her, his eyes full of sorrow. "I had to do something, Jo, to make up for what I did that night. I couldn't have faced you otherwise. I'm damn sorry."

"Clint! Hey, Clint's back and he's got Mrs. Masters's horses!" Larry shouted.

"Shut up and leave them be," Jo heard Hugh yell at the young man. "Everybody stay right here for a bit."

Jo clung to the ropes that held her horses, reddening as Clint's dark eyes held her own. "It was just the whiskey," she answered, finally dropping her eyes.

"Not completely. Whiskey or not, I had no right. I made an ass out of myself." *"God, how I wanted you,"* he wished he could add. "I hope getting the horses back makes up for it."

Tears stung her eyes. *"You've only made me love you more, against all my better judgment,"* she thought. *"If*

*only you hadn't touched me. How much do you remember,
Clint? How bad did you want me, Joline Masters? How I
wish I could trust your emotions.*" She met his eyes. "The
horses more than make up for it. You shouldn't have done
this. You could have been killed."

He smiled sadly. "I seem to have a way of surviving
things, sometimes against my own will." He sighed deeply,
his dark eyes moving over her. "I didn't . . . hurt you or
anything, did I?"

She turned away to hide her tears. Why was it so easy
to convince herself she should have no feelings for him
while he was away, only to have painful needs and desires,
and this surging love, ripple through her the moment she
laid eyes on him again? She petted her horses. "No. And
I'm sorry I . . . hit you like that. I didn't know what else
to do."

"Right now I wish you had had a gun and had stuck it
right to my head and pulled the trigger." He stepped a
little closer. "Jo, I . . . when we get the chance . . . I'd
like to explain . . . about Millie and Jeff."

She nodded, refusing to look at him, afraid he would see
the love in her eyes. *"Damn you for doing this to me!"* she
thought. "Yes," she said aloud. "I think it might help you
to tell at least one person . . . someone who . . . cares
about you . . . as a friend. You can't hold things in forever,
Clint." She hugged Star. "Oh, Clint, thank you. You keep
doing these things for me that I'll never be able to repay
you for."

He watched her lovingly. "You've more than repaid me
just by speaking to me. That won't ever happen again, Jo.
I'm not touching any whiskey the rest of this trip. That's a
promise. And you, uh, you did a fine job the day those
Indians attacked. You stayed calm, even shot a couple of
them. You're a hell of a woman, Jo. That day . . . all I
could think of was Minnesota—how I'd feel if those warriors somehow got hold of you. We're . . . good friends.
I'd feel . . . real bad . . . if something happened to you. It
just . . . made me think about what happened before . . .
and every time I do that I try to drink away the memory."

"I know." She faced him again. He looked beautiful
standing there so tall and strong. Memories of his kiss, of
the feel of his hands against her breasts, moved through

her painfully. She knew she should be angry with him, maybe even hate him. But she felt nothing but love and sorrow.

"Tie the horses, will you? I've got to watch the rabbits." She walked past him and turned again. "I'm glad you got here before we reached Montana. Hugh says it will just be a couple of days. I . . . I didn't want to get there without you along. I mean, it just seems like . . . after all we've been through . . . you should be with me when we cross into Montana Territory."

He grinned the handsome grin that melted her heart. "I'll be with you. That's why I rode like hell to get back here. I knew you had to be close."

She smiled in return and their eyes held a moment longer. "I'm so damn sorry, Jo. I didn't behave any better than the man who attacked you back at Cottonwood Springs."

"It was nothing like that and you know it. I think I understand, Clint. And somehow I have trouble staying angry with you for long. I was angry that night, but I wasn't afraid—not then and not now."

He watched her closely. "It won't happen again."

He turned away with the horses, and Jo returned to the fire. *Maybe I want it to happen again,* she thought.

The other men returned, joking and congratulating Clint over getting the horses back, asking for details about how he did it. They all ate, and Hugh played his fiddle. The men took turns dancing with Jo—all except Clint. And with an aching heart, Jo knew why he wouldn't dance with her. He was afraid to touch her again. She also knew it was just as well, for she was as much afraid of her emotions as he was.

That night Jo slept in her wagon, half expecting Clint to come and tell her about Millie. But he did not come, and he seemed to make a point from then on of never being caught alone with her. They had little chance to talk as they traveled the next three days, until finally he rode up beside her and caught hold of her horse's bridle. He slowed her and pointed to a river.

"That's the Yellowstone—the river we've followed and crossed a time or two already," he told her. "Once we cross it here, we're in Montana."

Jo's heart raced. It seemed to help her concern over her feelings for Clint to know she was finally reaching her intended home.

She sat and stared for a moment while the others passed them.

"Once we get into Montana, we'll ride up past the Ruby River and into Virginia City. That will be two or three more weeks yet. You can stock up on supplies and visit the land office, then I'll help you get settled." He put a hand on her shoulder, his first personal gesture since the night they were both trying to forget. "You've made it, Joline Masters. How does it feel?"

Her eyes teared. "Wonderful! It feels wonderful, Clint! I feel like I've really accomplished something . . . like I really belong out here. It's so beautiful. I could never go back to Lawrence now. Never!"

"Well, then, you've probably done the right thing. But it's not going to be easy, you know. What you've already been through was the simple part."

"I don't care. I'm going to make it, I just know it."

The others were already crossing the river, a dangerous task with the high spring waters.

"Hang on to that mount," Clint told her. "The water will come up to your waist. We'll have to build a fire and dry out once we get across."

"I don't care. Let's just get across," she answered, kicking her horse into a gallop. She screamed as the cold water hit her when they splashed into the river.

Chapter Fifteen

They rode into a broad valley filled with thick, green grass and an array of wildflowers, their colors of red and yellow, violet and white rippling in the wind like the waves of the ocean. Jo halted her horse, turning to drink in the beauty of this place, near what Clint called the Ruby River. The surrounding mountains were magnificent, capped with snow, their ridges splashed with purple and gray, their lower levels a carpet of deep green from pine trees. An eagle winged its way overhead, and from somewhere in the distance Jo could hear the rush of water.

Jo rode away from the rest of the travelers, circling the area, taking in its glorious beauty and feeling a wonderful sense of belonging. A wave of exquisite peace moved through her, and she felt like a wild thing, like just another form of life amid this array of nature's beauty.

The others continued on while Clint rode out to Jo. "What are you doing? Stay with the rest of us," he called out to her.

She turned to him with a smile, and for a moment Clint's breath caught in his throat. For that moment, sitting there astride one of her Appaloosas, her dark hair blowing away from her face in the wind, her form set against the magnificent backdrop of mountains, he saw her as the most beautiful creature he had ever set eyes on. He could still feel the round fullness of her breast in his hand, still smell her sweet scent, taste her mouth.

"This is it, Clint," she said as he came closer.

"This is what?"

"This is where I am going to settle. Right here in this valley. It's the most splendid, most beautiful place I've ever seen." Her dark eyes sparkled with excitement.

"Jo, it's too far from Virginia City—too remote."

"I don't care. Remote is what I want. This could be mine, Clint—all mine. It's so beautiful!"

"Indians roam through here. And so do outlaws."

"I don't care what you tell me. This is where I want to settle. Tell the others to stop. We'll camp here and you can ride the perimeter with me. We'll write down certain land markers so I'll have something for the Land Office when we get to Virginia City. I'll file right away under the Homestead Act. I just hope this doesn't already belong to someone else. But surely it doesn't. There's no house here—no sign of settling."

"And for good reason. Nobody else is crazy enough to settle here. A *man* wouldn't settle here, Jo. For a woman to consider it is ridiculous."

"Not for this woman. This is where I want to be."

"It's another ten miles to Virginia City."

"I don't care if it's fifty." She rode off, heading for a distant hill. "Come on! I've got paper and pen in my gear. I wanted to be ready in case I found the right spot."

He watched her for a moment, a lump rising in his throat at the thought of some day leaving her. But he was determined to do it. And if she was foolish enough to settle in a spot like this, that was her problem. His was to get her here, and he had completed that task. He looked around at the surrounding mountains, and he realized that if he too were looking for a place to settle, this would be it. But he had tried that once, and it had ended in tragedy.

He rode out to catch up with the rest of the men, telling them to hold up and make camp.

"What for?" Randy complained. "We've still got over half a day's riding to do."

"Our female companion has decided this is where she wants to settle," Clint answered, sarcasm in his voice. "She wants to mark out the boundaries before we go on to Virginia City."

"Here? Settle *here*?" Happy asked, his surprise evident.

"Yeah, here," Clint grumbled. "There's no figuring a woman, is there? They can be brave and smart and beautiful and independent—then do something dumb as a stump." He grabbed a hammer and the can of red paint that he had advised Jo to buy to use for marking rocks and stakes when she found a place to settle.

"Go ahead and make camp, Hugh. I'll be back in a few hours."

He left then to catch up with Jo, the other men watching after him and shaking their heads.

"She's some crazy woman," Moose mumbled.

"Hell, she'll probably end up better off than most of those men up there in the mountains tryin' to find gold," Ben put in.

Clint had to hunt for Jo at first, since she had not waited for him. She had ridden up a hill on the east side of the valley, and by the time he reached her, she was all the way to the top of the ridge, which looked out farther east over a smaller valley and to the mountains beyond.

"A hundred and sixty acres isn't as much as I'll really need, but maybe once I get settled and get an income coming in, I can buy more instead of waiting five years to claim more," Jo told him as he came closer. "Oh, you remembered the paint. Mark that big rock there, the one with the funny point on top. I'll make a note of it on paper. That will have to be my primary eastern marker for the moment."

Clint reluctantly dismounted and slapped a red X on the stone.

"Write my name on it. I want to be sure people know who's going to own this place," Jo told him.

Clint looked up at her with a scowl. "This is ridiculous."

She just smiled. "This is the most exciting thing I've ever done in my life. Don't be a grump about it. It's my decision, not yours."

He wrote her name—J. Masters. "Better just use the initial," he warned. "Then outsiders won't know a woman is settling here. They'll think it's a John or Joseph or whatever." He looked up at her again. "You intend to build fences and a house, dig a well and build a windmill all by yourself—plus cut wood—all before winter sets in?"

"Oh, I'll figure something out. I'll hire some men in Virginia City."

He rolled his eyes. "You'll find plenty of volunteers who will expect something in return, figuring any woman who'd settle alone in a place like this is easy pickings."

Jo reddened. "Well . . . there must be *some* decent men there, like Hugh and Moose and the others."

"Men like Hugh and Moose are wandering mountain men. They know about as much about building a windmill and building fences as an antelope. But if you *can* find some decent men, how do you intend to pay them? With a smile?"

She frowned, looking away. "I don't know yet. I'll find a way."

"This is all impossible, Jo. I shouldn't even be marking these stones for you. I should chain you to a post at Virginia City and forbid you to come back here."

"You'd have no right!" She whirled her horse around. "Stop trying to spoil it, Clint. This beautiful place is going to be mine, and nothing you can say will discourage me. As far as building fences and . . . building a cabin . . . I'll find a way. God means for me to be here. I know it in my heart. I'm staying, and I'll make it. You said so yourself. Why are you trying to discourage me now?"

"I care what happens to you, Jo. If nothing else, we're at least damn good friends, aren't we? What's wrong with caring about a friend? My God, you're ten long miles from the nearest civilization. I just want you to be sure about this."

"I *am* sure. Even if for some reason I can't make it this first year, the land will still be mine. It will be registered in my name. I want this valley to belong to *me*, Clint. Please help me mark it off."

He adjusted his hat and, clinging to the can of paint, hoisted himself back onto his horse using one hand. "Let's go find your next marker."

She smiled through tears. "Thank you." She turned her horse and headed north, following the rim of the lower foothills. "Do you think I'll be able to find a surveyor in Virginia City?"

"No doubt. With all the mining going on, claims to

stake and such, there's bound to be more than one surveyor around."

"Good. He can make this more accurate. This will
just have to be good guesswork for now. I think I'd want it
in a kind of rectangular shape—taking in most of the valley
below."

"If I were you, when you get a final measure, make
sure it includes some high ground. Out in these parts you
can never trust a river. The Ruby can get pretty mean
sometimes. I'd build my cabin on higher ground."

She nodded. "That's a good idea. Thanks for offering
it."

"Sure," he answered, still scowling. *"I ought to dump
this paint, pull you off that horse and make you remember
you're a woman,"* he thought. If he weren't so afraid to
love again, he'd take her to Virginia City and marry her.
Then he'd have plenty to say about what she was doing.
"You're a goddamned fool and a coward, Clint Reeves,"
he grumbled inwardly.

They spent the next five hours riding the rim of the
valley, Clint splashing red paint and the name J. Masters
on rocks and trees, while Jo wrote down approximate
locations and made a rough drawing of the valley, showing
how the Ruby River wound through it. From their high
perch, it was easy to get a rough picture of the boundaries,
and to see the river rushing in zig-zag fashion through the
center of "her land." She halted her horse near a waterfall.

"Oh, Clint, isn't it beautiful?"

He rode his horse up beside hers. "I'll grant you that.
A man couldn't ask for a prettier place to settle—or a
woman."

"Or a man and woman together," she thought. "With
all that wonderful grass down there, and the buffalo grass
farther up in these hills, maybe I'll just ranch," she said
thoughtfully. "I could handle that more easily than farming. I wouldn't need near as much help, and I do love
animals. Maybe I can find me a good stud horse in Virginia City to mate with Red Lady or Star."

"Maybe. Men up in these parts always need horses.
But good horses are a prime target for Indians and outlaws. I'm not trying to discourage you, Jo. I'm just stating

hard facts that you'd better consider. Men are going to figure you're an easy take."

"Well, then, they'll find out different. I've shot an outlaw and two Indians already. I'll shoot down anybody else who wants to give me trouble."

Clint grinned, well remembering the sock she had given him in the ear. "You probably *would* be a hell of an opponent."

She grinned herself then. "Clint, I'll bet there are plenty of deer and elk and such animals up here in these foothills. I'll have plenty of meat."

He nodded. "Antelope and bighorn sheep, too. Come fall, you'll hear the banging of their horns, like I told you a while back. It will echo through this valley like some giant is up here cracking rocks. And you'll hear the call of the elk."

His voice lowered thoughtfully on the last words, and for a moment they both sat there quietly, listening to the sad groan of the wind as it whistled down out of the mountains.

"I had no choice, Jo," he said then. She looked at him with a frown, wondering if he was talking about his wife. For some reason he was opening up to her again, and she was afraid to say one word for fear of breaking the spell. She simply turned her gaze back across the valley and listened, letting him tell her in his own way, his own time. Whatever had compelled him to suddenly talk, she could not imagine, unless it was the memory of another time when he picked out a place to settle, like she was doing now.

"I was wounded bad," he continued. "All I could do was watch as they dragged Millie and Jeff away. I knew . . . the mood the Indians were in during that time . . . what lay ahead for my wife and son. I'll never know how I did it, but I managed to get to my feet and get onto a horse. I held my rifle in my left hand, but that's all I could do with that side of my body. I couldn't use my arm. The pain was like nothing I had ever experienced before or probably ever will again. Strangely enough, I didn't bleed as bad as you'd think with a wound like that, although I lost enough blood by the time it was over that I finally did pass out.

"At any rate I tracked the Indians. I found their camp. By the time I did . . ." His voice choked, and he cleared his throat. "It wasn't like with your horses, Jo. I couldn't wait till dark and try to get them out of there. They were . . . being tortured. If I'd waited till dark, they would have suffered more than any human being should be allowed to suffer. Even if they would still have been alive, they wouldn't have been able to walk—and I was in no condition to carry them out of there. I knew I had no choice—absolutely no choice. I had to shoot them to end their suffering. If the Indians came for me after that, I didn't care. I wanted to die anyway."

He stopped for a moment, taking a thin cigar from his pocket and lighting it. He puffed on it, and Jo still said nothing; but her throat ached with a need to cry.

He cleared his throat again. "I . . . leveled my rifle on a boulder for support, since I couldn't lift my left arm to hold the gun. Then I just . . . took aim. I knew Jeff . . ." He stopped again, his voice breaking. Jo waited, silent tears spilling down her cheeks. "Jeff . . . would be the hardest for me. I loved Millie so much . . . but a son . . . he was only three. His crying tore at my guts like someone was ripping them out. I made . . . damn sure that first shot would hit its mark." He sniffed and wiped his hand across his eyes. "I guess the shot kind of stunned the Indians. They all just halted in their tracks and turned in the direction of the shot. I managed to cock the rifle by pressing it between the rock and my right shoulder . . . cocked it with my right hand, then positioned it again. The Indians . . . just stepped back . . . like they knew what was coming next. Millie was half dead already. She never really knew . . . what hit her."

He removed his hat and ran a hand through his hair, then wiped at his eyes again. "If there hadn't been so damn many of them . . . and if I wasn't so bad wounded . . . maybe I would have had some other choice. I, uh . . ." He sniffed again. "I passed out after that. When I came to, someone had cleaned and bandaged my wound. Millie and Jeff were all laid out beside me, wrapped in blankets for burial, a feathered lance shoved into the ground beside each of them. I knew it was a sign of honor. Apparently what I did impressed the Indians. They dressed

my wound and left the bodies for me to bury. One big
hole had been dug. They knew that's how the white man
buries his own. I guess they realized I never could have
dug the hole myself. I managed to . . . hold each of them
for a little while and I . . . buried them together. Millie
would have wanted . . . her baby boy . . . beside her."

His voice broke again and he turned his horse, heading downward toward the valley. Jo sat and wept alone,
her tears not just for his loss, but for all such useless
death. She had already read that thousands had died from
the war back east, and she prayed for Anna's husband.
Why did there have to be all this killing? But poor Clint.
Few suffered a horror that traumatic. It was no wonder he
turned to whiskey and fits of depression. But his story only
made it more clear to her that he was a deeply troubled
man who had personal problems to solve before he could
truly commit himself to anyone else.

She let the tears flow, suddenly realizing it felt good
to cry. She hadn't wept openly and deeply in a long time.
She wondered how Clint could live with the memories.
She wished there were some way to comfort him, but
there was no erasing such events. Only the passage of time
would help, but the wound would never completely heal.

She fished for a handkerchief in the pocket of her
skirt and blew her nose, wiping at her eyes while looking
at the glorious horizon—the sprawling valley with its brilliant colors, the deep green foothills beyond, and the
rising granite peaks that outlined those hills.

Life might be hard here, but at least there was a kind
of peace that could not be found anyplace else. This surely
was one of God's favorite places. Here a man or woman
could find his or her soul, could be one with God and
nature, could leave behind the heartache of the past. She
felt as much a part of this land as the trees and animals. It
was almost as though she had been here before, perhaps
in another life. She wondered how much of what a person
did was from choice, and how much was God's will. Surely
God willed her to be here, and if He willed it, He would
help her find a way to survive here.

But what was His intention for her meeting Clint
Reeves? Did He mean for her to fall in love with him, as
she knew deep inside was happening? Why did God have

to present her with such a complicated man, when she didn't really want a man at all. Had He taken Greg from her so that somehow she could become a part of Clint Reeves's life? Still, she didn't really want that responsibility, and Clint certainly was not ready for it himself.

She wiped at her eyes again, not wanting the men to know she had been crying. She waited a moment longer to let the cool air dry her eyes. A dull ache pressed on her heart at the thought of Clint's story as she headed down the hill toward camp. She saw Clint riding hard then, heading through the valley toward the north. She rode up to camp.

"Where is Clint going?" she asked.

Hugh shrugged. "Don't know. Rode up and left the paint and said he was goin' ridin' alone for a while. You know how he is."

Jo closed her eyes and sighed. "Yes." She dismounted and poured herself some coffee. "No sense keeping any food warm for him," she added. "He probably won't be back tonight."

Hugh held out a bottle of whiskey. "He gave me this. Said to tell you he wouldn't be needing it this time." He gave her a wink, as though he understood what both of them were going through. Jo smiled. She felt like celebrating with the whiskey herself. For once Clint Reeves wouldn't try to drown his memories in it. She was glad for that much.

When Jo awoke in the morning Clint was already in camp, hitching her oxen to her wagon. She brushed her hair and climbed out of the wagon, already dressed. The nights were still too cold to undress or even to remove fur jackets. She dipped a ladle into a water barrel, pounding on a thin crust of ice first to get to the freezing-cold water. She rinsed her mouth, then noticed a fire already lit and a coffee pot sitting on it. A familiar figure was hitching the yoke around the oxen.

"Good morning," she said.

"Morning," Clint answered without turning around. "It's my turn to walk with the oxen. I figured I'd go ahead and get them hitched."

She watched him quietly for a moment, deciding to

say nothing about what he had told her the day before. After all, what could she say that would make any difference. And no matter what she said, it would only dredge it up for him again.

"Will we reach Virginia City today?"

"Possibly—if nothing happens to put a dent in our travel. But it's mostly mountains all the way. Might take till the next day." He turned to face her finally, and she struggled not to show her astonishment. His face looked haggard, with circles under his eyes. He needed a shave but apparently hadn't bothered this morning. "You'd be best to pay attention to the way," he told her. "There will be times when you'll make the trip alone. The last thing you want is to get lost in these mountains. They'll kill you quicker than any Indian or outlaw could do. We'll be making the trip several times until your cabin is built and you're all settled. By then you should be pretty familiar with the way."

He left her then, saying nothing more. They were soon underway, making most of the distance but slowed by steep pathways that were slippery with lingering, hard-packed snow. It was a precarious trip for the animals, and some of the roads hung onto the side of mountains, making it imperative to go slowly. They camped high in the mountains that night; the lanterns, gas lights, and camp-fires of Virginia City were visible, but too far away to try to reach before dark.

The next day brought them into the city. They rode through muddy streets, where horse dung mixed with the slippery mire. The oxen strained at the wagons, and Randy cursed and whipped at them to keep going, his boots buried past his ankles. Happy brought up the rear with Bill Starke's wagon. His curses filled the air and mixed with a general din caused by wagons, horses, and a variety of men, most of them unshaven, a few in suits and sporting gold watches. Piano music flowed from nearly every saloon, and Jo wondered how on earth they had got a heavy piano this far into the mountains.

A wagon rattled past in the other direction, and the dog Spirit chased after its wheels, almost getting caught under them. Happy quickly picked up the dog and plunked it in Starke's wagon, tying it so it couldn't run loose and get hurt.

Whores meandered on the boardwalks and leaned on railings from upper balconies. They shouted suggestive remarks to Clint and the others. One in particular recognized Clint and called out to him by name. He looked up at a dark-haired woman who appeared to be about his age but who was prettier than most of the other women; Jo thought they were hideously painted, some much too fat, and most with homely faces. But the dark-haired woman was attractive. She leaned over a railing as Clint rode up to talk to her, and her breasts billowed over her low-cut dress so that Jo thought they might fall right out.

"Come see me later, honey," the woman called out to him as he rejoined the others.

Jo quickly looked away, a painful jealousy burning at her insides so that her stomach actually hurt. She told herself it was just as well. That was the kind of woman Clint Reeves belonged with for now. Still, the thought of some other woman enjoying his kiss, his touch, his strength . . .

"Hey, you bring us a new one?" A grizzly, poorly dressed man ran up between Clint and Jo, a whiskey bottle in his hand. "Say, you're the prettiest thing we've seen up here in months," he told Jo, putting his hand on her leg.

Jo jerked her horse away and Clint's foot came up under the man's chin, knocking him flat into the mud and horse dung. He left him lying there, and the rest of the men rode around him while people laughed at the sight. Jo felt the rush of blood to her face and she refused to look at Clint.

"The land office is just ahead on the left," he was telling her. "Don't let these men bother you. Soon as they understand you're a respectable woman, they'll leave you alone."

Their little group pulled up in front of the land office.

"Well, I reckon, this is where we part, ma'am," Hugh told Jo, riding up beside her. "Me and the others, we've got some catchin' up to do." He glanced at a redheaded woman who passed by, her face heavily painted, her dress red taffeta. He grinned and nodded to her, and Jo knew what he meant by "catching up." "And we've got to see about stakin' out our own claims and such." He tipped his hat. "It's been an honor knowin' you, Mrs. Masters. I truly mean that. Me and the others here, we wish you the best. And if you ever get in any trouble and need help, just send somebody after us. People will know where we are, one way or another. People in these parts, we have our own system of gettin' messages to each other."

"Thank you, Hugh." Jo's eyes misted as she turned her horse and looked at all of them. Happy finished tying her oxen and waded through the mud to his own horse. "Thank you, all of you," Jo told them. "If you hadn't been along when the Indians attacked—" She swallowed back tears. "And thank you for taking turns driving the oxen. I'm grateful to all of you. I'm going to miss you."

"We'll miss you, too, ma'am," Larry answered, his eyes passing over her appreciatively. "You're one hell of a woman. Everybody in Virginia City is gonna be rootin' for you, once they find out why you're here. You can bet on it."

Frenchy rode closer and put out his hand. "*Au revoir, Madame.*"

Jo took his hand and squeezed it. "Good-bye, Frenchy." Each of the others rode forward and shook her hand. "I feel like hugging all of you."

"There's nothing we'd like more, ma'am, but if you did that here, the men watching would all get the wrong idea and you'd have a problem," Ben answered with a grin.

Jo blushed again. "I do hope I'll see some of you again. You're all welcome to come and visit me any time you want. You know where I'll be. Please come and see me."

"We'll make a point to do that, ma'am." Happy tipped his hat to her. "And there *are* some decent men in this town. You just have to hunt around a bit. Clint will find somebody to go back with you and help build your cabin and such. In a mining town there are always men from back east who've hit on hard luck and are down to their last dime—men who had trades back east. Some will work for you just for a meal and a place to stay."

"You stay alert and keep that rifle handy," Moose told

her. "If you use it like you did against those Indians, you'll be all right."

They all grinned at the remark and bid her a last good-bye, then said their various farewells to Clint. They rode off in different directions. Jo watched after them, thinking what a strange breed they were, close in spirit, but men who were loners and didn't keep any one friendship for long. They knew it didn't pay to get too close to anyone. Death was always close at hand, ready to rip people apart in this land. She looked at Clint, who had dismounted and was tying his horse. He was like the rest of them, a man with whom it was almost impossible to get close. He had allowed that only once, and it had ended in disaster.

Jo dismounted, realizing she would have to get over her womanly need for permanency in friendships and home. This was a wild land full of wandering nomads. There would be no longtime neighbors for her here, no family, no close friends for life. The land would become her friend. The dog Spirit would be her closest companion. He barked from inside the wagon, but Jo left him there tied, worried about letting him run loose in the streets of Virginia City.

Clint tied her horse while Jo walked up onto the boardwalk, relieved to set her feet on something solid. Another painted woman walked by, eyeing her intently, as though trying to figure out if she was proper, or perhaps some new competition. Jo nodded to her. "Hello."

The woman smiled, then glanced at Clint. "Hello, hello," she said seductively, her eyes running over his fine physique. She turned back to Jo. "He yours?"

Jo wished the red wasn't showing in her cheeks, but she knew it was. "No. He's my guide."

The woman grinned more, glancing back at Clint. "You can guide me anyplace, anytime." She held out her arms then. "Hello, Clint!"

They embraced, and to Jo's chagrin, she realized they already knew each other. A miserable jealousy ripped through her when Clint kissed the woman's neck before letting go of her.

"It's been a long, long time, you worthless wanderer," the woman told him.

In spite of her heavy makeup, Jo could see she was beautiful. Her hair was a natural blond and was swept up in beautiful curls, decorated with fancy pins. She glanced at Jo again as she stepped back, then looked back up at Clint. "She need a place to work?"

Clint pushed back his hat, looking the woman over. "She is Mrs. Joline Masters, a widow from Kansas and a proper lady—and a very good friend, I might add. She's come here to settle—over by the Ruby River. She's going to file her claim right now, under the Homestead Act."

The woman's eyebrows arched, and she looked back at Jo. "All the way over by the Ruby? Alone?"

Jo straightened. "Yes," she answered, holding her chin proudly.

The woman chuckled. "Well, little lady, you've got courage, I'll say that much. By God, I wish you luck. Lord knows you'll need it. But if you change your mind and want to get rich, come on back here and look me up. A pretty little thing like you could make a fortune in this town."

Jo eyed her boldly. "I'd die in the wilds first."

The woman laughed harder and Clint grinned. "Well, that's what most likely will happen. But us women have to stick together." She put out her hand. "My name is Sally Turrell. My place is the first fancy house you saw coming into town—the one painted pink. You got a need, you come see me—any need. And I'm not talking sinful. I mean supplies, trouble, sickness—whatever. Any friend of Clint's is a friend of mine."

Jo was surprised at the remark. She cautiously took the woman's hand. Sally was a buxom woman, perhaps in her late twenties. Jo imagined that if Clint knew the woman from earlier years, she must have started her career at a very young age. There was a hardness to her green, wide-set eyes, as though she had already seen more of life than someone much older. It seemed to Jo that she would be much prettier without any of the extra colors she drew on her lips and eyes, and wearing a simple dress and hairdo.

"Thank you, Miss Turrell," Jo said aloud.

"Used to be Mrs. I'm a widow, too. Took back my

maiden name after my husband died in a barroom brawl. How about you?"

Jo let go of her hand, surprised to hear the woman had been married. "The war," she answered. "Shiloh."

The woman frowned. "Sorry about that. What on earth made you decide to come to this godforsaken place?"

Jo smiled a little. "The challenge, I guess. I wanted to get away from everything. Confederates raided Lawrence, burned my farm and ruined my crops. It was all I had left. I met Mr. Reeves here, and he was coming to Montana—so I asked if I could come along."

Sally looked up at Clint. "Well, what red-blooded man would turn down a request like that from something this pretty?" She smiled a crooked smile. "You two make it all the way up here without . . . well, I mean, traveling together and all . . ."

"There is nothing improper between us," Jo answered quickly, holding her chin defiantly again.

Sally's eyebrows rose, and she caught the grin on Clint's face. She looked at Jo. "Well, you're stronger than I thought." She looked Clint over. "Personally, I would have taken advantage of the situation." She patted his side. "How have you been, honey?"

"It could take a day to tell that one," he answered.

"I've got lots of time. Come see me. We have some years to cover."

Clint nodded. "I didn't know you'd got married. Sorry about your husband."

Sally tried to hide her sorrow. "Yeah, well, people like you and me, we aren't meant for such things, I guess. I heard from others what happened to you. Must have been pretty terrible." She leaned up and kissed him lightly. "Don't wait too long to come see me," she said softly. She gave him a wink, then nodded to Jo again. "I meant that about help. Don't you hesitate."

The woman walked off and Jo watched after her, her face red and her lips turned in a pout.

"Don't mind her," Clint told her. "Sally's a good woman at heart. She means it about helping you if you need it."

"But I don't want you to go see her!" Jo wanted to scream. But she reminded herself that that part of his life

was none of her affair, and she had vowed to forget about her feelings for Clint Reeves and turn all her attention to her new home. "Let's go settle my claim," she said aloud, turning away and opening the door to the land office.

Clint followed her inside, thinking how he would much rather share Joline Masters's bed than Sally Turrell's. But for now the only women he felt safe with were the ones who didn't matter, the ones who didn't expect emotional involvement. He almost looked forward to getting Jo settled and getting the hell out of her life. But he knew that leaving her would be the hardest thing he would ever do.

Chapter Sixteen

"It's mine, Clint, it's all mine!" Jo said excitedly, clutching the papers that granted her the valley. "I was so afraid someone else had already claimed it."

"No one else wants to take the chance with Indians and outlaws," he grumbled.

"Well, I don't have anything of much value for them anyway. It's not as though I'm mining gold or something. And I'll keep a good eye on the horses."

She walked a little ahead of him, and he studied the long hair and remembered how she looked naked in the river when she was sick. The value, to outlaws at least, was the woman herself, and she didn't even realize it. The thought of men abusing her, destroying her pride and happiness, brought a rage to his soul that created an equal rage at himself for caring so much. A part of him wanted to own her, protect her, possess her himself and make sure every other man who came along knew she was Clint Reeves's woman. But another part of him, the part that ruled him more firmly, told him never to care that way again. Jo went around to the back of Bill Starke's wagon, climbing inside and rummaging through some of his things. "We'll sell Bill's wagon and everything in it that I won't need, plus the oxen," she was saying. "I'll have to sell Brute and Goliath, too, much as I hate to. When it comes to plowing up land, I can handle draft horses better. But I won't buy any right away. I'll hang on to the money to pay men to help me build a cabin and fencing. The material

for both will come from my own trees, so that won't cost
me anything. And I have enough money to buy the extra
supplies I'll need to get through one winter. I'll wait till
next spring to worry about planting and such. By the time
we get a cabin built and dig a well, put up a windmill and
all, it will be too late for me to do any planting. But I can
at least have a small garden for myself. My biggest problem will be feed for the horses over the winter. Lord
knows there is plenty of beautiful grass there for them in
the summer."

She rattled on as she began holding up various items
Starke used to make boots. Clint just watched her, still
fascinated by her obstinate determination to settle in the
valley, still amazed that she was really doing this. "I don't
even know what this is," she said, studying an odd-shaped
tool. "There's no sense keeping it. Is there a bootmaker in
this town? Maybe he would want to look at some of these
things."

Clint grinned, shaking his head and feeling like a man
who had just been beaten at some kind of game. "You sort
through those things and I'll go find out," he answered.
"And I'll ask around about selling the wagon and oxen and
I'll find a place to put up the horses for the night. Then I'll
get you a hotel room."

He walked off, and Jo leaned out of the back of the
wagon, her heart pounding with excitement at all the
activity of Virginia City. In the distance were the purple
mountains, and somewhere to the west was her valley.

"*My* valley," she said aloud. "You're here, Jo. You
really made it!"

Finding a hotel room was not an easy task, with so
many men flowing into town looking for a grubstake, or
looking for guides to lead them to places where gold was
most likely to be found. It was obvious Clint could easily
find work here, and Jo felt guilty to be still taking up so
much of his time. But it was Clint who insisted on hiring
the men who would help build a cabin and dig a well,
convincing Jo that he knew a lot more about what men
could be trusted than Jo did. Jo's only objective was to get
back to her valley and get to work, so she didn't argue; but

selling off what she didn't need and rounding up the right
men took time.

Clint finally found her a decent room, after bribing
someone to leave it. But there was still no room for Clint.
He simply disappeared at night and returned the next
morning, and Jo had a pretty good idea where he probably
stayed. The thought of it kept her awake nights, struggling
with needs and with jealousy at the thought of Sally Turrell
enjoying Clint Reeves's body. A man as handsome as Clint
always found a place to stay, and the room itself probably
didn't cost him a cent. It was only the "extras" that came
with it that would cost him, but Jo guessed Sally didn't
even charge her old friend.

Clint never mentioned where he spent his nights, and
Jo never asked, determined to prove to him that she didn't
care. It took a week to get the supplies she needed and to
sell what she wanted to sell, but Jo was finally ready to go
"home."

Clint had gathered six men, two of them carpenters,
the other four farmers who knew about building fences
and digging wells. All of them were from the east, and
most even had families waiting for them. All had been
quickly discouraged after arriving at Virginia City—several
two years earlier, one only a few months ago. Finding gold
was not as easy as picking up rocks along the side of the
road, as some had described it. It took hard, hard work
and most of the time did not yield near enough gold to
make the work worthwhile. When a strike was made, most
prospectors didn't have the knowledge or the money to
properly mine it. Developers stepped in then, buying up
claims for a minimal fee, only to turn around and make a
fortune off another man's backbreaking work.

"Trouble is, once you get out here, the land kind of
grabs you," a carpenter called Jim Backus said as they
moved along the remote road to the valley. "Now I don't
want to go back east. I'm going to bring my family out
here and settle. I figure with all the people who are going
to keep coming out, I can stay plenty busy at my own
trade."

"You'll probably do better than most of the prospectors," Clint answered. "That's how it usually goes around
gold towns. It's the suppliers and builders and investors

who make the big money. Most prospectors never do hit it big, and those who do turn around and sell it—spend all the money and still end up broke. Some men make a career out of hunting for gold. I've seen men who have dug around in the mountains so long they're like crazy men—men who have lost all touch with reality."

"It can happen," Backus answered. "I can understand it after the few months I spent up there. A man can't live like that forever. It's no good being alone all the time."

"That's a fact," Clint answered. "But then sometimes a man can be surrounded by people and still be alone."

Jo looked up at him from her wagon, which she drove by herself now. The wagon was pulled by the big, shaggy gelding, and Red Lady, the roan mare. *Yes,* she thought, *that's the kind of man you are, Clint Reeves. Always alone on the inside.*

The conversation turned to questions from the hired men about what brought Jo to Montana and how she thought she could survive there. They all seemed to hold her in awe. They appreciated her beauty; but her independence had a way of keeping them at bay. She was more an object of conversation and fascination than one of sexual attraction. And her strength and determination encouraged considerable respect from the men she and Clint had hired.

Backus, who had a wife and three children in Illinois, was a nice-looking man, with dark hair and a trim build, his hands callused from hard work. The second carpenter was Newt James, a single man of perhaps thirty. The farmers, Weston Rivers, John Mason, Matt Simms, and Lucas Adams, were all married men with families. Mason had sold his farm in Missouri, and his wife and two children lived with his in-laws while they waited for word from him. Simms had three grown children who were taking care of his farm in Iowa. Adams, who had four children, had left his family behind in Illinois and come to Montana with Jim Backus. Wes Rivers had a wife and three children, who were waiting for him in Kentucky.

"It might be pretty out here, but it's too wild for me." Mason spoke up. "I'm going back to Missouri soon as we're finished building the fence and all. I'm only doing it for a little extra money to get me back."

"Me, I'm staying, just like Jim," Luke Adams put in. "I've never seen such country. Me and Jim came out here together, and we're staying. Maybe we'll take advantage of that Homestead Act, like Mrs. Masters did."

"I'm heading back," Matt Simms told them. "I'm getting too old for this. My three sons are running the farm. I miss them and the grandkids. I think I'll go back and just sit on the porch and watch them work."

They all laughed, and Jo felt excited and happy. Clint had picked some good men, men who honored and respected her, men who knew what they were about and would help build a fine cabin and sturdy fencing. Next spring, when she was ready to increase her herd and do some planting, she would probably have to hire at least two men, but she would worry about that when the time came. She told herself that if she let her mind swim with too many future plans she would be a nervous wreck. All that mattered now was that she get the cabin built. Comments from the others had made her a little faint of heart before they reached the valley. Had she really done the right thing? It seemed someone was perpetually telling her how foolish she was. Even some of these men wanted to go back east rather than settle here.

But as soon as they approached the valley and it came into splendid view, all her doubts again vanished. "There it is!" she told the others, her eyes misty. "Isn't it beautiful?"

A couple of them removed their hats and wiped at their brows. It was an unusually warm day for May, and they all had removed their jackets.

"Mrs. Masters, that's the prettiest piece of country I've seen, even around here where *everything* is pretty," Backus replied.

"Yes, ma'am, it's a right fine place to raise horses, or farm, either one," Wes Rivers added. "Look at all that grass."

"And water running right through the middle of it," Luke Adams put in.

"We have a lot of work to do," Clint told all of them. "Let's get down there and get started. Mrs. Masters wants the cabin built on this side and up the side of the hill here, in case of flooding."

"My porch will face the west, so when the sun rises I

can see it lighting up the mountains across the valley," Jo told them, her heart pounding with happiness. She thought how perfect all this would be if her feelings for Clint weren't so confusing and painful. "I love the mornings."

Clint thought how nice it would be to wake up with her on a chilly morning, to hold her close under warm comforters, to make love to her just as the birds woke up and started to sing.

"Clint, look at all the wildflowers, set against all that green. Did you ever see anything so beautiful?"

He studied her as she drank in the scene. "No," he answered, watching how her hair shone in the sunlight. He urged his horse forward, and Jo whipped her own horses into motion, already picturing her cabin and how she would decorate it.

The following weeks were filled with hours of hard work from dawn to dusk. Mason, Simms, and Adams camped in the pines of the foothills surrounding the valley, felling trees and trimming branches from the trunks all day long. Then they split the trunks into rails. Clint and Weston Rivers had the job of hauling wood, either to various sites for fencing, or to the site where the cabin was being built by Newt James and Jim Backus. All the men would work at building split-rail fencing once the cabin was done.

Jo spent part of her days hoeing up ground for a small garden and cooking for the men; but the major part of her time was spent mixing water and gravel into a thick mud to use for chinking the logs of her cabin, a chore she did mostly herself. James and Backus fitted the logs as closely as possible, but where the spaces between logs were too great, Jo shoved smaller branches, hewn from the bigger trees, stripped of green and piled near the cabin. The smaller branches took up more of the space, and then the chinking was added. Jo was careful to plug every crack and space she could find, determined to properly seal the little house that would have to keep her warm in the fierce Montana winters.

Newt fashioned sturdy shutters to be closed over the windows against wind and Indian attack. There would be only three windows, two in front and one off the bedroom of the two-room cabin. Jo could not afford glass for more than that, and Clint advised that too many windows only meant that many more entrances for intruders.

Rough, unbarked poles were pegged at the apex of the roof and at wall braces to form sturdy rafters, over which flat boards were nailed for roofing, the only lumber Jo had purchased at Virginia City. Jim Backus split pine into thin sections for wood shingles.

Within a month the cabin was finished enough to start the roofing, which Backus worked on while Newt and Weston Rivers began the task of building a stone fireplace at one end of the cabin. They had left an opening for the chimney, and now chinked stone against log, rigging a hoist with rope and boards on which to haul the heavy stones higher as the chimney rose. Clint, and the three men who had been cutting wood, stopped their cutting long enough to spend several days collecting good-size rocks, plentiful in the foothills, for the chimney, before returning to the task of cutting more timber for the fencing.

Jo was grateful for all the hard work. There was little time to talk alone with Clint, and by the end of the day everyone was too tired for much conversation. Sleep came easy. Jo's horses grazed happily in the valley, grateful to finally be through with the long journey, and getting fat on the sweet grass. Jo relished the sight of the horses grazing quietly, set against a backdrop of mountains and wildflowers. There was an occasional call of an eagle as one of the majestic birds left its nest high in the mountains and drifted over the valley. At night wolves howled to each other, but Jo had got used to the sound. Still, there were times when she wondered just how brave she would be once Clint and the other men left. On the entire journey she had managed to take care of herself most of the time; but she realized now that she had never truly been alone. In another month or two she would be. She didn't mind the others leaving, although she had come to call them friend and would miss them, just as she would always miss the people she traveled west with, and the mountain men with whom she had traveled to Montana.

But then there was Clint. Could she really bear to watch him ride away for good? And would he really do it? Of couse he would, as long as she insisted on it. And she *would* insist on it. After all, he was not the kind of man a

woman could really depend on for settling, not the way he
was now. There was always the whiskey to worry about.
When would he turn to it again? She wasn't even sure how
he really felt about her, if he cared about her for herself,
or if he was just reaching out to her the same as the
whores, trying to forget Millie Styles. How could a man
who had suffered what he had suffered ever be the same
again?

It brought a terrible pain to her chest to think of him
leaving; but he would go, she was sure, and she would let
him.

The cabin was sturdy, snuggled against a foothill over-
looking the valley. Jo got out of bed, a homemade struc-
ture with a rope spring on which she put her feather
mattress. She took a deep breath, smelling the wonderfully sweet smell of pine from the fresh-cut logs.

It was mid-August, and the fencing was almost com-
plete. Jo pulled on a robe and walked into the main room
to open the door and let in some fresh air. She loved the
summer weather here—none of the sultry humidity they
always got in Kansas in late summer. There weren't even
as many mosquitoes. The air was dry here, clear and fresh.

She stepped out onto the porch and smelled coffee.
Someone had already put some on over a fire outside. This
time of year it was cooler to cook outside, rather than
make a fire in the fireplace. Far across the valley she could
see the men working on the last section of fencing, a
zig-zag design of split rails nailed sturdily to posts by men
who were good at what they did. They had also built a
corral near the cabin, and a shed for the horses; and
nearby a softly squeaking windmill pulled water from the
depths of the ground into a stone well just a few yards
from the cabin, another accomplishment of Newt James
and Jim Backus.

Jo squinted, trying to see Clint across the valley. He
was usually easy to spot, taller than the other men and
broader, but she couldn't see him. Just a couple of days
were left now, before he rode out of her life. The summer
had gone by so quickly.

She walked down the steps to the fire and poured
herself some coffee, looking up at a brilliant blue sky,

breathing deeply of the cool morning air. This was where she belonged. She was more sure than ever. She had a new home, a place that was all her own. She could put the past behind her—the agony of losing Greg, the horror of watching her farm burn. She had a long letter ready for Anna, one she had been working on all summer so she could tell her sister everything about this place and about how her cabin was built. The only thing she didn't know how to explain was her feelings for Clint, for she didn't know herself just what they were.

She walked farther down the hill, watching the men work.

"Jo?"

The voice came from behind her. She turned to see Clint standing there. She reddened, pulling her robe closer, still wondering how much he remembered from the day he took her to the river, and from the night he had touched her breasts. "Clint. I thought you were with the others."

"I made an excuse to come down later."

"Excuse? Why?"

"I, uh, I wanted a little time alone—to say a few things to you—before I head out."

Her heart seemed to fall to her feet, and she hoped it didn't show in her eyes. "Oh." She swallowed. "I . . . guess it will be soon, won't it?"

"Tomorrow, I think."

She felt her heart quicken. "Tomorrow!" She had hoped for more notice. In a way she had hoped it would be never. "My goodness." She smiled to hide her disappointment. "I guess I hadn't realized how finished everything is."

He nodded, standing there looking almost nervous, fingering the hat he held in his hand.

"It's a good, sturdy cabin they built you. That fencing, it's good and strong, and it should keep the horses in, but just remember it won't keep wolves out. Keep the horses in the smaller corral near the cabin at night."

She nodded. "And close the shutters at night, keep the rifle loaded, keep the door bolted," she mocked, rolling her eyes. "I'm a prisoner in my own cabin at night."

He grinned a little, his dark eyes moving over her then as his smile faded. "I'll miss you, Jo."

She quickly looked away, sipping some of the coffee. "I'll miss you, too. I intend to . . . pay you something . . . although it could never be enough for all you've done."

He studied the cascading waves of her dark hair, gently blowing in a morning breeze. "You know I don't want any pay." He sighed deeply. "Jo, if things . . . were different . . . if I could get over certain things—"

"Don't say it."

"I have to say it. Damn it, Jo, I have feelings for you. What happened that one night . . . it wasn't all because of the whiskey. But I just . . . can't let myself care that much again."

"I understand," she answered, trying to sound matter-of-fact, strong, while all the time her heart pounded so hard it hurt. "It's the same for me," she told him. "The first thing I have to do is find Joline Masters, find out if she can really survive on her own, learn to depend on just herself. That's what it usually comes down to in the end, doesn't it? All we have is ourselves. We can't depend totally on other people, because death or some other circumstance could take them away at any time. We've both learned that." She turned and faced him, surprised at the look of love she caught in his eyes before he managed to force one of mere casual concern. She swallowed, trying to find her voice again. "We're damn good friends, though, aren't we, Clint?"

He smiled a little again, but his eyes looked watery. "Yeah, we're that, all right." Her heart ached at the loneliness she knew he suffered inside. He was trying to give her a casual good-bye, as though she were just another mountain man. "I'm proud to have known you, Jo. I, uh, didn't know helping you out that day of the raid would lead to all of this."

She stepped closer. "You're a good man, Clint Reeves. I never got the chance to tell you that day you told me about Millie, but it has haunted me, and I'm so sorry that had to happen. I hope . . . I hope you can learn to live with it some day . . . go on with your life . . . find love again."

He smiled nervously, walking over and pouring himself some coffee. "Men like me aren't meant for those things. I learned that lesson real quick."

"That isn't true, Clint. You'll find that out someday."

He rose. "Maybe."

Her eyes filled with tears. "Set the cup down, Clint. At least I get one good hug out of this, don't I? I feel like . . . like I'm saying good-bye to my brother, someone much closer than just a casual friend . . . or just a . . . guide. . . ." Her voice broke and he quickly set down the cup, walking closer and taking her into his arms. She reached her arms around his neck and he folded her against himself in a strong, wonderfully comforting embrace, so tight she could barely breathe.

"Jo," he whispered.

She turned her face up and their lips met in a kiss unlike any he had given her before. It wasn't the quick, sweet kiss he'd given her in the wagon; nor was it the almost brutal kiss he'd given her the night he had been drinking. It was the kiss of a man desperately in love, a man who desired the woman he held, worshipped her. He continued to hold her close with one hand, his other hand moving up to grasp at her hair while his lips parted her mouth hungrily in a hot, passionate, searching kiss. Jo returned the kiss with equal passion, every womanly need rudely awakened. She wanted a man again, and she wanted him to be Clint Reeves.

He stopped kissing her then, pressing her head against his chest. "I'll worry about you, Jo."

How she wished he would say "I love you." "I'll be all right," she answered aloud. "I will, Clint. I know it in my heart. This is what I want for now. Maybe some day . . . some day things will be different . . . and you'll come back . . . and we'll both be ready for something more. But if you never come back . . . I'll understand."

She could feel him trembling as he continued to hold her. "I'll send men out to check on you—men I know I can trust. And you need some feed for winter. I'll have a load sent to you."

"I'll give you some money. I've got barely enough left—"

"I'll help pay for it."

"Clint, I can't let you—"

"I want to. Please let me do it."

He slowly let go of her, glad there were other men around who could come back at any time. If not, he wasn't sure he'd be able to control himself, and he sensed it wouldn't take much to convince Joline Masters to let him come to her bed. But it wouldn't be fair to her, for he honestly wasn't sure if his feelings were real or if he was just reaching out to her out of his own loneliness.

"All right," she was saying. He let go of her and her face was flushed as she pulled her robe even closer around her. "I'll say it now, Clint, before someone comes back," she said, looking up at him. "I have feelings for you, too. You surely know that, or I never would have let you—" She put her fingers to her lips. "But it's the same for me. I need some time alone." Her eyes welled up again, and one tear slipped unwanted down her cheek. "God bless you, Clint. And thank you . . . for everything . . . everything."

Spirit ran up to her, wagging his tail. Jo quickly leaned down and picked him up, holding the dog close and running into the cabin. She realized in that moment that if Clint Reeves touched her once more, he would not sleep alone this last night. She couldn't let that happen. She closed the door, and sat down, hugging Spirit; her chest ached fiercely and the tears came then with almost the same grief as if Clint Reeves had died. Spirit licked at her tears and whined.

Chapter Seventeen

Jo put another piece of wood on the fire. The nights were already getting cold, and she was glad for all the wood Clint and the others had cut for her before heading back to Virginia City. The first few weeks after everyone left had been the loneliest she had ever experienced, even more lonely than when she had learned her father and Greg had been killed. At least then she had been near a town and among friends.

She knew the heart of her loneliness was the fact that Clint was gone, possibly forever. She realized his fear of loving could cause him to move on to another territory, to stay out of her life completely. Yet he had become so much a part of her life that sometimes she considered going to Virginia City and begging him to come back. But pride and common sense always convinced her it would be the most foolish thing she could do.

She walked back to the table, another piece of furniture the men had made for her. She began kneading some bread dough and glanced down at Spirit as she did so. He sat looking up at her with big brown eyes. "I don't have any scraps, if that's what you're after," she told the dog. "You might as well go lie down in the corner where you belong. You know you aren't supposed to be near the table."

The dog cocked its head, then got up and trotted off to lie on an old braided rug in the corner. Jo grinned, wondering how she could have stood the loneliness if not for the dog. At least she could talk to him, even though he couldn't answer. But he seemed to know what she was saying most of the time, and he was a comfort to have around.

She divided up the dough and dropped it into bread pans, then slid the pans into the little stone oven built into the side of the fireplace. She opened an iron door under the oven and added some wood to the fire there. She thought about Jim Backus as she closed the door, grateful for his inventive idea. Smoke from the fire under the oven was directed around the little iron enclosure through spaces between it and the rocks of the fireplace, pulled by air from the fireplace and sucked up the chimney. The extra iron insert created a very fine oven for baking.

Jo washed her hands and pulled on her bearskin coat. "Come on, Spirit." Woman and dog stepped outside, and Jo walked behind the cabin to pick the remaining squash from her garden, afraid the cold nights would freeze what was left and ruin it. She was glad now she had bought the seeds on her journey west, but she couldn't remember where she had been when she bought them. Was it Willow Bend? Rock Creek? Julesburg? What a long, adventurous journey it had been. She wondered if everyone from that wagon train had made it safely to Oregon. Oh, how she wished she could see them all again, especially Sarah.

She busied herself with the garden to put aside her loneliness. The garden had not turned out as good as planned. Most of the green beans didn't do well, and she had harvested only a few tomatoes. But she had cabbage and squash, as well as potatoes, carrots, and lima beans. She realized she would have to get used to a whole new way of farming in this land, and she would be doing a lot of watering by hand, since the summer rainfall was not as plentiful as in Kansas.

She put the squash into a basket and carried it around to the porch, taking in the view again. She never got tired of it. The horses grazed peacefully in the valley, and so far she had had no trouble with Indians, outlaws, or wolves, although the wolves howled nightly in the distant hills. The only thing she was out of was meat. She realized that even Spirit needed meat, and if she could shoot a deer or an elk, she could give the unusable parts to Spirit.

She went inside and set down the squash, then did some mending while the bread baked. As soon as it was done she set it out to cool, stoked the fire, and pulled on her winter moccasins and the bearskin coat. She picked up her rifle and shoved some extra ammunition into her coat pocket, then opened the door. Spirit hurried over to the door but she ordered him back.

"You stay inside. If I find anything, you'll just scare it off. A hunter, you aren't," she chided the dog. She closed the door and walked into the nearby forest of pines, the sound of Spirit's whining becoming dimmer as she walked farther away from the cabin. She made a point to keep the valley in sight to her right so that she could easily find her way back.

The cabin quickly disappeared from sight. Jo walked for several hundred yards, invigorated by the cool, clear air and the brilliant blue sky. She still could hardly believe this was all her own, and she prayed she would find a way to make enough money to buy more land next to her small spread. She really didn't have enough land if she was going to raise more horses, and she also needed to buy a good stud horse. She decided as she walked that she would plant a much bigger area next spring, and hope to have enough extra food to sell some in Virginia City.

She finally spotted deer tracks beside a little creek that flowed down from the mountains into the Ruby River. She guessed she was a half mile or more from her cabin now. She could see the valley, but she couldn't see her horses, and she could only pray everything was all right. She had to get some meat stored up for what she knew would be a long, cold winter, with days when she probably wouldn't even be able to leave the cabin. She had plenty of salt and lard for preserving, but she would smoke most of the meat in the little stone smokehouse Newt James had made for her. It had taken most of the money she had left to pay the men, but it had been worth it. She realized already she never would have survived here with just the wagon.

She moved behind some boulders and hunkered down to wait, hoping some deer would come along soon, since she hated being away from the cabin too long. The wind was at her face, coming across the valley from the west. Any animals that came to the stream would not catch her scent.

She thought about her hunting adventure with Clint, that first elk she had shot. Its head was mounted over her fireplace, just like Clint had said it would be. Frenchy had been the one to clean it out and stuff it, and it was one of her proudest possessions.

She put her head back against a rock and closed her eyes for a moment, remembering so many things: getting her horses back from Bart Kendall, the long journey west, the confrontations between Mrs. Boone and Clint, the way Clint had taken care of her attacker, the kiss—that first kiss in the wagon. She remembered the feel of Clint Reeve's big hand caressing her breast the night he had grabbed her in the woods, and most of all she remembered that last kiss. It would burn her mouth and her insides forever.

She thought about Anna, wishing she was here to talk to. What would Anna think of Clint Reeves? She hoped her sister would get the letter Jo had given Clint to find someone to take it to Columbia. She had no idea which, if any, of her letters had reached Anna. And now Columbia, even Lawrence, sounded so far, far away.

Still, whenever she had doubts about missing Anna or wondering if she should have left Lawrence, all she had to do was walk out and watch the sunrise lighting up the purple hues of the mountains to the west, and she knew she had done the right thing. This place had so quickly become home to her, and she knew that given the chance, she could not leave it now. Her thoughts were interrupted when she heard a rustling sound. She cautiously sat up straighter, peering over the top of the rocks to see two female elk drinking from the stream. She quietly raised her rifle and took aim at the biggest animal. The gun butted her shoulder as she squeezed the trigger, and both elk started running.

Jo came from behind the rocks and chased them a few yards downhill until the biggest one finally fell. She breathed a sigh of relief, having thought at first that she had missed. The animal was still alive, and it kicked wildly, its eyes wide with fear. Jo stepped closer and closed her eyes. "Thank you, spirit of the elk," she said softly. The little prayer made her feel better about putting the rifle to the animal's head and firing again to put it out of its misery.

She set the gun aside and took her butcher knife from a sheath she wore attached to the inside of her fur coat. The sun had brought an unusual warmth to the day, considering it was November, and she began to sweat as she started gutting the animal. She took off her bearskin coat and tossed it aside before continuing. It took nearly an hour to finish the bloody task, and she stood up then and walked back to the stream to wash her hands and arms. She hoped she would be strong enough to drag the carcass back to the cabin, realizing she should have brought a horse along for that job. But a horse might have scared away the elk.

She had turned to go back to tie a rope on the carcass when she heard a high-pitched, screaming growl unlike anything she had ever encountered before. It was no wolf. Her eyes moved toward the sound and she saw a mountain lion crouched in a tree above the carcass of the elk.

Jo's heart seemed to stop beating. At first she just stared at the mountain lion, trying to remember what Clint had said about them. *"Most of the time they're more afraid of you than you are of them,"* he had told her. Jo doubted at this moment that the statement was true. She had never known such fear. And with fresh meat at stake, she doubted the wild, hungry-looking cat would let its fear of one small woman preside over its desire for fresh meat.

She cursed herself for walking to the stream and leaving the rifle behind. She slowly rose, wondering if she could get to the rifle before the mountain lion could get to her. It growled again, crouched on a branch that didn't look strong enough to hold it. Jo's heart pounded wildly as she forced her legs to move, realizing her only chance was to get to the rifle. Anger and determination rose in her soul. That cat was not going to get the meat she so dearly needed. She thought of shouting at it, but she could not find her voice.

She kept her eyes on the menacing animal as she drew nearer to the rifle. She remembered Clint saying a cat would not pounce on a human unless it felt trapped.

Did this one feel trapped, seeing her approach? She suddenly wondered what on earth she would do out here if she were badly wounded.

"*God, help me,*" she prayed silently as she neared the gun. She slowly crouched and got hold of it, while the cat watched her, growling almost continuously, its tail still, its huge paws clasping the branch. Jo wondered at how quickly it had scented the meat. But then perhaps the animal had been nearby all along, planning to pounce on the two elk at the stream, now angry that a human had got to them first.

She felt the rifle in her hand and she slowly raised it. That final movement was all the cat needed. Jo had barely managed to cock the rifle and get it to her shoulder when the mountain lion leaped from the branch. Jo fired, and in the same instant the cat landed on her. She felt one paw rip down her left arm, catching the left side of her chest. She heard her own scream.

In the next moment the cat lay writhing on the ground. Jo cocked the rifle and took aim again, shooting it in the head. Her eyes teared with relief and with the aftereffects of the worst fear she had ever known. She staggered back from the dead animals and looked down at her arm. "Dear God," she muttered, watching blood pour down over her hand. It had all happened so fast she was nearly in shock, and she still felt no pain.

She knew it would be impossible for her to drag the elk back now. The first thing she had to do was clean her arm and get it bandaged. She could bring a horse back for the elk. She wondered if a person could eat mountain lion, and she decided she would at least clean the animal. If she didn't like the meat she could feed it to Spirit.

She picked up her coat and began walking back. The half mile she had covered seemed more like two miles as she made her way over the rugged ground, her heart still pounding wildly, her eyes burning with tears. By the time she reached the cabin she felt faint, and she knew it was because she had lost so much blood.

She went inside the cabin, closed the door, and stood against it, breathing deeply to gain control of herself. She could smell the fresh bread, and the squash still lay on the table. Somehow the sight and smells inside the cabin helped still her heart and brought back a sense of safety.

She walked to a cupboard where a pan sat empty, and ladled some water into it from a bucket on the countertop. She ripped off the rest of the torn sleeve of her dress and pulled down the left shoulder of the garment to expose the wounds. She winced at the sight and wondered if she would have scars.

Then she took a clean towel, dipped it in the water, and wrung it out, pressing it to the deep gashes left by the mountain lion's paws. She hunted around for a whiskey bottle and uncorked it, holding her arm over the pan while she poured whiskey into the wounds. She cried out at the stinging pain, but there was no one to hear. Spirit looked at her strangely, then proceeded to sniff around the floor, licking at blood that had dripped from her arm as she came in.

Jo poured more whiskey over the wound, then rummaged through the cupboard until she found some gauze. She used her chin to hold one end of the gauze against her arm, wrapping the rest tightly around the wound. She took more gauze and pressed it against the cut on her chest, which crossed over part of her left breast.

Her arm already ached, and she felt dizzy. She bolted the door and went to her bed to lie down, praying the horses would come to no harm while she slept. She didn't have the strength to go down and bring them up into the corral.

The room seemed to whirl when she put her head back, and the last thing she remembered was Spirit lying down on the rug beside her bed and looking up at her curiously.

When Jo awoke she realized the sun was already setting behind the mountains to the west.

"Oh, no!" she muttered. Darkness would soon settle over the valley, and the horses were still below. Not only that, but her elk carcass was still lying in the woods. "I've got to get that meat."

She sat up, gasping with pain, only then remembering her arm and why she had lain down. She looked down at the gauze and saw blood staining it. The wound ached fiercely and it hurt to bend her arm. She told herself she had to be strong, had to get the horses in and get her meat. She had determined to survive in this land. She couldn't let a wound defeat her after being here alone for only two months.

She forced herself to her feet and stood still a moment to get her bearings, then walked into the outer room and managed to pull on her coat. Spirit lay by the door, wanting to go outside.

"You poor thing," she told the dog. "How long have you been waiting for me to get up? You've been in this house all day." She grabbed her rifle and went outside, shivering as a cold wind hit her. She grabbed a bridle from where it hung on the porch and walked down to the valley, wanting nothing more than to get back into her warm bed. But she had said she could do this alone, and there was a job to get done.

With one hand she managed to get the bridle over Star's ears, and with great pain got the bit into the animal's mouth and buckled the bridle. She led the horse to a rock and mounted the Appaloosa without needing to use her bad arm. She rode the animal toward the other horses then, whistling and yelling, herding them up the hill and into the corral.

Jo felt hot in spite of the cold weather, and still lightheaded. She grabbed a rope and closed the gate to the corral, riding Star toward the place where she had left the elk. But already she could hear Spirit barking wildly, and distinguished the growl of wolves. Star whinnied and balked, and Jo got down, tying the horse and walking closer with her rifle. Tears stung her eyes when she noticed a pack of wolves ripping at both the mountain lion and the elk she had shot. Her day's work and her success at fending off the mountain lion had all been for nothing. There were far too many of the hungry animals for her to try to shoot them and send them away, and they had ripped so badly at the carcasses there was nothing left. Nor could she have trusted the meat after the wolves had got into it.

Three of the wolves turned and growled at her, eyeing her narrowly as though to warn her to stay away. For the moment Jo was almost glad for the raw meat. It was far too delicious a distraction to the wolves for them to waste their time on either her or Spirit. She backed away, calling to Spirit, who was yipping at the wolves and sparring with them, enjoying causing them irritation. But Jo knew what would happen to the dog if any of the wolves got serious.

She hurried back to Star, shouting at Spirit to come with her. The dog finally appeared and trotted beside Jo as she walked Star back to the cabin and put the animal into the corral. She decided that with the fresh meat to attract them, there should be no trouble from wolves tonight, and she knew that even if there was, she was in no condition to do much about it. She went back inside the cabin and Spirit followed. She closed and bolted the door, then sat down wearily in a homemade chair, realizing this truly was a land of survival of the fittest. In this land people were no different from the animals, all searching for ways to stay alive. She decided that next time she hunted she would take a horse along. If she had had one with her earlier, she could have dragged the carcass to the cabin and found a way to hang it high in a tree where no animals could get to it.

She put her head down on the table then and cried tears of anger: anger at herself for not being more aware of her surroundings when she shot the elk; anger at not taking a horse with her; anger at the wolves for taking what belonged to her; frustration that she would have to spend another day hunting. She wondered just when that would be. Her arm was much too sore to raise a rifle and shoot it quickly, which she had to be able to do if she was going to venture out alone into the woods again. She thought about Clint for a moment, realizing how badly his wound must have hurt him when he went searching for Millie, what pain he must have gone through trying to position and fire a rifle. Now that her arm hurt so badly, she realized how difficult it must have been for him to make his shots so accurate. She was glad he was not here to see what a mess she had made of her first hunting venture. Still, she could see the sly smile on his face, see the teasing look in his eyes.

Over the next two days a fever developed from Jo's

wound, and she wondered if she would die here alone, to be found as a bloated, smelly corpse in the spring. It was all she could do to get up and let Spirit outside and to keep a fire going. She subsisted on bread and raw squash, unable to find her desire or energy to cook, and eating only because she knew she had to keep up her strength.

Her arm hurt so badly she couldn't move it, and she knew it had to be infected. She kept pouring more whiskey on it and changing bandages, and she prayed her body would beat the infection, or she would die. Every day she watched for the telltale red streaks down her arm to her hand, or for the ugly dark color to come into her arm to tell her it was beyond help. She wondered if she would have to find a way to chop off her own arm, and she knew she would never be able to do it and didn't have the strength anyway.

She left the horses to graze in the corral, begging God not to let anything happen to them; begging Him to provide enough grass until she could get to the feed; and praying enough water would remain in the trough that the animals wouldn't die of thirst. The wind picked up and the cabin grew colder. She managed to keep putting wood on the fire, and each time, she whispered a thank-you to Clint and the other men who had chopped all the firewood.

After five days the pain in her arm lessened. It was easier to bend, and she still saw no sign of advanced infection. Her fever let up, and she wept with relief that she apparently was going to live. It took another five days to fully regain her strength, but during that time she managed to walk to the shed and carry buckets of feed to the horses with her good arm. On the seventh day she opened the corral gate and let the horses out to find more water and to graze, putting their care in God's hands. She couldn't keep them in the corral any longer, since she wasn't strong enough yet to carry water to them.

Twelve days after her attack she went out hunting again, this time taking Star with her. It took longer the second time to find meat, and this time it was a big deer, a buck. It wasn't nearly as much meat as she would have realized from the elk, but it was better than nothing. She decided she would cut it into very small pieces and eat it sparingly, since the skies were growing darker, and winter

could settle in at any time, burying her in the little cabin.
She smoked most of the meat, dried some of it, put
unusable parts into potato sacks and hung them high in
trees to let them freeze so they wouldn't attract the wolves.
She would lower them by rope and chop off what was
needed occasionally to feed to Spirit.

At night she studied her arm and chest in a small
mirror, wondering if Clint would think the scars were
ugly. She chided herself for caring what Clint would think,
realizing he would never see the scars anyway. Clint was
gone.

The skies grew more gray and the nights colder, and
Jo could see a long, lonely winter ahead. Her journey
west, those months with Clint, all seemed like such a long
time ago now. It was all just another part of her past, and
that was where she had to leave it—in the past. She had to
concentrate all her thoughts now strictly on survival.

A month after her attack her arm was still tender, the
claw marks still pink. But she knew she would be all right.
She decided she might go hunting one more time before a
blizzard came along to end her chances of going anywhere.
She had checked her rifle and reached for her coat when she
heard horses and the clattering of a wagon outside. She
kept hold of her rifle and went to a window, peeking
outside.

"Moose!" she shouted, going to the door.

Chapter Eighteen

Jo threw open the door to greet Moose Barkley, who was dismounting his horse. Behind him, driving a wagon, was Happy Strickland.

"Good to see you, ma'am," Moose greeted her, removing his hat. "We've brung you more feed and supplies. Sorry we didn't get here with it sooner, but they're short up at Virginia City and we had to wait for more to come in."

Jo grabbed Moose's hand and pulled him to the porch, overjoyed to have the company. "Come inside, both of you," she told them. "I thought maybe no one was coming. I suppose I could come into town, but I hate to leave the horses and the cabin for that long. I suppose there will be times when I'll have to."

Moose followed her inside, touched and surprised by her eager reception. Happy shook his head and chuckled. He climbed down from the wagon and followed Moose and Jo. Once inside, the men looked around the neat cabin, while Spirit barked and jumped at the men.

"My, my, look at this, Happy," Moose spoke up. "Ain't this a fine house, and fixed up so pretty." He turned his attention back to Jo. "Ma'am, you look real good. It's good to see you're doin' okay. We've all been worried about you." He put an arm around her shoulders and squeezed, showing his happiness for her, but Jo winced with pain. Moose let go of her and frowned, stepping back. "What is it, ma'am?"

She put a hand to her arm. "Nothing, really. I . . . had a little accident."

Moose frowned. "Accident? What kind of accident?"

Jo reddened slightly. "It's a little embarrassing, actually. It was a hunting accident."

"Now you tell us what happened," Happy insisted. "You healed? You need some doctorin'?"

Jo went to the cupboard and took out some bread and honey. "I'm fine now. I learned a good lesson, that's all. A mountain lion and I got into a tussle over the carcass of an elk I had just killed and cleaned."

"Mountain lion!" Happy looked her over as though she were a ghost. "You got attacked by a mountain lion?"

"Not exactly. He jumped me, but I shot him. His claws managed to dig into my arm as he was falling. I had some infection, but it's cleared up now. It's been over a month already since it happened, so it's obvious I'm not going to die."

Moose and Happy looked at each other. "Ma'am, that could have been real bad," Moose told her. "You sure as hell *could* have died. Clint ain't gonna like hearin' about that."

Jo plunked the bread on the table. "He *won't* hear about it, because the two of you aren't going to tell him. I want your promise, or I won't consider you my friends anymore. I don't want Clint to come running back here thinking I can't take care of myself. I said I could, and I'm doing it. I'm not going to let the first problem I have spoil all this for me."

Both men knew her temper and her determination. Moose fidgeted with his hat. "You sure you're all right?"

"I'm just fine. I got a deer a couple of weeks ago and I'm set for meat."

"Well, me and Moose spotted a whole herd of bighorn sheep on our way here. We've got more meat for you, if you want it," Happy told her.

Jo sighed deeply and sat down. "Oh, thank you, Happy. Yes, I'll admit I can use it. Sit down, both of you. I'm sorry I was so short, but everybody is just waiting for me to fail at this, and I'm not going to. The same thing could have happened to a man, couldn't it?"

Moose grinned a little. "I reckon it could have. Fact is, me and Happy have both had our share of accidents and close calls. So has every man who ever lived out here, and that includes Clint."

Jo began slicing some bread. "How is Clint?" she asked, trying to sound casual.

"All right, I reckon. Spent the first couple of weeks in a saloon after he left here."

Jo's heart fell at the words. He had gone back to drinking. She wondered if it was Jo Masters he was trying to forget this time rather than Millie Styles. Even so, she couldn't accept the drinking.

"He seems to do that occasionally," she said aloud.

"Me and Happy figure he's missin' you. He never said nothin', but we know he had a real likin' for you."

Jo blushed as she poured honey on some bread and handed it to Moose, then prepared another piece for Happy. "Clint doesn't know what he likes or doesn't like right now." She handed a piece of bread to Happy. "I'll get you some coffee." She went to the fireplace and picked up the coffee pot from the grid. "Where is Clint now?"

"Gone up into the mountains. He's been leadin' men to mining sites, takin' up supplies, things like that."

She poured some coffee. "Well, you can tell him I'm doing just fine. I got in some squash and potatoes and carrots. And with these new supplies, I'll be all right for the winter."

"No Indian problems? No strange men lurkin' around?"

"None." She put on a smile for them. "Spirit keeps me company. But it is good to see the both of you, to have humans to talk to again."

"We'll be the prettiest thing you ever saw come next spring," Happy told her. "You sure you want to go all winter up here alone?"

She rolled her eyes. "I'm sure. But I do appreciate your concern."

"There's quite a bit of feed out there," Moose told her. "Clint said we should set you up real good."

She turned away to set the coffee pot back, not wanting them to see the sudden tears in her eyes. She remembered Clint's promise before he left, and she knew he had paid for most of the feed. "I appreciate the supplies."

"Either us or some of the other men will check on you at times over the winter," Moose told her.

"Everyone except Clint," she thought.

"We respect what you're doin', ma'am," Moose added, "and we don't doubt your abilities. But it's a practice out here to check on each other. If you were a man, we'd do the same, so don't take it personal. Fact remains you'll be goin' for weeks at a time alone, so if you survive the winter, it will still be your doin', not ours. Hell, everybody in Virginia City is talkin' about the widow woman livin' along the Ruby River. Some call you brave, some call you crazy, most want you to make it."

Jo smiled. "I don't know about the brave. Crazy is probably the better description." She sipped some coffee and reached down to pet Spirit. "It's just that once I decided to do this, I couldn't go back on my decision. That's just the way I am. If I had turned back, I would have felt as though I had somehow failed at life—let myself down. When I think about Lawrence, I realize I could never go back there. But I don't like the thought of never seeing my sister again. I hope she'll be all right."

"Is she like you, ma'am?" Happy asked.

Jo stared at her coffee cup. "On the inside I guess we're a lot alike. But Anna is blond and blue-eyed; and she always liked pretty things, fancy dresses and such. She was never much for working the farm. But she's strong, and she can work hard when she has to. Her husband is a wealthy doctor from the South. If he survives the war, Anna will have a good life, and I wish her the best. I just hope her husband . . . comes back."

"You lost your man to the war, didn't you?" Moose asked.

Jo nodded. "Shiloh. You probably haven't heard about Shiloh."

Moose shrugged. "Out here anything east of the Bighorns and the Great Plains is like foreign country to us," he answered. "We don't pay a whole lot of attention to what's goin' on. We've got enough trouble handlin' the Indians out here. That's somethin' for you to remember.

Just because you ain't been bothered don't mean you won't be. I reckon you're safe for the winter. Indians tend to hole up in one place in winter, spend their time fixin' up their weapons and just tryin' to stay alive. It's spring and summer you've got to worry. You keep an eye out."

"I will." She looked at Moose. "What are you and the others doing? I thought you were going to prospect."

Moose shook his head. "I don't have the constitution for such things. I like to move around. We help deliver supplies, like Clint. But we'll be movin' on to other parts come spring. Some of the others will, too. But we'll always find somebody we can trust to come check on you."

"I'll probably need one or two men to stay on next year, if I can afford it," she answered. "I want to buy a good stud horse and start raising horses. Good horses will be needed up here. If I can raise some money through breeding and maybe planting enough vegetables to sell in Virginia City, I'll buy more land instead of waiting five years to claim more for free. I'll be needing the land for grazing."

Happy shook his head. "Well, I'll be. Already you're plannin' on expandin'. You'd better wait till you've got through a whole winter before you make them kind of plans."

"I have to think ahead, Happy. I'm tired of dwelling on the past. That's a lesson Clint hasn't learned yet."

"I expect not," Moose answered. "But then when a man like Clint decides he loves a woman enough to marry her, it's a pretty powerful love—not one he gets over very soon."

Jo's heart tightened. "No. I expect not." She took a deep breath and put on a smile, wondering if Clint Reeves could ever love her that way. "Well, how about some more bread and honey?"

"Sounds good to me," Happy answered with a grin. "That's mighty good bread."

Jo prepared some more for him, finding their company welcome, in spite of their uneducated rawness. It felt good to have people to talk to again. But she couldn't help the dull ache in her heart over the fact that Clint was not with them; and he had apparently turned to whiskey again

when he first got back to Virginia City. Was it because of
his feelings for her? If he had admitted to those feelings,
she would have considered giving up her dream of surviving here alone. She could have settled here as Clint Reeves's
wife. Together they could build their own little empire in
Montana. But Clint Reeves apparently didn't want any
part of settling again.

The wind blew out of the northwest with a driving
force that piled up snow at the rate of two feet a day. Each
day when Jo went out to check the horses in the shed, she
had to shovel her way again; so that by now the wall
of snow on either side of her pathway was becoming too
high for her to throw the snow onto. She could only
shovel it up against the sides, making her pathway even
more narrow.

Jo was almost grateful the snow had got so deep. The
walk between the walls of snow was at least out of the
wind, which howled constantly through the thick pines
and roared across the valley with a force she had seen only
in tornadoes. Clint and the others had been right. Winter
in Montana was long and cruel. She had taken advice
Moose Barkley had given her and tied a rope from the
house to the horse shed and the well.

"You think it can't happen, ma'am, but many a person
has died out here not ten feet from their house. They
couldn't see it because of the wind and snow."

Jo was not about to ignore the advice of men experienced with mountain winters. Twice a day she donned
every piece of warm clothing she owned and made her
way first to the well, then carried two buckets of water to
the horse shed, returning for two more, with Spirit trotting faithfully behind her. The horses had to be watered
daily. She couldn't fill the troughs and leave them because
within twenty minutes the water would freeze. She would
clean out the stalls as best she could, and she kept straw
piled deep for warmth.

Never had she been more grateful than now for the
care Newt and Jim and the others had taken in building
her cabin and the shed. The horse shed was built against
an earthen hill on its north side, so that winter winds

could not penetrate the building. A stone wall was built
against the western side to protect it from western winds,
and the roof was doubly reinforced to help keep it from
collapsing under heavy snows. The shed doors had a good,
tight fit, and when Jo closed them even in the daytime,
she had to use a lantern to see inside.

"How are you doing, Sundance?" She patted the buckskin gelding's rear. "You poor babies, out here in the cold.
I'll put out more straw for you."

Sundance whinnied as though to say thank-you. Jo
climbed a wooden ladder into the loft above and dragged a
bag of oats to the opening in the floor, throwing it down.
It was too heavy for her to lift down. She descended the
ladder and opened the bag, dragging it to each stall and
shoveling some of the oats into feed troughs, giving each
horse a pet and talking to each one as she fed them.

The animals were all she had for company, and she
wondered if she could have kept her sanity through the
winter without them. There were times when the droning
of the wind seemed more than she could bear. It was a
sound that never let up, night or day, a constant roaring
and moaning, an endless whistle through the pines and a
continuous reminder that she was totally alone.

She had known loneliness before, but never of this
magnitude. She noticed that she hadn't even heard wolves
howling lately. Was it because she was so buried in snow
that all sound was gone? Or did wolves hibernate in winter, like some other animals? It seemed amazing that any
wild animals survived this kind of weather. In spite of
their danger, she actually missed hearing the howl of the
wolf. It at least let her know there was other life in these
mountains besides herself and her horses.

She finished feeding and watering the horses, then
blew out the lantern and went out, making sure the doors
were tightly closed. She pulled the hood of her bearskin
coat back over her head and was almost grateful it would
be next to impossible for anyone to come visiting in this
weather. Not only did it mean she needn't worry about
outlaws or Indians, but in spite of how big a fire she built
inside the cabin, it was never warm enough to take off her
clothes to bathe. She was sure she must be a sorry sight,

bundled in several layers of clothes and not bothering to try looking feminine. She had no beets left for making rouge, and she had no milk at all to make buttermilk for a skin bleach. She had only a little rosewater left for refreshing the skin, and a tiny bit of cream; but she didn't want to use either until she could bathe and dress normally. She liked to make soap from honey, which was milder to the skin than lye soap. But for now the honey had to be reserved as a treasured food, in case she ran out. The same went for corn starch, which she sometimes used to hide a shiny nose but now needed for cooking purposes.

Out here a person had to be practical. There was no room for vanity and luxuries. Survival was the first word of the day. As far as washing without freezing, the best she could do was wash by hand. She couldn't even wash her hair as often as she would like, since a wet head made her shiver, and she was frightened of getting sick like she had on the journey west. There would be no one to help her now. There would be no Sarah to nurse her, no Clint to take her to a stream and cool her fever.

She thought of that day at the oddest moments. It seemed strange to have a male friend to whom she had felt so close; to feel so comfortable with a man who was not her own husband that it had not upset her when he saw her naked. Surely all of that meant something. Did Clint ever give her much thought anymore? She worried about him, wondered where he might be in this horrible weather.

She made her way back to the cabin, which was also dark even in daytime because snow was piled so high that it covered her windows. She went inside and spotted another mouse skittering across the floor, disappearing behind a cupboard. She had long got over being frightened by the pests, since killing them had become a daily task. She realized that even mice had to find someplace to go in this kind of cold, but she did not appreciate their choosing her cabin for warmth.

She threw more wood on the fire while Spirit chased after another mouse. Then she picked up the heavy fireplace shovel and pulled out a chair, sitting down to wait and struggling against tears of loneliness and despair.

"Don't you dare cry, Jo Masters," she thought. *"You*

said you'd make it out here, and you will." She spotted
another mouse. "You stay," she told Spirit.

The dog cocked its head and watched eagerly as Jo sat
still and waited for the mouse to come closer. She whacked
it then with the shovel, and Spirit yipped excitedly.

"Well, maybe I shouldn't hate these things so much,"
she told the dog as he came over and picked up the
mouse. "What else would I feed you if not for the mice?"

Spirit trotted to the door and looked up at her, the
mouse hanging out of his mouth. He had quickly learned
through scoldings that he was not to eat mice inside the
house. Jo opened the door for him and he scampered out
between the rocklike walls of snow.

Jo closed the doors and sighed, another wave of tears
wanting to come. Again she refused to cry. She decided
she had to look at the good side of everything. The deep
snows made all her chores harder, which made the days go
faster. Spare time was spent killing mice and inventing
ways to make food go farther. The mice provided food for
Spirit. And, after all, she was still alive and well, and if she
was careful, she would not starve before spring.

She marched into her bedroom and took out paper
and a quill pen, coming back into the main room to sit
down by the fire and start another letter to Anna. It would
be spring before she could send it, but it would surely be
an entertaining letter to read when she finished explaining
what it was like to spend a winter alone in the mountains
of Montana.

"Dear Anna," she wrote. "I could never fully describe the winters here in Montana. The wind coming out of the mountains howls and screams as though
alive. I am buried here under several feet of snow,
and it is a frightening feeling, as though I am lost to
the world, or perhaps the only person left alive in
it."

She had written only a few words when she caught some
movement from the corner of her eye and saw a mouse
sitting on its hind legs in front of the fireplace, as though
to warm itself. Suddenly her battle against the small in-

truders seemed amusing and she laughed aloud, deciding to let the mouse sit there.

"I'll get you another time," she said quietly.

"Even the mice find it hard to keep warm in this weather," she wrote. "And they have apparently decided my cabin is a fine place to find shelter. Pesty as they are, I find myself sometimes feeling sorry for them."

Spring came with a myriad of sights and sounds. The singing of early birds was mixed with the distant thunder of snowslides in the mountains. Some were so violent that Jo actually felt the cabin shake. The cabin itself creaked and groaned as snow around it melted, exposing logs that had been sheltered by the snow for months. Dry air and sunshine hitting the logs caused cracking and constant creaking sounds.

The river in the valley swelled far beyond its banks, and again Jo was grateful for good advice. If she had built her cabin in the valley, she would have been flooded out. After all these months, she was still experiencing reminders of Clint's expertise, and his warm concern for her.

When Jo went outside to care for the horses, she walked through ankle-deep slop, and she wondered if the walls of snow would ever melt all the way so that she could see grass again. What a welcome sight that would be! She was getting low on feed, and the horses were much too fat for their own good. They needed to be turned out to pasture in the valley. Outside she could hear the rushing waters of the Ruby, and she began to hear the howl of the wolves again. She decided that as soon as she was able she would go hunting, since her meat supply was running low.

Every day the snow seemed to go down another foot, and the constant sound of wind was replaced by the continuous dripping of water. It ran from the rooftop, splashed onto porch railings, ran off into puddles on the ground. It dripped from trees and ran down mountainsides in swollen streams and waterfalls. The valley became a small lake, but as the waters receded, lush green grass appeared, a wonderfully relaxing sight to eyes nearly blinded from seeing nothing but white snow for months. Jo wondered if

she had developed new, permanent wrinkles from squint-
ing so much.

In late April the weather warmed enough that Jo opened
her door to let in fresh air. She began a rigorous cleaning
of her cabin, hoping the spring air would get rid of the
smoky smell that had accumulated over the winter months.
And she decided that as soon as the cabin was cleaned, she
would have her first full, hot bath since last autumn.

She wiped cupboards, cleaned out the fireplace, swept
down the entire cabin. She scrubbed clothes and blankets
and hung them outside over fences and railings; and after
that first day of more continuous work than she had done
all winter, she was too weary to haul in water for a bath.
She slept soundly and spent the next day cleaning out the
horse shed. She turned the horses out into the corral near
the house, and they pranced and whinnied, and seemed to
enjoy the spring as much as Jo.

"It's time to get that fat off you," she told Star. "You'll
be no good to me all fat and lazy like you are now." She
smiled and closed the gate, and Spirit ran around inside
the corral, dodging hooves. They all reminded her of
children playing. The thought brought an unexpected wave
of depression, as she suddenly realized that in a way her
animals took the place of the children she wanted deep
inside. She often wished she had got pregnant before Greg
went away. At least then she would have his child with
her.

She sighed and reminded herself she had come here
to put the past behind her. She marched back to the
cabin, drinking in the sights and sounds of spring. Wildflowers were springing up everywhere, as though to pro-
fess there really was life after death. Jo picked a few of
them and put them into a vase, setting it on her table. She
hauled in water and heated it over the fireplace. She
dragged out the big, wooden tub in which she would
bathe, and she laid out a yellow dress, something more
feminine than the dull homespun she had worn for months.

Today she would bathe and feel like a woman. For
some reason she had the need to feel her femininity, to
remind herself she was still a woman, in spite of having
lived like a man—sometimes more like an animal—through
the winter. She dug out some old pieces of material and

her sewing box, deciding that later that evening she would start a quilt. For a day or two she would be a woman, before pulling on more practical clothes and going hunting again. Before long she would have to go into Virginia City. She was in desperate need of supplies, and she couldn't count on Moose and the others to keep bringing her things. For all she knew some of them had left for other places, including Clint. The thought made her chest hurt, but she told herself she must face the truth. Clint Reeves had been gone for months. He wasn't coming back. As soon as the snow was melted enough that a journey to Virginia City wouldn't be dangerous, she would go.

She poured the hot water into the tub and tested it. It was too hot to get into, so she picked up two buckets to go back to the well and get some water to cool off the bath. She had been so lost in thought that she only then realized the horses in the corral behind the house had been whinnying nervously. She had been thinking it was just playful cavorting, but she realized it was a more frightened sound.

It was then she heard the deep roar. It was not the growl of a mountain lion. It was not like anything she had ever heard. Her eyes widened and she set down her buckets near the door. She could hear Spirit barking wildly now, heard the roar again, this time closer. She grabbed her rifle and stepped outside, moving cautiously to the end of the porch to peer around the side of the cabin.

Her eyes widened and her breath caught in her throat. A huge grizzly was backing up toward the porch, moving on its hind legs and growling at Spirit. The dog continued to yap at the bear and the bear growled back, its hair standing on end, the hump between its shoulders seeming to rise.

The bear was as tall as the corner of the cabin, which sat on two feet of rock under which Jo stored her vegetables. She guessed the animal to be at least ten feet high, and at the moment its paws looked a mile wide. She could see its huge claws, and for a moment she stood frozen in place. Another roar brought her out of her stupor, and she cocked her rifle.

"No, Spirit, stay away!" she screamed at the dog.

Her voice seemed to surprise the bear. It turned and looked at her. Jo remembered someone telling her how vicious a bear could be in the springtime when it was just out of hibernation. *"And grizzlies are vicious any time of year. They're just one mean bear,"* Clint had said.

Suddenly the grizzly was on all fours and lumbering toward the cabin. Jo stood her ground and took careful aim, hoping her rifle was powerful enough to kill such a big animal. She fired, and the bear roared again and stumbled, landing half on the porch and half on the ground. Jo backed away and cocked the rifle again. The bear growled at her and rose up, pulling itself onto the porch. It came at Jo, trying to rise on its hind legs. But the porch roof hung too low for the bear to stand to its full height. Just as it came back down on all fours, Jo fired again, then managed to get inside the cabin just in time to shut and bolt the door before the bear could reach her.

Jo closed her eyes and struggled with terror as the bear landed against the door, growling and scratching. She quickly ran around closing the shutters to the windows, while the bear kept on clawing and pushing at the door. She felt every nerve end come alive as she stared at the door, clinging to the rifle and ready to fire again. She wondered how many more bullets it would take to kill the animal if it broke through the door.

The scratching and growling, mixed with whinnying and barking, seemed to go on for hours; but it was only perhaps thirty minutes before things suddenly grew quiet outside. Jo waited, tears of fear in her eyes. She wondered if the bear was playing a trick on her, ready to pounce on her the moment she opened the door. She slowly went to a window and opened the shutters, peering out. She could see a big paw lying still on the porch. She went to the door then and very slowly raised the heavy piece of wood that she used to bolt it. She opened it a crack, and another wave of terror swept through her at the sight of the great, hulking mass of bear lying in front of the door. She stood still a moment, realizing finally that the animal was not moving and did not appear to be breathing. She opened the door a little more, then all the way.

Slowly she lowered her rifle and breathed a deep sigh of relief. The bear was dead. Spirit stood below the steps of the porch, wagging his tail.

"You could have been killed!" she scolded. "One of

these days you're going to get it from some animal, you stupid dog!" She set the rifle aside. "Or I will," she muttered.

She kneeled down beside the bear, studying its huge claws. "Well, I guess I don't have to go hunting," she told Spirit. "But this isn't going to be an easy project."

She looked over at her tub of hot water. The bath would have to wait. So would being feminine again. She had a bear to skin and clean, and from the size of this one, it would take two or three days to do the job right.

Chapter Nineteen

It was early May and a very warm day when Jo heard the shouts of men and the clatter of wagons. She looked up from her garden to see several wagons passing through the valley. They stopped and shouted something about good grass, and Jo hurried to a tree where her rifle stood. Her grazing land was too precious to her own horses to allow others to come through and use it. These men had apparently just opened her fence and came on through as though they owned the place. But they didn't own it. It belonged to Joline Masters!

She ran to Sundance and mounted up. She had got into the habit of keeping one horse saddled every day in case she needed it, alternating horses so they all had a turn at grazing. Spirit was already far ahead of her, dashing down the hill to bark and growl at the intruders. Jo urged Sundance toward the wagons, and several men looked up from unhitching their teams to see a pretty woman with long, dark hair and wielding a rifle riding toward them. It was such an unexpected sight that their only reaction at first was to stare.

"What the hell?" one of them muttered.

"Are we dreamin', or what?" another put in. "Who'd ever expect to see somethin' like that way out here?"

Jo rode closer, halting Sundance and leveling her rifle. "You men are making camp on private property. I need this grazing land, so just move on."

A big, bearded man in soiled clothes removed his hat and stepped a little closer, holding out his arms in an indication he meant her no harm; but Jo kept her rifle steady.

"Ma'am, we figured out here grass is grass."

"You must have seen the fence. It surrounds my whole place."

"Yours?"

"Yes. I'm Joline Masters, and this is my spread."

The man looked past her and up toward the cabin. He noticed a bearskin stretched out between two trees in front of the cabin. "Just you? Alone?"

"Don't get any ideas. I've killed several men, including Indians; and I've killed a mountain lion, elk, and deer, and a grizzly. I'm not afraid to use this gun."

A couple of the others removed their hats, one man scratching his head and looking up at the bearskin. Jo eyed them all carefully. There were six of them, and they all looked tired and dirty and a little thin.

The apparent leader grinned. "Well, ma'am, I'm Rubin Keats. We've come up from Fort Bridger, and we've been through a damned mess tryin' to get up to Virginia City to the gold fields. Your place lies right smack in our pathway. When you've come as far as we have, you don't feel much like goin' way out around a fence. We took down a section, but we put it back after we passed through. We just figured it would be okay to go on through here. We won't bother nothin'—but our animals need to graze. We got socked with a freak snowstorm farther back in the mountains, and they're pretty wore out and hungry."

Jo glanced at their horses. The two wagons they had brought were pulled by mules. All the animals looked bony.

"We've been pushin' these same animals all the way from Missouri," another told her. "We're all done with our volunteer service in the war—had our fill and decided to come west."

Jo lowered her rifle slightly. She realized she had almost forgotten about the war. "What is it like back east?" she asked. "Isn't the war over yet?"

The men looked at each other. "Ma'am, ain't there a telegraph up to Virginia City? Don't you get no news?"

Jo kept her finger over the trigger of her rifle. "I haven't been to Virginia City since I first got here about a year ago."

Their eyes widened. "You mean you've been right here, all alone, all that time?" one man asked her.

"This is my place. I claimed it under the Homestead Act. I can't leave it untended. But I suppose I'll have to soon. I need supplies. What about the war? And whose side did you men fight on?"

They all looked at each other again. Feelings ran high back east regarding North and South. This woman was holding a rifle on them and apparently knew how to use it. Their answer could mean their lives.

"We, uh, we fought on the Union side, ma'am," Keats said cautiously. "When we got out, the South was pretty much beat. Sherman had took Atlanta, and we heard he intended to sweep the whole South from there. The war could even be over by now. Indians cut the telegraph lines to Fort Bridger, so we don't know for sure. We heard there's been more Indian trouble up these parts. Ain't you had any problems with Indians?"

"Not so far." She lowered her rifle a little. They seemed like decent men. She could understand their reason for taking a shortcut through her land. "Were any of you . . . at Shiloh?"

"No, ma'am," one answered.

She lowered her rifle more. "My husband was killed there. I came here last year from Kansas." She looked over their horses and mules once more.

"Sorry about your husband, ma'am," one of them told her.

She met Keats's eyes again. "All right. You can camp here, but for a fee. I've got to get some use of my land. I'll have a look at your horses. If they look healthy, except for being so worn out, I'll consider selling you fresh ones." A lump rose in her throat at the thought of getting rid of any of her horses, which had become like friends to her. But again she told herself she must be practical. Here was a chance to make some money and also build her herd. She had to learn not to get so attached to her animals if she was going to go into the business of raising and trading horses. She realized she could take these sorry-looking horses and mules, fatten them up on her own grass, and sell or trade them to others who came through needing rested, healthy animals.

"If you men would like a woman-cooked meal, I can provide one—fifty cents each. It will cost you three dollars each to graze your animals here; you can trade a couple of your horses for my healthier ones—ten dollars plus your worn-out horse. I can't sell more than two right now. I only have five, but I intend to buy more in Virginia City later this summer; and I'll hire some men to round up mustangs for me. Any of you who will go into Virginia City and bring back some supplies I need will be reimbursed for what he pays for his meals, as well as get paid for the supplies. I can't give you the money first because I don't know if I can trust you ever to return. If you come back with the goods, you'll get paid then."

Keats grinned. "Ma'am, you seem like a woman who means business."

"I am. I'll not let strangers spoil what I've done here, and I can't afford to let your animals eat up my grass for nothing. I have to buy feed for my own animals."

Keats looked at the other men. "What do you say, boys? You willin' to fork up the money?"

"We can pay to have the animals graze here a day or two if it means gettin' a woman-cooked meal," one of them answered.

Jo kept her rifle in her right hand while she picked up the reins. She backed Sundance a little. "There is a well up there by the windmill. You can wash there and set up camp. I'll fix you something to eat and bring it out to you." She eyed all of them again and saw only friendly looks; some seemed more surprised and amused than anything else. "I'm sorry I don't seem overly friendly. Out here a woman has to be extra careful. I don't want to see any of you carrying a rifle or wearing a gun when he comes near the house. Is that clear?"

"Oh, yes, ma'am," they answered almost in unison.

Jo turned Sundance, riding farther out into the valley and whistling and calling out to her horses to herd them back closer to the house.

"Did you ever see anything like that?" one of the men spoke up.

"Never in my life," another put in.

"I don't have any desire to cross her the wrong way," Keats said.

"That's some woman," another answered. "Woman like that deserves too much respect for a man to do her wrong." They all watched as Jo herded her horses up the hill and into a corral near the cabin.

"Let's get busy," Keats ordered then. "We've got to unhitch and unload these horses and mules. I'm anxious to taste some home cookin'."

The others gladly obeyed.

Jo counted her money: thirty dollars in grazing fees and for meals; twenty dollars and three horses and a mule, in exchange for Red Lady and Shag. She went into the bedroom and moved aside a chest of drawers Newt James had made for her, shoving the money into a hole in a hollow log behind the dresser. It was a good hiding place, for she knew she had to be aware of the danger of outlaws.

She felt like dancing. The unexpected encounter with Rubin Keats and his men had given her an idea that could quickly net her enough money to expand her land holdings. She got out the can of red paint Clint had used the year before to mark her borders, and retrieved a board from a pile left over from roofing; then she proceeded to paint a sign. HORSES FOR SALE OR TRADE. ALSO MULES. GOOD GRAZING LAND. VEGETABLES FOR SALE.

She went outside and loaded the sign onto her wagon, then added more lumber, wire, and a hammer and nails. She hitched Sundance to the wagon and drove to the southern end of her land, Spirit running behind her. She propped the sign against the fence and nailed it in place. Then she took the hammer and began prying loose a section of fence, after which she took the boards from the wagon and hammered them together to make a gate. She had watched Newt James do this and knew how gates were built and hung. And she was determined she could do chores like this without always needing a man.

After two hours of work, with her blouse drenched in sweat, she managed to pull up the gate, drag it to the opening in the fence, and lean it against the two fenceposts that bordered the opening. Spirit lay in the grass, stretched out and sleeping in the sun, totally unconcerned about his mistress's labor.

The gate was slightly longer than the opening, but good enough as far as Jo was concerned. She wired one end to a fence post so it could swing open, then wrapped wire around a horizontal post on the other side, as well as a board on the gate. She took a smaller piece of wood and slid it through the two sections of wire so that it created a boltlike lock.

She stood back and surveyed her work. The gate hung slightly crooked, but it would serve its purpose. She smiled at her accomplishment and walked over to pet Sundance.

"I'm sorry about Red Lady and Shag, but I've got to do things I won't like in order to survive out here, Sundance. But I don't think I'll ever sell you."

The horse whinnied and nuzzled her. Jo opened her gate and led horse and wagon through, while Spirit quickly up and followed. She closed and locked the gate, thinking about her money again. She decided the first thing she had to do was go to Virginia City and buy a good stud horse, as well as hire some men to round up some mustangs for her. She was advertising horses for sale. Now she had to find some. The horses traded for Red Lady and Shag were a start, but they needed some fattening up before they could be resold. At least she had ended up with more animals than she had before.

She urged Sundance into a slow trot, gazing at the beautiful wildflowers and distant mountains as they headed back to the cabin. "It's going to be a good summer," she said to the horse. "Mr. Keats will return soon with food and supplies, and maybe we'll get more customers soon, boy." The buckskin gelding snorted and nodded its head as though he understood. "By the end of summer maybe I can buy a stud horse. Last summer Luke Adams said he saw some wild horses over that other rise. If I can find some men to round them up for me, I'll have a real ranch started. I guess I'll have to stop naming my animals and quit getting so attached to them. I'll miss Shag and Red Lady." She sighed deeply. "But by next year I can probably buy more land." She wondered if spending the winter alone had made her a little crazy. She was talking to Sundance as though he were a person. "Before you know it I'll be hiring permanent hands. Maybe I should start branding my horses."

She thought about what kind of brand she could use. She would have to decide before she went to Virginia City. She would have to visit the blacksmith there and have the branding iron made.

"How about a big *J*, Sundance?" she said aloud. "Wouldn't you like my initial displayed on your rump?"

The horse whinnied and shook its mane, and Jo laughed.

"I wouldn't want something burned into my rump either, boy, but it only hurts for a second. That's what they say, anyway. All it will do is burn your hair off." She sighed as she pulled the wagon up in front of the cabin. "I just wish I could talk to Clint about all of this," she said quietly, gazing out at the valley. "I wish he could see how well I survived the winter." She climbed down from the wagon. "I wonder where he is, Sundance. Think we'll ever see him again?"

The horse nuzzled her again and she patted its neck. "Right now I guess you're my best friend, aren't you?"

Spirit barked and leaped up at her jealously, and Jo picked him up, laughing away tears that had come to her eyes. "I'm sorry, Spirit. *You're* my best friend, aren't you?"

She put the dog down and began unhitching Sundance, praying Keats would keep his promise and return with the supplies she needed.

The blackjack dealer dealt Clint another card and he turned it over, showing a queen to go with his ace. The dealer matched his five dollars and Clint left all ten lying on the table while the dealer whisked out another round of cards, turning over a king for herself. Her full breasts billowed above the ruffles of her low-cut, purple dress, and she watched the handsome Clint Reeves with hungry eyes, while a man plunked out "The Battle Cry of Freedom."

> "The Union forever!
> Hurrah! Boys, hurrah!"

A group of men started singing the Unionist patriotic song, celebrating the fact that the Civil War was over. The news was just about all anyone was talking about, and the streets were wild, a sea of mud created by so many men on horseback riding up and down and shooting off their guns, churning up the spring muck and mixing it with horse dung. Lee had officially surrendered at a place called Appomattox Court House in Virginia, after General Sherman swept the south, destroying everything in sight.

> "Down with the traitor,
> Up with the star.
> For we're marching to the field, boys,
> Going to the fight,
> Shouting the battle cry of freedom."

Clint wondered how long it would take for the west to fill up with people from the South; destitute, broken people who would want to take advantage of the Homestead Act and start over. Jo was lucky to have grabbed up such a good piece of land when she did. But there was going to be more Indian trouble as soon as more people started coming west. It was a sure bet. He tried to tell himself not to worry about Jo; he had managed to stay up in the mountains the whole winter trying to forget her. But it hadn't worked as well as he had hoped, and now he reasoned the best thing to do was to leave Montana, get as far away as he could.

He won another hand at blackjack and scooped up his money, going to the bar and ordering another beer. All the talk of the war being over brought Jo more forcefully to mind. She had lost a husband in that war. Had it been worth it? Word was that hundreds of thousands of lives had been lost. Jo ought to know it was over, he thought. It might relieve her worry over Anna and her sister's husband. And it would probably make her feel at least a little better to know the Union had been the victor. If her husband had to die, at least he died for the winning side. But he supposed there was no real winner in the bloody conflict, and hard feelings were going to run high for a long time to come.

The saloon was a din of voices and singing, laughter and piano playing. Whores danced with hungry men, and the bar was packed, everyone talking at once.

"She wasn't like no woman I ever met," he overheard a man nearby saying to another. "All alone out there, tryin' to build a ranch. And I got a feelin' she can do it. She ain't one to mess with, I'll tell you."

"How can one woman run a ranch way out there in the wilderness?" the man asked. "There's Indians and outlaws and wild animals. . . ."

"Hell, she killed herself a mountain lion and a grizzly. And she wasn't lyin' about it, neither. I saw the grizzly's hide, stretched out to dry. And she's got an elk's head hangin' over her fireplace."

Clint was all ears. He moved a little closer to hear better above the rest of the noise.

"Name's Joline Masters. I'm takin' back some supplies for her 'cause she don't want to leave her place untended."

"She must look like a horse and be muscled as a man," the other man replied.

Several others laughed at the remark.

"That's the best part," the bearded man told them. "She's the prettiest thing this side of the Missouri River—a lot prettier than these painted dogs in town here." There was more laughter. "And she can cook, too, damned good. She'd make one hell of a wife for any man, but I got a feelin' she ain't lookin' for no husband. Seems to be real happy bein' on her own. Said she lost her husband in the war and come out here from Kansas."

"Whooee! I'd like to get a look at her," one man put in.

"Well, she's one respectable lady," the bearded man told him. "So don't go gettin' no ideas. She's a fine woman, but she ain't afraid to use that rifle of hers. Claims to have already killed a couple men with it, includin' Indians."

"I know who you're talkin' about," a man farther down the bar shouted. "She come into Virginia City last spring. We've all been waitin' to hear how she was doin'. For my part, I'm glad to know she's doin' okay."

"That she is," the bearded man answered.

Clint finished his beer and moved closer to the bearded man, putting down some money. "Buy you another drink?"

The man looked up at him. "Sure! Why not?" He put out his hand. "Keats is the name, Rubin Keats."

They shook hands and Clint ordered the drinks. "Clint Reeves. I overheard you talking about Jo Masters. I'm the guide that brought her out last year. You say she's doing all right?"

"Looks like it to me. And she's a fair horse trader, too. Squeezed me out of three good mares and a mule in return for only two of her horses. Charged me and my men to use her grass, and charged us for meals. She's a smart woman—took us pretty good. I'm takin' some supplies back to her tomorrow."

Clint drank some of his beer. "How about letting me do it? I haven't seen Jo in months. I'm heading down to Fort Laramie soon anyway. I can take the supplies on my way."

"Well, I reckon that would be all right. I'm anxious to get to prospectin', anyway. If that doesn't work out, I aim to settle out here under the Homestead Act, like Mrs. Masters did."

"Well, I won't see her again once I leave this time. Figured I'd go see how she's doing for myself before I go. She give you a list or something?"

"Right here." Keats took a piece of paper from the pocket of his calico shirt. " 'Course I wouldn't mind doin' it myself, mind you, just to get another look at the woman and taste some more of her cookin'. Besides, she's supposed to reimburse me for my meal money if I bring the supplies."

"How much would that be?"

"One dollar. She charged us fifty cents a meal, and we ate two meals each—six of us. She made herself six dollars just off that."

Clint grinned, picturing Jo boldly telling the men if

they wanted to eat they would have to pay. "I'm not surprised," he said aloud. "You say she shot a grizzly?"

"Sure did." Keats shook his head. "Had the skin hangin' out to dry. Big one, too. And she said she killed a mountain lion, only it clawed her pretty good on one arm."

Clint lost his smile. "That's too bad." The old protective feelings returned again, mixed with painful desires he had hoped would go away. He wondered if he was playing a dangerous game by going to see her again. He knew it was probably a stupid decision, but he felt that he was the one who should tell her about the war being over; and, after all, he was leaving Montana for good. He finished his beer and slapped a dollar's worth of silver on the bar. "Here's what Jo owed you. That's for being good enough to take the supplies. But I'd like to do it myself."

Keats laughed and shook his head. "Go right ahead, Reeves. I don't mind makin' a dollar for doin' nothin'."

Clint nodded, adjusted his hat, and went out into the street. He looked over Jo's list and headed for a supply store.

Jo rose and brushed her hair, then pulled on a dress. She was getting a little worried now about Keats coming back with her supplies, as he had been gone six days now. She stirred the fire and set a pot of coffee on, then sat down at the table to do more figuring before going outside and do her chores.

A whole wagon train had come through a few days earlier, with men on horseback besides. She had sold Patch, one of her Appaloosas, for forty dollars and two mares, plus collected forty dollars in grazing fees. With the fifty dollars she had made off Keats's men, she now had a hundred and thirty dollars, plus sixty dollars she already had left from the year before. That was almost enough to buy another hundred and sixty acres. But she warned herself she had supplies to pay for, and she needed a lot more horses than those she had now. She also needed a good stud horse, and she needed men to round up mustangs for her and break them.

But she had a good start. She studied the figures, her

heart pounding excitedly at the prospect of truly becoming a big rancher all on her own. The long, lonely winter didn't seem so terrible now. She had learned many lessons this first year, and she would use that knowledge to get through another year. She decided she could only take a day at a time and thank God for what she had this day. Today she had sunshine and warmth, and she would go out and hoe her freshly planted garden.

She pulled on a sunbonnet and picked up her rifle, opening the door to go outside. It was only then she saw them; at least twenty painted warriors, sitting quietly on horseback in front of the cabin.

Chapter Twenty

Jo froze in place. Spirit bounded outside, barking at the Indians, and Jo realized they had snuck up so quietly that even the dog had not known they were there until now. She gripped her rifle, suddenly envisioning poor Millie Styles being tortured by the Sioux. Were these Sioux? Her breath came in such short gasps she felt dizzy as she backed toward the door. She grasped the rifle in both hands then, summoning all her courage.

"What do you want?" she asked, wondering where the voice came from. Surely it wasn't she speaking out to these Indians.

One of them rode forward, a powerful-looking man of perhaps thirty. "Where is your man?" he asked.

Jo swallowed, for once wishing she had one. "There is no man. I'm here alone."

"When will he come back?"

"He won't. I told you. There *is* no man. This is my place."

The Indian scowled and glanced around. "Yours? Alone?"

Jo slowly nodded. The Indian turned to the others and said something in their own tongue. Several of them grinned and a few laughed. The one who had ridden closer looked back at Jo.

"It is amusing how you lie," he told her. "But why would you?"

"I'm not lying. My name is Joline Masters, and I've

settled here. This is my place. I might add that I have
done you no harm, so if you wish to harm me, you will do
so without honor, unless your people consider it bravery
to attack one lone woman." She took a deep breath for
more courage. "I know how to use this rifle. I might not
get all of you, but I'll get a few. I'll die fighting, just like
you and your warriors would do."

The Indian's eyebrows shot up in amusement. He
glanced at her rifle, her size. "I have never faced a white
woman who did not run in fear, screaming and calling out
filthy names."

"Why should I run? You would only catch me. I
prefer not to die like a coward."

He frowned, then said something to his men again. A
few grinned, others just stared at her strangely.

"The bearskin," their leader said then. "There must
be a man here. Someone killed the great bear. To kill the
grizzly is most honorable. It wins a warrior great respect."

Jo stood a little straighter. "*I* killed the bear. And
when I took his meat, I thanked his spirit."

He watched her a moment, then said something to the
others, keeping his eyes on Jo. They all muttered in
their own tongue and nodded. One held up his lance and
let out a warcry that startled Jo, and she backed away
farther, not realizing it was a shout of honor.

"I am called Yellow Wolf," the Indian told Jo. "I
learned the white man's tongue from men of black robes
who come to teach us about the white man's God."

"Priests?"

"When I was a boy, they tried to teach me white
man's ways. But I soon saw the foolishness of their way—
much waste—broken promises—no respect for the land
and the animals. I think perhaps you are not like them.
You thanked the bear spirit, like the Indian would do."

"Oh, thank you for teaching me that, Clint," Jo thought.
"It's only right," she answered. "When an animal offers its
life so that we can eat, we should be thankful."

Yellow Wolf nodded, his dark eyes drilling into her.
An old warrior behind him grunted something and Yellow
Wolf answered. Jo kept hold of her rifle, ready to shoot if
necessary. She prayed that showing bravery, and knowing
the tiny bit she knew about Indian ways, would help her.

"Red Beaver says to tell you we are looking for food."
He glanced over at her corral. "And horses. It was a hard
winter. The white man kills our game, and the snow
buried the grass. Many of our horses died of cold and
hunger, as did many of our old people and children.
Others have hungry bellies, but so many white men have
invaded our land, we cannot travel to all the places we
once roamed to get food. And people—like you—who
settle here . . . we chase them out—kill them—burn their
buildings and take what we need to survive. It is right.
This is our land."

"One woman alone can't mean you any harm. How
much can one woman eat? I hunt very little. My meat lasts
very long. I have been here many months now. I survived
the terrible winter alone. Killing me won't begin to solve
your problems with the white men. Why not make friends
with those who are willing to be your friend? I am willing.
I can give you food—plenty of bear meat. I smoked it. I
don't have much else. I'm waiting for some supplies myself. Like you, my food is scarce now because of the long
winter. Just please don't take my horses. I ask you as one
honorable person to another. I have only a few, and I need
them for survival. I sell them . . . trade them."

Four of the warriors were already circling the corral.
Jo forced herself not to be distracted by them. She kept
her eyes on Yellow Wolf, seeing behind the paint and
defiance a tiny light of compassion. She tried not to think
about the horror story of what had happened to Clint's
family. Every situation had to be different. Surely there
were ways to deal with these people, just as they had dealt
with the band of Sioux on their journey west.

"How much meat?"

"All you want, especially if you're telling the truth
about hungry children."

He frowned in surprise. "Why should you care about
our children?"

"I am a woman. All women care about children."

"You have children?"

"No. My man was killed in the white man's war back
east before we had any children."

He looked her over as though she were a wasted
woman. "You are a strange white woman. But I think you

are honorable. Set aside your rifle, and we will not harm you."

She moved her eyes to look at all of them then. Those around the corral were inside it now, laughing and talking, sizing up her horses as though they owned the place. She looked back at Yellow Wolf. "What about my horses? I would never steal yours. Why would you steal mine?"

"I have not said that we would. For now you have no choice, white woman. Put down the rifle so that I know you speak the truth about honor, and so that I know the bravery you show in your eyes is real."

Jo swallowed, realizing she didn't have a chance either way. Her only real chance of surviving this was to win their respect. She slowly lowered the rifle, then leaned it against the side of the house.

"I can . . . make you some apple pie," she said then, amazed the thought had come into her head and thinking how silly it sounded.

Yellow Wolf frowned again. "Pie? What is this . . . pie?"

"It's . . . it's very good. I have some dried apples in storage below the cabin. Have you ever eaten apples?"

"Once, I think, at a white man's fort. They were sour."

"Apple pie isn't sour." She forced a smile. "Let me make some for you. And you can have some of your men look in the smokehouse and take whatever meat you need."

Yellow Wolf turned and said something to Red Beaver, who, Jo realized, was actually the leader while Yellow Wolf was simply a spokesman. He looked back at Jo.

"Red Beaver says he will try this . . . apple pie. Where is it?"

Jo took another deep breath, hoping she could get through all of this without fainting. "I have to make it. It will take a while. There is plenty of water—" She pointed to the windmill. "There . . . in the well. I would give you vegetables, but it's too early. Nothing has grown yet. The smokehouse is over there, beyond the corral. And I have oats. I need them very badly, but the grass is high now. If some of your horses are weak, take a bag or two of oats for them. The feed is in the loft over the horse shed, around the side of the hill behind the house."

Yellow Wolf raised one leg and brought it around in front of him, sliding off his horse. He shouted an order to the others, then walked closer to Jo, rifle in hand. "I will think about the things you have offered, and your wish about the horses. We will see if there is really meat in the smokehouse. You make your apple pie and we will see if it is sour."

Jo nodded, struggling not to be totally overwhelmed with terror as he drew closer. He sported an array of weapons, and what looked like a human scalp hanging from his belt. His face was painted in red and black, and in spite of his fierce look, he was handsome and clean; beaded rawhide strips were wound into a braid at the side of his head.

"What . . . what kind of Indian are you? I . . . don't know about Indians."

He stood a little taller. "We are Sioux—Oglala. Surely you have heard of Red Cloud." He tossed his hair proudly, and Jo felt her heart sinking.

"Yes," she answered. "He is a great leader. White men fear his name."

Yellow Wolf grinned a little. "*Ai*. And for good reason."

Jo thought of Clint. "Yes . . . for good reason." She struggled not to show contempt or hatred, something she was sure would light the fuse to the present volatile situation. She told herself there was surely a way to reach this one called Yellow Wolf. "I . . . have to go to the side of the house to go into the fruit cellar and get the apples."

"I will follow you."

Jo turned. "As you wish." She walked on rubbery legs to the door to the fruit cellar, remembering that day back in Lawrence when she hid in a similar cellar inside the pickle barrel. There was no chance for hiding now. At least Quantrill's men had made so much noise she had heard them coming. Now she knew what Clint meant about being quiet as an Indian.

She opened the cellar doors and went below, feeling Yellow Wolf behind her. She picked up a small basket of apples and turned, but he stood in her way, looking even more threatening in the near darkness.

"I have been with white women," he told her with a

sneer. "I pay the white man back for what he does to *our* women."

Jo felt a tingling dread move up her spine. "You have been with white women who were afraid of you. I am not afraid," she said boldly, hoping she sounded truthful. "I am offering you food and friendship. And I have killed the great bear. I am a friend to the Indian. I have shown you this. Come up into my house and I will show you something that will prove this to you."

She moved past him, intuition telling her she must not show an ounce of weakness. To her relief he let her go and followed her up the steps and into the house. Outside, the others had dismounted and were lounging around; some looked at the bearskin, others inspected the smokehouse, while more jumped on the backs of her horses and rode them, using no riding gear of any kind. Jo went inside, setting the apples on the table and stoking up the fire under the stone oven. When she turned she noticed Yellow Wolf staring at the elk's head hanging over the fireplace.

"That was the first animal I ever killed," she told him. "I kept his head like a trophy . . . like you would take a scalp or a skin, or perhaps use the claws of a bear to make a necklace."

His dark eyes watched her then as she picked up a paring knife and turned back to the table. She saw the doubtful look in his eyes when he saw the knife. She held it up.

"I have to peel the apples first."

He nodded. "You said you had something to show me."

She set the knife down for a moment, wondering what gruesome ways these warriors had of torturing someone. She walked into her bedroom and Yellow Wolf followed. Jo opened a drawer of her chest and took out the necklace the young Sioux woman had given her back on the trail west. She held it out to Yellow Wolf.

"From a woman of your own people," she said. "It was a gift. I gave her some ribbons, and I admired her baby." She thought about showing him the belt Old Woman had given her, but she vaguely remembered something about the Shoshone and Sioux being enemies. She was

afraid that showing Yellow Wolf the belt would rile him.
He studied the necklace a moment, then met her eyes.

"You are a strange white woman."

"You told me that. Others have also said so. But I
don't care what they think. This is a beautiful land, and
I want to live here. I have no man to take care of me, so I
take care of myself. It's the way I want it. I hope you will
let me live here in peace. If you do, you will always be
welcome here, and I will always be willing to share my
meat if your children are starving."

He only frowned, his dark eyes unreadable. He handed
her the necklace and stepped back. Jo put away the necklace and walked into the outer room, picking up the knife
and beginning to peel the apples. She was so shaken that
every muscle ached, her back and shoulders so tense it
was difficult to work. Yellow Wolf watched her every
move. Old Red Beaver came inside the cabin, looked
around and grumbled something before leaving again.

"He says in here he is shut away from the Great Spirit
and the sun. We do not like hard walls and something
above that shuts out the light and the air. A man's spirit
cannot be free inside these man-made caves."

Jo sliced some of the apples. "You have your way of
living. We have ours."

Four more warriors came inside then, walking up to
the table and watching Jo. She prayed they wouldn't see
her hands shaking. She knew she had made some kind of
sense to Yellow Wolf. But how much control did he have
over these others? One of them came around beside Jo
and she turned to face him boldly. He took out a knife,
and Jo stood frozen, waiting for him to plunge it into her
belly. She felt him slip it close to her side. Then she felt a
jerk as he ripped it through the ties of her apron.

He held up the apron and let out a war whoop,
running outside with it. Jo grasped the table for a moment
while she waited for the feeling to come back into her
legs. A second man came around behind her. Yellow Wolf
barked something to him. The man answered angrily, then
left. The other two moved away from the table and began
looking around the cabin, pointing to the elk's head and
walking around inspecting things, picking up utensils, rugs,

curtains. One picked up a braided rug and walked out with it, while another left carrying two pans.

Jo decided not to argue about it. She just kept peeling and slicing the apples until she had enough for two pies. She quickly threw together some lard, flour, and water, wondering if she had ever made pie dough this quickly before. She rolled out the dough with Yellow Wolf still watching. She put it into pie pans, then mixed some sugar and cinnamon with the apples and poured them into the pie shells. She topped the pies and poked them with a fork, then placed them into the stone oven.

"It will take . . . about an hour," she told Yellow Wolf. "Do you know how long that is?"

"I know. Come and sit."

"I . . . have to clean up this mess."

"Sit!"

She met his eyes, her pride and anger beginning to overtake her fear. "I intend to clean up the mess on my table first," she answered, forcing her voice to be strong. To her relief Yellow Wolf did nothing as she cleaned off the flour and piled apple cores into a bowl. She carried them to Yellow Wolf. "Would you like to feed these to your horses? Horses love apples."

He took the bowl from her, looking almost like a wounded animal. "My men will thank you," he told her, walking out with the apples. Jo frowned, wondering if her persistent courage and her bold answer a moment earlier had changed something.

She walked to the door and watched as the warriors eagerly fed their mounts, laughing and talking among themselves. Yellow Wolf spoke to them, then pointed to Jo. The two men who had taken her utensils and rug, and the man who had cut off her apron, walked up to her and handed back the items. Jo took them, totally surprised at the gesture. She glanced at Yellow Wolf, who actually looked somewhat sheepish.

Jo decided it was best to ask no questions, but just to be grateful she had somehow impressed them and was still alive and untouched. But her mind still raced with visions of horror, and she decided she would never make it through the next hour if she didn't keep busy. She quickly got out her sewing basket and began working on her quilt, struggling to remain calm as she tried to thread a needle.

Outside she could hear the Indians whooping and laughing, apparently still riding her horses. She prayed they didn't have any whiskey with them. She knew what whiskey could do to a normally rational man. But these men were far from rational and predictable even when sober. She knew they could change their minds about her at any moment, and she wished she understood Indians better. She was acting on pure instinct, along with the tiny bit she knew about Indians from what Clint had told her.

The next hour seemed more like a whole day. She had finished several pieces of quilt by the time the pies were done. She took them out and set them on the table, praying the painted men outside would like them. She went to the door and saw some of the men carrying smoked meat to the parfleches on their mounts. Yellow Wolf was sitting by the well. When Jo walked outside he got up and approached her.

"They take only some of the meat," he told her. "They leave some for you, because you have killed the bear and have shown no fear; and because you offered the food with kind eyes. Your heart is true, white woman. You do not need to fear us—now, or if we should return."

Jo didn't know whether to believe him or not. "Thank you," she told Yellow Wolf. "You are an honorable man. Some have told me an Indian cannot be trusted. But I have always believed there are men of all colors who can be trusted, and those who cannot. Such things cannot be judged by the color of our skin. You have seen today that some whites can also be trusted."

A hint of bitterness came into his eyes. "Some. But not many, especially not the ones who come to us representing the Great White Father in the land of the rising sun. They have lied to us too many times."

Jo held his eyes. "Yes. I suppose they have. But I know a white man who is a good man, a man who can be trusted, a man who understands and respects your people and even called some of them friend. Yet your people burned his home and murdered his wife and son."

He frowned. "I am told that back in the land of the rising sun, where white men fight, sometimes brother

murders brother, son murders father. Who is to say why
men do these things? In times of war, hunger, great
sorrow, times when pride and revenge must be satisfied,
men do strange things."

"Yes," she answered, watching him carefully. "It is
sad, isn't it?"

Jo saw intelligence in his eyes, and she decided he
would be a good man to know, if they were not such
worlds apart. "The pies are done," she told him. "I'll cut
them as soon as they have cooled a little." She turned and
started toward the house, then looked back at Yellow
Wolf. "What about my horses?"

His dark eyes were difficult to fathom. He seemed to
be weighing his thoughts. "We will not take the horses,"
he finally answered.

Jo gave him a slight smile. "Thank you." She went
back to the house, wondering how things might have gone
if she had shot at them or screamed and acted terrified.
She glanced at her rifle on the way inside, but she left it
standing against the wall. It was then she noticed some of
the others circling Spirit, one of them holding a knife in
his teeth.

Jo ran right into the circle of warriors, grabbing Spirit
up into her arms. "No!" she shouted. "Don't you kill my
dog!"

They all looked at her curiously. Jo looked over at
Yellow Wolf. "I gave you meat!" she shouted at him.
"Don't let them kill my dog. Take more meat if you want.
This dog is a pet. He's not for food!"

Spirit licked at her neck, as Yellow Wolf came closer.
He suddenly grinned. "The dog is special to you?"

"Yes." She remembered the incident with the other
Sioux. "Our spirits are like one," she told him, remembering what the other Sioux warrior had told her months
before. She hugged Spirit close as Yellow Wolf told the
others something in their own tongue. They backed away,
and the one with the knife took it from his mouth and
shoved it back into its sheath.

Jo quickly walked to the house with Spirit, carrying
him to the bedroom and closing him inside. "God help
me," she whispered as she closed the door against the

dog's barking. "Please keep giving me courage until they're gone."

She half stumbled to the pies and began cutting them. Then she carried them out onto the porch, and each warrior took a piece in his hands and ate voraciously, licking palms and fingers and grinning with pleasure. Jo prayed that once they were finished, they would be on their way.

Clint halted his train of packhorses, listening. He heard laughter in the distance, and what sounded like a war whoop. Old, trained instincts told him something was wrong, and his heart quickened. Indians? What were they doing to Jo!

He climbed down from his horse and tied it, then took his rifle from its boot and moved the rest of the way down the pine-covered hill on foot toward Jo's cabin. He cursed himself the whole way for not getting here sooner, but he had taken time to pack a few extras Jo didn't have on her list, wanting to bring her some special things she could remember him by. He had even brought her a milk cow.

He made his way quietly toward the cabin, approaching from behind. He could see its roof now, as well as several Indian ponies outside. "My God!" he whispered. Horror moved through him as old memories returned. He quickly moved farther around the south side of the cabin, the end that was exposed. He crouched behind a large boulder and removed his hat, carefully raising his head up to see.

Jo was standing on the porch of the cabin, and at least fifteen warriors stood nearby, all of them eating something and talking among themselves. Clint raised his rifle, taking careful aim, filled with a horrible dread that he would have to relive the past and shoot Jo instead of the Indians.

It was then he noticed Jo smile. One of the Indians walked to his horse and retrieved a blanket, handing it to Jo. Clint watched carefully. It appeared as though Jo was fine, and the Indians were apparently giving her a gift of the blanket. He noticed the bearskin stretched out between two trees and he grinned a little. So, the story about the bear was true. And it looked as though she had

found a way to make friends of the warriors below. How
she had done it, he couldn't imagine.

He kept a close eye on them as they all mounted up.
One of them rode forward then, ramming a lance into the
ground in front of the cabin. "As long as the lance is here,"
Clint could hear the Indian saying, "no harm will come to
you from our people, white woman. Your eyes are true,
and your heart is good."

The warriors mounted up and rode around the cabin
and corrals for a few minutes, whooping and yipping before they finally rode off. Clint watched Jo sink to the
porch steps and put her head in her hands. He rose,
walking down the hill toward the cabin.

"Jo?" he called out. "You all right?"

Jo looked up, tears on her face. She slowly rose.
"Clint!" she whispered.

Chapter Twenty-one

Jo could not imagine a more welcome sight at that moment than Clint Reeves. She rose as he came toward her, and in the next moment his arms were around her. All the pent-up terror and strain of the morning, along with relief at seeing a familiar face, welled up into a torrent of tears she had wanted to shed for months. She clung to him, for the moment not caring about appearing weak. Sometimes it felt better to cry. She often found renewed strength after crying, and she wondered why she had held it in for so long.

"My God, Jo. Did they hurt you? Touch you?"

She only cried for several more minutes before pulling away slightly to take a handkerchief from the pocket of her dress. "I'm all right. This is ridiculous. I'm . . . so sorry." She blew her nose. "I just . . . oh, Clint, I've killed a mountain lion, and faced a grizzly and strange men; but this was the most frightening experience of all. You have . . . no idea how good it is to see you . . . at this moment." She sank back down onto the steps of the porch.

"I met Rubin Keats in town and told him I'd bring back the supplies myself. I was just coming over the hill when I spotted the Indian ponies." He sat down beside her, putting an arm around her shoulder. "I hid and watched, ready to shoot. But it looked like you were all right, and I saw they were leaving. I figured it would be pretty stupid to start shooting."

She nodded. "I don't know how, but . . . I think I

269

managed to befriend them. One of them . . . spoke English. He's called Yellow Wolf. I remembered what you said . . . about showing no fear . . . and showing respect. I pretended I wasn't afraid of them . . . stood my ground . . . asked Yellow Wolf if he considered attacking a lone woman an act of bravery, something like that."

Clint grinned, all the old feelings flooding back unwanted. "I should have known," he told her. "If anybody can talk her way around wild Indians, you can." He glanced at the bearskin. "They were probably impressed by that skin. That would mean a lot as far as their respect for you."

"I guess. I showed them the necklace that Sioux woman gave me. I offered them meat from my smokehouse, and I baked apple pie for them."

He grinned. "Apple pie? Where did you come up with that one?"

"I don't know. All I know is it apparently worked. Yellow Wolf tried to buffalo me a couple of times, but I talked right back to him. All of a sudden he acted almost like a scolded little boy." She blew her nose again, taking deep breaths to regain her composure.

Clint rubbed her shoulders. "Don't you know that inside the tipi an Indian woman is boss? Indian men don't like being scolded by their women. They usually get the hell out. And most of them have to put up with mothers-in-law living with them. That's something few men enjoy."

Jo smiled then and wiped her eyes. "Yellow Wolf left the lance. He said as long as it's here none of his people will harm me. Apparently I did something right."

He grinned, almost absently stroking her hair. "And here I worried about you all winter. How stupid of me. The place looks great. You've even got that bearskin hanging out there. And Keats tells me you're a hard-nosed businesswoman already making money off newcomers."

She shrugged, suddenly aware of his strong hand stroking her hair. "I'm just thinking of ways to survive, that's all. We don't always do things by choice. Sometimes simple necessity forces us to do things we would never normally think to do." She faced him then, and he seemed more handsome than ever. "Why did you come in Keats's place?"

He took his hand away then, sighing deeply. He rested his arms on his knees and looked out at the bearskin. "I wanted to see you once more. I'm, uh, going away, maybe for good."

Jo's heart fell painfully.

"I'm heading for Fort Laramie. I figure with the war over and all—"

"The war is over?"

He nodded and met her eyes. "I just heard in town. Lee has surrendered. But I guess the South is in pretty bad shape. I figure a lot of ravaged, homeless people are going to head west to start all over. That means there will be more Indian trouble. I already talked with a colonel and another good scout who were up this way—promised my services. The army needs scouts pretty bad now. They'll be sending more soldiers out now that the war is over."

Jo stared at her lap. "So, it's really over," she said quietly. "I wonder how Anna is—if her husband will make it home." She sighed. "I wish there was a way to let Greg and my father know—to tell them they didn't . . . die in vain. But sometimes I wonder if that's true. It's all . . . such a waste, isn't it, Clint?"

"Seems that way."

She met his eyes again. "I missed you, thought about you often. And now you're . . . going away for good." Her eyes filled with tears again and she quickly rose, realizing that even though he had been gone many months, nothing had changed between them. She almost wished he hadn't come back at all. "I need to freshen up," she told him. "I'm sorry . . . about all the tears. What a way to greet you."

Clint rose beside her, his eyes full of pain when he looked at her. "I missed you, too, Jo," he said softly. Their eyes held for a moment before he turned away. "I'll go get the supplies. I left the packhorses tied farther up the hill." He put on a grin. "I brought you a milk cow—a gift from me."

Her face lit up with gratitude. "Milk! Oh, that sounds wonderful!"

He smiled softly. "Don't worry about the tears. Not

many women would have handled that situation the way you did. One gunshot, a hint of panic, one insult, and things might have been different." His gaze traveled over her. "You never cease to amaze me."

Clint went off to get the supplies, and Jo walked on rubbery legs into the cabin. This time her weakness was not from fear of Indians, but fear of Clint Reeves—fear of being close to him, fear of touching him. What an odd time for him to appear. She struggled against the old feelings, realizing that the ordeal with the Indians had left her vulnerable, emotional, more aware of her loneliness.

She quickly washed her face, then went into the bedroom to get her brush. She changed into a clean dress, the one she wore being soiled from baking pies and from the perspiration of pure terror. She sprinkled on some rosewater, then suddenly wondered why she was worried about her appearance. She scowled at herself in the mirror and marched into the outer room to put on some coffee, smiling again at the sound of Spirit barking at Clint and Clint's voice talking back to the dog.

Clint called out to Jo then, and she went to the door to see six packhorses loaded down, trailed by a cow. She laughed and walked out to greet the cow. "Oh, Clint, you shouldn't have. I can't afford her." Spirit sniffed around the cow, then ran off to chase a mouse he spotted skittering toward the horse shed.

Clint walked closer to Jo, catching the scent of rosewater. "I told you she's a gift from me."

She looked up at him. "You've already done enough for me."

He studied the beautiful face that needed no coloring to enhance its charm. How fresh and clean she looked compared to the whores in Virginia City. "I can never do enough for you." He quickly looked away. "You must have chores. What can I do for you while you unload these things?"

"Clint, you don't have to—"

"I want to. I figured it would be better if you unloaded so you can see everything that's here. The only thing I couldn't bring enough of was feed for the horses, but you won't need that so much till winter nears again. You'll need your wagon for that. If you want, I can talk to a few men in town who I know can be trusted and send them out to see what you need, maybe to watch the place while you go into town. You can't just leave it, Jo. Indians or outlaws would strip you clean."

"I know. I want to hire some men anyway, to round up some mustangs for me and break them. I've decided to go into the business of raising and selling horses to newcomers. I intend to make enough this summer alone to buy more land."

He grinned. "Well, knowing you, you'll do it." He pushed back his hat, suddenly looking nervous. Jo noticed he was clean shaven and she caught the scent of leather and man. "So, what can I do while you unload?"

She put her hands on her hips. "Well, if you insist, you can turn the horses out into the valley and clean out the stalls in the horse shed. And you can get me my first bucket of milk. Do you know how to milk a cow?"

He grinned. "Yes, ma'am." He walked toward the cow and began untying her. "I had to learn. Jeff was a big milk-drinker. He used to—" He stopped short and met her eyes, his own filled with the old agony. "You have a bucket?"

"I'll get one." She went inside and came back out with a wooden bucket, handing it to him. "I've got coffee on, and I have some bread baked fresh yesterday. I'm afraid the pie is all gone, thanks to Yellow Wolf and his friends."

Clint laughed lightly. "Thank God for apple pie."

Jo felt her own gratefulness. "Yes." She turned back toward the house, then looked at him again. "Whenever you're through, we'll sit down and talk. It's been a long time, Clint."

He nodded. "Yeah, a long time."

He led the cow away, and Jo watched after him, wishing she fully understood all her feelings. She began unpacking the supplies, finding surprises like perfume and delicate soaps and creams. There was a new frying pan, a set of flatware, a lovely yellow crocheted blanket, and material for making new dresses. A lump rose in her throat as she realized he had deliberately thrown in things she had not written on her list, presents from a man showing his love the only way he knew how for the moment. Would he really go away forever?

The thought brought a terrible ache to her chest. Surely it was all just a ruse, just another effort at fighting his real feelings. She could see those feelings in his eyes; and although she had been certain she was over her own feelings for him, it had taken only that first sight of him today to make it all come flooding back into her heart and soul.

Clint was here again, and she had missed him more than she realized. His presence brought a certain warmth and happiness to her being that had been missing all winter. She felt a new energy as she unloaded supplies and put things away: flour, sugar, salt, spices, jellies, lard, yeast. And now she would have milk!

She piled things inside, deciding to find a place for them later. The morning had been too traumatic for her to worry about it now. She poured herself some coffee and went to the doorway, gazing out at the mountains across the valley, a sight she never grew tired of watching. What a strange day it had been—the visit from the Indians, and now Clint. The lonely boredom of winter was suddenly replaced by sunshine and warmth and visitors, a welcome relief, even if some of the visitors had been Sioux Indians. She breathed deeply, still calming her heart from the terror of the morning.

"Surely God is with me," she thought. "He's brought me this far." She closed her eyes. "Now if He would only help me know what to do about Clint Reeves."

Over an hour had passed, and Clint finally headed toward the cabin carrying the wooden bucket. "Here's your milk," he told her. "The stalls are raked out and the horses are having a good time in the valley."

Jo took the bucket from him. "I can't wait to drink some!" she said happily.

Clint followed her inside. "You know, you're going to have to build another horse shed if you're going to round up mustangs."

"I know. I'll find a way."

His eyes surveyed her while her back was to him. "That

I don't doubt." A painful surge of desire moved through him, and he cursed himself for ever deciding to do this. "All the supplies unloaded?"

"Yes. I tied all the horses. You can turn them out in the valley if you want." She hesitated and turned to look at him. "I mean, you'll be staying a little while, won't you?"

Aching needs pressed deep inside him. "Sure."

She smiled. "Good." She walked closer. "Clint, how can I thank you for all the extras? You can be so thoughtful—the perfumes, the creams, the material. I didn't order any of those things."

Their eyes held. "I know. I just figured after a long winter up here alone, it would be nice for you to have them. You're too beautiful to just let yourself go, even if you're out here alone most of the time." He pulled at a piece of her hair. "You might be as handy as any man, but don't forget you *are* a woman, Jo Masters, and I mean that in the most respectful sense. I'm not saying you can't do this because you're a woman. You've already proven otherwise."

She reddened, still holding his gaze. "Thank you." She had a terrible desire at that moment to feel his kiss again, the kind of kiss he had given her before he had left the last time. Did he remember that kiss? She turned away, walking to the fireplace and removing the coffee pot. "Sit down. I'll pour you some coffee. We can put milk in it if we want. Oh, that sounds so good to me. I'll love you forever for bringing me that cow."

He just watched her for a moment, seeing her redden at the remark. He knew she loved him, just the same as he loved her. Why was it so hard to say it? Why did these feelings terrify him so? If only he could get over the past, stop having the nightmares.

Jo was still blushing as she set coffee on the table and refused to meet his eyes for the moment. "I'll cut some bread and we can try some of the fresh jellies you brought."

"I've got to go back outside and wash my hands first. You have some soap?"

She retrieved a bar of lye soap and handed it to him. Again each of them felt the urgent needs long denied when their eyes met. He turned and walked out, coming back minutes later to sit down at the table. Jo brought a loaf of bread to the table and cut a slice for him, then opened a jar of strawberry jam. "I feel like a little girl in a candy store!" she said, sitting down across from him. "This day started out to be the worst day in my life, and now it's turning into the best. God must have brought you, knowing I'd need the comfort of a friendly presence right now."

Clint smiled softly. "Well, I'm glad I came then." He drank some of the coffee. "Now, tell me about this mountain lion and the bear. Sounds like you had a couple of close calls."

She rolled her eyes. "I did! The bear I don't mind telling you about. But the mountain lion—he was just a good lesson, and I feel foolish telling you."

"Just be glad you're alive. What the hell happened? Wildcats don't usually attack humans."

"Well, in this case it was a fight between him and me over who got the meat of a young elk I had just killed. Apparently the smell of fresh blood far outweighed his fear of me. As it turned out, the wolves won in the end—made a meal out of both the mountain lion *and* the elk! If I hadn't had to come back to the cabin and nurse my wounds, I wouldn't have lost my meat. When the mountain lion leapt at me and I shot him, his claw got my arm pretty good on the way down."

Clint's eyes filled with concern. "You could have died," he said then. "You realize that, don't you?"

She set down her coffee cup. "Death comes when it's time," she told him. "I know what you're thinking. You or someone else should have been here. But I wouldn't have wanted it that way, Clint. And whether or not I was alone wouldn't have made any difference in whether the infection killed me. I had something to prove to myself over this past year, and I've proved it. Now I've even faced my first Indians. I'm going to be all right, Clint."

He looked at her with eyes full of pain and anger. "Why do you insist on placing yourself in dangerous situations? You've proven all you need to prove, Jo. Why don't you get the hell out of here and move closer to town?"

Her eyebrows shot up in surprise, and her own pride and anger welled within her. "Why? So you can go running off without having to worry about me? Why should I make it so convenient for you?"

"*Convenient!* What the hell is that supposed to mean?"

"It means I know you're just running away from the truth again, Clint Reeves. It means I know you have deep feelings for me or you wouldn't be here right now. You're afraid to face those feelings, so you're going to run again, as far from me as you can get! But at the same time you want the convenience of knowing I'll be all right while you're gone so you won't have that on your conscience."

He got up from the table, scowling. "I came here out of friendship, to see how you were doing, to say good-bye. You're taking an awful lot for granted." He turned away, heading for the door.

"Am I?" He hesitated at the door, and Jo rose and walked up behind him. "Maybe you can leave without expressing your feelings, Clint Reeves, but I can't let you go without expressing mine. If you're serious about not coming back, I might never get another chance to tell you I . . . I could have loved you." She felt the tears coming again and she cursed them. "No. What I really mean is . . . I *do* love you."

Why did the words suddenly come so easily? She was caving in to her vulnerability from the strange, eventful day. The long months of loneliness, the brush with death she had just incurred, and the realization that she might never again get the chance to tell him, all culminated in this sudden need to tell the truth, to get it off her heart and her mind for once and for all.

Pain filled his eyes as he turned to look at her. "Don't say it, Jo. I didn't come here for that."

She touched his arm. "Didn't you? You can run, Clint. But wherever you go, I want you to remember you have a friend here—not just a friend, but a woman who loves you." A tear slipped down her cheek. "And right now I . . . I suddenly want to do whatever I have to do to make you come back."

His face looked flushed, and his jaw flexed with repressed emotions. His own eyes filled with tears. "Not that way, Jo. I've never wanted it to be that way."

"What other way is there for us right now?" She could hardly believe her own words. "It's better than this awful

need . . . this . . . this vague, unsettled . . . something . . .
we both feel. It's all so clear to me now, Clint. It's something we both need as surely as we need to breathe. It's
why you came here, even if you won't admit it. And right
now . . . I don't care what you'll think of me. I only
know . . . I love you . . . and I want you to come back . . .
and I need . . . to be a woman . . . to—"

He suddenly leaned down and covered her mouth with
his own, while his arms came around her. His tongue
softly probed in a hungry kiss, and she flung her arms
around his neck; her whimpers mingled with his groans as
he pressed her tight, lifting her feet from the floor. His
lips never left hers as he grasped her bottom and lifted.
Her legs came around his waist while their kiss grew more
heated and passionate, and she felt him walking, carrying
her to her bed.

Nothing mattered now—not the Indians or bears or
mountain lions—not the chores, or the pleasure of having
cream in her coffee. All that mattered was to satisfy this
terrible, urgent, long-neglected need that only Clint Reeves
could satisfy. He laid her on the bed with her legs were
still wrapped around him. His kiss turned into many passionate, hungry, warm, wet kisses, not just to her mouth,
but to her eyes, her nose, her ears, her neck; all quick,
desperate, searching kisses mingled with the groaning of
her name.

She breathed deeply, feeling faint when his lips traced
over her throat and downward as he unbuttoned her dress,
pulling one side away to expose a breast. She closed her
eyes and cried out at the feel of his warm tongue tasting
her nipple, while already his hands had moved down and
were grasping at her bloomers. She lifted up, helping him
get the bloomers off, neither of them wanting or needing
to take the time for preliminaries. This was a need too
long denied. He pushed her dress to her waist, his fingers
probing just long enough to feel her silken moistness and
know she was already ready for him. In moments he had
his buckskin pants unlaced and his long johns unbuttoned.

Jo cried out his name when she felt the huge, soft,
warm manhood touch her groin, and in the next second he
was surging wildly inside of her. She arched up to him,

tossing her head while he kissed at her madly, then grasped
her under the hips, pushing hard into her while he again
found the exposed breast and sucked at it as though he
took nourishment from it.

It was all quick and hard and beautiful. Jo had never
felt this kind of ecstasy, never like this with Greg. She felt
faint at the touch of Clint Reeves's big hands grasping her
bare bottom, his lips hotly tasting her breast, the very
embodiment of his manhood surging inside her, finding
comfort and satisfaction there. It was over in moments, for
Clint's needs were too demanding for him to hold off.

He touched her hair, kissing at her neck, and she could
feel his tears trickle past her ears. "Jo, Jo!" he groaned. "I
still have to go. Tell me you understand."

She ran her fingers through his hair. "I understand,"
she said softly. "It doesn't matter. Just stay . . . today . . .
tonight. I love you, Clint."

He met her lips again, and she could feel his trembling.
His lips moved to her neck again. "I want . . . to say it.
It's so hard."

"I know."

"Just let me make it nice for you," he said then, his
voice husky with desire. He pulled away the other side of
her dress and kissed the other breast, kissed her scars.
"You didn't have a chance to enjoy it the way you should."
He met her mouth again, his hand trailing down to find
her lovenest, his fingers probing more softly then, working
a wonderful magic that made her moan, made her want to
open up to him. He left her lips then. "Jo, my Jo," he
whispered. "I want to see you, Jo, all of you. I never
forgot the sight of you . . . that day at the river."

She closed her eyes while he undressed her. She felt
brazen and wanton, and she didn't care. She heard him
undressing too, and she opened her eyes to feast on his
magnificent build. Her eyes fell to that part of him that
had so achingly awakened her womanhood. She touched
him there, feeling on fire. Her fingers trailed up to the
ugly scar near his chest.

"My poor Clint," she whispered.

He took her hand and kissed it, then bent down to
kiss her breasts again. His lips trailed over her flat belly,

and he kissed at the hairs of her lovenest while his fingers again worked magic with her until she felt the climax that made her arch up to him wildly. He moved back on top of her, grasping the calf of each leg and pulling them up over his shoulders. He entered her then, able to probe even deeper this time. He remained raised up on his arms, drinking in her brazen beauty, while she ran her fingers over his nipples and the hairs of his chest, meeting his eyes boldly, seeing the tears there, mixed with fiery need.

He reached back around her legs and lowered them, coming closer, again pushing his hands under her hips, whispering her name while her fingers dug into his back and she buried her lips against his strong shoulder.

This time the mating lasted several beautiful, ecstasy-filled minutes, as they moved in perfect rhythm, each lost in the glory of making love with true emotion. It could only be that way for Jo. But Clint had been with whores, his needs filled mechanically. This was so different. This was so much more satisfying. When his life finally spilled into her, he felt weak and spent. He let out a long sigh and sank down beside her, keeping her in his arms, her legs still wrapped around him.

"Stay right where you are," he told her, kissing her hair. "I just want to stay in this bed all day, Jo."

She kissed his chest, his scar. "And I want you to stay here. It feels so good to let it out, doesn't it, Clint?"

He kissed her eyes. "I've never felt this way in my whole life. It scares the hell out of me." His voice choked and she kissed at the tears that lingered on his face.

"I know it does. It's all right. You've faced so many things, Clint, without fear. But there is one fear you'll have to conquer if you're ever going to be a whole man again, be happy again."

He put fingers to her lips. "Don't talk about it—not today or tonight. Let's just enjoy each other, enjoy the moment."

She smiled softly, kissing his fingers, remembering how she used to send him running by talking too much. She didn't want that to happen now—not now. He cupped a breast in his hand, pushing up on it and leaning down to gently kiss the nipple. She closed her eyes and breathed deeply, shuddering with wonderful desires.

"You're so beautiful, Jo. I've never known a woman like you." The light kiss turned to a gentle sucking as his warm mouth closed over her breast and he groaned with manly ardor. He pressed against her, and she could feel he was already eager for her again. She grasped at his hair as he lay on top of her, gently forcing her legs apart once more. He moved inside of her, and Jo lay back and enjoyed the moment, forcing herself not to think about tomorrow. There was only today and tonight, and Clint Reeves in her bed.

Chapter Twenty-two

Dawn broke with the sweet music of larks, robins, and thrush. Jo turned her back to Clint, snuggling against him. His arm came around her, and she studied his strong hand. She knew he would go away today, yet somehow it didn't matter. She was almost astonished to realize she had gained enough confidence in herself that she knew she could build her ranch with or without a man. It was not for the ranch or for protection that she needed him. Her need of Clint Reeves went much deeper. She needed him for a special fulfillment, for the woman inside herself that wanted a home with children and a man in it. Clint Reeves was not ready for that, and until he was, she would rather run her ranch alone. Letting him leave now would be the hardest good-bye of all, but insisting that he stay would be her biggest mistake.

She kissed his hand and he stirred sleepily, nuzzling her hair. "Morning," he mumbled. His hand moved over her bare breasts and down over her belly. Her body was warm and soft, and he moved his hand around to caress her hips. He kissed at her neck. "Once more, Jo," he whispered.

She did not resist. She turned to him, and nothing was said as he moved on top of her and took her gently, quietly, moving first in rhythmic thrusts, then in circular motions that made her break the silence with a whimper of ecstasy. The thrill of being bedded by this man who was also her best friend, this man she had wanted for so long without admitting it even to herself, again brought on the shuddering climax that rippled through her insides and pulled him even deeper. Again she felt the throb of his life pouring into her belly, and she took it gladly, caring not for tomorrow.

When they finished they lay quietly beside each other for the next several minutes. "When will you leave?" she finally asked.

"Soon as I eat a little something. I'll have to take the packhorses back to Virginia City first. They belong to Hank Tremble, the man I worked for all winter. You might get another visit from Moose and Happy. They're still around. The others left. Newt James is still nearby. I'll see if he'd be interested in working for you. Luke Adams and Jim Backus left to get their families in Illinois. They'll be back next year. You might end up with some neighbors that you know, come next spring." He kissed her hair. "If you can get through another winter—and you shouldn't have any trouble if you hire a couple of men to work for you—you'll probably have neighbors a lot closer than Virginia City to turn to if you need help."

"I managed without help or neighbors last winter."

He sighed deeply. "Damn it, Jo, will you quit being so stubborn? I'm perfectly aware of your abilities. But everybody needs help at one time or another, no matter how strong or skilled or whatever. It's a fact of life. Don't be so damned proud that you won't get help when you need it. That's just plain stupidity."

If you're so concerned, then why are you going away? She wanted to blurt out the words, hurt him with them. But she knew why he was going away, and it had nothing to do with how much he loved her. She knew she should feel used, but she didn't have any such feelings. She had given in to her own vulnerability, had wanted him brazenly. Why should she blame him for what happened? And she knew Clint Reeves well enough to know he had not bedded her for pure manly pleasure. He had a terrible, deep need for the emotional fulfillment that being with her had brought him; and she had had the same need.

He kissed her shoulder. "I'm getting better, Jo. I'm learning to live with it. And I'm going to try real hard to get through this next year without the whiskey. I might have a few beers now and then, but if I can stay off the whiskey and prove to myself I can live with the memories without any crutches, I'm coming back. I just . . . I don't want to think I can't handle the memories without you or booze. I hope to God you can understand that. I always had a certain . . . inner strength. I've got to know I still have it."

She snuggled against him. "I know. I knew it yesterday. I didn't invite you to my bed to try to make you stay, Clint. I don't even *want* you to stay if you're still full of all that bitterness, and I'll not live with a man who goes on drinking binges. I love the Clint Reeves you are right now. But I couldn't love the Clint Reeves you become when you turn to whiskey; and until you learn to get along without it, we can't be together." A lump rose in her throat at the realization that he had not actually said "I love you." She knew that he did, but she needed to hear the words, and it was still too difficult for him to say them. "If you . . . don't come back . . . I'll understand that, too. Just don't . . . ever forget me."

Her voice broke, and he pulled her even closer, hugging her tightly. "My God, Jo, how can you think that I would?" He kissed at her hair again. "If I don't return, and you meet another man—"

"There will never be another," she sobbed. "No one can match you." She breathed deeply to regain her composure. "I don't need a man the way most women do. I can take care of myself, and I'm not interested in . . . in sex and children unless the man is very special. The special ones don't come along very often."

He smiled through tears. "The same goes for women. I'll probably never meet another one like you. Just the thought of you will help me stay away from the whiskey. But I can't have you there in person always preaching about it. If I do this, it will be on my own, and for me, not you."

"That's the way it should be." She turned and faced him, wondering how she must look by now after a day and night of lovemaking. "My hair must be a tangled mess."

He smiled, but she saw the tears in his eyes. "You look beautiful, more beautiful than I've ever seen you—radiant is the better word. Being fulfilled as a woman for a little while has put a special glow in your eyes."

She reddened, realizing how intimate he had been with her, and how boldly she had allowed that intimacy. Making love with him had seemed as natural and right as breathing. Now it was done. There was no changing it, nor did she care to.

"I'd better get up and wash and start breakfast." Her eyes shone with tears again and her throat ached. "We might as well . . . get this over with."

He pulled her close and kissed her eyes. "It's going to be all right, Jo. I know it is."

She kissed his chest and quickly moved out of the bed, pulling on a robe before she stood up. She went into the outer room, glad she had left some water over the fire the night before. Most of it had steamed away, but there was enough left to mix with some cold water to wash with. She refilled the water kettle and set it back over the fire for Clint, then quickly washed. She walked back into the bedroom, keeping the robe tied around her, and began brushing out her hair, while Clint watched.

"You mean I don't get one more look at what's under that robe?"

She glanced at his reflection in the mirror. "You've seen plenty. If you want another look, you'll have to come back for it next spring."

He grinned. "That's a cruel remark."

She smiled then herself. "It might be cruel, but it's sincere. It's your turn to go and wash while I get dressed."

He sighed deeply. "I could stay another day."

Her own smile faded. "No. What difference would it make, except to make the leaving even more difficult? I think it's right that you go, Clint. I want you to be whole again; and I want you to love me for me—not just use me to pretend you still have Millie. I want you to be clear in your own heart and mind that it's Joline Masters you want and love." She turned and faced him. "What we've done was just something that had to be, Clint—something that had been burning at our insides for a long time. Now comes the real test. If you come back, it will be because you love *me*, Joline Masters." She rose. "Now go get washed while I dress."

He looked at her a moment, then got out of bed. She studied his naked splendor, feeling warm and satisfied at being a woman again. He was a beautiful specimen of man, and she wanted him to be her man, her partner. He was that rare breed of man who would recognize her independence, let her have as much a hand in running the ranch as he. She would be glad and proud to share with him whatever she managed to build on her own, and Clint Reeves had great possibilities for running a much bigger enterprise. But he was not ready for all of that. He walked up to her, leaned over and kissed her cheek, then left the room.

Jo quickly pulled on clean bloomers and a lavender-checked dress. She fastened her hair at the base of her neck with combs. When she walked into the main room, Clint had pulled on some long johns, which he had retrieved from his gear the night before during one of their brief respites from lovemaking. Jo tried to remember at that moment just how many times they had made love the day and night before, but she wasn't even sure.

Clint pulled on some buckskin pants while Jo made coffee, but he remained shirtless. "I'll help you with chores again before I leave," he told her, sitting down to the table.

"It isn't necessary."

"I want to."

She set the coffee pot on the grate of the fireplace. "I would rather you didn't, Clint. I'll need to keep really busy the first few days after you're gone. I'll look forward to the work. Just do me a favor and send a couple of good men back here. And try to find Newt James. I'll need another horse shed, like you said, and maybe even a bunkhouse. Newt's a good carpenter."

"I'll see what I can do."

"I'll fry some pork when the coffee is done. You can do one thing if you want—go milk Margaret so we'll have milk for our coffee."

"Margaret?"

"The minute I looked at her I thought of the name Margaret," she answered.

Clint chuckled. "You still naming animals?"

"Only the ones I know I'll keep, like Margaret and

Spirit. I'm going to quit naming the horses, since I'll be constantly trading and selling them—except Sundance. I promised him I wouldn't sell him."

He was still grinning. "And I suppose you think he understood you?" He rose to pull on a shirt.

"Of course!" Jo answered. "All my animals understand me."

Clint just shook his head and chuckled again, picking up the wooden bucket and going out to milk the cow.

The morning was beautiful. Jo stepped out for a moment to watch the sunrise, as she always enjoyed doing. She thought how nice it would be to do this every morning, make breakfast while her husband did a few chores. Then together they would mend fences and round up mustangs, smoke meat, hunt. She could hire men, but it wouldn't be the same as sharing this place with a man who truly understood how much she loved it, a man who respected her independence but still knew how to draw out the vulnerable woman who lay beneath her stern outer shell. Clint was that kind of man. But he was going away, and there was no guarantee he would ever come back.

Already she was building her defenses, forcing herself to face facts and accept them. Again she would have no one but herself, and it might always be that way. She glanced at the bearskin and took a deep breath of pride. She would make it just fine without Clint Reeves. But it would be so much nicer, so much more fulfilling, to share all this with him.

Clint returned with the milk, and they shared a quiet breakfast, talking about everything and anything but the fact that he would soon leave. Jo cleaned up the table, then began packing some food into his parfleche. "I wish I had something to give you to think of me by," she told him. "But maybe it's better you don't have any reminders." Her eyes misted as she wrapped some biscuits into a cloth and put them into his supply pouch. "I have . . . plenty of reminders of you . . . all those nice extras you brought out."

She met his gaze then, a tear slipping down her cheek. "Take care of yourself, Clint. You'll be exposing yourself to danger."

"No more than you are by being here—probably less,

considering a man is a less likely target than a woman alone. You'd be wise to leave that bearskin hanging outside. It will make men think twice about giving you trouble."

They both grinned a little. He strapped on a weapons belt and walked closer to her, grasping her arms. "I'm going to have one hell of a guilt to live with if something happens to you, Jo. Just tell me not to leave and I won't."

She shook her head. "No. I don't want you that way. You do what you have to do, Clint. You know where I'll be. I don't intend to leave this place. I already love it too much."

He leaned down and kissed her cheek, then found her mouth. She wrapped her arms around his neck and he pressed her close, kissing her gently, sweetly. His lips left her mouth and he held her close a moment longer. "Forgive me, Jo," he whispered.

"There is nothing to forgive. I'll pray for you. And I'll pray you'll come back well and whole."

He reluctantly pulled away from her, quickly wiping at a tear that had strayed from his eye. "You're some woman," he told her then, giving her a supportive smile. He turned and walked out, and Jo went to the door to watch him herd the packhorses out of her corral and tie them together. He saddled and mounted his own horse, then took up the reins of the lead packhorse. He faced Jo, who was still standing in the doorway, and tipped his hat.

"Good-bye, Jo Masters. Something tells me that even if I don't come back, you'll have your own little empire here some day—Joline Masters, queen of the Ruby River valley."

Jo smiled for him. "I hope you're right."

His own smile faded. "I am. And right now I'm not worthy of sharing any of this with you. The day I feel I am, I'll be back."

She put her hands on a porch post, hoping he couldn't tell how difficult it was to keep her legs from giving way beneath her. "You're a good man, Clint. And you *are* worthy. I'll be looking forward to next spring."

She saw the pain in his eyes as he nodded. "So will I." He turned his horse and quickly rode off, followed by the packhorses. Jo watched until he disappeared into the thick pines behind the cabin. She struggled with a terrible urge to run after him, beg him to stay. He would, if she asked. But she knew it would be wrong.

She walked back inside on shaky legs, heading into the bedroom. The bed was a rumpled mess. How strange it felt to realize she had only recently spent hours in it with Clint Reeves, brazenly offering her naked body to him in wanton desires, being a full woman in the most beautiful way. And it had happened so suddenly, so easily.

She sat down on the bed. "Clint," she whispered, the tears coming then. Spirit bounded into the room and jumped into her lap. She hugged the dog close, lying down on the bed and weeping, grabbing Clint's pillow and breathing in his lingering scent. She wasn't sure how long she wept before she forced herself back up and tore the bedclothes from the bed, carrying them out to the porch. She would fill her washtub and wash everything.

"First come the horses," she told herself. She blew her nose and wiped her eyes and went back inside to put on a plainer dress, then pulled on her old work boots and marched to the horse shed. There was work to be done.

It felt good to ride, to float across the open valley on Sundance and ride up the next ridge, getting a sense of how it must be for the Indian, or for men like Clint, men who fit this magnificent land. But, Jo reasoned, a woman could fit it, too, for a woman's soul could be as much a part of the land as any man's. She had earned her right to be here and this might be all she would ever have now.

She rode with Moose Barkley, Rubin Keats, and a man by the name of Jason Darnell. They had covered at least thirty miles in the last five days, tracking a herd of mustangs. The horses had taken them in a circle, until they were within a few miles of the ranch again. They had finally spotted the herd just this morning, and the four of them rode at a gallop now, chasing the mares toward a box canyon.

Jo was grateful for the help. Moose had worked on a ranch once and knew more about horses than most mountain men.

Rubin Keats had returned to work for Jo, quickly deciding there were enough men grubbing for gold and not finding it. He was enjoying just being in new country, away from the ugly war he had left behind, discovering new places. A man who had little self-determination, he found it was easier working for someone else than toiling away at something that might never gain him a dime. The mountains were already overrun with miners, and he wondered where newcomers would go to stake new claims. Rounding up mustangs was easier work, and his pay was to keep one horse for every four he found for Jo Masters. He was quickly gathering enough horses to sell for a tidy profit.

Jason Darnell was a young man of only seventeen, who had also seen all the war he wanted to see. His parents had both been killed in Mississippi, and he and his best friend had fought with the Confederates for a short time at only fifteen. When his friend died after having a leg amputated, Jason had come west and left the war and its bad memories behind him. Jo was skeptical of him at first because he was from the South; but he could not help what had happened to him, and she decided that if she were going to ask Clint to leave bad memories behind, she had to do the same.

There was a lot of healing left to be done now that the war was over, and it had to start somewhere. It wasn't Jason's fault Greg had been killed, and somewhere back east she had a brother-in-law she would also have to learn to forgive. Jason was a hard worker and eager. Jo felt sorry for the loss of his parents, for he was barely more than a boy, with a slight build and a face that still didn't need shaving.

The three men had been sent out by Clint, and Jo decided that if Clint trusted Jason, so would she. Back at the house Newt James worked at building a log bunkhouse, from trees taken from Jo's own property. There would be little cost to Jo, and already she was making good money on her horses. Rubin and Moose had broken a few, which she had sold to travelers who came through her ranch. More had been herded to Virginia City and sold by Moose earlier in the summer.

In a few weeks Jo planned to go to the city herself to buy more land, and now as Sundance splashed through creeks and galloped over rolling green foothills, Jo found herself wishing she could own all of Montana, every pine, every grand mountain, every blade of lush, green grass. She had been sleeping under the stars the past few nights, getting a better feel of the land. As soon as these mustangs were captured, she would mark off the new section of land she would like to buy.

She loved the work, since it helped keep her from thinking about Clint. The weeks since he had left had been the loneliest she had suffered, in spite of the presence of four extra men. She had been busier than ever, and she thanked God for it. No chore was too hard, no hours too long. And she was actually grateful for the nights she didn't have to sleep back home in the bed alone.

It had not been as easy to go on with her life as she had supposed she could make it. She had been sick every morning the first month after Clint left. She was sure the sickness was due to the emotional upheaval of having Clint ride out of her life, combined with working harder than ever.

But now she felt fine, and she enjoyed riding Sundance at a fast gallop, feeling the wind in her hair, working Sundance around the small herd of mustangs she and the men were chasing into the canyon. Moose let out a howl when the horses were finally cornered and they began to settle down, realizing there was no place left to run.

"Ain't that the prettiest bunch of mares you ever set eyes on?" he shouted to Jo.

Jason grinned and chased after a roan mare with a sleek body but powerful-looking shoulders. "This one's the best," the boy shouted. "Look at how she's built. Nice and healthy." He rode closer to Jo. "Ma'am, this is the best lot of horses yet—no sickly-lookin' ones or ones with crooked legs or their ribs stickin' out."

"They're beautiful," Jo answered. She looked at Moose. "We'll go into Virginia City in a few days. I want the blacksmith to make me a branding iron, Moose, in the shape of a J. And I want to take four of the best mares and see if I can trade them for a good stud horse. What I'd really like is another good buckskin like Sundance. I'll need your advice. I don't have enough experience in raising horses." She looked at the herd of mares. "What I don't know I suppose I'll learn the hard way."

Moose grinned. "I expect so, ma'am. I'll be glad to

round up a few of these mares and see what I can do in
Virginia City."

"Take one for every four, like always. While we're gone
I'll have Newt and the others build a special shed and
corral for the stallion, away from the mares, so he won't
bother them until we *want* him to bother them."

They all laughed, and Jo reddened a little. She wondered if Moose suspected anything had happened between
herself and Clint. Surely not. Clint would never give it
away deliberately.

"I hope we can get a few mares pregnant yet this
summer," she continued. For a brief moment a flutter of
dread moved through her chest, an unexpected anxiety at
the word. Pregnant. Women got pregnant the same way
mares did. Only then did she realize she had gone a long
time without a period. She had been so busy, so full of
thoughts about Clint's leaving and what she would do with
the ranch, that she had not paid any attention. She quickly
dismissed the concern, turning to Moose and avoiding the
sudden panic that had momentarily overwhelmed her.
"You think you'll start your own ranch eventually, Moose?"

He shrugged. "I'm just takin' the money. I'm not much
for settlin'."

"I will some day," Jason put in. "I like it out here. I'm
gonna have my own place."

Jo smiled. "I hope you do, Jason. You're a good worker."

Rubin Keats whistled and shouted to the herd of mares.
"Let's run them back."

They all joined in keeping the herd together, and Jo
hoped she could keep up the pace of continuous riding it
would take to get the horses back to the ranch. She felt
tired, but she was not about to admit it to the men. She
thought again about the sudden awareness that she was
very late for her time. She tried to remember back, as she
slowed her horse for a moment and let the men ride ahead
of her. Had she had a period since Clint left? No!

She put her hand to her chest, telling herself to be
calm. After all, she and Greg had made love often, and
there had been no pregnancy. Spending one day with a
man couldn't possibly—

She kicked Sundance into a fast gallop. Perhaps a good
hard ride would bring on her time. Besides, she had been

sick those first weeks after Clint left. That was probably all
that was wrong—just too many emotional changes over
the past year. God surely wouldn't let this happen, not
with Clint gone, maybe forever. Besides, she had a ranch
to run, more fences to build, a herd of mares to brand and
sell.

She caught up with the others, again pushing away the
dreaded thought. She decided she would have Newt make
a sign and hang it over the gates to her land. It would be a
J lying partially sideways, and below that would read THE
LAZY J RANCH. It was time to give her place a name.
Some day the LAZY J would be so big a man would have
to ride a whole day or more to get off the land.

Chapter Twenty-three

Jo was amazed at how Virginia City had grown. It had been well over a year since she was here last, and the wild, bustling town was a startling contrast to the near silence of the valley. She didn't realize until she arrived that she had missed being around people, and she decided that now that she had some help, she would try to get to town more often. She had come with Moose, driving her wagon for supplies and leaving Jason and Rubin back at the ranch to keep an eye on things.

Moose led four good, sturdy mustang mares, which Jo hoped to use to trade for a good stud horse. Jo followed behind him in the wagon, the noise of the town almost hurting her ears as she followed Moose and the mares toward the claims office. The street was still a mire of mud and horse dung. Horses tied to hitching posts lined the street on either side, and an assortment of people, mostly men, trooped up and down the boardwalks, some already drunk even though it was barely noon. Painted women laughed and pianos played from inside saloons, which far outnumbered any other business establishments in the town.

Jo wondered how she could keep coming here if her condition was what she suspected. How could she come to town with a swollen stomach and no husband? Clint and the others had tried so hard to make sure men in this territory knew she was a respectable woman. What would they think of her if they knew? Even now men were waving to her and smiling.

"Glad to see you made it, Mrs. Masters!" someone shouted.

Jo smiled back, her heart slowly shattering inside. Clint! If only he knew. Now that she was in town she could probably get a message to him, but the stubborn, determined side of her told her she would never know if he had come back for the right reason if he knew about the baby. He had to come back for her alone. And if he did come back, it would be several months yet. She had no doubts now that she was pregnant, and the baby would likely be born before she saw Clint Reeves again. What should she do in the meantime?

She noticed a few respectable-looking women farther up the street where the supply stores were located. Apparently families were beginning to move in; men were bringing wives to the territory. She realized she missed the company of other women. But what could she share with any of these women? Her life was so different from theirs. One of them turned to stare when a man said something to her and pointed to Jo. She looked at Jo as though she were some kind of rare animal. How could she make the average woman understand her need for independence, her compelling desire to prove she could survive in the wilderness alone? Yet she often yearned for women's conversations—sharing recipes, quilting bees, talk about children.

Children! She put a hand to her stomach. What did she know about babies? She supposed most of it came naturally, but the company of other women would surely help. She wanted to hate Clint Reeves for doing this to her, for totally disrupting her well-planned life. But she couldn't blame Clint. She had asked him to stay, thrown herself at him freely. Her pregnancy was no one's fault but her own. And if Clint knew about the baby now, he would be here as fast as he could ride. But she didn't want him that way.

How she wished Anna or a good female friend were close by with whom she could share this terrible dilemma, to whom she could spill her feelings for Clint, someone to whom she could turn for advice. Anna! How would she feel about her sister if she knew she had gotten herself pregnant without a husband? And how was Anna, now that the war was over? Had Darryl come home yet?

"Well, hello there!" came a woman's voice. "So, you survived after all."

Jo glanced in the direction of the voice to see Sally Turrell smiling and waving, her blond hair looking even whiter in the sun, her green taffeta dress fitted perfectly to her lovely shape. Jo felt a sudden stab of jealousy, wondering how many times Clint had visited the woman. She wanted to hate her, even as she waved to her, yet she realized Sally Turrell was the only woman in Virginia City that she knew, at least slightly. And she was a woman experienced in life, the only kind of woman who might understand Jo's painful situation.

She followed Moose to the land office and climbed down from the wagon. "Go ahead and take the horses to that horse trader you told me about up the street," Jo told him. "Check out his studs and leave the mares in his corral."

"You want to pick out a good stud yourself, don't you?" he answered.

"Yes, but you have as good an eye or better, Moose. Besides, I know you're itching to get to a tavern for a couple of beers. Go ahead and do what you want for a couple of hours. I'll meet you at the supply store in about three hours. Then we'll go back to the trader together."

He tipped his hat. "Fine with me."

Jo tied her horses and approached the land office, her precious, hard-earned money tucked into her handbag.

"Howdy, Mrs. Masters." An old man nearby spoke up, nodding to her. He sat in a chair that leaned against the outside wall of the land office. "You gonna get ya some more land?"

Jo smiled. "If I can."

The old man studied her pretty, young face, her hair neatly rolled at the sides and tucked with combs. She wore a blue skirt and a flowered blouse, and she didn't look anything like the kind of woman one would think it would take to survive alone through a Montana winter.

"Did you really shoot yourself a grizzly?" the man

asked. "Talk's all over town you killed yourself a bear out there."

Jo reddened slightly. "Yes. I killed him. It was more an act of desperation and luck than skill and bravery."

The old man laughed. "Ain't that how it usually is? But it don't matter. Fact remains you got yourself a grizzly. Why, you're practically a female hero in this town."

Jo just grinned and shook her head. She walked inside the land office, clinging to her handbag, unaware that farther up the street a man in a black coat was watching her. Inside the land office she greeted a man behind the desk, the same one who had handled her original claim. He looked up at her with total surprise in his eyes.

"Mrs. Masters!" He put out his hand. "I've heard rumors you did just fine this past year. But I didn't believe it until now."

Jo shook his hand. "Hello, Mr. Wade. I've come to claim more land."

"Well, have a seat. You know, of course, that to claim more land this soon you'll have to be able to pay for it. You haven't occupied your present claim for the five-year requirement yet." Jo sat down in a chair across from his desk. "It's one thing to manage for one year," he was saying. "But five years is a real test."

Jo reached into her handbag and plunked two hundred dollars on the man's desk, watching the shock in his eyes.

"I know the rules, Mr. Wade," she told him. "I'll be here for another four years. In fact, I'll be here for the rest of my life. That money is to claim another hundred and sixty acres on the west side of my place. I have a drawing with me showing the approximate boundaries. I would like you to send out a surveyor as soon as you can to measure off the entire three hundred and twenty acres so I can be more exact when I put up more fencing."

Wade counted the money and shook his head, saying nothing. He unfolded the drawing Jo handed to him and studied it for a moment. "You're sure about this?"

"I wouldn't spend two hundred dollars on something I wasn't sure of, Mr. Wade."

He glanced at her over his spectacles. "No. I suppose you wouldn't." He removed his glasses and frowned. "Did you really kill a grizzly out there?"

Jo smiled and blushed again. "Yes. I'm amazed at how fast that story traveled."

"You're an enigma to the men out here, Mrs. Masters. They can't quite figure a woman like you."

"I'm nothing so unusual, Mr. Wade. I simply chose Montana as a place to settle. I love it here and I'm staying. I'm still a woman like any other." She thought about Clint, and the life in her belly. Yes, she was still a woman. And right now she had a bigger problem than grizzlies and fencing.

Wade grinned and put his glasses back on. "Well, let's get to the details then."

For the next forty-five minutes Jo sat explaining landmarks and signing papers. She left the land office with her new deed and said her good-byes to Mr. Wade. When she stepped outside, she hesitated before unhitching the horses, remembering Sally Turrell's smile and wave. She desperately needed to talk to a woman about her problem. And intuition told her that in spite of Sally's tainted reputation, she was a woman who would understand, and a woman who knew how to keep her mouth shut when necessary. In some ways they were probably not so different: both of them independent, both of them choosing unusual paths in life, far from the norm for the average woman, neither of them having a lot in common with women who quietly submitted to husbands and rocked their babies by the hearth.

Yet Jo realized she did want to rock her baby by the hearth, but not with a man sitting across form her who felt obligated to her because of that baby. She lifted her skirt and made her way across the street, picking the most solid ground she could find. When she reached the other side of the street she went inside a shoe store, and while the owner was helping a customer she snuck toward the back of the store, into a storeroom, and out the back door into an alley. It was difficult enough in this town not to be noticed when you were a woman; but she had built a reputation that made her stick out like a rose in a thorn patch, and she didn't want any man seeing her go to Sally Turrell's house.

Bart Kendall moved around the corner of the land office, old feelings of vengeance welling up in his soul at the sight of Joline Masters. He watched her walk across the street and disappear into a shoe store, then headed for the door of the land office.

"Hello there," he spoke up to the man sitting inside.

Wade looked up at him and smiled. "How do you do." His eyes shifted for a moment to the odd lump at the side of Kendall's head where an ear should be, but he kept his smile and said nothing.

"That woman that was just in here," Kendall asked. "I think I know her. Her name Joline Masters?"

"Why, yes, it is."

Kendall removed his hat. "Well, I'll be damned. I knew her back in Kansas. She live here now?"

"Well, not right here in Virginia City. Would you believe she actually owns three hundred sixty acres along the Ruby River—all her own?"

Kendall grinned and shook his head. "Is that a fact?"

"Yes. She's been here nearly a year and a half already—filed for her land under the Homestead Act. She's started herself a horse ranch—doing all right, especially considering she's a woman."

Kendall shook is head. "Well, I remember she was pretty independent. But that seems like awful dangerous country for a woman alone—what with Indians and outlaws roamin' all over." He scratched his head. "Seems to me like I heard somethin' about her and a Clint Reeves. They didn't get hitched or anything? I think Reeves brought her out here—was kind of sweet on her, wasn't he? I know him, too. He, uh, he around?"

Kendall put a hand self-consciously to his missing ear. He would not forget the day Clint Reeves carved it off. He had not gone near Joline Masters since then, but his thirst for vengeance had won out over his better judgment. He had spent the last couple of years with outlaws, looting the South, robbing from broken and defenseless people, enjoying his share of women left alone by their men who had gone off to a hopeless war. And all the time he had been thinking about Clint Reeves and Joline Masters—about the pain and humiliation of losing his ear at Julesburg.

"I don't think Reeves is around," Wade told him. "I wouldn't know if they ever got hitched, as you put it. Mrs.

Masters filed under her own name, though. I believe Clint
Reeves left Montana."

Kendall had trouble not showing his delight at the words.
"That so? Well, that's a surprise. You say Mrs. Masters
settled along the Ruby?"

"Yes, sir. I doubt her place would be hard to find. It's
the only one for miles around in that area."

Kendall nodded. "Well, thanks for the information. "I'll
see if I can find it."

He turned and left, watching carefully as he opened the
door to be sure Jo was not around. He didn't want her to
know he was in town. He took a look at the fine horses
that were hitched to her wagon, and he grinned bitterly.
"You owe me a couple of horses, woman," he muttered.
"And you're going to pay me back—and then some."

He headed toward a saloon where the men with whom
he had been riding were gambling and drinking. Their
leader was a cocky young man named Sonny Morrow.
Kendall liked Sonny, whom he had met in Laramie. Sonny
was thought of by men of his breed as the most ingenious
horse thief west of the Missouri River. With Sonny and his
gang Kendall had helped steal horses and rob from miners
and Mormons all over Utah and Wyoming on their way to
Montana. Riding with Sonny made a man feel important,
and it had filled his pockets with a lot of money. One day
soon he would return to Lawrence and live like a king. He
would show people there who Bart Kendall was! No one
would scoff at him again or boot him out of their place of
business or off their steps.

But there was someone who needed to be taught a
lesson before he returned to Lawrence. Joline Masters
would pay for humiliating him the day she got her horses
back from him; and getting back at Joline Masters was the
ideal way to also get back at Clint Reeves. If Clint was
gone, he was not around to defend the uppity Mrs. Masters.

Kendall walked inside the saloon and joined his outlaw
friends. This was going to be a fine winter. They would
take their herd of stolen horses, which was kept hidden in
a canyon west of Virginia City, to Canada soon, then hole
up in Virginia City for the winter, laying low for a while
until those who might be searching for them gave up.

In the spring they would go on another expedition of
raiding ranches and stealing more horses, again taking
them to Canada. And by next spring Joline Masters's
herd should have grown some. Kendall couldn't wait
to see her face when he took every horse she owned, let
alone the other things he intended to do to her. He
ordered a drink and joined in the conversation, proud to
be part of Sonny Morrow's gang. His pride swelled even
more at the thought of showing Sonny how important and
informed he was, when he told the man about a place
where it would be easy to get some fine horses—a ranch
along the Ruby River, run by one little woman.

Jo hurried toward the other end of town, staying behind
the buildings and ducking back more than once when she
thought someone would see her. The short distance seemed
like ten miles, but she finally spotted the pink frame house
of "ill repute," which was kept surprisingly neat, with rose
bushes planted around a veranda that surrounded the
entire house. The three-story building was trimmed in
white, and there were porch swings on the veranda.

Jo cautiously approached a back door and knocked. A
young girl of perhaps fifteen opened the door, startling Jo
with her youth. She wore a white maid's cap and an apron.
"Yes, ma'am? You wanting a job with Miss Turrell?"

Jo's eyes widened. "No! And I don't want any men who
might be in there to see me. I need to talk to Miss
Turrell."

The girl opened the door. "Come on in. This is just the
kitchen. Ain't no men in here."

Jo stepped inside, breathing in the scent of fresh-baked
bread. She was suprised at the domestic atmosphere in
the kitchen. But beyond the kitchen walls she could hear
women's laughter, mixed with the louder guffaws of men.
Some woman was singing to the accompaniment of a piano.

"I'll go get Miss Turrell," the young girl in the kitchen
told Jo. Jo had a sudden urge to stop her and run away
from this place, wondering why she had been stupid enough
to come at all, but the girl was already going through a
door, and Jo didn't want to attract any attention. When
the door opened she noticed a man carrying a half-naked

woman up a stairway. Jo just stared wide-eyed until the door closed, then sat down at the kitchen table, shuddering at the thought of what the women here did for money. Still, how different was she from them? She was unmarried and pregnant, a situation almost as bad as being a whore.

She waited for what seemed an eternity before the door finally opened and Sally Turrell walked inside, still wearing the green taffeta dress. She closed the door behind her, staring dumbfounded at a blushing Jo Masters. She sauntered closer, frowning. "What on earth are you doing here, of all places?"

Jo looked at her lap, fingering her handbag. "I'm not sure myself."

Sally's eyebrows arched and she came closer and sat down. "Is it about Clint?"

Jo met Sally's green eyes then, her own eyes showing a flash of jealousy. Sally grinned a little. "If you want the truth, your Mr. Reeves did more talking than anything else around here, and it was usually about you." She leaned back in her chair. "I know about Clint—what happened in Minnesota and all. But I always had a feeling he wasn't telling me everything. There was something more— something he tried to bury under too much whiskey. My guess is you know what it is, which means Clint must think a lot of you to bare his soul to you." The woman sighed, folding her arms. "I know one thing. He thought you were the prettiest, strongest, bravest, best all-around woman he'd ever known and he had damn strong feelings for you. Only he was afraid certain problems he had would make him mess things up." She watched Jo closely. "You wanting to know if I've heard from him? I'm afraid I haven't."

"That's not why I'm here," Jo answered quietly, dropping her eyes again. "I know his problems, Miss Turrell. I don't know what he told you when he left, but he . . . he promised . . . to come back in the spring . . . if he could stay off whiskey until then. Of course, there's no guarantee I'll ever see him again."

"So? I could guess all that. That still doesn't explain why you're here."

Jo met Sally's gaze again, swallowing for courage. "I just . . . needed to talk to someone . . . another woman . . . one who understands things and . . . knows about life; not some busybody who'd repeat everything she heard over a quilting bee."

Sally frowned. "What's wrong?"

Jo looked around the room nervously and blinked back tears. "I'm, that is, I *think* I'm . . . carrying Clint's baby." She waited for the gasp, the exclamation; but Sally only leaned forward, resting her arms on the table.

"So," she said, thoughtfully staring at a sugar bowl. "He *did* come to see you before he left. Couldn't stand the last good-bye, hmmm?"

Jo swallowed, staring at the checkered tablecloth. "Something like that." She met Sally's eyes. "I love him. And Clint loves me. It was . . . I don't know . . . almost the natural thing to do. It seemed so right, even though I knew Clint could make no promises. It didn't matter. I thought maybe . . . maybe you'd understand." She sighed deeply. "All I know is I feel better just telling you."

"You want my approval? My advice? I'm still not sure what you're looking for. If you want to know I understand I do." Her eyes moved over Jo, appreciating her beauty. "And I can understand why Clint was so weak."

Jo shrugged. "I was, too. I had just spent the morning bargaining with some Sioux Indians and I was pretty shaken by the time Clint got there. The Indians had left, but . . . I was so scared and relieved at the same time. When I saw Clint, nobody ever looked better. I knew in that moment I loved him a lot more than I realized. And I had missed him . . . so much. It was almost easier letting him go . . . afterward . . . than if I had let him go without . . . without . . . being with him that way." She met Sally's eyes again. "Do you know what I'm saying?"

Sally grinned a little. "Sure I do. I'm human and I'm a woman. There are reasons why I do what I do for a living, Mrs. Masters—"

"Joline."

"Fine. Call me Sally. At any rate, there is a human being behind this face and paint, Joline. But I'm still not sure if you expect something from me."

Jo shifted in her chair, setting her handbag on the table. "I suppose I don't expect anything, except any advice you might have. I'm staying in Montana. I just bought more land next to my ranch, the LAZY J, and I'll be buying a good stud horse before I go back. But here I am—a single woman who is about to grow a big belly. How do I explain it? And what do I do if Clint doesn't come back?" She closed her eyes and put her head in her hands. "I don't want the men around here to think I'm a loose woman, and I don't want my baby to be called dirty names."

"You should try to get hold of Clint."

"No!" Jo met the woman's eyes again. "If he comes back it has to be for me, just for *me*, not because of the baby."

"He has a right to know."

"And he *will* know—when he comes back. If he doesn't return, maybe he's better off not knowing. I'll have to decide then. But I have to give him that chance to come back on his own, Sally. Can you understand that, too?"

The woman sighed. "There aren't many things I *don't* understand. But you're right about how people would talk—and that baby can't be born a bastard."

Jo shuddered at the word, closing her eyes and holding her head again. "So, what do I do?"

"Find a man to marry you—someone you trust not to force his husbandly rights on you—someone who'll give the baby a name and be willing to give you up once Clint comes back."

Jo shook her head. "That's a lot to ask of any man. Where am I going to find someone like that?"

"That's an area where I can't help you. How far along are you?"

"About three months, I guess."

"You could try to get rid of it."

"No!" Jo's heart pounded wildly at the mere suggestion. "I'd never do such a thing! It's a baby, a live baby growing inside of me. And it's *Clint's* child. I could never tell him I had done such a thing to his child, especially after he's lost a wife and son! If Clint comes back a whole man, he'd want this child more than anything."

Sally nodded. "I suppose he would." She put up her hands. "Well, you've heard my suggestion."

Jo glanced around the room. "I don't know. I've survived a lot of things, Sally. And I daresay I've bluffed my way out of a lot of things. There have been times when I've forced myself to appear confident and brave, made strange men realize they'd better not give me trouble, bluffed my way out of a sticky situation with those Indians. I've shot a mountain lion, elk, a grizzly—shot a few men, too. I survived the winter alone out there and made enough money this summer to buy some more land." She shook her head. "You'd think there would be a way to get through this, too, without having to use some poor soul to take part in a lie with me. I've handled everything else alone. I should be able to handle this alone, too."

Sally grinned. "Still determined to be independent, are you? Don't forget you're going to have another little life depending on you in a few months. By the way, you planning on having the baby out there all alone, too? Might as well add that to your record of accomplishments."

Jo rose and paced. "You think I'm crazy, don't you?"

Sally sobered. "No. I think you're one hell of a woman— and deep inside that's exactly what you are—a *woman*, with all the needs and emotions of any woman. That's why you took Clint Reeves to your bed, and that's why you'll have this baby of his and love it a whole lot more than you ever loved Clint or this land or anything else."

Jo felt the crimson come into her cheeks again at the comment about taking Clint to her bed. Such words came so easily to women like Sally. But she was exactly right, and that was the hell of it. She walked closer to the table. "Sally, are there any crooked preachers in town?"

Sally's eyes widened and she laughed lightly. "Crooked *preachers?*"

Jo sat back down. "Sure! This town is crawling with every kind of lowlife who ever walked. There must be some preachers in town who are technically, legally preachers, but who wouldn't hesitate to accept a little bribe to do someone a favor—a Christian act that would help them out—like a fake marriage license?"

Sally just stared at her, then grinned even more. "And I thought you were so innocent. You're quite a woman, Joline Masters, just like Clint said."

Jo leaned closer. "If I could get a marriage license, dated back to this spring, saying Clint is legally my husband, that would solve the problem, wouldn't it? Are there any preachers in town who got in only a couple of months ago—someone who could say he was passing through my place and Clint and I asked him to marry us?"

Sally chuckled. "Honey, this town is full of Bible-carrying hypocrites, gamblers, cheating speculators, outlaws, panhandlers—you name it, this town's got it."

"Do you think you could find someone to make up a fake marriage license for me?"

"How are you going to explain Clint's absence?"

"He had already promised to do some scouting for the army. People in town won't think anything of it, since neither Clint nor I has been back to town to say anything one way or the other. The only ones I really need to convince are the men working for me. I think I can do that. I'll just tell them Clint will be back in the spring— that he wasn't worried because he knew I'd be hiring good men—that he obviously didn't know about the baby. I'm sure I could make it work, Sally. I can't leave Virginia City before tomorrow anyway. I'm getting a room at the Mountain Inn. You could have the marriage license delivered to me there. I'll pay you, and whoever you get to do it. But you have to swear never to tell the truth."

Sally just grinned and shook her head. "I don't want any money. Clint was a good man—troubled, but good deep inside. He'd *want* me to do it. I'll see what I can do. How much can you pay?"

Jo rummaged through her handbag. "Ten dollars is as high as I can go."

"That's plenty," Sally lied, knowing it would take much more. She liked Joline Masters. More than that, she liked Clint. She would pay the difference herself. She got up from her chair. "You go take care of whatever business you have to take care of. I'll see what I can do."

Jo sighed with relief. "I don't know why, but I just knew you could help me, Sally. Maybe it's because we both . . . cared about Clint."

Sally smiled resignedly. "Yes. We both did. But to me he was just a little more special than all the others. For you there *were* no others. It's the same for Clint. To him I was just a sounding board, someone to relieve his need for you. But you—you're everything to him." She walked to the door. "Now you'd better get going. And make sure no one sees you. Decent women don't usually come calling on women like me."

Jo stepped closer. "I've chosen my way; you've chosen yours, both for reasons we don't need to explain to the other." She turned and laid ten dollars in silver coins on the table. "Thank you, Sally." She faced her again. "If circumstances were different, we might be good friends. I miss the company of women."

Sally blinked, looking for a moment as though she were struggling with a touch of emotion. "Well, maybe you'll get some neighbors eventually. Once you have that kid you'll want to share talk about raising the little devil—and being Clint's kid, it *will* be a little devil—boy or girl."

Jo smiled. "Now all I have to do is explain to Moose Barkley and the other two men working for me."

"Well, the rest of the town will be easy to fool, since this is the first time you've been back since you first arrived. In fact, I'll start spreading the rumor myself that you and Clint got married last spring. What about when you have the baby? Somebody besides a bunch of no-good cowhands should be with you."

Jo put a hand to her stomach. "I suppose. I . . . don't know a whole lot about birthing a baby, let alone my own. I've watched it with animals." She smiled nervously. "But I have to admit I'm a little frightened. I think I'd rather face that grizzly."

Sally put a hand on her arm. "When you think you're getting close, send Moose for me. I've helped with several—my girls, once in a while they get careless. They usually find a husband. Out in a place like this, lonely men will settle with anything to have a wife to turn to in the night. Lots of my girls end up getting married, even without having to." She let go of Jo's arm. "At any rate, nobody has to know where I've gone. I'd be glad to come help you, if you don't mind having me in your house. You can tell Moose you told me about the baby because I was the only woman in town you had met—and because I was a friend of Clint's. I know Moose Barkley. He'll understand."

Jo nodded. "I'll send for you. But I'm afraid it's pretty lonely out there."

"No matter. Fact is, I guess I wouldn't mind getting away from all this craziness for a while anyway."

Jo hugged the woman spontaneously. "Thank you, Sally."

Sally opened the door. "Get going. I'll be in touch sometime later tonight."

Jo quickly headed outside, turning to wave before hurrying for two blocks behind some buildings, then ducking up a narrow alley to the main street. She walked casually then, nodding to men who stared or gave her their greetings. A few followed her, enjoying the sight of a pretty woman. Some men were dressed in suits, businessmen come to town to take advantage of the prospectors. Jo passed a few respectable-looking women, and all of them had a man on their arm. They stared at her as though she were insane to be walking alone, but Jo felt no fear. She was Clint Reeves's woman, a fact that was respected even if Clint wasn't around. Soon they would know just how serious a statement that was, when they all found out she and Clint were "married." She would only pray her scheme would work, and she was determined to give her child Clint's last name.

She lifted her skirts and had to wait several minutes for horses and wagons to pass before she could dart across the street again. She unhitched her horses and climbed up into the wagon, driving it to the supply store. Moose was inside waiting for her. "Where you been?" he asked. "I figured you'd have been here by now."

Jo looked up at him. "I . . . I thought you were going to have a couple of beers."

"I was. But I checked first at the telegraph office, and they had this here letter for you."

Jo took it from him, thinking it might be from Clint. But it was from Anna. She smiled, clutching the letter. "Anna!" She looked up at Moose again. "It's from my sister. This is my first letter from her since I left Lawrence." Jo put the letter in her handbag. "I'll read this when I get to my room tonight. Would you do me a favor and see if you can get me a room at the Mountain Inn?"

"Yes, ma'am."

"I'll order my supplies and wait for you to get back,

then we'll go see about the horses. Did you find any decent-looking studs?"

"Yes, ma'am, one fine black one and a buckskin."

"Good. And, Moose . . . ," Jo touched his arm. "I . . . need to talk to you about something later tonight."

"Sure thing. I'd better try to get that room first. You go ahead and order up the supplies and we'll load them up in the mornin' before we leave." He gave her a nod and walked out.

Jo watched after him, anxious to read Anna's letter; but there were things to take care of first. She wondered if Sally would come through for her with a marriage license, and how Moose would take the news. Most of all she wondered how Clint would react when he came back and found out he had a child—if he came back at all.

Chapter Twenty-four

Jo carefully opened the letter, praying the news inside would be good. Seeing Anna's handwriting made her miss her sister even more.

"Dear Jo," she read. "I would have written sooner, but I had to wait until you were settled in one place. I'm sorry you had to leave Lawrence so quickly, but I think I understand, and sometimes I envy you being far away from all the turmoil here. Still, I worry so much about you, what with all the stories you told me in your letters. What has happened between you and your friend and guide, Clint Reeves? He sounds like quite a man, but also a very troubled man. If you have found love again, I am happy for you.

"How I wish we could be together to share our adventures and heartaches. It is such a brave thing you have done, and I pray every day that you are well and happy and have realized your dream of having your own land in Montana.

"Now, I must be brave. By the time you get this letter, a Union victory will probably be in all the headlines, as I am sure it is coming soon. But I sometimes wonder if it will ever really be over. There is still so much hatred and bitterness left. My own Darryl is not the same man who left to go to war four years ago. I cannot explain what has happened. It is still too painful for me. Perhaps some

day I will find the courage to tell you, once I understand fully myself what went wrong. I can only tell
you that Darryl did survive the war, but our marriage is over, and the love we once shared is gone.
Besides this heartache, outlaws and raiders have been
running rampant, jayhawkers and bushwhackers who
continue their devious crimes in the name of revenge. Without a war for an excuse, they are simply
criminals, which I feel is all they ever were.

"I am sorry to burden you with this terrible news.
At least you know I am still well and safe. I wish this
war would end, not just on paper, but in the hearts
of men. I fear that will take much, much longer. I
pray every day that Darryl will come to his senses
and return to being the fine young doctor I married.
I know this sounds terrible, but sometimes I feel I
would have been better off if he had been killed in
battle like Greg, than to come back the man he is
now. May God forgive me for such a thought.

"For now, I am compelled to support myself
through my own efforts. I am leaving Columbia and
all things familiar. For now I intend to go as far west
as the Kansas-Pacific will take me. Maybe I will
come all the way to Montana and join you. Whatever
happens, I will let you know where I am.

"Please pray for me, Jo, as I pray for you. Write
again soon and tell me how you survived the winter.
I have heard winters are bitterly cold where you are.
I do hope you're all right. For now you can continue
to write me here in Columbia at the boarding house
where I live and work. The address is on the envelope. I have left my employment at the restaurant
with Fran Rogers. Her husband, Darryl's best friend,
was killed in the war. Fran considers me a Yankee
and treated me so rudely I was forced to quit.

"I will leave a forwarding address if and when I
settle someplace new. I so look forward to your
letters, and I save each one, so do keep writing and
keep me informed.

"All my love,
"Anna."

Jo carefully folded the letter, tears welling up in her eyes. What terrible things were happening to her sister? She knew Anna well enough to realize she was not exaggerating. If anything, things were much worse than she had even described in her letter. Was Darryl abusing her? What kind of man had he become?

She laid the letter on a dresser next to the hotel bed. It seemed the war had disrupted people's lives in ways unrelated to actual battle. Anna's life had been turned as upside down as her own. Because of the war she was waging her own battle here in Montana just to survive, and she was carrying the child of a man she probably never would have met if not for Quantrill's raid.

There came a light knock at the door, and Jo rose from the bed and made her way to the door, hesitating before opening it. "Who's there?"

"It's me—Sally," came the soft reply.

Jo quickly opened the door and let the woman inside. Sally wore a cape and hood. "I don't think anyone noticed me," she told Jo, removing her hood.

"It's all right."

"No. It's better this way." She handed Jo an envelope. "There it is. Don't ask questions and don't ask to meet the man who prepared it for me. His name is Joseph Sneed, and he wandered into Virginia City a couple of months ago. He preaches in the streets and uses his white collar and Bible to get people to trust him—preaches by day and robs miners by night. When he isn't robbing miners he's at my place taking his delight in some young girl."

Jo's eyes widened.

"Some preacher, huh?" Sally snickered with disgust. "The license inside that envelope is real, though, and Reverend Sneed signed it." She said the word "Reverend" sarcastically. "Of course, it's a lie, but the paper is genuine enough. All you have to do is sign your name and Clint's at the bottom. Forge in whatever witnesses you want. Sneed used the date of last May first."

Jo clutched the envelope, "I suddenly feel like such a criminal," she said quietly.

"Well, don't. And don't you dare feel ashamed. If Clint got you pregnant, then that's what God meant to happen. The baby could be the best cure for him once he comes back, his best insurance against the whiskey bottle." She put a hand on Jo's arm. "He *will* come back, Jo. The way he talked, anybody could see how much he loved you. He won't be able to stay away. You just be sure to send for me when your time is close, you hear?"

"I will. Thank you so much, Sally."

"I didn't do much of anything. I liked you from that first time I met you, Jo. I told myself—there's a woman with guts; I hope to hell she makes it. So far you have." She put the hood back up. "Get some sleep and I'll see you in a few months. I just hope there isn't too much snow for me to get out there." She turned and opened the door before Jo could say another word. After peeking out to be sure no one was about, she quickly left.

Jo closed and bolted the door, staring down at the piece of paper. She still had not talked to Moose about any of this. The afternoon had been spent picking out the stud horse they would take back with them. He was a big, sturdy buckskin with black mane and tail, a feisty, eager animal that was obviously ornery and unpredictable, but the finest horse Jo had ever set eyes on. Already the name "Buck" seemed the only reasonable one for him as far as Jo was concerned, and she couldn't wait to get him back to the ranch and put the Lazy J brand on him.

She sat back down on the bed, thinking again about Anna. How could she explain the baby to her sister? Should she lie about the marriage to Anna as she would do with everyone else? Or should she just tell her the truth? She got a piece of paper and pen and ink from her supplies and lay across the bed, turning up the nearby lantern to see better. This would be a long letter, but it would help her through what she knew was going to be a sleepless night.

She set the fake marriage license aside. She would look at it later and fill in the names. There was still a chance she was not pregnant at all, though she knew that was only wishful thinking. She sighed, a lump rising in her throat.

"Please come back, Clint," she whispered. Every part of her ached for him. But she wondered now if, even in her present predicament, she might not be better off than Anna. She suspected Anna was not telling her the worst of it. She wondered what Greg might have been like now if he had lived. Would he have come back a changed man, too? What a terrible thing, to have a husband still alive but to look at him as a stranger.

She decided Anna had enough problems for the moment. She would not tell her sister about her pregnancy until Clint returned and the baby was born. There was no sense worrying Anna with her present situation. There was nothing Anna could do about it.

"Dear Anna," she wrote. "I hope you receive this letter, as I have only your Columbia address, and you said in your last letter you would be leaving. It is July, 1865, and yes, by the time I got your letter, the war was over. I am so sorry to hear the bad news about the trouble that continues there, and especially sorry about you and Darryl. Out here the war doesn't matter much. All that matters is surviving a typical Montana winter, and I will tell you what that is like . . ."

It was called the Powder River Expedition. Clint was glad for the immense project that lay ahead. Scouting for the army on this particular venture meant being more alert than he had ever had to be, which meant no drinking. He would much rather be lying next to Jo than heading out on this mission for the army, but he had to be sure he was free of the past, be sure it was Joline Masters he loved and wanted, and not just a memory. His bones and nerves ached for a swallow of whiskey, but he refused to touch it. He knew it was whiskey that kept his past alive rather than helping him bury it, whiskey that kept him from Jo.

He moved out of Fort Laramie the first of August with three thousand troops, all headed toward the Powder River in northwest Wyoming. More troops were headed toward the Black Hills and the Tongue River, and fourteen hundred more men should this very moment be heading out of Omaha to circle the Black Hills and the northern edge of the Bighorn Mountains, where they would all meet near the Tongue River.

The Sioux and Northern Cheyenne were on a rampage that had settlers terrified from mid-eastern Colorado all the way to the Canadian border. Clint could hardly blame the Indians, after hearing about the massacre of peaceful Southern Cheyenne at Sand Creek, Colorado, by Colorado Volunteers under a Colonel John Chivington.

Since hearing about Sand Creek, he had been able to think more clearly about the Indians, to understand their hatred and bitterness. What had happened to women and children at Sand Creek was no different from what had happened to his wife and son. The worst part was it had been done by supposedly civilized men. At least when the Indians murdered and tortured, it was part of their culture, their way of fighting. But for white men to do what had been done at Sand Creek . . . to cut babies from mothers' bellies and carve up bodies while still alive and screaming . . . to kill tiny children in cold blood. . . .

He could find no reason for it. But the massacre had helped him put what had happened to his own family into clearer perspective. Now Red Cloud and his Sioux, inspired by the horrors of what had happened to their Cheyenne friends and brothers, were causing havoc for settlers for hundreds of miles. In spite of the lance that Yellow Wolf had left in front of Jo's cabin, Clint was worried about her, and he had already decided that as soon as this expedition was over, he would go back.

Being away from Jo was worse than he had expected. His nights were restless, his need of her agony. It had not taken long for him to realize more and more that it really was Joline he hungered for, Joline Masters he loved and needed. Bedding her had given him more pleasure than he had known before, and knowing she was waiting for him gave him a new strength.

"Figure we'll find Red Cloud and his devils?" a soldier riding beside him spoke up, interrupting Clint's thoughts.

"Hard to say," Clint answered. "Indians can be damned tricky, and they know this country better than any white man ever will."

"Even a man like you?"

"Even me." Clint puffed on a thin cigar.

"You've fought Indians a lot, I'll bet."

Clint thought about Minnesota. "I have. Didn't always come out ahead, though."

"I've never fought them before. Kind of scary."

Clint looked over at the young recruit, who looked as though he didn't even need to shave yet. "It can be. But I hold a lot of respect for them, Private. They're as cunning in battle as the best soldier—and they ride a hell of a lot better and faster. You soldiers carry too much gear, and you make too much noise coming in—all those swords clanking and saddles squeaking and supply wagons rattling. But, that's the army."

"That's what we have men like you for, isn't it? To ride on ahead and see what's up there so we don't ride right into something?"

Clint nodded. "Soon as we get closer to the Powder you won't see much of me or the other scouts."

The private turned to look back at a large band of Pawnee who accompanied them. "Can those Indians be trusted?"

Clint glanced back at them himself and grinned. "The Pawnee? They've got a great hatred for the Sioux and Cheyenne. They can be trusted. We run into trouble, they'll be fighting right by your side, and gladly."

They rode on in silence for the next few minutes. "Kind of strange, isn't it?" the private spoke up then.

"What's that?"

"Indians fighting Indians. And in the Civil War it was us whites fighting each other. Now that the war is over, we all band together to fight Indians. Seems like men just have it in their blood to fight, doesn't it? If we can't find good reason, we invent one."

Clint sighed. "It does seem that way. It's all kind of a stupid waste, isn't it? Actually, I don't blame the Sioux for what they're doing. I suppose I'd do the same thing, if—" He stopped short and puffed his cigar. "At any rate, they've got to be stopped. It's too bad, because this land really was theirs first. But how are we going to stop more whites from coming in? It's like trying to hold up a huge crack in a damn with just a finger. As long as whites insist on coming out here, somebody has to protect them, I guess. It's gold that started the whole thing, gold and free land."

"I guess the Indians will just have to learn to accept it, won't they?"

"I suppose."

"You got family, Mr. Reeves?"

Clint stared straight ahead. "Did have," he answered. "My wife and son were killed by the Sioux up in Minnesota." Somehow the words came out a little easier; and he didn't feel the awful need to drink and forget. *"You have to face the past and accept it,"* Jo had told him. Being with her, making love to her, hearing her words of love had given him a strength he had not felt for a long time.

"Gosh, I'm sorry, Mr. Reeves. No wonder you volunteer to hunt them down."

"What?" Clint looked at him, only then realizing what the boy had said. "Oh, it isn't because of that." He looked straight ahead again, keeping the cigar at the corner of his mouth as he spoke. "A man can carry that kind of hatred and sorrow only so long, Private. Then there comes a time when he has to shed himself of it or go crazy and destroy his life. I have other reasons for being here, and I have someone special to go back to. In fact, if I hadn't given General Connor my word to scout for him, I'd go back to her right now. I thought for a while it was best to leave, for personal reasons. But I was wrong. Soon as this expedition is over, I'm going back. A lot of things have become more clear to me lately."

The young soldier grinned. "What's her name?"

Clint puffed on the cigar again for a moment. "Jo. Joline Masters. She's one hell of a woman, I'll tell you. She's the kind who could get along just fine without a man at her side, and then again she sure knows how to make a man feel like a man."

"I haven't had time to find one special woman yet," the private said. "All I got time for are the women who follow the soldiers and put up their tents outside the forts, if you know what I mean."

Clint laughed. "I know exactly what you mean." The conversation stirred aching needs deep inside, needs only Jo could satisfy now. He had given no thought to the whores since leaving Jo, had no desire for any other women.

"You think the rest of the soldiers will meet us like they're supposed to?" the private asked then. "I mean, what if we get caught out here all alone and a few thousand Indians surround us?"

Clint gave him a wink. "That's why you've got me and Jim Bridger along—to make sure that doesn't happen." He

took the cigar from his mouth. "Buck up, Private. Lieutenant Colonel Walker and Colonel Cole will both make it
to the Tongue in time. My guess is we'll never find the
biggest share of the Sioux anyway. They're too smart. I
tried to tell your officers that, but they won't listen. This
whole campaign could be useless, but Washington has
spoken, so here we are. But Red Cloud has this whole
area pretty much bottled up."

"Aren't you afraid to go out ahead alone?"

"Sometimes. I just have to read tracks and try to think
like the Indians so they stay only one step ahead of me and
don't circle around behind me."

The private glanced at the array of weapons Clint wore—
knives, guns, an ammunition belt, a rifle in its boot attached to his saddle. "Well, I sure wouldn't want to go up
against you."

Clint just grinned. "You take care of yourself, son. It's
time I rode on ahead."

"But we only left Fort Laramie two days ago."

"That's far enough to start being careful." Clint finished
his cigar and kicked his horse into a faster gallop, riding
past column after column of soldiers. He hoped this expedition wouldn't move into the winter. He had planned to
stay away from Jo until the spring. After all, she had
Moose and other responsible men working for her now.
But everything had become much more clear for him now.
He was in love—with a real woman, not a memory.

He rode to the crest of the next rise, gazing out over
vast, open country. Red Cloud and his thousands of Sioux
and Cheyenne could be anywhere. The army's plan was to
encircle the area most used by the Indians in late fall and
winter, then close in. Clint rode with General Connor's
troops. Lt. Colonel Samuel Walker would approach from
the west, Colonel Nelson Cole from the east. If plans
worked right, the bulk of the Sioux and Cheyenne force
would be trapped in the Powder River area. But Clint
knew trapping Indians could be like trying to net a fast,
slippery fish or grab a bird. He headed north, beginning
his own search.

Jo and Moose watched Buck prance and shake his head
as he investigated his new corral. "He's beautiful, Moose,"

Jo commented. "I think I made a really good deal. As soon as we know some of the mares are ready to mate we'll bring them to him and see what happens. I should get some fine fillies and colts out of him, shouldn't I?"

"Yes, ma'am, you surely should. You did right buyin' that one."

Jo sighed and faced him. "Moose, I need to tell you something."

Moose pushed back his hat. He was never clean shaven, and his beard was gray and white, his shoulder-length hair also turning white. Moose Barkley was an aging, rugged mountain man who seldom bathed, but Jo knew his heart was good as gold and his appearance never offended her. "Well, ma'am, I was wonderin' when you'd get around to it. You told me back in town that you needed to talk to me about somethin', but you never brought up anything unusual. What is it you've been havin' on your mind? You upset with somethin' I did?"

"Oh, no! It's nothing like that, Moose. You've been so much help." She turned to look at Buck again. "I just thought you should know . . ." She swallowed. "Clint and I . . . the last time he was here, a traveling preacher came through and . . . well . . . we decided to marry."

There was a long silence. Jo glanced at Moose and saw him frowning. "Marry?" He finally spoke up. He thought it through another moment. "Well, that's just . . . just fine. I'm real happy for you. But . . . I don't quite understand, ma'am—I mean . . . Clint went away."

Jo dropped her eyes. "Yes. He was already committed to a scouting job for the army."

Moose watched her closely. He knew Clint well, knew the man had personal problems. "Ma'am, excuse me, but if I had just married you, I sure wouldn't want to be leavin'. That don't sound like Clint."

Jo refused to meet his eyes, looking back at Buck. "Nevertheless, it's true. Clint . . . had some personal things to straighten out. I told him it was all right. He's coming back . . . in the spring. Everything will be all right then." She sighed deeply. "Moose, I need you and at least one of the other men to stay on through the winter. I can't afford to pay all three, so one will have to leave. I'd try to make it through the winter alone again, but . . . I don't have just myself to worry about now. I'm . . . I'm going to have a baby."

Moose's eyes widened, and his mind raced with confusion. Clint had married her, then left her? And now she was carrying his baby? "Does Clint know about that?"

"No."

"Well, you're going to get word to him, ain't you?"

She shook her head. "No. I . . . I don't want him to have it on his mind when he's supposed to be tracking Indians or whatever he'll be doing. All his senses have to be alert."

"But, ma'am, he ought to know."

"This is the way I want it, Moose." She finally met his eyes. "I know it all sounds strange, but please just accept it and try to understand. I . . . I have a marriage license, if you don't believe—"

"Oh, no, ma'am, I don't doubt what you're tellin' me! I just . . . well, it just seems like Clint should know."

Jo turned away again. "He'll be back and everything will be fine. Come February or so I'll have a fine baby for Clint, and next summer some of my mares will deliver, and Clint will be here. We'll fence off that new land." She faced the man again. "Will you stay the winter?"

Moose removed his hat. "Yes, ma'am. Sure."

"And I'll need a woman around when my time comes. I'll want you to go and get Sally Turrell around the first of February."

"Sally Turrell! Ma'am, she's a—"

"I know what she is. But I met her once, and she's the only woman who has taken a moment to talk to me and to say that if I ever need help here I should tell her. I expect a woman like that should know about birthing babies, considering some of her own girls must surely get in that kind of trouble at times. Other women—family women—they look at me like I'm some kind of oddity. At least Sally Turrell has taken the time to show some kindness and concern. Will you get her for me when the time comes?"

"Yes, ma'am. Whatever you want."

She put a hand on his arm. "Thank you, Moose. And . . . tell Jason and Rubin for me, will you? Make them understand."

Moose nodded and watched her walk back toward the

cabin. The whole story about her and Clint marrying seemed strange, and he still couldn't imagine Clint marrying her and then leaving—unless they hadn't really married at all. Clint had brought out her supplies last spring. They had been alone together.

The man sighed and shook his head. He suspected the truth, and Clint ought to know. But Joline Masters had spoken, and Moose respected her too much to voice what he thought was the real story. Joline was carrying Clint's baby, all right, but there had been no marriage. How she had got a license, he wasn't sure, but he was not going to question it or let her know he didn't believe her. He'd known all along how she felt about Clint Reeves and how Clint felt about her.

"He never should have brought out them supplies," he muttered.

Chapter Twenty-five

The wind blew bitterly cold, stinging Clint's face with a cutting, wet sleet. As he had suspected, the entire expedition to find Red Cloud had been fruitless. For weeks General Connor's troops had searched for the other two columns that were supposed to meet them. By the time they were located, the soldiers under Lt. Colonel Walker and those under Colonel Cole were together but starving. An early fall snowstorm had confused their march and had killed several of their horses, and as they struggled on, they were harassed daily by close to a thousand Sioux and Cheyenne warriors. The only thing that had saved the soldiers was that the Indians did not have enough guns to attack full force.

Clint had helped Connor lead the weak and footsore soldiers back to Fort Connor, a hastily built stronghold near the Tongue River where some soldiers remained while others went back to Fort Laramie. Clint stayed with the soldiers at Fort Connor, which he realized now was a mistake. The fort was constantly under siege from Indians, so intense that a hunting expedition of only a few miles required fifty men, several days of rations, forty rounds of ammunition per man, and more ammunition in wagons.

Lately the weather prevented such expeditions, and hay and oats for the few horses left alive was running low. Reinforcements and new supplies were supposedly on their way, but a few men, terrified that the Indians would overrun the fort completely, had deserted. Some had died of scurvy, others were literally starving to death. It was December, 1865, and the bitter winter was only making things worse for the isolated soldiers. In spite of the weather, the Indians managed to remain camped in the hills around the fort and continued to harass and attack any men who exited the fort to hunt for food.

Clint had taken it upon himself to go out alone to hunt, figuring one man alone who knew Indian ways might have a better chance at success than an entire regiment. He guided his horse silently through deep snow, keeping to thick pines, his keen senses on constant guard. He saw no sign of tracks of Indian ponies or moccasined feet as he guided his horse up a treacherous incline and into even thicker pines.

He couldn't help wondering how Jo was managing this winter. He was glad she at least had Moose with her, but spring couldn't come soon enough for him now. In fact, he intended to head back to Virginia City—and the woman who waited for him in the Ruby River Valley—just as soon as relief came for the men at Fort Connor, even if that was much sooner than he had originally intended. The fact that it was the middle of winter didn't matter. Alone, with just his horse and a packhorse, he could make it to Montana even in the dead of winter. But for now the Indian threat was a much greater deterrent than the weather.

Right now, with the sleet beating against his face, he could not imagine anything nicer than lying in a warm bed with Jo, the little cabin warm from a fire in the hearth, the howling wind outside unable to reach the man and woman snuggled under blankets inside. He wondered now why he had ever left. Jo was right. He had been running for years, but it was a useless flight, since all he was running from was himself, his own memories. He had to learn to live with both, and he was no longer going to use whiskey to dull the hurt or help him pretend the hurt wasn't there at all. It *was* there, and it was never going to change. He simply had to go on from here, just as Jo had learned to do.

It had been seven long months since the day and night he had spent in her arms, and he had gone longer than that without whiskey. It hadn't taken the year or more he thought it would take for him to know for certain what he

wanted. In fact, he had known it the minute he rode away
from Jo, but the lingering fear of caring again had kept
him riding, and giving his word to General Connor had kept
him away.

He finally spotted what looked like deer tracks and he
followed them for close to two miles, realizing he was
dangerously far from the fort but also knowing that if he
didn't bring back some meat, more men could die. The
wind picked up and the sleet began turning to snow. Clint
looked up at a dark, threatening sky, then caught sight of a
cavelike cutout in the bank just above. He pulled his hat
down farther to keep the sleet and snow from biting at his
eyes, and turned up the collar of his wolfskin coat, heading
his horse up the hill. He maneuvered the animal into the
little cavity, but it was not high enough for man and horse
together. He ducked his head and dismounted as the wind
rose and snow swirled over the opening to the cave with
an angry howl. He was glad he had found shelter; the
snow was already coming hard and fast. His only worry
was how long he would have to hole up here.

He kept hold of the reins to his horse and settled back
against the wall of the cave, closing his eyes and thinking
of Jo, and how beautiful it was in the Ruby Valley. He and
Jo had come a long way together, both emotionally and
physically, since they made that trip west. He wondered
what he would be doing now if he hadn't helped Joline
Masters the day of the Quantrill raid. He remembered
that day as vividly as if it were yesterday.

The storm raged for several hours. The sun sank behind
the Bighorn Mountains, and Clint removed a bedroll and
buffalo robe from his horse and made up a place to sleep.
He took a dried apple from his gear and fed it to his horse.

"That's it for now, boy. I'll help you dig through the
snow to find something to eat come morning."

The animal whinnied quietly and nuzzled him for a
moment, and Clint took out a piece of jerked meat and
settled into his crude bed for the night. In spite of cold
and hunger, he managed to doze off, his rifle beside him.
As he moved in and out of sleep he was aware that
sometime during the night the howling wind had stopped,
and he woke at sunrise to see huge, fat snowflakes drifting

quietly to the ground, piling up snow at the rate of several inches an hour.

"Damn weather," he grumbled. He wasn't sure if he should go on or just return to the fort. At the rate it was snowing, he might get stranded for days and starve to death, although going back wouldn't help much. Everyone there was starving, too, thanks to the wily Sioux.

He rose, throwing off the buffalo robe and rolling it up with his bedroll, tying everything back onto his horse. It was then he heard the soft call, like an owl. He frowned, his keen ears telling him it was not an owl at all. He quickly removed his gloves so it would be easier to handle a gun. He picked up his rifle, grimacing at how cold it felt in his hands. He cocked the gun and moved closer to the cave entrance, pushing his horse farther back. Clint watched the thick pines surrounding the cave, then suddenly caught sight of feathers and buckskins as a Sioux brave darted from one tree to the next.

Clint raised his rifle, took careful aim, and waited. The brave peeked from around the trunk of a huge pine, and Clint fired. He heard a man cry out. Now he saw more Indians darting back and forth, looking up from behind boulders, and he knew he was outnumbered. He fired twice more, hitting another warrior. Again he cocked and fired, killing a third man, all the while thinking how ironic it was that now that he had finally decided what to do with his life, it would probably end here in the Bighorn Mountains, and he would never get back to Jo.

Suddenly several warriors jumped down right in front of the cave entrance, having apparently moved in from above. Clint fired twice more, killing one and wounding another, but there were too many, and in seconds they moved in to wrestle his gun from him and grab his arms. Clint fought violently as several warriors dragged him out of the cave, taking his knife from its sheath while others took his horse. Clint managed to wrench free for a moment, and he landed hard fists into the two closest warriors. But he was soon held tight again, and he knew the struggle was useless. He waited as the apparent leader of the small band approached, decked out in buffalo-skin leggings and moccasins, a heavy bearskin coat draped over his big shoulders. His face was painted in black and white, but the paint did not hide the heavy scar that ran through the center of his face from his forehead to his chin.

Clint's eyes widened, full of fire and hatred. He stopped struggling and just stared as the man came closer. It was a face Clint Reeves had never forgotten.

"Two Moons!" he said bitterly.

The Indian stopped and stared back at him for a moment. His eyes moved over Clint and he came even closer, ripping off Clint's coat and pulling aside his deerhide shirt and the heavy woolen shirt he wore under it. He studied the scar for a moment, then muttered the Sioux name for "Man Who Looked At Death."

"My old friend," the Indian said with a strange smile.

"I have not called you friend since the day you attacked my home and dragged off my wife and son—the day you gave me this scar!" Clint growled.

Some of the warriors stepped back, whispering and staring. Two Moons grunted an order to the men who held Clint, and they let go of him.

Clint shook with rage and remembered horror. "So," he hissed. "Again you have me outnumbered! But there is just me this time, Two Moons—no helpless woman and child for you to torture!"

Two Moons seemed to flinch. "We do what we must do. Our own women and children suffer. The white man tells us we must live in peace. Black Kettle and his people tried to do so, at Sand Creek. The white man showed us what happens to us even when we do as he asks. It is the same as it was in the land to the north so many seasons ago. Nothing has changed."

Clint shook his head. "I suppose it hasn't. I'm sorry for what is happening to your people, Two Moons, but the *Wasicus* are going to keep coming, and nothing you and Red Cloud and the others do will stop it forever. I want there to be peace, Two Moons; but when I look at you, I realize I have one feeling, one need that will never change! I want to *kill* you!"

Two Moons watched him closely. "Stories have been told around our campfires about that day—how you found our camp in spite of your terrible wound—how you killed your own woman and son so they would no longer suffer. Today we saw a white man. We came here to kill him, take his scalp and his horse and supplies. But we have found The Man Who Looked at Death. You are an honored warrior, and you have the right to finish what you wanted to do the day we took your woman and child and left you for dead. When I kill you, I will be considered a great warrior."

"I see no honor in murdering a man when he is helplessly outnumbered, like I was that day in Minnesota!"

Two Moons shook his head. "It will not be that way." He snapped another order and one of the other braves walked up to Clint, handing him his knife. Two Moons drew his own knife and threw off his bearskin coat. "The Great Spirit has led us to this place because something was left unfinished," the Indian told Clint. "Today we will finish it."

He stepped back, crouching and waving his knife. Clint stared at him for a moment in surprise. The man was giving him a chance to win back some of the honor he felt he had lost by not being able to help his wife and child. Before him stood the man who was responsible for all the hurt, all the nightmares, the horror of putting a bullet into his wife and another into his little boy, then burying them together in that deep, dark hole, both of them so bloody and beaten they hardly looked like Millie and Jeff anymore.

The morning was soft and peaceful; the heavy snow muffled all sound and glittered in the morning sun. But rage welled in Clint's soul, and he lunged at Two Moons. The rest of the warriors stepped back, grinning and shouting war whoops as Clint and Two Moons lashed out at each other. Clint darted back from the wicked plunge of Two Moons's knife. His foot caught on a rock hidden by the snow, and he fell backward. In an instant Two Moons was on top of him.

The two men rolled in deep snow, while the other Indians stepped out of the way. The snow continued to fall in thick flakes that made it difficult to see when it landed on hair and face. Clint and two Moons struggled almost silently in the fluffy white bed of snow, muscle straining against muscle as Two Moons managed to roll on top of Clint and Clint held off the big Indian's knife hand.

In strength they were well matched, but Clint had an

edge, a hatred and a desire to kill that gave him an added power. He suddenly butted his head upward, landing it hard into Two Moons's mouth. The man grunted and released his grip enough so that Clint managed to shove the man off and get to his feet while Two Moons tumbled down a low bank. Clint crouched, arms spread, as Two Moons struggled back to his own feet.

The big Indian glared at Clint, blood pouring from a split lower lip and loosened teeth. He charged Clint again, lashing out with the cunning of a man who had fought this way many times.

Clint darted back skillfully from every thrust, glad Two Moons had already ripped off his wolfskin coat, giving him more freedom of movement. He did not notice the cold now, or feel the snow that had collected down his neck and shirtfront when he had tumbled in it with Two Moons. Nor did he feel pain at first when Two Moons's knife suddenly sliced a deep gash across his middle. Clint Reeves was primed for a kill, numb not just from the cold but from grief and revenge. He lashed back, gauging the big Indian, waiting for just the right moment.

Now blood dripped all the way down Two Moons's shirtfront. Clint felt a warm wetness against his own belly, but there was no time to wonder how deeply he had been cut. Blood from both wounds began staining the fresh snow as Clint charged Two Moons again, grabbing the man's right wrist to keep the knife away; but at the same time Two Moons grasped Clint's wrist and the two men shoved back and forth until Two Moons brought a foot up and rammed it right into Clint's wounded middle. Clint grunted and doubled over.

It all happened in what seemed only seconds. Clint was aware that his own knife was still in his hand as his grip weakened on Two Moons's wrist. He felt Two Moons trying to pull away, taking advantage of the sudden blow to Clint's middle. Somewhere deep in his mind a voice told Clint to hang onto the man's wrist while he forced himself not to buckle to the blow to his belly. He immediately came up again and came up hard, deliberately slamming his head again into Two Moons's chin.

Clint heard Two Moons cry out, felt the man's grip on his wrist weaken so that Clint managed to wrench his arm

free. His head was still slightly bowed, and he rammed
Two Moons hard, causing the man to stumble backward.

In the next moment Two Moons was on his back. Clint
ignored his pain and landed into Two Moons before he
had a chance to get up again. His knees came into Two
Moons's chest, so hard that the man was momentarily left
breathless. Two Moons raised his knife hand, but without
air he had no strength. Clint managed to lay his knife at
the Indian's throat before Two Moons could grab his arm.
At the same time he grabbed Two Moons's knife hand and
slammed it down hard against a small rock, over and over,
until Two Moons let go, still struggling for breath. Clint
grabbed the knife and tossed it aside.

With Clint's weight on his chest, and already knocked
breathless, Two Moons's color darkened in an effort to fill
his lungs with air. Clint grinned, grasping hold of the
man's hair and jerking his head back, pressing his knife
against Two Moons's throat. "It's *my* turn now, Two Moons!"
he growled.

Two Moons stared at him a moment, his eyes wide, his
mouth making motions with no sound coming out. Clint
plunged his knife straight into the Indian's Adam's apple,
pushing deep until he could feel the tip of the knife touch
the ground at the back of Two Moons's neck. He stared at
the Indian for several seconds, trembling with a mixture of
rage and sorrow, realizing in that one quick moment that
there was no satisfaction in revenge. Killing Two Moons
would not bring back Millie and his little boy. Tears stung
his eyes as he tore his knife from Two Moons's throat and
slowly rose. He wiped off the knife on the dead man's shirt
and shoved it back into its sheath, backing away from Two
Moons.

The rest of the Indians just stared at Clint for several
long seconds, then quietly picked up Two Moons, gathered
their horses, and left. They said nothing to Clint. The
fight was between Two Moons and Clint Reeves, and the
Wasicus had won.

Clint watched them go, feeling strangely remorseful,
and wondering how long the killing would go on. He went
down on his knees, overwhelmed by a sudden grief. "I
killed him, Millie," he groaned. "For what it's worth . . . I
killed him." He grasped his belly and bent over, weeping.

It was over. He knew as surely as he breathed that all the
bitterness was gone from him now. He could go to Jo, and
there was nothing he wanted more at this moment than to
be with her.

He threw back his head and breathed deeply, warning
himself that if he didn't get back to the fort and get help,
he would never see Jo again. He wiped at his eyes and
looked at his wounded middle. His shirt and the front of
his pants were soaked with blood. He managed to get to
his feet and stumble to where his coat lay. He pulled it on
and staggered to his horse, using his last bit of strength to
pull himself into the saddle.

"Come on, boy," he mumbled, ". . . got to . . . get back
to the fort . . . get back to Jo."

The day was treacherously lovely, giving no hint of the
impending storm. February had brought an unusual warming trend, and a chinook wind had melted most of the
snow in the valley. Jo walked out onto the porch, watching
Rubin herd the mares to the valley below for an early
feeding on the recently exposed grass. Jo was grateful for
the break in the weather, as grazing the horses in the
valley would save her dwindling supply of winter feed; and
the mares, especially the pregnant ones, needed the
exercise.

She put a hand to her swollen belly, thinking that the
horses were not the only ones to be giving birth, although
they wouldn't deliver until much later in the summer. Her
own "foal" was due soon, as far as she could figure, and
the temporary thaw seemed like a good time for Moose to
go get Sally Turrell. The man had left this morning, and Jo
felt a little more relaxed knowing another female would be
with her.

The warm wind whistled through the pines, and Jo
wondered how much longer it would be before Clint returned. The more the baby grew in her belly, the more she
had made herself believe he would come. After nearly
nine months, there were times when a little voice deep
inside would try to tell her Clint had only used her to
satisfy his desire before going away for good. But she
could not forget what it had been like to be in his arms, or
forget the feel of his tears on her neck. It had meant much

more to him than simply meeting manly needs. There was a special bond between them, one that had been strengthened on their trip west. They were good friends long before they were lovers. She felt she understood Clint even better than she had known or understood Greg.

She pulled her shawl around her shoulders and walked outside to the corral where Buck was held. She never tired of watching the proud stallion, and he trotted toward her, tossing his head and whinnying. He was as unpredictable as the Montana weather, but a healthy, strong animal that Jo was sure would father some fine, sturdy fillies and colts.

"You're going to help my little ranch here grow real fast, boy," she said to the horse.

Buck tossed his head and pranced away. It was then Jo noticed that he seemed to be limping. Jo frowned. She went to the gate of the corral and unhooked it, closing it partway behind her as she entered. She took a rope from a nearby post and approached Buck quietly, talking softly to him.

"Come here, boy. What's wrong with your leg?"

The horse approached her, softly neighing. Jo slipped the rope around his neck, still talking to him as she held the rope in one hand while she ran her other hand down Buck's left shoulder and forearm, over his knee and shank. She felt nothing out of the ordinary, and the horse didn't seem to be in pain. She gently felt the fetlock, then raised his left front leg, noticing a sharp stone lodged in his hoof.

"Oh, you poor thing." She grasped the stone, but it was too tightly lodged to remove it with her hand, and when she tried the horse whinnied and jumped away, his foot coming forward into her swollen belly with such force that it knocked her backwards. The feisty Buck suddenly broke into a run, yanking the rope out of Jo's hand. Jo grasped her stomach and shouted to Buck, but the animal seemed to sense he had a chance for freedom as he headed toward the gate.

"Buck! Come here, Buck!" Jo shouted.

The big horse bumped into the gate and it swung open, and before Jo could struggle to her feet Buck was gone. "Damn!" Jo swore, holding her stomach. She felt a light cramping sensation, but she told herself it was nothing. After all, if a baby was coming the pain would be much

worse, wouldn't it? She cursed herself for being so stupid
and she hurried down the hill, hollering for Rubin. She
felt another cramping, but she forced herself to ignore it.
The only important thing right now was to get Buck back.

Rubin rode up from the valley at a gallop. "What is it,
ma'am? The baby ain't comin', is it?"

"No, Rubin. But— I noticed Buck limping and I went
inside the corral to see what it was. The next thing I knew
he was out the gate. You've got to get him back, Rubin!
He's got a rope around his neck. He could get tangled
and hurt. And there's a sharp stone lodged in his left
front hoof. He could injure himself."

"Which way did he head?"

"Up behind the cabin. Please get him back, Rubin!"

"You okay? He didn't hurt you, did he?"

"No. I'm fine. Just go get him back."

Rubin nodded, riding past her and up the hill. Jo sighed
with disgust, looking out over the valley at the mares and
deciding they would be fine until Rubin returned. She
noticed some dark clouds appearing on the western horizon over the peaks of the mountains, but it was such a
pleasant, pretty day, she paid no attention. She went
inside the cabin, grasping her stomach as an even stronger
contraction hit her. She struggled to a chair and sat down,
breathing heavily and forcing herself not to panic. After
all, she had just been kicked by a horse. She just needed
to rest a little while. Besides that, Moose had already gone
for Sally. Sally would be here in another three days.

She sat taking deep breaths, reminding herself that she
had survived many things and this was just another challenge. After several minutes with no more contractions
she decided she was just fine. But in those few minutes
the air coming in the front door had changed. There was a
sudden, cold nip to it, and Jo smelled snow in the air. She
rose and walked to the door to close it, and noticed that
the dark clouds seemed to be moving fast. She felt a small
panic building in her chest. She was well aware how fast
the weather could change in these mountains, and she
only hoped Rubin would find Buck quickly and get back
before the storm clouds reached the valley. The mares
would have to be brought back up to the horse shed.

Another contraction hit her with sudden, unexpected

force and she doubled over. "My God," she whispered.
"Not now!" She waited until the pain subsided, then made
her way to the bedroom, overwhelmed with a sudden
need to lie down. She made it to the bed and lay down on
her side. Another pain came, and suddenly Buck, the
mares, the possible impending storm didn't matter. The
baby was coming. This was the first time she had experienced such a thing, but it was something a woman knew.
A terror gripped her more real and fierce than when she
had faced Quantrill's men, or faced the mountain lion, or
Indians, or the grizzly. This was not something she could
prevent, hide from, hold a gun on. This was happening to
her whether she wanted it to or not, and there was not a
soul around to help her.

The wind howled down the side of the mountains and
across the valley, bringing snow to its ragged, biting edge
and whitening everything in sight within an hour. The
storm hit with savage rage while Jo lay in labor, her agony
making her nearly oblivious to the weather outside. Perspiration covered her entire body, in spite of the fact that
the cabin was getting colder by the minute. She loosened
the buttons of her blouse and untied the rope belt she
used to hold up her skirt above her belly.

Images floated in her mind: Buck rearing, the horses
grazing in the valley. She cried out when she envisioned
the horses still standing there but turning to blocks of ice.
No! Not her mares! Everything she had, her whole future,
was tied up in those horses. Who would bring them in?
Rubin was surely lost in this blinding snowstorm, and Buck
would die, too. Everything would be gone, and Moose
would never make it back now from Virginia City with
Sally.

Clint! If only Clint were here. Perhaps she had been
foolish after all not to tell him. For hours she lay in pain,
made worse by her own terror over having her first baby
alone, as well as the agony of thinking she would lose
everything she had worked for. Morning stretched into
late afternoon, then early evening. She thought she heard
the door open.

"Clint?" she called out between gasps. No. It wouldn't

be Clint. "Rubin? Rubin . . . Buck . . . did you . . . find Buck?"

A tall figure of a man stepped into the bedroom. "Clint?" she moaned. Her pain subsided and she forced her eyes to focus. Her eyes widened then with added terror. It was Yellow Wolf! She tried to get up, but strong hands held her down.

"We will help you," she heard him say. "My woman is with me. Her mother is also with me."

Another pain ripped through Jo's belly, and at the moment it didn't matter to her why Yellow Wolf was there, or that Indian women might help her instead of Sally. Jo knew she was in no position to argue. A woman was a woman, and Indian women had their babies in the wilds all the time, with no one special to help them.

"My . . . horses . . . the storm," Jo muttered. "They'll . . . die."

"I travel with many others. They bring the horses to the house you made for them. They will not die. I go now. It is bad for a man to be near at birth of child."

Yellow Wolf left her, and she heard him talking to someone in his strange Sioux tongue. People were moving around, and Jo thought she heard a small child's voice. A moment later two women were propping her up, making her sit up slightly. She realized it felt a little better to raise her shoulders. Blankets were piled around her shoulders while someone pushed up her skirt and gently massaged her belly. She heard women talking in a language she could not understand.

The next several hours were the worst Jo had ever known. She drifted into a world far removed from the real, where faces and past events mingled into strange dreams; where she envisioned a horrible witch grasping at her belly with gnarled fingers and trying to rip out her insides. There were moments when she was vaguely aware that the cabin was warmer, aware of someone forcing her legs apart, coaching her in a language she didn't understand. There was a moment of deep, deep pain, and a sudden relief, after which she passed out for several minutes before waking up to someone massaging her stomach, pushing, talking quietly.

Again she floated off, awakened later by the sound of a

baby crying. It took her a moment to realize that a tiny, red, wrinkled piece of life lay squalling beside her. It reminded her of a baby bird. A young Indian woman urged her to turn to her side, and blankets were propped behind her. The Indian woman opened Jo's blouse and positioned the baby. Jo felt the child lightly suck at her breast, and the infant was instantly quiet. The Indian woman said something and Jo looked at her, truly seeing her for the first time. She was lovely, and she was smiling at Jo.

Jo put a hand on her arm. "Thank you," she said, her voice weak.

The woman nodded. An older Indian woman came to stand beside the young one, both of them watching the baby feed. They said something Jo did not understand, then left the room.

Jo studied the baby, her eyes misting. She had always wanted this, somewhere in the future. She never dreamed it would happen this way. Who would have thought when she left Lawrence . . . She stopped to count the months. Two and a half years! It had been two and a half years since that day Clint helped her after the raid. Now his child lay feeding at her breast. If only he knew!

She carefully opened the Indian blanket in which the child was wrapped. The umbilical cord was cut off and tied with rawhide. She opened the blanket farther and saw the child was a boy—another son for Clint Reeves.

"Oh, Clint," she whispered. "You've got to come back. You have a new family."

She studied the toes, the fingers. Everything was there. She covered the child, then felt a presence in the doorway of the room. She looked up to see Yellow Wolf, then quickly covered herself, reddening. Yellow Wolf acted as though he had seen nothing and came a little closer.

"My woman says it is a boy—a son."

Jo nodded.

"The father will be proud." He eyed her closely. "When I was here last, you said you were a woman alone."

Jo dropped her eyes. "I was—then. There was a man I . . . cared for . . . the man who brought me here. He came to see me . . . the same day you were here. He came right after you left. We were . . . soon married."

"Where is your man?"

Jo cuddled her son closer. "He . . . had to go away for a while. He'll be back in the spring."

"He left you here alone?"

She met his eyes again. "No. I have men working for me. One went after a woman who was going to be here when I had the baby, but it came too soon. The other . . . left this morning to find a horse that had run away. Please tell your men not to harm him if he comes back."

"We are not a war party. This time we travel with family. Many soldiers have been searching for us. Red Cloud tells us to go into many groups so that the soldiers cannot catch all of us in one place. We were going even farther north when the storm came. We stopped here for shelter, and we heard your cries of pain."

Jo closed her eyes. "Thank God," she whispered. She wondered if Clint was among the soldiers chasing the Sioux. She met Yellow Wolf's eyes again. "My horses?"

"They are all right. We stay until the storm ceases and you feel strong. Then we go." He came a little closer. "I wish to see your son."

Jo pulled the baby away from her breast, keeping herself covered as she moved the blanket away from the baby's face. Yellow Wolf touched the baby's hand, his own skin looking even darker against the baby's soft, thin skin. Jo noticed Yellow Wolf smile slightly, saw in that one brief moment the human side of the Sioux warrior who called himself Yellow Wolf. For the moment he was just a man, no different from Clint or any other man. She realized she had never allowed herself to understand that Indians were as human as anyone else, as capable of loving and as caring about their families as any white man. Those families were being threatened; their children were starving. Could they be completely blamed for some of the things they did?

"He is a fine son." Yellow Wolf straightened. "I go now."

"Yellow Wolf." Their eyes met and he waited. "Take whatever you need when you go. I pray you'll be safe."

He nodded slowly. "Yellow Wolf is grateful." He walked out of the room and Jo stared after him, her heart torn between Clint's horror story and what these Indians had just done for her. They had saved her life, and her baby's.

Indians had taken Clint's first family away from him; and now Indians had saved the woman he loved and his new son.

She looked down at her baby again, her heart brimming with love. She had not been sure she wanted this child at this time in her life. But now, here he was, looking up at her with big, brown eyes, a healthy boy. "What shall I call you?" she said, touching the baby's soft cheek. Several names passed through her mind, but she wanted a name that represented everything about Montana, for Montana was where her son was going to grow up. It had to be a strong name, one that fit the land.

"Montana," she said softly. She lay back, terribly weary again. "Montana. Why not Montana! Montana Reeves. I like the sound of it—sounds like a big, strong man—a man just like your father." She pulled the baby closer, kissing its cheek. "I could call you Monty. Yes, that's going to be your name, Montana."

Chapter Twenty-six

Clint rode ahead of the miserable contingent of soldiers who straggled out of Fort Connor and headed south toward Fort Laramie. The Sioux had kept Fort Connor completely cut off from aid for most of the winter. Many soldiers had died of starvation and disease. Reinforcements had finally arrived from Fort Laramie to accompany the remaining forces back to their fort.

Clint scouted for the returning soldiers, anxious to get them to Fort Laramie so he could be on his way to Montana. He would take the southern route, back up past the Tetons, hoping to avoid the biggest concentration of Indians. After a long, painful recovery from the wound inflicted by Two Moons, and a hard winter of near starvation, he did not care to run in to any more Indians if he could help it. His original intention had been to go straight to Jo after he was wounded, but infection had set in and had nearly killed him. He also felt a responsibility to stay with the starving soldiers until help came.

"What do you think of this Indian situation, Mr. Reeves?" The question came from a Sergeant Scott, who rode beside Clint. The man's eyes had deep circles around them, and his cheeks looked caved in. Like Clint and most of the others, the winter of little food showed in his gaunt face.

"I think it's going to get worse before it gets better," Clint answered. "Red Cloud is winning and he knows it. He'll close the entire Bozeman Trail before he's finished."

The sergeant shook his head. "Word is, General Sherman himself is coming out to Fort Laramie this summer. He took care of the South. Maybe he can take care of the Indians."

Clint watched the horizon, his eyes keenly aware of every strange movement. "Maybe. But fighting Indians is a whole different matter. This kind of war is going to go on a lot longer than the Civil War, Sergeant, mark my words. There is too much distrust. Some of the miners up in Montana shoot an Indian down on sight, without question or reason. We haven't held true to one treaty we've ever signed with the Indians; and there are always men low enough to sell whiskey, and guns to them. Besides that, the Indians consider all of this their land. You can hardly blame them for fighting for it. Their survival depends on being able to migrate, follow the seasons and the buffalo."

The sergeant frowned. "You sound like you're on their side. Hell, they almost killed you a few months ago. And I hear that's not the first time they tried. Word is, Indians killed your wife and kid, up in Minnesota."

Clint rode on in silence for several seconds. "They did." He finally spoke up. "The same thing has been done to their own by white men." He realized more clearly than ever that he was finally free of the bitterness and hatred. "Revenge killing can go on forever, Sergeant Scott. It has to end somewhere. So does the hatred. That kind of hatred can kill a man from the inside. It made me turn away from someone who loves me very much." He turned to look at the sergeant. "There are two sides to everything, and usually each side thinks he's right. That's the hell of it."

He rode on for several minutes in silence, thinking of Jo, how nice it would be to be sitting with her right now in the quiet little cabin, talking about the horses, or maybe how many children they wanted. He realized he loved the land around the Ruby River as much as Jo did. Together they could have a good life. With a wife like Jo, a man could build a hell of a ranch. With a wife like Jo, a man could do anything.

He rode on ahead, catching up with a lieutenant. "Lieutenant Bloom," he called out.

"What is it, Reeves?"

"My job is done here. We're far enough south that I think I'll head on west. I've got to get back up to Montana."

The lieutenant frowned. "You sure you're strong enough? You ought to rest a while at Fort Laramie, Reeves, put on a little more weight, build your strength back up."

"I'll be all right. All I need is permission to take some of the supplies you have along, and I'd like my pay. Just give me a note or something that's good at a bank in Virginia City if you don't have cash. And take out enough for a horse. I'll be needing a packhorse. The Indians stole mine up at Fort Connor."

The lieutenant looked him over. Reeves was a big man, a man accustomed to this kind of living. "Well, Reeves, I suppose if anyone can make it back to Montana alone in your condition, you can. You've done a good job. The army will miss you. Think you'll come back and do more scouting for us sometime? I have a feeling this thing with the Indians is only going to get worse."

"I've got a woman waiting for me in Montana. I doubt I'll be back."

The lieutenant grinned. "Well, pick out a horse from the remuda and pack some supplies then. Come to my tent tonight and I'll see you get paid."

"Thanks, Lieutenant."

The soldier pushed back his hat. "You say this woman is up in Montana?"

"Yes, sir."

Bloom frowned. "She's right up there in Indian country. Hell, man, you just rode out of that mess. What's the woman doing up there?"

"She runs a ranch along the Ruby River."

"Alone?" The shock on the lieutenant's face was almost humorous.

"It's a long story, Lieutenant, and I don't have time to tell it. But if anybody is in danger, it's most likely the ones who try to give *her* any trouble. She even shot a grizzly last year." Clint grinned at the expression on the man's face. "I'm riding back to the remuda, Lieutenant, to look the horses over. I'll come by tonight."

Clint rode off and the lieutenant turned to watch after him a moment. He frowned, thinking about a woman in Montana who shot grizzlies. He imagined she must be as tough as any man, and he wondered what she must look like. But then men like Clint Reeves needed a strong woman who didn't mind living in the wilderness. He chuckled, picturing a hard, rough woman who stood as tall as Clint and had arms as big as a man.

Jo laid Monty in the wooden cradle Rubin had made for the boy. At two months old it was already obvious Clint's son would take after his father in size, and sometimes Jo worried if she would have enough milk for the constantly hungry infant.

She knelt beside the cradle, patting the baby's bottom. Monty was a good baby who slept through the night and seldom cried. When he was awake his big, brown eyes were constantly alert, and he grinned at the slightest touch or spoken word. It had not taken long to forget the pain and terror of the day he decided to come into the world. She only knew she would be forever grateful to Yellow Wolf and his wife and mother-in-law. She thought of Clint's remark about Indians and mothers-in-law and she laughed aloud.

"Oh, Clint," she said softly. "When are you going to come home and see your son?"

Her eyes teared as she rose. She was worried now. Maybe something had happened to Clint. She decided she would ask Moose to go to the telegraph office the next time he went to Virginia City and wire Fort Laramie. Now that Monty was here and more real to her, she realized it was only right to tell Clint about the baby. It was possible he was already on his way to Montana; she prayed that he was. More than anything she wanted him to come back without knowing about the baby—to come back for her alone.

She walked outside, breathing deeply of the sweet, spring air. It was nearly the end of April, and most of the snow had melted. But she knew full well how quickly a late, spring snowstorm could kick up out of the mountains. She thanked God that Rubin had found Buck that awful day. He and the horse were stranded for four days after the storm, but they made it back. It had taken nearly a week for Moose to arrive with Sally, and by then Jo was on her feet and feeling just fine. She could still remember the shock on the faces of Moose and Sally when they walked in to find her nursing a baby.

She gazed out at the valley below, where her mares, several of them pregnant, grazed peacefully. She could hear the rhythmic chopping of an ax. Several yards to the south of the cabin Moose was cutting some trees to begin building more fencing. This summer, when Clint returned, Jo intended to fence in her new land. Everything seemed so perfect, except for Clint's absence. Every day she watched for him, but every night she went to bed with only little Monty at her side.

Spirit bounded past her skirt then, darting outside to chase a squirrel, his ears flopping up and down as he ran. The squirrel scampered up a tree, and Spirit half climbed the tree trying to reach it.

"When will you ever learn?" Jo told the dog, laughing. "You've never caught a squirrel yet and you never will."

She went back inside to prepare some bread dough, glad to have Moose around to help with chores, now that she had Monty. She didn't like leaving him alone in the house for too long at a time. Rubin had taken Sally back to Virginia City a few days after her arrival, and Jo had told him he could stay there until later in the spring. The lonely life on the ranch was hard on Rubin, who longed for some livelier company. Moose didn't mind staying. He was a man who for most of his life had lived alone in the wilds.

The morning passed quietly. Monty slept soundly, and Spirit stopped barking at the squirrel and lay down to bask in the welcome sunshine. Jo baked her bread, hoping she had enough flour left to get by until Moose could go into town again. She washed her hands and untied her apron, and it was then she heard the gunshot, somewhere in the distance. It seemed to come from the direction where Moose was working. Her heart quickened and she frowned and went to the door, picking up the rifle she kept beside it.

She walked outside, her ears alert, her eyes searching. Everything looked normal. The horses still grazed in the valley, and Margaret was slowly walking toward the horse shed, nibbling on grass here and there. But Spirit's head was up, his ears cocked. The dog got to his feet and trotted toward the direction where Jo had heard the gunshot.

Jo walked down the steps of the house and followed only as far as Buck's corral. The big horse whinnied and pranced as though disturbed.

"Moose!" Jo called out. "Moose, are you all right?"

There came no reply. Jo clung to the rifle, watching and listening, an odd panic building in her chest. She wanted to go and see if something had happened to Moose, but she couldn't leave the cabin.

"Moose!" she called again. She could no longer see Spirit, but now she could hear him barking. She cocked her rifle and waited, but saw no one. Suddenly she heard another shot, and just as suddenly Spirit stopped barking.

Never had the silence of the mountains seemed suddenly so threatening to Jo. There was only the soft, constant sound of wind rushing through the pines. "Spirit?" she said quietly, her eyes tearing.

"I reckon he's dead," came a voice behind her.

Jo gasped and whirled, ready to fire. But at least six men walked from the side of the cabin. She recognized the one who had spoken, recognized the ever-present black coat.

Bart Kendall stepped closer, holding his rifle on Jo. "Throw the gun aside, little lady. I done heard how good you can use it."

Jo wanted nothing more than to fire. How she would love to see Bart Kendall die! But the men with her would surely fire back, and she couldn't shoot all of them. Nor could she take the risk of getting hurt or killed. She had to think of Monty now. Her stomach churned at the sight of Kendall's several-day-old whiskers and the tobacco stains at the corners of his mouth.

"What the hell are you doing here, Kendall?" she spit out at him, throwing her rifle aside.

He only grinned. "Well, now, I reckon you can guess." His eyes moved over her. "I come to take back what you took from me. You took them horses way back when. Now me and these men here are gonna take yours." He stepped up close to her, reaching out to touch her breast with the back of his hand. Jo jerked back, hitting out at his hand.

Kendall returned with a solid blow to the side of her face, knocking Jo to the ground so hard that she got dirt in her mouth. She spit it out furiously, paying no attention to the pain of the blow as she quickly scrambled back up, picking up a handful of pebbles as she did so and throwing them in Kendall's face.

Kendall cried out and stepped back, and the men with him laughed. Kendall threw down his rifle and came at Jo, grabbing her wrists and pushing her to the ground, planting a knee into her stomach. "You ain't got no Clint Reeves to help you now, Missy. I know he's gone. And that man who's been helpin' you is dead. There ain't nobody, and you ain't gonna boss me aside this time!" He leaned closer, using his shoulder to knock off his hat and turning his head to show her his missing ear. "Look at this! See this? See that ear, or what's left of it? Your stud Reeves did that to me, sayin' I'd best leave you alone. Well, now he ain't here to do nothin' about it!"

Jo stared for a moment at the ugly stub of an ear. "I'm glad . . . he cut it off!" she sneered through gritted teeth, gasping for breath. Kendall's knee pushed harder so that she thought she might pass out. "He shouldn't . . . have stopped there!" she added before spitting at him.

Kendall let go of one of her wrists and slapped her hard. Jo tasted blood in her mouth, and her head reeled in confusion. She thought she heard someone barking an order to Kendall to get up. Suddenly the pressure on her middle was relieved. Someone was helping her up.

"We came here for horses and supplies!" someone was shouting. "You got need for a woman, Kendall, there's plenty of whores in Virginia City!"

"This one owes me," Kendall sneered.

"If she was smart enough to get her own horses back from you, that's your tough luck, Kendall. This bunch rides under *me*, Sonny Morrow, and you take your *orders* from me, you hear?"

Jo clutched at her stomach, struggling to get her breath. She spit out blood and could taste a cut on the inside of her right cheek. A swelling bruise on the left side of her face began to throb with pain. She struggled to keep her bearings and her head clear, for Monty's sake. She clung to a fence post then for balance, as her vision cleared. A tall, rather good-looking man stood near her, but his eyes were a cold blue.

"You all right, ma'am?" the man asked.

"What kind of men . . . are you?" she asked, keeping a hand to her stomach.

The man pushed back his hat, looking her over. "Name's Sonny Morrow, ma'am. Bart, here, said you had a ranch here in the valley—and you worked it all alone, except for one or two men." He shook his head. "That's not very smart, ma'am. Sooner or later, somebody's bound to take advantage of that."

She turned her gaze from Morrow to Kendall, and then the others. "What fine, brave men you are, to steal from a woman!" She looked back at a grinning Morrow as three more men approached from the direction where Moose had been working. They led the horses of the other men, who had sneaked up to the cabin on foot. "They killed Moose, didn't they?" she hissed at Morrow.

The man shrugged. "Got to clear away all obstacles," he replied.

"Includin' that damned barkin' dog," one of the others added.

It took all of Jo's strength not to break down at that moment. Moose and Spirit! Dead? Moose was such a good man, had been so loyal. And Spirit . . . Spirit. She held Morrow's eyes, wanting to remember his face. "Take what you want and get off my land! You're scum! Cowards!"

Morrow frowned. "Ma'am, you keep talkin' like that, and I might be prone to lettin' Kendall do what he wants with you." His eyes looked her up and down. "Fact is, you're so much prettier than I expected, I might have to go against my own rule about not forcin' myself on a proper woman."

"You'll do what you want no matter what," she sneered. She spit out more blood, wiping at her mouth with a shaking hand. "You intend to kill my baby, too? He might give you trouble! Or maybe you'd like to abuse me in front of him. That should make you feel like a real man!"

Jo studied the slight change in the man's eyes. "Baby?"

"My son is in the house. Take what you want. I just want to go to him."

Morrow shot a look of surprise at Kendall. "You said she was a widow woman with no children."

Kendall looked even more surprised. "She was, the last I knew. That Clint Reeves who brought her here is long gone. Everybody in town says he's been gone a long time and ain't comin' back."

"Clint Reeves is my *husband*," Jo shot back at Kendall. "The little boy inside that house is his *son*, and when he comes back and finds out about this, you'll wish you were dead, Bart Kendall!"

With satisfaction she watched fear pass through Kendall's eyes. The man looked at Morrow. "I didn't know."

Morrow walked closer to him and suddenly backhanded Kendall, knocking him to the ground. "You stupid sonuvabitch! You said this would be easy. You said the woman was alone—and that there wasn't anyone else on the ranch who'd bother coming after the horses."

Kendall got to his knees, rubbing the side of his face. "Well, there *isn't* anybody else. Do you see Reeves any place?"

Morrow turned to Jo. "Where is your husband?"

Jo put a hand to her bruised face, trying to think. "He's an army scout. He's due back any day. It could even be today, for all I know."

Morrow grabbed her arms and jerked her closer. "Oh, yeah? Well, I think you're lying, woman. I think he left you and isn't coming back at all. Either way, we'll be long gone before he has a chance to do anything about it." He grabbed her hand and held it up. "Where's your wedding ring?"

Jo jerked her hand away defiantly. "I don't have one! A traveling preacher married us last spring. We never had a chance to buy a ring. What difference does it make to you?"

"The difference is I want anything you have of value."

"Well, I don't *have* anything of value!"

Morrow turned his eyes to the valley. "Except some damn nice horses."

Jo was so full of rage she felt like she would choke. The horses! She thought how ironic it was that she was in far more danger from men of her own kind than she had been from Yellow Wolf and his warriors.

"I've worked for two years to build up what I have," she told Morrow, her voice husky with rage and sorrow. "I did it on my own—helped round up the mustangs, saved and traded, and did what I had to do to get that herd started. How dare you just come here and take it!"

Morrow shrugged. "We all have to make a livin', ma'am. You're just damn lucky I'm not a rapist. Just a horse thief, ma'am; just a horse thief. And that herd you've got down in the valley will fetch us a pretty penny up in Canada. Now you go on up to the house there and make my men a nice meal. Then we'll be collectin' food and anything else we'll be needin' before we leave. Go on up here now and stay with your kid."

Jo just stared at him a moment, hardly able to believe anyone could be so vile. "I won't forget you, Mr. Sonny Morrow. And neither will Clint Reeves. Moose Barkley was his good friend."

Morrow pushed back his hat. "Yeah, well, I don't think your Mr. Clint Reeves is comin' back anytime soon, and I'm not much afraid of one little woman with a babe sucklin' at her breast. And if you try anything, it will be more than the babe, if you get my meanin'. The sooner we eat, the sooner we're out of here, ma'am—and the easier it will be for me to hold back my men. You understandin' me?"

Jo refused to cry. "I understand you perfectly, Mr. Morrow. I understand you're all lower than the filth under your boots." She turned and marched into the cabin, praying Monty would stay asleep as she set tin plates on the table.

"You men check the smokehouse," she heard Morrow ordering outside. "We'll round up the horses when we leave."

Jo felt nauseated. Moose! Poor Moose! And was Spirit dead, too? Losing the dog was like losing the best friend she had ever had. Her throat ached fiercely with a need to cry, but she was not about to show fear to these men any more than she would to the Indians. After a few minutes several men wandered inside, all of them staring at her with much hungrier eyes than Yellow Wolf or any of his men. She dipped some stew from a kettle that hung over the fire from the night before and began setting plates of stew on the table. She said nothing as she slammed some spoons onto the table and stood back. Monty began to fuss then.

"I'm going to be with my baby," she said boldly. "If you want more, get it yourself."

She marched into the bedroom and picked Monty up from the cradle, deciding her own person was not safe just because Sonny Morrow had said it was. She decided holding a baby might be further insurance against being attacked. Morrow seemed to have something against raping a woman who was a wife and a mother. But she didn't doubt he had raped before, and they were probably all as unpredictable as the wind. If it were up to Bart Kendall, they would all have a turn with her.

She carried the baby into the main room, not wanting any of them to come into her bedroom. She sat down in a chair and waited for them to finish eating. They talked about other raids, and she soon realized these men had been raiding and stealing and killing all over Wyoming and Utah. She was not surprised Bart Kendall had taken up with such men. She could not think of worse scum than the men who trooped around her house now, eating her food, rummaging through her cupboards, and filling their saddlebags with her food.

Kendall came inside, his face still flushed from being clobbered in front of Jo. He glared at her as he ate some stew, then threw his plate on the floor. He came closer to her then, wiping a little blood from the corner of his mouth. "I think you're lyin' about Reeves," he told her.

"I'm holding his child right here in my arms."

"Maybe so. Maybe it's some drifter's kid. How do we know? Maybe you ain't the proper lady you make yourself out to be. If you got married, how come you filed for more land under Joline Masters instead of Joline Reeves?"

Jo struggled not to look guilty. "I filed under Masters because that was the name I used for my first piece of land. Clint understands how important this place is to me. It makes me proud to have it in my own name."

"That's a crock. I think Clint Reeves just had himself a good old time under your skirts and then lit out!"

She held his eyes, unflinching. "And maybe you're wrong, Bart Kendall," she answered calmly, grinning slightly.

"Now that I've seen your ear, I do hate to think what Clint will do to you when he finds out about this." She watched him pale slightly. "He's a good tracker, Kendall. He'll find you. As sure as you're standing there, he'll find you. And heaven help you when he does."

"You shut your mouth, woman, or I'll use that baby for wolf bait!"

"Leave her alone, Kendall." One of the others spoke up. "You heard Sonny."

Kendall glowered at her a moment longer, then turned to see Morrow coming inside. Jo wondered how a man got to be like Sonny Morrow. If he were shaved and cleaned up and better dressed, he would be a handsome man. Was he a remnant of the war, a changed man like Anna's husband? She thought about Anna again for a moment, wondering if Darryl had turned mean—if he was some kind of outlaw. She had written to Anna, but there had been no more letters from her sister.

Kendall walked up to Morrow, his fists clenched. "You got to let me get some kind of revenge, Sonny!" he hissed. "I'm the one who told you about this place. Everything is just the way I said it, and I've got dues comin' from this woman! She's a smart-mouthed bitch who needs a lesson!"

Morrow glanced from Kendall to Jo. He grinned slightly, then looked back at Kendall. "You don't touch her or the baby. Anything else you want to do is fine. I don't like this thing about a husband who's a scout. A man will let a lot of things go, but you touch his wife or kid, and we might have a hard time getting shed of him. I don't want an angry husband on our tail."

Kendall drew in a deep breath, looked around the cabin for a moment, then turned to Jo. "All right," he told Morrow, his eyes on Jo. "I won't touch her or the kid. But I'm burning down this cabin."

Jo just stared at him, refusing to cry and beg.

"Just remember the torching is your idea," Morrow answered. "Let the woman get some clothes and baby things out first."

Jo could hardly believe her ears. They were actually going to burn down her house! Everything she had worked for was going to be destroyed—her horses stolen, all her furniture and dishes and clothing destroyed.

She rose and walked calmly into the bedroom, laying Monty back in his cradle. She quickly threw her Indian necklace and belt into the beaded parfleche the old Indian woman at Fort Bridger had made for her. She took out some clothes and stuffed those into the parfleche also. She threw a couple of dresses and most of Monty's baby things onto the bed, then wrapped everything into the bedspread.

She stared at the bed a moment, remembering again the wonderful hours she had spent there with Clint. "Come back, Clint," she whispered. "Come back and see what they've done." Her eyes watered and she quickly blinked the tears away, telling herself she had to think fast. If they burned down her house, she would need a way to keep warm. Somehow she had to get to Virginia City for help. The nights were still bitterly cold. She had to think of the baby. He could die.

She put out her hand, touching the bearskin, which now hung on the wall in her bedroom. "What better protection?" she muttered, ripping the thick, furry skin off the wall. "I owe you one after all, old grizzly," she said, fighting tears as she kissed the fur. "I knew there was a reason God sent you."

She thought of the money then that she kept hidden in the wall behind her dresser. She glanced toward the outer room to see Morrow and Kendall both staring at her. From where they stood, they could not see the dresser. She turned and began slamming dresser drawers to confuse any other sound they might hear. At the same time as she opened a squeaky drawer, she pulled the dresser out just far enough to reach quickly into the hole and take out as much money as she could manage in one grasp. She quickly pushed the dresser back and shoved the money into the cradle under Monty's blankets and little feather mattress. She picked up Monty's cradle then and carried it through the outer room to set it outside.

She looked at no one as she marched back inside the house and picked up the quilt full of her belongings, wrapping everything into the bearskin. She lifted the heavy bundle and carried it outside while Morrow and his men watched curiously, chuckling at her stubborn refusal to cry or show fear. She came back inside to take down her bearskin coat from a hook near the door. She met Morrow's eyes then. "I'll be needing some food."

He grinned. "Take a loaf of bread. You're lucky to get as much as you're getting. And you're damned lucky all Kendall is doing is burning this cabin. Don't worry about those horses. We'll take good care of them. Just be glad you and the kid are alive."

"How kind of you," Jo sneered. She walked around the table to wrap a loaf of bread into a towel, then headed out the door with her coat and the bread. Kendall grabbed her arm.

"I told you a long time ago I'd get you, woman. And you just remember I can come back—alone!"

Jo jerked her arm away. "When Clint gets through with you, you won't be going anywhere, ever!" She hurried out the door, still afraid Morrow would change his mind about not hurting her and the child. She carried her belongings out under a big Ponderosa pine away from the house, then came back to take Monty and his cradle under the tree, where she sat down to wait. She covered the cradle with her old bearskin coat and sat against the tree for what seemed hours before the men exited the cabin.

"Yahoo!" she heard Kendall shout. "This is gonna be a pretty sight!"

Jo closed her eyes as the rest of the men mounted their horses. "Hurry it up, Kendall!" one of them shouted. "Let's get the hell out of here and get the horses."

"Clete, you go get that stud horse. He's a fine-looking animal. Ought to bring us a pretty penny." Jo recognized Morrow's voice.

"Buck!" she thought. She was so proud of him. Now they were taking everything away. She heard the crash of a lantern, and she knew it was Kendall, using her lamps to set her house on fire. Moments later she heard the crackling sound. It was not long before her nostrils caught the scent of smoke, and she remembered that awful day in Lawrence. Again everything she owned was being stolen or destroyed by fire. It seemed that bad luck had a way of following her.

Kendall proceeded to ride to the new bunkhouse and the newer horse shed Rubin and Jason had built just a few months earlier. He torched those buildings also. Jo kept her eyes closed and rocked Monty's cradle, telling herself she had started over once—she could do it again. After all, she at least had her little boy.

"Thanks for the supplies and horses, ma'am," she heard Morrow saying. For several minutes there was the lingering sound of men shouting and horses being herded together, whistling and joking.

Kendall rode up to Jo, leering. "It's been a real pleasure, Mrs. Reeves, or is it Mrs. Masters? Far as I'm concerned, that baby is a bastard, and you ain't worth bein' treated like some kind of proper lady. I'll be back, woman, to get the rest of what's owed me."

He turned his horse and rode off with the others. Jo waited for the sound of horses to die away. She heard things falling inside the house, then heard a crashing sound. After a while she managed to look toward the cabin. The roof had fallen in, and the fire had crept up behind the house to the older horse shed behind it, which was also now on fire.

Her heart felt like stone. She told herself there was nothing to do now but try to think rationally and protect little Monty. She had to get help, but first she had to do the right thing by poor Moose. She would not let him and Spirit lie in the open to be eaten by wolves.

She realized then that the newer horse shed didn't seem to be burning hard. Smoke poured from only one end. She grabbed a bucket of water from near the well and ran to the shed, dousing a lazy fire that licked at one end of the building and thanking God that the wood was apparently too green and still too wet from winter snows to burn well. It was obvious the fire was not going to do much damage, and she closed her eyes, breathing a sign of relief that at least one building was saved. She took hope in the tiny bit of good luck.

She looked around the shed then and found a shovel, then dragged it outside to where Monty lay in the cradle.

"We've still got one good shed left," she told her son. She looked down at the shovel. "And one tool. You and I are alive, and we have a few possessions—and I saved most of the money. We're going to be all right, Monty, you'll see."

She bent down and wrapped the baby in her bearskin

coat. It was already getting cooler as late afternoon put the
sun down behind the distant mountains, but she knew she
would keep warm from the exercise of digging a hole for
Moose and Spirit. It was more important to keep Monty
warm. She carried the baby and the shovel into the woods
where Moose had been working. When she reached the
spot, she stopped and stared, slowly setting Monty down
onto a pile of wood chips, which would protect him from
the cold, damp ground.

Moose's body lay over a log, a bullet hole in his back.
Spirit lay nearby, his head covered with blood.

"Oh, my God," Jo muttered. The tears came then. She
walked over to Spirit, picking up the dog and breaking
into great sobs of grief as she carried him over near Moose.
She knelt beside Moose, then, still clinging to the dog,
and she put her arm around the dead man.

"Oh, Moose, I'm so sorry," she wept. "I'll . . . get them
. . . somehow," she promised. She bent her head and
kissed Spirit, choking in a sob that welled up from somewhere deep in her soul. What better friend was there than
a faithful dog? He had been the only thing that kept her
from insanity that first terrible winter.

She laid the dog down carefully beside Moose, then
walked over to pick up the shovel to start digging. She
knew she wasn't strong enough to drag Moose's body
closer to the house. She would bury him right here. Tears
streamed down her face as she struggled with the still
partly frozen ground. Once she got deeper, the earth was
softer, but it took hours of digging to create a hole big
enough for Moose's body. Still, it didn't seem deep enough,
but Jo ached everywhere.

She glanced in the direction of the cabin and saw the
smoke was not as thick. She thanked God the ground and
trees were still wet enough to keep the fire from spreading
into the timber. If that happened, she and Monty would
be in great danger, depending on the winds.

She tossed the shovel aside and grabbed hold of Moose's
body, which was nearly stiff already. It remained in a bent
position as she managed to drag it to the hole and push it
in. "I'm sorry, Moose," she said through her tears. "It's
the best I can do." She sniffed and wiped at her eyes with

the sleeve of her dress, then picked up Spirit and gently laid him next to Moose.

"Good-bye, my precious friends," she said to them both, petting Spirit one more time. Her arms tired and sore, she picked up the shovel and filled the hole as best she could. Monty started crying from hunger, but she had to finish the grave first since it was getting dark and she feared the wolves would come.

A pile of logs lay nearby waiting to be split. With every ounce of strength Jo had she began rolling the logs over the grave; sometimes she had to pick one up by the end to position it right. She covered the grave with as many heavy logs as she could get over it, hoping it would hinder wolves from digging up the fresh dirt. By the time she finished making the grave she was sweating. The cold air against her perspiration chilled her, and she walked over to Monty, wondering where she found the strength to pick him up and carry him back under the tree.

"It's too late in the day and I'm too tired to start for Virginia City today, baby," she told the boy, holding him close. "We'll start tomorrow."

She leaned against the tree, putting the bearskin coat over herself and Monty. She felt underneath and opened the front of her dress to feed Monty, then sat back in the mountain silence. In the distance she spotted her rifle still lying on the ground. Her mind raced with the need for survival. Again she was challenged with the elements, only this time it was not just her life that was at stake. She had Monty to consider.

First she had to find a way to get to Virginia City. She knew she wasn't strong enough to carry both baby and belongings, and there were no horses to pull her wagon. Morrow's men had taken all of them. She remembered the contraptions the Indians used to pull their belongings. Clint had called them by a french name—travois. She knew how they were made, and she was sure that from branches Moose had cut down, and from her blanket and leather harness left in the other horse shed, she could rig up a travois on which she could pack Monty and her precious few belongings and pull them to Virginia City herself. At least she had a rifle, and there were a few extra bullets in a saddle bag in the remaining horse shed, if

Morrow's men hadn't found and taken them. The cabin was burned, but the Indian lance still lay in front of it, where one of Morrow's men had ripped it from the ground and thrown it down. She decided she would take it along, hoping it would help protect her if she came across Indians who were not a part of Yellow Wolf's band.

She breathed deeply for self-control. She had survived a lot of things. She could survive this. She would not be beaten. She shivered against the cold air and held Monty closer.

"We'll sleep in the hay in the horse shed tonight, Monty," she told the baby. "We've got the bearskin to keep us warm. Tomorrow I'll see if I can get to any of the food in the root cellar. I'll make up a travois and we'll go to Virginia City. It's a long trip, Monty, but maybe we'll run into someone on the way who can help us. Somehow we've got to get there and get help. We can't stay here. Kendall might come back."

She felt Monty's tiny hand pinch at her breast, and the tears came again.

Chapter Twenty-seven

With healthy horses and a wagon, the ten-mile trip into Virginia City had not seemed such a terrible journey to Jo before, especially after walking across half the country to get to Montana. But this journey was far different. She walked dragging a travois behind her, tied around her waist. She was tired and hungry and in pain from the blow to the side of her head, as well as from what she feared was a cracked rib where Bart Kendall's knee had pushed against her middle.

The road to Virginia City was slippery and muddy most of the way, and at times she was so dizzy she wasn't even sure she was still on the right path. She only knew she had to get help for Monty's sake. The fact that her little boy would die if anything happened to her was all that kept her going, but she made little progress each day. She subsisted on the loaf of bread Morrow had let her take, as well as early berries. The cabin had caved into the root cellar, and she had found no salvageable food there. On the second afternoon of her journey she spotted a rabbit, but her senses were so rattled from her ordeal that she missed her shot and the rabbit bounded away.

"Please come back," she whimpered.

The rest of the day she saw no game, and by night she slept in whatever kind of shelter she could find, under overhanging boulders, on beds of pine needles, wrapping both herself and little Monty under the heavy bearskin, keeping the baby close to her for warmth. Her only com-

fort was that Monty was such a good and healthy baby,
and he seldom cried. He seemed unaffected by the bitterly cold mountain air that hit their faces each morning
when Jo climbed out of the bearskin.

Jo trudged on over high passes and through areas of
deep, slushy snow that made the journey even more difficult and dangerous. On the third day she barely missed
being buried by a snowslide, managing to drag the travois
against a rock wall over which hung a ledge that kept the
snow from dumping on Jo and the baby. Jo grabbed Monty
from the travois and stood holding him close, hunched
over and terrified of the thunderous tumult just over their
heads.

By the time it was ended, the snow lay deep in front of
the little overhang. Jo stepped out, her foot sinking up to
her thigh in the fresh slush. A cold wind hit her face, and
she looked up to see gloomy dark clouds kicking up from
the northwest. She knew what that could mean. Her eyes
clouded as she struggled with indecision. Everything seemed
to hurt, and if a spring snowstorm was coming, she was
not sure she had the strength to survive if she was caught
in the open. She knew full well what a mountain storm
could be like.

Again she had to think of Monty. Above all, the baby
had to be kept warm and fed. She had milk for him, and in
the little shelter she had found—even more protected
from the wind by the fresh snowslide that had piled in
front of it—they could stay relatively warm as long as they
had the bearskin.

She came back inside, deciding to wait out the rest of
the day and see if a storm hit. It was already late afternoon, and her legs ached from trudging through deep
snow. She settled into the little cove, pulling the bearskin
over herself and Monty and letting Monty feed at her
breast while she lay resting beside him. She wondered at
how easily this land could turn from friend to enemy and
back to friend.

There were times when she hated this land as much as
she loved it, yet she knew she would never leave it. She
had a ranch in the Ruby Valley and she would go back to
that ranch. Men like Sonny Morrow and Bart Kendall

were not going to stop her. Somehow she would find them
and get back her horses, and she would find men to build
her another cabin. She had survived too many obstacles to
be stopped now. A raging anger gave her the strength she
needed, and keeping her son alive gave her the will.

"We'll be all right, Monty," she told the baby, stroking
his soft cheek. "Mama will get you to Virginia City and
somebody there will help us."

She winced with the pain that pierced her left side and
struggled against tears of panic. This was not the time. She
had to continue convincing herself she could rise above
this latest setback, that she would get to Virginia City. She
closed her eyes, again feeling a dizziness that sometimes
made everything around her seem dark, as though the sun
were setting. "We'll be . . . all right," she told Monty
again, before dozing off.

Clint pushed on through the snowstorm, worried about
Jo. He was close enough now that snow or no snow, he
was determined to get to her. He was still not back to full
strength, and the journey had not been easy. The nights
were bitterly cold, and he had driven himself harder than
normal, determined not to waste one minute of time getting back to Jo. Snow and sleet and mountain winds had
plagued him all the way through Jackson Hole and Yellowstone, yet just being deeper in the mountains gave him
added incentive, for he was closer to Jo, and he was in the
country he loved best.

All the way he cursed himself for leaving. How could he
have ever doubted that his feelings for Jo were real? Of
course they were real. He loved her, and he would take
the chance on caring again; for risking those feelings was
far less painful than forcing himself to stay away from Jo.
And, after all, God had led him to Jo, hadn't he? It
seemed so right to be with her, as though it were destined.

Now the Ruby Valley was just ahead, and his heart
quickened like a younger man in love for the first time.
He kicked his horse into a faster gait, reaching the southern end of Jo's fencing and the gate she had made herself.
He urged his horse closer, noticing the gate was already
open, and wondering if Jo knew about it. He rode through,
then closed and locked the gate. Here in the valley it was

snowing heavily, but the wind was not as fierce as he knew it must be farther up in the mountains, where the peaks were totally hidden by what looked like a fierce snowstorm, its howling winds echoing in the valley. He pulled his hat farther down over his eyes and headed toward the ranch, glad to see the horses had not been caught in the snow. They were nowhere to be seen, apparently in the horse shed above.

He urged his horse uphill then, toward the cabin. It was still early morning, and he pictured Jo just out of bed, her hair still tangled, her body still warm, wrapped in a robe while she stirred the fire and made coffee. He prayed she still wanted him, still loved him. He pushed his hat back a little, looking up toward the cabin, expecting to see smoke wafting from the stone chimney. But all he saw was the stone chimney standing alone—and no cabin surrounding it.

It seemed as though his heart suddenly stopped beating. Where was the cabin? He kicked his horse into a gallop, staring at the naked chimney. He could see now that a fresh snowfall had covered burned ruins of what had been Jo's cabin. The blackened logs lay in a smelly rubble, and a wave of dread engulfed Clint as he drew closer. He halted the horse and dismounted, noticing that the Indian lance was gone from in front of the cabin. Had Indians done this?

"Jo!" he called out desperately. "My God, no!" He noticed the original horse shed was also burned, but a new one was still standing. "Jo!" he called out again. He tied his horse and took his rifle from its boot, walking to the newer building, calling Jo's name over and over. He searched the newer horse stalls, finding a coat he was sure belonged to Moose.

"What the hell?" he muttered.

He walked back outside, realizing then that there was not one horse in sight, none of Jo's original horses, none of the mustangs. He heard a low mooing and ran in the direction of the sound to find Margaret the cow pawing through snow to find some grass.

"Margaret!" He walked up and petted the cow's head for a moment, then called for Jo again. He noticed an inden-

tion in the snow that led into the woods, as though there
had been some kind of path made in older snow. That
meant someone had walked there. He tracked it for a ways,
keeping alert for any sound, any trace of Indians lurking
nearby. The snow continued to fall in huge flakes, and he
cursed it for covering whatever tracks he might have been
able to follow. He traced the indentation to an opening
where several piles of logs and smaller wood chips were
stacked. He noticed what looked like a crude cross near an
awkwardly stacked pile of logs. He walked closer, his heart
pounding with dread at the sight of piles of dirt around the
logs where it looked as though animals had been digging.
He knew the sign—wolves digging at something dead. He
was almost afraid to look at the cross.

"Moose and Spirit," was all it read.

Clint frowned, kneeling closer, his heart aching at the
words. Moose? Dead? How? Why? And how would a dog
manage to die at the same time as a man? Had they been
caught in the fire? He looked back toward the cabin,
which he could not even see from here. It couldn't have
been a fire. Why would someone have dragged their
bodies all the way out here to bury them? And *who* had
buried them? Jo?

He looked around, poking at the other piles of wood to
be sure there weren't any other graves. But there was only
the one. He called out for Jo again, but his ears met with
silence, except for the distant howling of wind farther up
in the mountains.

There was no time for grieving. He had to find out what
had happened to Jo. Since she and the horses both seemed
to be missing, his first thought was that Indians must
have stolen both away. But Indians would not have stopped
to bury Moose and the dog. He studied the grave again,
noticing the snow was melted around it. The melted snow
and the fact that there was enough scent for animals to
have dug around it could only mean the grave was still
fresh, enough heat and scent still coming off the bodies to
attract the wolves. That also meant it was a shallow grave,
hastily dug. With the ground still partially frozen, a woman
would have difficulty digging a very deep grave. A stranger
couldn't have done it. No stranger would have known
Moose's and Spirit's names.

He tried to make sense of the situation. If it was Jo who had dug the grave, that meant she was still alive somewhere. Perhaps she had left to get help. If she did, she would head for Virginia City; and if the grave was as fresh as he suspected, she could be caught right now higher up in the mountains in the snowstorm that raged. He hurried back to where he had tied his horse, searching around the cabin ruins but finding no signs that helped him.

It was then he noticed it—a cradle sitting under a big pine tree. He frowned, walking over to the wooden baby bed, kneeling beside it. He touched it, rocking it in the snow for a moment. What on earth would a cradle be doing here? Had white visitors come by and left it? Another thought entered his mind then, one he didn't want to imagine. Jo? He examined the cradle closer, turning it over, and saw the names carved into the bottom.

"For Jo and Monty, from Rubin."

"Jo and Monty?" Clint murmured. His heart tightened. Jo and Monty. Who was Monty? Surely Monty was the baby that had occupied the cradle. Jo's baby? If Jo had had a baby . . . had she married someone else? No. His memory of that day and night he had spent with her was too vivid, her words of love too strong in his mind and heart. How many times had he made love to her? He couldn't even remember. He had filled her over and over, feeling as though he could never get enough of her.

He rose, closing his eyes. "My God," he whispered. "It must be mine." He threw back his head, blinking back tears. Had she had the baby up here all alone? Where were they now? Was his worst nightmare revisiting him? Were the woman he loved and the child that apparently belonged to him in the hands of Indians? His only hope was was the fact that Moose and the dog had been buried, apparently by a woman. Yellow Wolf had promised Jo no harm would come to her, but Clint knew full well the slightest affront could change an Indian's mind. If it was Indians, maybe for some strange reason they had allowed Jo to bury Moose and the dog before they took her and the horses away. But that was very unlikely, again meaning it was possible Indians didn't have her at all.

He struggled with the horror of what it could mean if she *was* with Indians, feeling his ability to overcome the past being tested in the most cruel way. He took a deep breath and cried out Jo's name in one long, deep, panic-filled call. But still there was no answer. His only hope was that she was all right and maybe had already made it to Virginia City!

He untied his horse and mounted up, riding off in the direction she would have to take. If he didn't find her in town, he would wire for soldiers and search every canyon and valley in Montana until he found her!

Jo had felt the fever coming through the night as she slept fitfully. Each time the pain in her side woke her, she felt hotter, until finally she pushed the bearskin to her waist, keeping Monty covered but longing, herself, to be cooler. Everything seemed unreal now, a strange nightmare—the howling blizzard outside, the pain in her head and side, the congestion in her chest. Somewhere in the recesses of her mind she knew she had a baby to care for. She had to find food, make a fire, find water to wash the baby's bottom when she changed him.

But her body would not cooperate. She changed Monty's diapers and fed him in a daze. She remembered she was supposed to be going to Virginia City, but the snow and wind outside kept her buried in the little alcove she had found. The first day spent in the cave turned into a second, as Jo moved between tossing and sleeping and feeding Monty. She was aware she was very sick, terrified she would die here—meaning her baby would die, too. She managed to get up and walk on shaking legs to the entrance of her little shelter, where she scooped up snow and ate it for moisture.

The second night her fever was worse, and she remembered how sick she had been on the journey west. Clint had been with her then. That was when he had carried her to the river to cool her. Should she go and lie in the snow? What if she never woke up? Poor little Monty would lie alone, crying and slowly starving to death. No. She had to stay alive for Monty. That meant she had to have food and water. But she was so weak, so hot. Tomorrow. She would go outside tomorrow and hunt for food. She stumbled back to the baby, lying down beside him again and praying through tears that God would not let Monty die.

Somehow she got through a third night. When she awoke she heard no wind. She rose, and through bloodshot eyes she saw sunshine peeking through the opening between the snow and the top of her small shelter. Monty began fussing and she managed to change him, then held him to her breast to be sure his belly was full before she went looking for food. She still felt hot, and her whole body ached fiercely. Breathing came hard, and her rib still gave her piercing pain whenever she moved the wrong way. Her jaw ached so badly she couldn't open it all the way.

Monty finished feeding and drifted off to sleep. Jo pulled away, covering him with the bearskin; then she found her own bearskin coat and put it on in a daze. It seemed to weigh a ton on her weakened body. She found her rifle and stumbled outside, stepping into the deep snow and falling forward. It took her several minutes to get back onto her feet and maneuver herself to a piece of ground where snow had been swept free by the wind. She stood there a moment, trying to get her bearings, trying to see where the road was that led to Virginia City, but everything was covered with snow, and in her confused state, she wasn't even sure in which direction she should go once she headed out again.

For now she had to find food. She glanced back at the cave, telling herself she had to keep it in sight or she might get lost and never find Monty again. Besides that, she had to be able to see the shelter in case an animal tried to get inside to her baby. She looked around the still pines; everything was made quiet by the new snow. She tried to remember just how far she had come, how long it had been since leaving the cabin. With great effort she cocked her rifle and walked a few yards from the cave.

The cold air made it even harder to breathe. She prayed an animal would come along and make her job easy so she wouldn't have to stray too far from Monty, but there was nothing in sight. She listened for the sound of water, but heard no sound of a rushing stream where she might get a real drink. Her mouth felt like sandpaper, and she worried her milk would dry up and she wouldn't be able to feed Monty.

She walked on a little farther, then sat down on a stump to catch her breath, hoping again an animal would come by. The cold seemed to penetrate her heated body like a knife, and everything ached even worse. After what seemed like hours she began to cry in desperation. She was very sick. There was no denying it, and suddenly it both angered and terrified her. Never had she felt this helpless since coming here. She wouldn't mind if it was just herself. But Monty! She had to think of Monty!

She rose to head back to the cave, wondering how she was going to keep from starving to death. It was then she noticed a couple of wolves sniffing around the shelter where Monty lay sleeping. "No!" she whimpered. A surge of needed strength moved through her body and she raised her rifle, then realized she couldn't shoot straight at them or a bullet could fly into the cave and hit Monty, or ricochet off a rock and hit him.

"Get away!" she screamed. She fired her rifle into the air, then cocked it and fired again. The wolves darted away. Jo staggered back toward the cave, but she could see the wolves crouching off to the side, waiting like the cunning animals they were, somehow sensing she was dying and all they had to do was wait for the end. She turned and fired at one of them and it ran away, but she knew it would come back.

Just before she reached the cave she again stepped into deeper snow, her foot sinking in to her crotch. She struggled desperately to get her leg out, but her strength was gone. When she put her hands down to pull up her leg, she only sank deeper into the snow. She pulled her hands free and looked for something to grab onto to draw herself up, but there was nothing. She dug desperately at the snow, but she simply did not have the strength to get out.

Jo could not stop the tears of desperation as she saw the wolves slinking closer again. "Monty," she whimpered. "God, save my baby!" She reached for her rifle, but some-

how she had lost it in the snow. "No! no!" she wailed.
"Not this way, God! Not now! Not this way!" Again she
struggled to get free, but to no avail.

Clint halted his horse at the sound of the gunshot. It
echoed through the mountains, seeming to come from
every direction. He turned his horse, scanning the hills
around him. There came a second shot. This time he got a
better idea of the direction from which it had come. It was
behind him and above, to the left. He headed the horse in
that direction, then was more sure of the location when
there came a third shot. Whoever it was, even if they
were shooting at him, he had to find out. How many
people would be up here just after a snowstorm? Most
likely it was someone in trouble—maybe Jo.

His horse's breath came in snorting gasps as the big
gelding trudged through snow so deep the animal could
hardly move. Clint headed him toward ground that was
clearer, while he searched the hills desperately. Finally he
spotted what looked like something alive and struggling.
Farther above he noticed wolves prowling about. He took
his rifle from its boot and fired at them, several shots that
made them run off.

The climb had become too much of a burden for his
horse. Clint dismounted, leading the horse by the reins,
heading for the struggling human. When he came closer
he saw the long, dark hair. "Jo?" he called out.

Jo was sure she had drifted into insanity. Maybe she had
died and in death was hearing Clint call to her. "Clint,"
she mumbled. "Why didn't . . . you come back?"

Suddenly she felt strong arms pulling at her. "Jo! My
God, Jo!" She felt herself being pulled free of the deeper
snow, and in the next moment someone was holding her,
pressing her so tight that it hurt her rib and she cried out.
"Jo! What is it? Where are you hurt? What happened?"

She opened her fevered eyes to a handsome face that
looked like Clint, but the face was so thin. "Clint," she
whispered. Her eyes were full of tears. "Clint." It was all
she could get out for the moment, she was so overwhelmed,
struggling to understand if this was real or a vision.

He was kissing her face over and over, smoothing her

hair. "Jo, I'm sorry. I'm so goddamned sorry," he was saying, sounding close to tears himself. "I never should have left. I've got it all figured out, Jo. I'm all right, and I love you, Jo. I would have come back sooner, but I was wounded. When I found the cabin . . . my God, Jo, what happened?"

She managed to reach up and touch his face, and Clint realized then that she was raging with fever. Her hand was hot against his skin.

"Jo, you're sick. I've got to find some shelter—"

"Monty!" she said, her voice weak. "The baby . . . up there . . . shelter. Find Monty."

Clint looked above her, seeing snow piled in front of what looked like some kind of opening. He got up and tied his horse to a nearby tree. He picked Jo up in his arms, carrying her up to the makeshift shelter and ducking inside with her. There he spotted the bearskin and heard a faint crying. His heart quickened as he carried Jo over to the bearskin and pulled it back. Under the bearskin was a blanket on a bed of pine needles, and on top of the blanket lay something moving under a quilt. He lay Jo down on the blanket and knelt beside her, pulling back the quilt to see an infant chewing on its fist, its feet kicking at a flannel kimono it wore.

Without a word Jo turned to her side and opened her coat and dress, pulling the infant close to feed at her breast. It was obvious she was hardly aware of Clint's presence. Her first thought was for the baby. Clint's eyes misted as he watched the infant suckle at her breast. He pulled the bearskin over both of them and leaned down, kissing Jo's cheek.

"God, I love you, Jo." He leaned closer and kissed the white of her breast, then the soft, fuzzy hair of the baby's head. Monty was a boy's name, and Jo was obviously this baby's mother. No one needed to tell him this was his son. He remained bent over them for several minutes, his arms around them both. "Why in God's name didn't you wire me, Jo?"

Her only reply was to whisper his name and ask him in her delirium to keep the wolves away. He petted her hair. "I'll keep them away. You just rest. I'm going to get my gear and get some food in your stomach."

"Water," she murmured. "So . . . thirsty."

He kissed her heated forehead. "I'll get you some water."

He rose and went out to get his gear. Right now it didn't matter how she had come to be here. All that mattered was keeping her alive. Explanations could come later.

Jo snuggled closer to Monty, somehow knowing in her confused mind that Clint was here. Somehow he had found her, and everything would be all right. Clint had come home . . . home to Montana.

Chapter Twenty-eight

Jo pulled her breast away from Monty as Clint supported her with one arm. She leaned up to gulp the water he offered her, but he seemed to draw it away too quickly. "Take it easy. A little at a time," he told her.

"Please, just . . . a little more." She drank a little more until he finally took the canteen away again. Jo studied his face, reaching up to touch it. "I can't believe you're . . . here," she whispered.

He corked the canteen and leaned down and kissed her cheek. "I would have been here a lot sooner, but I was wounded . . . and then we were trapped at Fort Connor—I'll explain it all when you're better." He took her into his arms and gently stroked her hair. "My God, Jo, what happened?"

She frowned, realizing how much thinner his face was. Her heart tightened at his words about being wounded. "You aren't well," she whimpered, her condition exaggerating her fears.

"I'm all right now. I just have to put on a little more weight." He held her close, and his arms comforted her. Already she felt stronger. He was here! He was really here! But was he here to stay this time? "Jo, don't worry about me. Tell me what the hell happened to you."

She grasped his shirt, the horror coming back to her. "They took everything, Clint," she sobbed. "They killed Moose . . . and my little . . . Spirit. He was . . . my best friend." The tears came harder and he rocked her lightly.

368

"Hush, Jo. It's going to be all right."

"But . . . they burned . . . my house . . . stole my horses. My horses! My pregnant . . . mares . . . and my stud horse. He cost me . . . nearly everything I had. I . . . I bought more land . . . but now . . . now I have to start all over. I don't know if I can do it all over again, Clint."

He watched his son for a moment. The boy slept beside her, a beautiful, healthy child.

"Not you, Jo. Us. *We* have to start all over, and we will." He kissed her cheek and looked into her fevered eyes. "I love you, Jo Masters. I didn't think I could say that to another woman, but it comes easy with you. I'm all right, Jo. Something happened while I was gone. . . . I looked the past right in the face and I conquered it. And then when I came back and saw that cabin burned, found those graves and thought you might be dead—" He held her closer again. "God, I love you, Jo. Can you ever forgive me for leaving?"

She moved an arm around his neck. "It's all right." Now she felt even stronger! He had finally said the words she knew were in his heart. For him to be able to say them was proof enough he was going to be all right. He was ready to love again. "Clint, I love you . . . so much. I knew . . . you'd come back. I gave the baby . . . your last name."

He hugged her tighter. "My God, Jo, you should have let me know."

"I wanted you to come back . . . just for me . . . not because of the baby."

He kissed her hair. "What a terrible thing to go through all alone."

"Moose . . . was gone . . . getting help for me when the baby came. And Rubin . . . Buck got away and Rubin went after him. I was . . . alone . . . but then . . . Yellow Wolf came."

"Yellow Wolf!" He moved to look into her face. "He came back?"

"Clint, you have to learn . . . not to hate them. Yellow Wolf's wife . . . and mother . . . saved my life . . . the baby's life. If not for them . . . neither one of us might be here. It was . . . so cold . . . and I couldn't make a fire. I had no help. They stayed . . . until I could get up and walk. They fed me . . . kept the house warm. They were good to me, Clint. You . . . owe them something. They . . . saved our lives."

"But look what they did to you—killed Moose, burned the house, stole—"

"Not Indians, Clint. Outlaws." She began coughing and he held her closer. She grasped her side, the coughing making the pain worse in her ribs.

"I'd better make a fire and get some food in your stomach," Clint was saying. "The first thing we have to do is get you well. How long ago did this happen?"

"I'm . . . not sure. Four or five days, I think. The storm came . . . I got lost and then . . . I got sick. I was so scared . . . for Monty. I was afraid I would die . . . and he'd be . . . all alone. I had no food, Clint. I don't want my . . . milk to run out."

Anger began to fill his eyes. "Who the hell would leave a woman and baby to die in the wilderness?" He gently laid her back, covering her better with the bearskin. "Did you know any of them?"

Her own fury at the memory was giving her even more strength. Clint was here now. He loved her. "Bart Kendall," she said, her bitterness evident in spite of her weak voice. She coughed again and leaned away from the baby, grasping her side as the agonizing pain returned to her rib cage. When she looked back at Clint, she wondered if she had ever seen such fury in a man's eyes.

"Kendall! I thought I took care of that bastard!" The anger in his eyes was replaced with horror as he leaned closer to her, only then noticing how one side of her face was oddly discolored. At first he had thought it was due to cold and exposure. "What did he do to you!"

Jo closed her eyes. "He hit me . . . knocked me down. They came . . . so fast . . . shot Moose down in cold blood . . . snuck up to the cabin on foot. There was nothing . . . I could do. Kendall . . . pushed me down . . . put his knee in my stomach. I . . . couldn't breathe. I think he . . . cracked a rib. My side hurts bad, Clint."

He pulled the bearskin back and reached inside her coat, gently feeling her ribs. She winced with pain. "What else did he do, Jo? I want the truth."

She saw the desperate fear in his eyes, and she touched

his arm. "He didn't do . . . what you think. He wanted to. One of the others . . . stopped him. I guess he was their leader. His name was . . . Sonny Morrow. He said he didn't stand for . . . raping proper married women. I think . . . it helped that I had . . . a little baby. He was a . . . strange man, Clint. He stopped Kendall from . . . raping me. But he let him burn my house . . . left me to die out there. The only things . . . he let me take . . . were a few belongings . . . and a loaf of bread. I . . . made a travois . . . tried to find some food, but . . . I was too weak to shoot straight."

His eyes filled with relief that she had not been raped and the baby had not been harmed. He grasped her hand and held it to his lips. "Damn!" he hissed. His dark eyes searched her own, and she saw determined vengeance there. "Did they give any indication where they might have taken the horses?"

"They said . . . something about . . . Canada."

He almost smiled. "They did, did they? And I'll bet they'll take their time, thinking you're back here helpless and unable to tell anyone what happened. This snowstorm probably held them up even more."

Her eyes teared again. "Clint, my mares. Some of them were pregnant. I . . . need those foals. They might . . . run them too hard. I'm afraid some of the mares will lose their foals, or die in the cold."

He rose. "You aren't going to lose any horses, Jo. We're going to get you to Virginia City and I'm going to get back those horses. And Bart Kendall will find out he guessed wrong if he thought he could get away with this one! I'll do more than slice off his ear this time!"

"Clint . . . you look so thin and . . . tired. You can't . . . go after them alone."

He grinned, shaking his head. "I won't have to go alone. Once the men in Virginia City hear about this, half the town will gladly come with me. You have a lot of people on your side, Jo, don't you know that? They aren't going to like what Kendall and his friends did to you—and they're going to really be in a rage when they find out Moose Barkley was shot down in cold blood."

Her heart felt lighter and she stopped crying. "Do you . . . really think you can . . . get the horses back?"

He looked down at her, and at that moment he was the most beautiful sight she had ever set eyes on. "I'll follow them all the way to Alaska if I have to! Now you just lie there and rest. I'll take care of everything from here on. I'll go get my gear." He turned away, then hesitated. "I'm so damn sorry, Jo. I should have been there."

"You're here now . . . and you came back . . . for me. That's all that matters."

He shook his head. "Maybe. And maybe you can forgive me. But it will take a long time for me to forgive myself."

He walked out, returning later with an armful of wood. He piled it near the entrance to the small shelter. After nearly a half-hour of fussing with the wet fuel he finally got it to burn. He went outside then and brought his horse closer, taking his supplies off the horse. He set a pan over the fire and dumped a can of beans into it, part of the army rations he had saved.

"I don't have a lot, but I don't expect at this point you're particular about what you eat," he told her. "The point is to get some food in your belly. I have a little smoked venison along. I'll throw it in with these beans."

Jo watched his every move, half expecting him to suddenly disappear when she woke up from this dream. He put on the meat and set a small coffeepot over the fire, filling it from a second canteen. He took some gauze from his supplies then and came over to Jo, kneeling down beside her. "Let's take a look at that rib. Can you stand for just a few minutes? It will feel a lot better if I wrap it good and tight."

"I'll try."

Clint helped her to her feet, then took off her coat and unbuttoned her dress, pulling it to her waist. For an undergarment she wore only a man's cotton undershirt that buttoned in front, so she could easily open it to feed Monty. Clint pushed it up to expose her ribs, but it also exposed her full breasts.

"Hold it up and keep your arms up," he told her.

Their eyes held for a moment as Jo self-consciously covered her breasts at first. He leaned down and kissed her cheek. Saying nothing, he pulled her hands away and gently kissed each breast, catching the taste of her milk. He knelt down, kissing gently at the bruise on her stomach.

"No one will ever hurt you again, Jo," he said softly.

She clasped his head, holding his face against her breasts. "I know." She stroked his hair. "I know."

He kissed her belly again, and in spite of her fever and aching weariness, old passions were reawakened, and she knew how wonderful it was going to be when she was well. Clint was back, and suddenly nothing else mattered, not even the stolen horses. After what she had accomplished alone, just think what they could accomplish together. She was satisfied now. She had proven she could do what she had set out to do. She was ready now to have a man at her side. *"We'll start over,"* he had said. She didn't have to do it alone.

He gently wrapped her ribs, and it helped the pain. She pulled her dress back up and pulled on her coat, and Clint took her chin in his hand and lifted her face to meet his eyes. "I do love you, Jo. I knew it when I left, but I just couldn't make the words come out."

"I know. I never expected you to stay. But I guess . . . I didn't expect I'd get pregnant either."

He leaned down and kissed her mouth gently, then cradled her head against his chest for a moment. "Do you think I could hold my son? I know he's sleeping, but—"

"It's all right."

He helped her lie back down, then moved around the other side of her, keeping the quilt wrapped around Monty as he gently lifted the baby into his arms. He sat down beside Jo, studying his son, touching the boy's soft cheek with a big, rugged finger.

"I've been calling him Monty," she told him. "That's short for Montana. I wanted a name that sounded strong and that fit the land. Montana was the best thing I could think of."

"It's a good name," Clint answered, studying his handsome son. "Hello, Montana," he said softly. His eyes brimmed over then, and he leaned down, nestling the baby into his shoulder, his back to Jo. He put his head down, and Jo could see his shoulders shaking. Her throat tightened at what he must be thinking at that moment. He had a family again. He had a son. She was glad now for the pain of giving birth, and she didn't care that she had had this baby out of wedlock. After all, they were as married in their hearts as any piece of paper could prove. And Monty was what Clint needed more than anything else in the world—the best medicine possible for such a broken man.

After several minutes Clint raised his head, breathing deeply and wiping at his eyes. He opened the quilt and studied the baby's hands and toes, giving the boy a thorough examination, as though he didn't believe he was real.

"He's beautiful, Jo," he said quietly. "You did a hell of a job." He cleared his throat and leaned down to kiss the baby's cheek. "I sure didn't expect to come back to this. Thank you, Jo."

His voice broke slightly and she put a hand on his back. "You're quite welcome . . . Mr. Reeves."

He laid the boy back down beside her, turning to her with reddened eyes. "We'll get married as soon as we get to Virginia City."

She smiled, and told him about the fake marriage license. "We'll have to marry in secret so no one knows we never got married the first time."

He grinned sadly. "I'm sorry you had to do that." He leaned down and kissed her eyes. "I want you to eat now, and then just sleep. Sleep as much as you need. Those horse thieves won't get so far in this weather that we can't track them. We'll go to an outlaw hangout north of here first and track them from there. They might have even held up there for a few days."

She settled back and watched him as he got her food. She felt so much stronger already, confident that if anyone could get back her horses, Clint Reeves could do it. He was thinner, but as handsome as ever, still tall and broad and strong. He brought the food to her and helped her eat. She swallowed some blessedly hot coffee.

"Come and lie down beside me, Clint," she told him when she finished. "I want you close. I still can't believe you're here."

He cleaned up the food and checked his horse first, then came back with his own bedroll, opening it up next to her for more room, covering them both with a buffalo robe so that most of the bearskin remained over Monty. He pulled Jo into his arms and she nestled against his shoulder, thanking God Clint Reeves was here beside her.

"We'll build the ranch even bigger, won't we, Clint?

Together we can own half of Montana, and we'll raise the most beautiful horses in the whole territory."

"We sure will. I got pretty good pay from the army, Jo. We'll do all right. I'll get those horses back, and we'll build a new house, bigger and better than the first one."

"And we'll have more babies—sons to help with the ranch."

He kissed her hair. "Yes. Lots of sons to help with the ranch. But first you have to get well. Try to sleep, Jo. There's nothing to worry about now. Just be glad you and Monty are alive. That's all that's really important."

She settled against him. How good it felt to know help was here and she didn't have to struggle through this alone. With her ribs wrapped and her belly full, lying in the arms of the man she loved, she drifted off into a deep, exhausted sleep.

It was nearly dawn when Jo awoke. She heard birds singing, and water dripping everywhere; the snow was beginning to melt from another chinook wind that brought welcome warmth again to the land. She felt a big hand gently caressing her breast, and she realized that the touch and Clint's warm lips at her neck had awakened her.

She turned to him and saw his eyes were closed. It was difficult to tell if he was awake or asleep, as his lips met her mouth and he groaned quietly. She felt his hardness against her thigh and he kissed her harder, moving his lips then to her neck, her ear. Jo realized her fever was gone. She was simply sore and weary, but not too weary to prove to herself he was really here; to reawaken the sweet joy she had found in Clint Reeves.

"Just once, Jo," he whispered. "I'll be gentle."

She said nothing in reply as his hand reached inside her dress, pushing it back to expose one breast. His lips found its sweet fruit and he gently tasted his son's nourishment, finding a kind of strength and comfort there himself. His lips moved back to Jo's throat as he pushed up her dress and reached inside her bloomers.

Jo shuddered at the gentle, perfect movements. He pushed the bloomers to her ankles and unlaced his buckskin pants, moving between her legs and carefully avoiding putting his full weight on her rib. He entered her in one quick gentle thrust, and in that moment she knew they would be united forever. He was here to stay, and after all they had both been through, they could survive anything, as long as they were together.

"My beautiful, strong, brave Joline," he said softly.

She simply closed her eyes and let him move, too weak to do anything but lie there and enjoy the feel of him inside her. He finished quickly, not wanting to make it difficult for her. He settled beside her then, pulling her close. "I'm sorry," he told her. "I just . . . I needed you, Jo."

"I needed you the same."

He sighed, stroking her hair. They lay there quietly for several minutes before Clint finally spoke up again. "He's dead, Jo. Two Moons is dead. I killed him myself."

"Two Moons! The Indian that led the attack the day Millie and your son were captured?"

"The same. It was as though . . . as though God meant for me to face that day all over again—to see it for what it really was. Two Moons seemed to know what had to be—we both knew. There was business left unfinished. He handed me a knife and we fought. That's how I got wounded."

"My God, what a terrible thing for you, to see that man again. How badly were you wounded?"

"Pretty bad. Took a knife across my middle. It got infected. I made it back to Fort Connor, and then we were stranded there most of the winter, cut off from aid and supplies by Indians." He turned onto his back.

"Seeing Two Moons—is that what you meant by looking the past right in the face?"

He sighed deeply. "Yes. It was strange, Jo, the feeling I had when I killed him. It wasn't like I thought it would be. I mean, I realized whether he was dead or alive, it wasn't going to change the fact that Millie and Jeff were gone. I realized what a crazy world this is—men always finding an excuse to fight and kill. I just wanted to forget all of it and come back here to you. How can anyone be blamed? Indians caused the death of my wife and son; but Indians saved you and Monty. It was white men who brought you harm."

He rose up on one elbow, meeting her eyes. "I'm all

right, Jo. I haven't touched whiskey in months. And I can talk about Millie without half losing my mind. For a long time I blamed myself, wondered if I could have somehow saved them. But I know I couldn't have. I did what I had to do. I didn't really kill them, Jo. They might as well have already been dead. If the same thing happened again, I'd do the same thing over to keep you and Monty from suffering."

She touched his face. "It won't happen again. God means for us to be together, Clint." She smiled for him. "I feel better. I think I can travel if you rig me up on the travois and keep me under blankets. The sun is out and it feels warmer."

He grinned and kissed her cheek. "Yes, ma'am. I'll make some breakfast and we'll head for Virginia City. I've got some horses to find, and a man by the name of Bart Kendall."

Jo smiled, imagining the look on Bart Kendall's face when he saw Clint Reeves again.

Jo could hear the ruckus in the street below. She picked up Monty and went to the window of her hotel room, looking down into the street to see at least fifty men gathered around Clint, all ranting about what had happened to Moose and to Jo, all ready to ride with Clint. She smiled to think of how good-hearted these men could be. So many of them were nothing more than uneducated drifters, wandering prospectors who would never realize their dream, some of them leftovers from the war, men who had suffered deep, personal losses.

She was glad so many were willing to go with Clint, for she knew he would go after Bart Kendall alone if he had to, and he still wasn't back to full strength. Never had she loved him more than at this moment. How many times had he helped her on her journey west, even to putting his own life on the line? He had struggled and won not only outward battles, but a very important personal battle. She had no doubt he would recover her horses. He would do anything for Joline Masters.

No, not Masters. It was Reeves now—legally. But she realized she had belonged to Clint Reeves almost from the

moment she had met him. That was just four months short
of three years ago.

She had begged Clint to take her with him, for more
than anything she wanted to see the look on Bart Kendall's
face when Clint caught up with the man. But Clint had
insisted she stay in Virginia City with Monty. She had the
baby to think about now, and she knew Clint needed to do
this alone, to somehow make up for what she had suffered
because he had not been with her.

*"For once in your life let someone else do something for
you."* She could still hear his words. *"You don't have to do
everything alone."*

No, she didn't. But she knew Clint Reeves would continue to let her be her own woman; would give her free
rein in decisions about the ranch; would be her partner
and gentle lover, not a man who expected her to suddenly
become his silent servant. He needed a woman who filled
his secret needs, gave him the inner courage to match his
outer strength. She would be that woman. And he would
fill all the voids of her own life, help her fulfill that
womanly side of her that wanted home and hearth and
more children.

She watched him mount up. He looked up at her window and she waved. He nodded, and several others looked
up and raised their hats before riding off behind Clint
Reeves, all eager to track down Sonny Morrow and his
gang.

Sonny lit a cigar, rubbing at his eyes and trying to get
the sleep out of them. It had been a cold night, and he
had slept hard under his heavy buffalo robe. He cursed
the weather, which had got worse as they headed toward
Canada. Of course things were warmer farther south, but
he knew some horse traders in Canada who would take his
herd, no questions asked. The brands would be changed
and the horses would probably end up being sold to the
Royal Canadian Mounted Police.

The horses they had collected from the woman by the
Ruby River were a fine addition to the stolen horses they
had brought up from Utah. He wondered what had happened to the woman, admired her spunk, almost hoped
she had survived and wondered why he hadn't brought

her along. Once tamed, she might have made a fine bed partner. But women like that usually meant trouble. And if she was telling the truth about a husband, the man was less likely to come after them if the woman was left untouched. At any rate, nearly a month had passed since they had left the Ruby. They were camped on the Canadian border. If anyone was following them, they would have reached them by now.

He got up from his bedroll and stretched, then walked behind a pile of fallen pine trees to relieve himself. He had just finished when he noticed a movement behind a huge boulder just above him to his left. He instinctively reached for his revolver, when he heard the voice. "Just throw it aside, mister."

Morrow looked up to see a tall man in buckskins and a wolfskin coat coming around from behind the boulder, wielding a rifle. "Who the hell are you?"

"Name's Reeves. Clint Reeves. You've got some horses that belong to my wife, and you and I have a score to settle."

Morrow's eyes widened. "Reeves! You're the husband?"

Clint grinned. "That's right. And you're Sonny Morrow, aren't you?"

Morrow stepped back a little. "Look, mister, it was all Bart Kendall's idea. I told the sonuvabitch I didn't like the idea of messin' with a woman."

"Didn't stop you, though, did it? If you had settled for just the horses, I might not be here. But you let Kendall manhandle her, and you let him burn her cabin—left her in the wilderness with my son to die." Clint cocked the rifle. "I really wish you'd go for that gun, Morrow."

Morrow eyed him narrowly. "You alone?"

"Might be. Then again I might not. I'll let you decide."

Morrow swallowed, inwardly cursing Bart Kendall. He carefully took out his pistol, throwing it aside and turning around. "You wouldn't shoot a man in the back, would you?"

"Why not? Your men did it to Moose Barkley. He was a good friend of mine. I'd like nothing better than to shoot you in the back, but I think I'll save you for the people of Virginia City. They all greatly admire Joline Reeves, Morrow. I'm sure they'd like the pleasure of watching your neck stretched by a rope."

Morrow suddenly plunged forward, rolling into camp and shouting to his men. "Up! Everybody up! Get your guns!"

"What the hell!" someone shouted. One man went for his gun and Clint fired. The man cried out as a bloody hole opened in his face. Morrow scrambled to reach his bedroll where he had another gun. Clint cocked his rifle and fired again, then ducked behind a rock as other men woke up and reached for their guns. Morrow lay near his bedroll, screaming from a gaping wound in his hip.

By then the camp was surrounded with men from Virginia City, who had all waited in hiding. They had tracked the outlaws for nearly three weeks, putting up with foul weather and hungry bellies, determined not to give up. Clint had found the camp the night before, and in the wee hours of the morning the men had moved in on foot.

The outlaws fired wildly, but their shots were returned with a volley of gunfire from the surrounding rocks and trees, and in seconds only four men were left alive, two of them wounded, including Morrow. They all tossed their guns aside, and Clint recognized Bart Kendall's black coat. The man's back was to him. Clint stepped closer.

"So, Kendall, we meet again. Too bad you didn't heed my warning about staying away from Jo."

Kendall turned, his face as white as the snow around him. "Reeves!"

Never had Clint seen such fear in a man's eyes. Just that look was satisfaction enough. He stepped closer and pressed the end of his rifle against Kendall's throat, its hot barrel burning the man's skin. "I'd love to pull this trigger, Kendall, but Joline Reeves deserves the pleasure of watching you die at the end of a rope. You're going back to Virginia City."

"I . . . it was Morrow's idea, Reeves. I wanted to leave her be . . . like you told me."

"Sure you did. You heard I was gone—figured maybe it was for good. You thought you'd get some revenge, didn't you? I'll bet you even figured on going back to pay Jo another visit once you got your share of money for the horses." Clint shoved the rifle then, momentarily cutting off Kendall's air by pushing in on his Adam's apple. Kendall sank to the ground, choking. Clint waited while the rest of the men rounded up bodies and horses. As soon as Kendall regained his breath Clint came down with the butt of his rifle against Kendall's neck, enjoying his cry of pain. He shoved the groaning man onto his back, putting a booted foot to his neck. "You're scum, Kendall. You should have listened to me. You'll die for this one, and you'll get to see the look of victory on Joline Reeves's face before you breathe your last breath. She's beaten you again, Kendall. She survived. You messed this one up good." He leaned down and grabbed the man by his coat front. "Now get up and get on a horse!"

"Let me go! Let me go and I promise you'll never see me again," Kendall told him, almost weeping. His answer was to feel a hard boot come up into his groin. He sank to his knees.

"That's for what you would have done to Jo if Morrow hadn't stopped you," Clint growled. He let go of the man, letting him crumple to the ground.

It was nearly the end of June when Clint and the others returned to Virginia City, leading the wounded Morrow and his other three men with them. Morrow was in obvious pain, having ridden nearly three hundred miles with a wounded hip. One of the men had dug out the bullet, but all they had for pain was whiskey, and Clint wouldn't let Morrow drink enough to completely kill the pain.

"We're only taking this thing out of you to keep you alive for a public hanging," he told Morrow.

All the way back Bart Kendall sweat and shivered, knowing full well what he would face in Virginia City.

Jo was sitting in the hotel room feeding Monty when she heard raised voices, the sounds of an angry crowd gathering. She rose, holding on to Monty, and rushed to the window.

"Clint!" she gasped. They had been gone a long time, and Jo was worried something had gone wrong. She could not imagine something happening to him now, after all they had been through. She had clung to the belief he would be back and now here he was, and ahead of him the men herded her horses.

Jo's eyes misted at the sight. There they were! She couldn't tell if they were all there, but most of them were. She spotted a couple of her pregnant mares, and Clint led Buck with a rope to keep the spirited stud under control. Someone knocked on the door to Jo's room and she hurriedly closed her dress, rushing to the door. Sally stood outside.

"He's back, Jo," the woman said, as excited as everyone else. "Come on outside! Clint shouted at me to come and get you. He wants you out there."

The days were warm now. Jo quickly brushed her hair and pinched her cheeks for a little color. She studied her dress in the mirror to be sure it was clean, then wrapped Monty in a light blanket and carried him down the stairs and outside, where Clint and the others had gathered, herding Morrow and Kendall and the other two men in front of the hotel. It seemed by the time Jo got to the front door that every man in Virginia City had gathered around the four men, who all looked frightened to death. Morrow was pale from pain and fear. Kendall swallowed when he saw Jo, but he glared at her with all the hatred he felt for her.

The crowd quieted when Jo exited the hotel doorway. She walked up to Bart Kendall's horse and met his eyes boldly. "I told you what would happen, didn't I?"

"You bitch!" the man sneered.

The rest of the men went into a roar of anger; some of them grabbed at Kendall.

"Hold it! Hold it!" Clint put up a hand and shouted down the crowd. Jo noticed he looked a little better. The warmer weather and sunshine had brought some color back to his face, and he had put on a little weight. He met Jo's eyes.

"Jo, do you recognize these men as the ones who stole your horses and shot Moose Barkley?"

Jo turned her eyes from Clint to Sonny Morrow—then back to Bart Kendall. "Yes," she said in a loud, strong voice. "And killed my dog and burned my house and horse shed and took all my food. They left me and my son to die out there!"

There came another uproar, and Kendall swallowed, already feeling the rope around his neck.

"Men, you know the punishment for murderers and horse thieves!" Rubin Keats shouted.

"Hang 'em high!" Happy Strickland yelled.

"We brought them back for Jo Reeves to identify," Rubin yelled above the crowd. "We already know they stole her horses. We brung them back with us. We know all we need to know!"

Men crowded around Morrow and his men, pulling them from their horses and dragging them away. There was such a crowd that Jo had to step back inside the hotel to keep from being overrun. She completely lost sight of the outlaws as men pulled them down the street toward a gallows that had been built with the expectation Clint and the others would find the men. Clint ordered some men to herd Jo's horses to the corrals at the end of town. He dismounted and walked up to Jo, pulling her inside the hotel lobby and embracing her and Monty together.

"Oh, Clint, I was getting so worried," Jo told him. She looked up at him and he leaned down to kiss her lightly.

"The weather didn't cooperate very well," he answered. "New snow kept covering tracks until May, and we had to be careful not to be spotted until we knew we had them cornered good."

She stepped back and looked him over. "Are you all right?"

He nodded. "We had a little shootout. The rest of Morrow's bunch are dead. Morrow took a bullet in the hip from my gun." He took Monty from her, holding the baby up and looking him over. "How are you, son?" He kissed the boy's cheek and held him close. "He's grown!" he told Jo.

"Babies have a way of doing that." She smiled, touching his arms. "Thank you, Clint, for getting the horses." She put her head against him and the baby and Clint put an arm around her. "I'm so happy you're back and all right. I want to get back to the valley, Clint. I miss it."

"I know. I missed it too, the whole time I was gone after I first left you there, even more when I left you the second time." The crowd still shouted down the street. "You can watch the hanging if you want, Jo. You've earned the right."

She shivered and pulled away. "No. I found satisfaction

enough in seeing Bart Kendall's face when the men pulled him from his horse. Suddenly all the hatred is gone. I don't want to watch."

He sighed, touching her hair. "Well, I do. You take Monty. I'll be back for you later. If you're strong enough, we'll head back to the valley tomorrow."

She took the baby, holding him close. "It sounds wonderful."

He bent closer, lightly kissing her lips again. "I've missed you," he told her softly. "When things are over I'll visit the barber and a bathhouse before I come back." He gave her a wink. A shiver of passion moved through Jo at the meaning of his words. He touched her cheek with the back of his hand before leaving.

Jo went back upstairs. She had thought at first she would want to witness Bart Kendall's punishment, but suddenly all the revenge had left her. She didn't want Monty's life to start out full of violence and hatred. Clint had managed to overcome the past. It was time to start fresh and new. She went into her room and sat down on the bed, trying to shut out the sounds of the shouting that continued outside. It seemed to go on for an hour. The violence made her shudder and hold Monty closer, but one thing she knew—she had a whole town full of men who would help her whenever she needed it. And she had Clint.

She heard the thud of the scaffold doors being shoved open from under the feet of the outlaws. Once, twice, three times, four. She closed her eyes and kissed Monty's cheeks, wondering when law and order would come to Montana—more than that, wondering if and when it would ever return to the rest of the country.

"I hope we can protect you from such things, Monty," she told her son. She wondered what had happened to Bess and Johnny Hills, Sarah Grant, Sidney and Marie Boone, and the others. Had they all made it all right to Oregon? And what was happening with Anna? She knew there was not much she could do for any of them. There was enough to do right here, and she couldn't carry the weight of everyone else's problems on her shoulders.

"We're here to stay now, Monty. Everything is going to

be all right now. Your daddy is home." She hugged Monty close. "Your daddy is home."

"Look at them, Clint!"

From the hill above, standing in front of their new four-room cabin, Clint and Jo watched the new foals romping in the valley below, three colts and two fillies. One foal had been stillborn, and another had died three days after it was born. But five had survived, five healthy horses to add to Jo's growing herd. Clint still referred to them as "Jo's horses."

"They'll do all right, Jo," Clint answered. "It's a pretty sight, isn't it?"

Jo looked over the valley at the mountains beyond. Wildflowers bloomed everywhere. Hammers pounded from six hired hands building a bigger horse barn. The sound was music to Jo's ears. She studied the purple mountains, the green valley, the romping young horses.

"It's the prettiest sight I've ever seen," she answered.

Clint grinned, putting his arm around her shoulders. "Not as pretty as you."

She smiled and leaned against him. "Let's go for a ride, Clint. Monty can sit up now. You can hold him in front of you with one arm while you ride. I feel so good today. Let's take a picnic basket. I haven't ridden the perimeter of my new property since I first claimed it."

He gave her a hug, realizing it would take her a while to talk about the land as theirs and not hers. He didn't mind. She had earned the right to call it her own.

Jo went inside and prepared some food, then got Monty ready. She carried the basket and the baby outside, while Clint brought up his horse and Sundance, both horses saddled. He helped Jo mount up, then handed her the baby.

"Just a minute," he told her then. He went inside the house and Jo waited curiously. Clint came out a moment later with Yellow Wolf's lance, which Jo had left standing in the corner of the bedroom. Clint shoved the lance into the ground in front of the new cabin. He met her eyes.

"I hope he comes back, Jo. I'd like to meet him—thank him."

Their eyes held. "I hope he comes back, too. He'd like

you very much, Clint, and you would like Yellow Wolf."
She smiled sadly. "It feels good to let go of the past,
doesn't it? You've done the right thing."

He moved his own horse, mounting up and taking Monty
from Jo. "Let's go, son. It's time you started learning
about this place. It's all going to be yours some day, you
know."

They rode off together, down the hill and into the
sprawling, green valley where the horses grazed peacefully.

Jo thought about Anna again, hoping her sister would
find the peace and love she had found. She realized she
needed to write Anna and tell her how wonderfully everything had worked out. If Anna could get Darryl to come
here, maybe things could work out as well for her.

"*God be with you, Anna*," she thought, feeling almost
guilty for being so happy. But she realized she should not
feel guilty at all. She had earned this happiness, and
nothing was going to take it away from her. She would
write to Anna, and she would pray for her; but for now she
would enjoy her husband and her son, and her home in
Montana.

If you would like to read about Joline's sister,
Anna Kelley, be sure to watch for

Embers of the Heart

by F. Rosanne Bittner

on sale now

Here is a brief excerpt
from Anna's unforgettable and moving story.

1860

Anna stopped packing for a moment and touched the pearl necklace that graced her slender neck, the little golden heart at its center representing Darryl's love for her. He had given it to her on their wedding day, hardly a year ago. It had been a year of blissful love for them, but things had not been so blissful on the streets of Lawrence, Kansas.

Her heart ached for Darryl and the way he had been treated just because he came from a plantation family in Georgia. Sometimes it seemed as if all of Kansas was ready to explode. She was sick of all the hatred, the fighting that seemed to go on daily in the streets between those for or against slavery and states' rights. Border wars with Missouri between bushwhackers and jayhawkers had devastated the countryside and had taken many lives needlessly.

"I feel like this is my fault, Darryl," she told her husband.

She heard a deep sigh, and in the next moment his strong but gentle hands seized her shoulders. He nuzzled her thick, strawberry-blond hair, then wrapped his arms around her from behind.

"Don't be ridiculous," he answered. He spoke with the heavy southern drawl that she had learned to love. "It's the prejudice of all the ignorant people in this town. Lawrence is full of jayhawkers, and I'm from Georgia. My parents own slaves. Most of these people can't see past that."

"It isn't fair," Anna answered, turning to look into gentle brown eyes. Darryl was a sturdy but slender man, always immaculately dressed, his dark hair neatly combed. She had been attracted to him the moment he had come to Lawrence, a new, young doctor, ready to devote his services to the Kansas frontier, where doctors were scarce. That was two years ago, and she had only been sixteen. Darryl was twenty-six then. Why did two years suddenly seem like ten? So much had happened, so much hurt and insult to a man who had come here out of a sincere desire to help.

"You tried so hard, Darryl. You've done nothing against any of these people. You've never taken sides—"

He put his fingers to her lips. "There's no sense going over it again and again, Anna." He studied her lovely blue eyes, loved the feel of her perfectly curved body against his own. She was only eighteen, but there was never anything childish about her, except her innocence when he married her. Anna was a strong young woman, raised in a rough frontier town, a creature of amazing grace and beauty that he had never expected to find when he came here to set up his practice. He had hoped they would have a child by now, but he never mentioned it to her. He knew that deep inside it worried her that she still had not conceived.

"I'm not going to stay here and continue to see you suffer insults because of me," he continued. "Let alone the danger to your very life. That burning torch someone tossed through the window two nights ago is as far as I'm going to let this go. I'm worried something will happen to you just because you married a southern man."

"But I don't think of you that way. You're just my husband, a fine doctor who could have helped this community."

"It doesn't matter what you think. Right now this whole country is full of hatred, Anna, and you and I can't do anything about it."

Her eyes teared, and she wrapped her arms around him, resting her head against his chest. "I'll miss Joline, and Father, even though right now I'm so angry with them. I hate all these hard feelings. Joline and I were always so close when we were growing up, especially after Mother died."

"I know. Some day this will all blow over, and you'll be close to your family again. In the meantime, your pa and your sister will be all right. They're both strong and stubborn." He smiled to himself. "Like you," he teased. He stroked her hair. "I would have liked to get along better with your pa, Anna. When I first came here, we seemed to do just fine. Then Greg Masters came along," he added, referring to Joline's new husband. "He started up with all that anti-slavery talk, still starts an argument every time we're with them."

He let go of her. "I can't make them understand, Anna. They just won't listen, not even your pa and Joline now. Sure, my folks own slaves. But they don't whip them and tear their families apart and all the other things most northerners think. I know that goes on, but not on my folks' plantation." He let go of her, running a hand through his dark hair. "Hell, without slave labor, my folks couldn't make ends meet."

Anna dropped her eyes, her emotions mixed. She didn't want to tell him that even she couldn't fully understand the concept of slavery. Even if the slaves were well treated, it still didn't seem quite right to "own" human beings. Sometimes when Darryl talked about them, it seemed almost as though he didn't really think of them as human at all; but because of the true compassion he seemed to show for his own race, his desire to be able to help and heal, she didn't want to believe he could think differently about Negroes. After all, here was a man who could have chosen to stay on that plantation and live off his wealthy parents. But he had chosen to be a doctor, had chosen to come to the frontier, where doctors were so badly needed. His parents had sent him money when he wrote to them of his marriage to Anna, but he had put that in a savings—"For our children," he had told her. Anna worried now whether she would be able to give him any.

Darryl came closer, touching her chin and leaning down to kiss her cheek. "Some day, when all this is over, I'll take you to Georgia, Anna. You can see for yourself the kind of people my folks are. You'd love it there. The plantation is beautiful. Somehow we'll get through all this." He ran his fingers over the pearl necklace. "You just remember who gave you this necklace and what it represents. You hang on to it, no matter what happens."

She met his eyes, frowning. "I don't like the way you said that. We're just going to Missouri to live with a friend of yours, right? I mean, if this country ends up in war, you wouldn't go off and leave me, would you?"

She saw pride and anger flash deep in his dark eyes, and her heart tightened with dread. "It's a possibility, Anna."

"Darryl—"

"Anna, it's becoming more and more obvious the Union is jealous of our southern wealth and our free labor. They want to crush us. The big factory owners in the North are out to destroy us—to destroy our whole way of life! My father and his father before him worked all their lives to build what they have. If the Union had its way, the South would be changed forever. My parents and others like them are about to face the possibility of losing everything they live for! Do you think I could sit by and let that happen?"

Her eyes widened with a mixture of astonishment and near-disappointment. "I thought . . . I thought we felt the same way about all this hatred, all this ridiculous rivalry between North and South. I thought we were both neutral in our feelings—that we just wanted to live our lives apart from all of it."

He stepped back, giving out an odd snicker of surprise. "Anna, what kind of fantasy world are you living in? I would *love* it if we could do that. But this thing is getting too big for both of us. It's going to be impossible not to get involved eventually." He threw up his hands. "Hell, I'm not saying I'd march off to war tomorrow. I'm just asking you to remember who I am, where I come from, what all this means to my family."

"But . . . you're a doctor. You save lives, you don't take them."

He nodded. "And I hope to keep it that way. If war should come, and if I decided to do my part in defending the South and states' right, I would volunteer as a doctor. That's all, Anna. I'd help the ones who get hurt."

She swallowed back a lump in her throat. "But . . . you'd still be in danger. You could still get killed."

He came closer, pulling her against him again. "Anna, it hasn't even come to that yet, and it might *never* come to that. I'm just trying to explain the worst possibilities. I want you to be ready, and I want you to understand and to support my beliefs."

She loved him, trusted him. What did slavery and states' rights and possible war have to do with their personal needs and passions? In fact, right now, what did her own doubts about slavery matter? She just wanted her husband to stay close to her. She didn't want him to go away or get hurt, and right now she didn't want to make matters worse by admitting she couldn't quite agree with his beliefs.

"I'll try to understand, Darryl. And I do support you, because I love you so much. I just . . . I don't know. After that burning torch came through our front window, I began to realize how serious this is. It frightens me."

He rubbed her back. "Well, it just so happens that it frightens me, too. Things will be better in Columbia. Missouri is having its own battle between jayhawkers and bushwhackers, but at least there the sympathy is for the South, at least for the moment. We'll live with Fran and Mark for a while, Anna, just till we see if this all comes to war, and see how dangerous things are. We'll be safer that way. After a while, if things calm down, we'll find our own place."

"I hope that won't take long," she replied. "You know how much I enjoy having my own home, fixing things up my way."

"I know. Right now I just figured Missouri was a reasonable compromise. You won't be so far from your pa that you lose touch. I'll be with an old friend from Georgia and from school. We'll just kind of wait things out in Missouri—see what happens. For the moment I don't think it's wise to go any farther east, either north or south."

She looked up at him. "I hope Fran Rogers likes me."

He grinned. "How could she *not* like you? You're beautiful and sweet and you get along with anyone."

She ran her hands along his upper arms, lowering her eyes. "You said you and Fran were close once."

"We were very young, and we lived near each other. It was a childish fling, that's all. Fran's father was an overseer on the plantation. Fran and I used to go riding together sometimes, and one summer when we were only about sixteen, I kissed her. I went off to school that year, and that was the end of it. The next summer we both realized it was just a childish thing. That's about all there was to it."

She met his eyes again. "Maybe she didn't take it all that lightly. Maybe she loved you more than you think— the handsome young son of her father's boss. She might still have feelings for you." She ran her fingers over the thin scar on his left cheek, put there at an early age in a riding accident.

Darryl chuckled. "She's married to Mark, Anna. I brought him home one summer from school and introduced them, long after I had broken things off with Fran. By the next summer Fran and Mark were married. End of story." He leaned closer then, touching his nose to hers. "Besides, she didn't turn into the beautiful woman you are. Fran took after her father, who was a big, mean sort of fellow. I'm not saying she took after him in personality, just physically. She's tall and strong and could probably out-do some men. But right now I don't want to talk about her."

He met her mouth tenderly. Tensions had been so high, it had been a while since they had made love. Darryl had made it beautiful for her on their wedding night, and she had quickly learned that lovemaking was something to be enjoyed, not dreaded. The kiss became deeper, warmer, both of them expressing a need to put aside anxieties and talk of war, and just enjoy their love.

He picked her up in his arms and carried her into the bedroom, neither of them caring that she had already stripped the bed and packed the blankets. For the moment she would forget about the hatred in Lawrence, forget about the fact that she was being forced to leave this lovely house Darryl had rented for them and the fact that they had sold the lovely furnishings he had bought for her. He had promised her a new home and new furnishings when they got settled in Columbia.

Darryl had always taken good care of her. He had money from his family, and he was capable of earning good money himself as a doctor. Perhaps in Missouri he would do even better. After they were married he had insisted she buy the best furniture, the finest clothing, and he had even hired a woman to help with cooking and cleaning.

Anna Barker Kelley had not asked for any of it, nor had she married Darryl because of his wealth. She simply loved him. She had been raised on a farm outside of Lawrence, the daughter of Tom Barker, a man who came from hardy stock in Illinois. Anna and her sister Joline had helped their father with the farm all their lives, Anna taking her mother's place inside the farmhouse and with general farm chores expected of a farm wife; Joline helping with the heavier chores. Their father had often teased that Joline was the "son he never had," and both sisters worked hard.

Anna was accustomed to living without the luxuries Darryl offered her now. But Darryl had insisted. For him, living amid the finest things was a way of life. Darryl Kelley came from another world—a world of wealth and slaves and a gracious, gentler way of living. Anna was learning to accept and enjoy the kind of life he wanted for her; and as she became lost in his gentle lovemaking, she gave no thought to the possibility that one day soon she might have to draw on the rugged Barker strength that had been bred into her.

*　　*　　*　　*

The new home in Columbia never came to be. Missouri was as full of strife and bloodshed as Kansas, and Darryl insisted it was safer to continue to live with Mark and Fran. He never even got around to setting up a practice. Instead, they both helped with the *Main Street Inn*, the restaurant the Rogers' owned. Fran and Mark had moved to Missouri to be closer to Fran's mother, who had come here to live with a sister in Centralia after Fran's father died. Mark had set up his business here in Columbia because it was a bigger town, only a short train ride from Centralia. The couple had done well. Mark had studied business in college, and he loved to cook. He had combined that love with his education and had a successful restaurant; but lately they had lost more than a few customers because they were "Confederates from Georgia."

Anna wondered how a whole year could have slipped by so quickly. And when and how, during that year, had she and Darryl lost the seemingly perfect love they had shared back in Lawrence during that first year of marriage?

Now she was packing again, this time for an even more heartbreaking reason than fleeing Lawrence to come to Missouri. This time she was packing a few things for

Darryl, who was going off to war with Mark Rogers. He had told her so matter-of-factly, implying she had no choice in the decision, a look in his eyes telling her not to argue the issue. Three months ago the Confederates, which the citizens of the southern secessionist states called themselves, had fired on Fort Sumter. Union soldiers had answered the shots. The United States was at war, and Darryl could not ignore his southern pride. The Union was already moving into southern territory, threatening his family's very way of life.

It seemed incredible to Anna that any state would want to secede from the Union, but several already had, including Georgia. A barrage of political game-playing and a test of Federal vs. State control had culminated in a dreaded war, with slavery emerging as the apparent key issue. Anna knew it went much deeper than that, but things had happened so fast, and there were so many misunderstandings and confused rumors and newspaper stories, that how and where the ugly mess had truly begun seemed vague to her now. She could see this was fast becoming a war of pride, of children at odds, each wanting his own way.

"I wish you would stay right here," she said to Darryl, keeping her voice low, since Fran and Mark were still in the house. The house itself had already been sold. Fran and Anna were to take rooms at a boarding house not far from the restaurant Mark and Fran owned. Fran planned to use the money from the sale of the house however she needed while Mark was gone.

"This should only take a few weeks," Mark had said at the dinner table last night. "Then again it could take a lot longer. You women will be a lot safer in a place where there are many people, and you won't have so far to walk to the restaurant, so you won't have to worry about thugs and outlaws."

"God knows there is enough fighting right here in Missouri," Anna continued aloud.

"We're needed a lot worse in other places," Darryl answered. "There are too many pro-Union forces here. Missouri is already a lost cause, as far as I'm concerned. You know what happened at Boonville. Governor Jackson was already retreated to the southern end of the state. I'll probably go to Georgia and check on my folks, then go on to Richmond and formally volunteer my services."

"You'll just volunteer as a doctor, won't you," she urged. "You won't get involved in the fighting?"

Their eyes held as he buttoned his shirt. "I'll do my best, Anna. It all depends on how ugly this whole thing gets."

She turned away. "You're only doing this because of Fran and Mark. They're both so . . . so adamant that the South is right . . . already so devoted to the Confederacy. Mark talked you into this. He rallied and ranted about going off to fight for the South, and he infected you with his patriotism. A disease, that's what it is. This whole thing is like an ugly disease that is festering and spreading." Her voice choked, and she could hardly see what she was doing for the tears in her eyes.

Darryl moved to the bed and sat down, pulling her down beside him. "It isn't that way, Anna. It's a matter of standing up for what a man believes is right."

"But what if you're *not* right," she gasped, tears running down her cheeks as she faced him. For the first time since she had known Darryl Kelley, she saw a flash of fury in his eyes.

"Do *you* think I'm wrong? Do you think the *South* is wrong?"

She looked at her lap. "I don't know what I think about anything anymore. I only know that I love you and I don't want you to go away. Missouri is exploding with gangs and thugs—jayhawkers and bushwhackers. The home we were going to have here was never ours, and the quiet happiness we shared when we first got married disappeared so quickly. I'm so sick of talk of war and states' rights and slavery, of Union and Confederate causes." She met his eyes again. "I just want to be with you, Darryl. I want our own home, my own kitchen, an office for you in one wing. I want my wonderful physician husband here, helping people get well, sitting at our own supper table every night. I can't stand the thought of never knowing where you are or if you're all right."

He grasped her arms as she broke into tears. He held her close, letting her cry. "I'll write, Anna. And if I volunteer as a doctor, I'll be behind the lines. I'll be all right. As long as you take a room at that boarding house and stay close to the restaurant, you'll be all right, too, while you wait for me. I suppose there are safer places you could go, but there isn't time to decide where, and I need to know exactly where I can find you when I come back. Besides, I promised Mark you'd stay here and help Fran at the restaurant."

"Fran doesn't like me." She pulled away and rose, wiping at her eyes with a handkerchief she pulled from a pocket on her blue cotton dress.

"That's nonsense."

"You know that it isn't," Anna answered, her voice stronger. "She knows my father and Jo's husband are pro-Union—that they've already left to volunteer. You saw how she shunned them when they stopped here to see me; you know how she has behaved toward me ever since. She looks at me as though I'm the enemy. And if it was just that, it wouldn't be so bad; but she was unfriendly even before that. She's always acted almost jealous of me, ever since we first came here, as though I've interfered with the friendship she and Mark shared with you."

Darryl rose slowly. "Anna, that's all in your imagination. I've told you that before. You feel out of place because Fran and Mark are from my past, from my home state, and because we're all Confederate sympathizers."

"It's not my imagination." She closed her eyes and turned away, and Darryl studied his wife's beautiful form, always surprised at how well she carried herself in spite of coming from a Kansas farm. She had all the grace and elegance of the most refined southern belle.

"Darryl," she said softly. "I don't want *you* to think of me as an enemy. I want you to understand that I don't take *anyone's* side in this war. I detest the fighting, on both sides. And I simply . . . love you. I want us to get back to the life we planned to lead when we first got married."

He put a hand on her waist. "We will, Anna. It might take a few more months, but it will happen. I can understand how hard it might be for you to stand staunchly behind the Confederacy, but I need you to stand behind me. I need your support, Anna. I need you to understand that part of me that compels me to do this. This is for my family, for a whole way of life, for Georgia."

She turned and met his eyes, realizing that for the moment Georgia and his family came before his love for her. To know that hurt, but it made her realize just how important this was to him. "Just come back to me, Darryl," she said in a near whisper. "We've had so little time. . . ."

He drew her into his arms, and they embraced tightly, desperately. "I'll come back, Anna. That's a promise."

FANFARE

Sandra Brown

☐ 28951-9 TEXAS! LUCKY ....$4.50/$5.50 in Canada
☐ 28990-X TEXAS! CHASE ....$4.99/$5.99 in Canada
☐ 29500-4 TEXAS! SAGE ....$4.99/$5.99 in Canada
☐ 29085-1 22 INDIGO PLACE ....$4.50/$5.50 in Canada

Amanda Quick

☐ 28594-7 SURRENDER ....$4.50/$5.50 in Canada
☐ 28932-2 SCANDAL ....$4.95/$5.95 in Canada
☐ 28354-5 SEDUCTION ....$4.99/$5.99 in Canada
☐ 29325-7 RENDEZVOUS ....$4.99/$5.99 in Canada

Deborah Smith

☐ 28759-1 THE BELOVED WOMAN ....$4.50/$5.50 in Canada
☐ 29092-4 FOLLOW THE SUN ....$4.99/$5.99 in Canada
☐ 29107-6 MIRACLE ....$4.50/$5.50 in Canada

Iris Johansen

☐ 28855-5 THE WIND DANCER ....$4.95/$5.95 in Canada
☐ 29032-0 STORM WINDS ....$4.99/$5.99 in Canada
☐ 29244-7 REAP THE WIND ....$4.99/$5.99 in Canada

Available at your local bookstore or use this page to order.

Send to: Bantam Books, Dept. FN 18
            414 East Golf Road
            Des Plaines, IL 60016

Please send me the items I have checked above. I am enclosing
$_____ (please add $2.50 to cover postage and handling). Send
check or money order, no cash or C.O.D.'s, please.

Mr./Ms._____

Address_____

City/State_____Zip_____

Please allow four to six weeks for delivery.

Prices and availability subject to change without notice.　　FN 18 1/92

★ WAGONS WEST ★

This continuing, magnificent saga recounts the adventures of a brave band of settlers, all of different backgrounds, all sharing one dream— to find a new and better life.

- ☐ 26822-8 **INDEPENDENCE! #1** $4.95
- ☐ 26162-2 **NEBRASKA! #2** $4.95
- ☐ 26242-4 **WYOMING! #3** $4.95
- ☐ 26072-3 **OREGON! #4** $4.50
- ☐ 26070-7 **TEXAS! #5** $4.99
- ☐ 26377-3 **CALIFORNIA! #6** $4.99
- ☐ 26546-6 **COLORADO! #7** $4.95
- ☐ 26069-3 **NEVADA! #8** $4.99
- ☐ 26163-0 **WASHINGTON! #9** $4.50
- ☐ 26073-1 **MONTANA! #10** $4.95
- ☐ 26184-3 **DAKOTA! #11** $4.50
- ☐ 26521-0 **UTAH! #12** $4.50
- ☐ 26071-5 **IDAHO! #13** $4.50
- ☐ 26367-6 **MISSOURI! #14** $4.50
- ☐ 27141-5 **MISSISSIPPI! #15** $4.95
- ☐ 25247-X **LOUISIANA! #16** $4.50
- ☐ 25622-X **TENNESSEE! #17** $4.50
- ☐ 26022-7 **ILLINOIS! #18** $4.95
- ☐ 26533-4 **WISCONSIN! #19** $4.95
- ☐ 26849-X **KENTUCKY! #20** $4.95
- ☐ 27065-6 **ARIZONA! #21** $4.99
- ☐ 27458-9 **NEW MEXICO! #22** $4.95
- ☐ 27703-0 **OKLAHOMA! #23** $4.95
- ☐ 28180-1 **CELEBRATION! #24** $4.50

Bantam Books, Dept. LE, 414 East Golf Road, Des Plaines, IL 60016

Please send me the items I have checked above. I am enclosing $_____ (please add $2.50 to cover postage and handling). Send check or money order, no cash or C.O.D.s please.

Mr/Ms _____

Address _____

City/State _____ Zip _____

Please allow four to six weeks for delivery.
Prices and availability subject to change without notice. LE-9/91

A Proud People in a Harsh Land

THE SPANISH BIT SAGA

Set on the Great Plains of America in the early 16th century, Don Coldsmith's acclaimed series recreates a time, a place and a people that have been nearly lost to history. With the advent of the Spaniards, the horse culture came to the people of the Plains. Here is history in the making through the eyes of the proud Native Americans who lived it.

☐ 26397-8	**TRAIL OF THE SPANISH BIT**	$3.50
☐ 26412-5	**THE ELK-DOG HERITAGE**	$3.50
☐ 26806-6	**FOLLOW THE WIND**	$3.50
☐ 26938-0	**BUFFALO MEDICINE**	$3.50
☐ 27067-2	**MAN OF THE SHADOWS**	$3.50
☐ 27209-8	**DAUGHTER OF THE EAGLE**	$3.50
☐ 27344-2	**MOON OF THUNDER**	$3.50
☐ 27460-0	**SACRED HILLS**	$3.50
☐ 27604-2	**PALE STAR**	$3.50
☐ 27708-1	**RIVER OF SWANS**	$3.50
☐ 28163-1	**RETURN TO THE RIVER**	$3.50
☐ 28318-9	**THE MEDICINE KNIFE**	$3.50
☐ 28538-6	**THE FLOWER IN THE MOUNTAINS**	$3.50
☐ 28760-5	**TRAIL FROM TAOS**	$3.50
☐ 29123-8	**SONG OF THE ROCK**	$3.50
☐ 29419-9	**FORT DE CHASTAIGNE**	$3.99
☐ 28334-0	**THE CHANGING WIND**	$3.95
☐ 28868-7	**THE TRAVELER**	$4.50

■ ■

Available at your local bookstore or use this page to order.

Bantam Books, Dept. LE 10 414 East Golf Road, Des Plaines, IL 60016
Please send me the items I have checked above. I am enclosing $_____
(please add $2.50 to cover postage and handling). Prices are $1.00 higher per book in Canada. Send check or money order, no cash or C.O.D.'s, please.

Mr/Ms._____

Address_____

City/State_____Zip_____
Please allow four to six weeks for delivery.
Prices and availability subject to change without notice.   LE 10 12/91

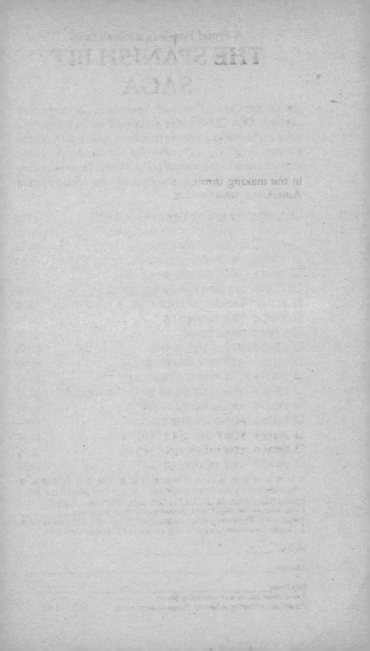